Like her heroine, Ann Granger has worked in the diplomatic service in various parts of the world. She met her husband, who was also working for the British Embassy, in Prague and together they received postings to places as far apart as Munich and Lusaka. They are now permanently placed in Bicester, near Oxford. SAY IT WITH POISON, Ann Granger's first Mitchell and Markby mystery, was also her first crime novel. Ann is currently working on her fifth Mitchell and Markby whodunnit.

Also by Ann Granger

Mitchell and Markby Crime Novels

Say It With Poison
A Season for Murder
Cold in the Earth
Where Old Bones Lie
A Fine Place for Death
Flowers for His Funeral
Candle for a Corpse
A Touch of Mortality
A Word After Dying
Call the Dead Again

Fran Varady Crime Novels

Asking for Trouble
Keeping Bad Company
Running Scared

Murder Among Us

Ann Granger

First published in 1992
by HEADLINE BOOK PUBLISHING

First published in paperback in 1993
by HEADLINE BOOK PUBLISHING

1

ISBN 0 7472 4043 4

Printed and bound in Great Britain by
Mackays of Chatham plc, Chatham, Kent

HEADLINE BOOK PUBLISHING
A division of Hodder Headline
338 Euston Road
London NW1 3BH

AUTHOR'S NOTE

The name only of Springwood Hall is taken from that of a Victorian country house in the annexe to which my husband lived as a boy. Sadly this old building was entirely demolished many years ago. I am not aware of any other house by that name and certainly no reference is intended to any such house, should it exist.

A.G.

lichen, tin... and weather it appeared oddly naked and had

Chapter One

'Springwood Hall Hotel Restaurant' announced a glossy brand-new sign. 'Opening shortly', read a smaller one hung beneath it.

The electricity board van rattled past disregarding both proud announcement and discreet promise. It turned through wrought-iron gates, freshly painted black and picked out in gold, and roared down the newly gravelled drive. This was just another call on the day's work schedule.

The van drew up before the front of the building and a young man in overalls got out of the driver's seat after first reaching for his toolbox. As he slammed the van door he glanced dispassionately at the rambling mid-Victorian Gothic Hall with its false turrets and drainpipes emerging from the open mouths of grimacing gargoyles. It was built of local honey-coloured stone and had been recently scoured clean. Stripped of the kindly patina bestowed on it by lichen, time and weather it appeared oddly naked and had lost its previous harmony with the landscape. The way in which its architectural style jarred with the medium chosen for its construction was unfortunately underlined. Technically, restorers had done a good job on the Hall, but the results weren't for the sensitive.

Clearly the young electrician saw nothing to impress him.

1

He shrugged and, whistling loudly, turned aside to approach a fellow artisan who was several yards away before a separate building labelled 'Indoor Swimming Pool'. Here plate-glass double-glazing on a grand scale had been installed and allowed those outside to see the pool inside, surrounded by white tiles, potted palms and wicker loungers and, in the background, the doors to changing rooms and showers. But the age, size and location of the pool block with regard to the Hall indicated that this smaller building had once been the coachhouse. The decorator applying a last coat of varnish to the doorframes saw the newcomer draw near but gave no outward sign.

'Electrician!' announced the man from the board.

'Nothing to do with me, mate!' returned the varnisher.

In some mysterious way this stalemate opened the way to casual conversation. The varnisher indicated willingness to chat by pausing, standing back and surveying his work, head on one side.

The electrician was at least impressed by the glimpse of the indoor swimming pool. 'Nice place!' he offered, adding with a wave of his free hand at the house, 'Done it all up a bit since I was here last. Creepy old dump, it was. Must've cost a fortune.'

'Money,' said the varnisher ponderously, 'is no object, as they say.'

'I suppose it'll suit wealthy old geezers but it beats me why they wanted to spend all that time and cash doing it up. I mean, it's still a tarted-up old ruin, innit? I can't see they've done nothing to modernise the place. Windows have still got wooden frames and that funny old boy over there in a cap mucking about with the roses just about sums it up, if you ask me! They'd have done better to have knocked the whole thing down and built something proper in its place.

When's it opening as a hotel and that, then?'

'Sat'day. Everyone's buzzin' round like a load of blue-arsed flies gettin' it all ready. Got a load of celebrities comin' down for it. Telly people an' all, I heard say.'

'That right?' The man from the electricity board perked up.

'No one you'd ever heard of,' said the varnisher in tones of disgust. 'Blokes in purple shirts what write about food in the heavies, architects and the like. Coupla high-class tarts with buck teeth and flat knockers, just to show the top punters is likely to drop in.' He deigned to turn his head. 'If you want to know anything, your best bet is to go round the back to the kitchens. That's very likely where you'll find them, though whether you'll get any sense out of any of them I couldn't say! It's like a bloomin' madhouse in there. You don't want to fall foul of the chief cook and bottle-washer. Swiss bloke. They got some very sharp knives lying about in that kitchen so I keep clear! Watch out for the bloke what owns the place, another one of them Swiss – but he ain't here at the moment.'

At that point a hideous noise shattered the air. Midway between a screech and a bellow, it gained in strength until it seemed some soul in torment screamed out in its agony, then faded away again.

'Blimey, what was that?' gasped the electrician.

The varnisher was unmoved and resumed his work with slow careful strokes. 'One of the mokes.' He nodded in the general direction of open land beyond the swimming pool. 'Got a field full of 'em down there. Not all donkeys, mind you. A coupla horses and a Shetland pony or two. All mangy-looking brutes and bite you as soon as look at you. I keep away from them an' all. There's a sort of stable, falling down, and a bird what looks after them.'

The electrician remembered why he'd come and that time on his work sheet had to be accounted for. 'See you, then!' he said and set off towards the back of the house and the kitchens.

Some ten minutes later a large Mercedes swept up the drive and stopped before the main entrance. The man who leapt out was only of middle height but solidly built, heavy in the shoulders, with a tanned complexion and neatly trimmed dark hair. He had the air of a prosperous businessman or, more likely, a former sportsman now turning his attention and talents to business. This was true. Eric Schuhmacher had been a formidable ice-hockey player in his day. Muscle was just beginning to turn to flab as it tends to do in such cases, but he was still an impressively fit figure and not one with whom anyone would lightly undertake to argue.

'There he is!' muttered the varnisher, watching Eric stride purposefully in expensive white calf loafers towards the kitchens. 'William Tell hisself!' He wiped his brush and carefully replaced the lid on the tin. 'Ho! "I shot an arrer in the air: It fell to earth I know not where!"' He chuckled happily at this shaft of his own.

Eric Schuhmacher, on his way to the kitchens through the narrow entrance vestibule at the back of the house, passed the open door at the head of the flight of steps leading down to the cellars. He frowned, wondering who was down there. It was a nuisance, having had to relocate the cellar entrance. The old entrance in the kitchens had proved inconvenient when the new work surfaces were installed and the new door had been pierced in this vestibule wall outside the main kitchen area. Awkward to get at when deliveries were made and, worse, out of sight of the cooks in the kitchen at other times.

He entered the kitchens themselves and beheld a scene Bruegel might have painted. At first sight a disorderly kermis, it resolved itself into scurrying sous-chefs, stacks of comestibles, huge shiny pans boiling away, mysterious bottles, and an odour compounded of garlic, sweat, wine, meat juices, onions and simmering bones.

He approached a short, stocky, swarthy man with long arms and a low brow. His rolled up sleeves showed muscular forearms thick with long black hairs which enhanced his simian appearance.

'*Gruotsi*, Ulli!' Eric hailed him and slapped one brawny shoulder. 'Saturday is going to be the greatest day of my career – our career, Ulli!'

'*Ja*, Herr Schuhmacher!' growled the chef.

But Eric had spotted something amiss. He suddenly darted forward and descended on a crate of peaches. 'Who accepted this delivery? What use will these be by Saturday?'

'I'm sorry, Herr Schuhmacher!' apologised one of the sous-chefs.

'Sorry isn't good enough, Mickey! You know what I want for this place eventually? Four stars! And perhaps even, one day, five! That's my ambition! And how will Springwood Hall Hotel get them? By attention to detail, Mickey, detail!'

He returned to Ulli Richter, crouched perspiring over a macabre decapitated animal head on a marble block.

'I can't keep my eye on everything, Herr Schuhmacher!' Ulli said. 'We'll be ready Saturday, but only with God's grace! That big oven is playing up again and someone keeps taking my knives!'

This was a serious accusation and Schuhmacher looked suitably wrathful. A master chef's personal set of kitchen knives was sacrosanct and everyone in the kitchen knew this. He turned to address his staff who all stopped working and froze in various attitudes, hatchets half-raised, wooden spoons at the slope, all attention.

'On Saturday afternoon the special guests will be here early to be shown round. So will the TV people. I want no mess, none of this chaos! I want order and complete cleanliness, no unwashed mixing bowls, no grubby rags! And everyone is to smile!'

'Yes, Herr Schuhmacher!' they all chorused obediently, except Ulli Richter who merely twitched his bushy eyebrows.

'Right, back to work!' Schuhmacher turned back to his chef. 'Everyone seems to be here, Ulli. Who then is down in the wine cellar? The door's open.'

Ulli reflected. 'A young man with a toolbox went down there, ten minutes ago. Electrician. That new lighting, it's playing up and without it down there, you can't see your hand in front of your face.'

Schuhmacher paled. 'Alone?' He started for the door, his voice rising to a howl. 'Alone in a cellar of fine wines! Some of them great classics! Almost unobtainable! No one went with him? Good heavens, must I do everything myself?' He vanished out of the door.

'I'll be bloody glad,' muttered Mickey the sous-chef, 'when Saturday night is over!'

Ulli Richter pretended not to hear. He picked up a meat cleaver, raised it on high and brought it down with a sickening thud. The calf's head, neatly cloven, fell open in two parts like a book, revealing a scrambled mess of pink brains.

'We're flogging a dead horse, my dears!' said Charles Grimsby. 'This battle's lost. Gird up your loins for the next one.'

'Rubbish!' said Hope Mapple firmly, in her capacity as chairperson of the Society for the Preservation of Historic Bamford.

Zoë Foster, eyeing Hope's ample figure, had a mental vision of her taking Charles's suggestion literally, and stifled a giggle.

'What's the matter, Zoë?' Hope demanded crossly.

'Sorry, hay fever. I've got the snuffles.'

'I hadn't realised the pollen count was very high today,' said Grimsby. 'I'm a sufferer myself and I'm usually the first to know about it.' His pale blue eyes peered suspiciously through rimless spectacles at Zoë.

Zoë sank back in her chair, the moment of humour gone, leaving only deepest depression remaining. Trust Charles to be so tactless as to talk about dead horses.

Its youngest member, Zoë had joined the society in its aim of saving such old monuments as survived around Bamford simply because it was campaigning against Eric Schuhmacher's plans for Springwood Hall. The Alice Batt Rest Home for Horses and Donkeys was on land belonging to the Hall. The rest home and its aged inhabitants were Zoë's life. She hadn't founded it. That had been done by Miss Batt many years ago. Zoë had been the last in a long line of helpers to toil willingly for Miss Batt and, when that lady had finally retired to a rest home for humans in Bournemouth, Zoë had taken over.

'I'm leaving it in your safe hands!' Miss Batt had said. 'I know you won't let me down, Zoë, or most importantly, you won't let our four-legged friends down!'

Zoë had done her best. The rest home never had enough money, of course, but it struggled along. A local vet gave his services free, which helped. But the animals tended to be unattractive from old age and various disabilities and several, owing to previous mistreatment, were very bad-tempered. It made fund-raising so much more difficult.

Good fortune had briefly shone on them during the time of the Hall's previous owner. As a horse-lover himself, he'd not only been happy to accept the peppercorn rent they paid but had even given them a modest subsidy.

All had changed with the arrival of Schuhmacher. As bad luck would have it, at the same time the lease came up for renewal. The decrepit collection of horses and donkeys and the ramshackle stabling, not to mention the distinctive odour, had not been seen by the Swiss as an asset, adjacent as they were to the landscaped gardens of his luxury hotel. He had no intention of renewing the lease. The rest home had six months to find new premises and if it didn't, which it probably wouldn't, it must close down.

Zoë closed her eyes and tried to shut out the dreadful vision of what would happen to all her poor, balding, grumpy, kicking, lop-eared, yellow-toothed and dearly loved charges.

'I'm sorry you're not feeling well, dear,' Hope Mapple said. 'But you can go on taking the notes, can't you? Would you rather Charles took over as secretary for this meeting?'

'No, it's fine really. It was just a bit of a sneeze.'

Robin Harding, losing patience with the whole lot of them as he frequently did – though not with Zoë – demanded, 'So what do you propose we do, Hope? The place opens on Saturday in a blaze of publicity! There'll be *cordon bleu* cooking, magnums of champers and celebrity guests in black tie and designer gowns. Concluding with a firework display to a background of Handel. Bad taste isn't in it, in my personal view. But the fact remains that you, I and the rest of our merry band would make as much impression if we turned up as a set of plaster gnomes. There's no point. Not until the day we can afford the grub,' he finished bitterly.

'Denis Fulton will be there,' said Grimsby, adding rather self-consciously, 'I've got one of his books.'

'The cookery fellow?' Robin dismissed Denis Fulton. 'A load of hot air!' Scorn crossed his freckled snub-nosed face.

'He's famous!' said Grimsby huffily.

'I don't think he's as good as Paul Danby,' Zoë put in, rallying to Robin's support. Besides which, Paul's daughter Emma regularly helped out at the rest home without demanding a penny in return, happy to muck out and groom for the pleasure of it. 'His cookery articles are practical and fun. I don't know why they had to get Fulton down when we've got our local man. Paul Danby's verdict on the new restaurant would mean a heck of a lot more to local people!'

'But not a damn thing to the society crowd Schuhmacher hopes will spread the word about his upmarket eating place. Paul's small fry – sorry, bit of a pun . . .' Grimsby looked quite pleased with himself. 'Fulton has a TV series and he's married to Leah Keller, as she was.'

'Look here!' ordered the chairperson firmly. 'Stop gassing on about food. It's disgusting! We're talking about our heritage! We're getting away from talking about our course of action!'

A slim dark-haired woman in the corner stretched her arms above her head, clinking a collection of silver bracelets and displaying to advantage her scarlet sweater. She murmured in a slightly nasal voice, 'We haven't got one, Hope!'

Hope Mapple gave Ellen Bryant a look of pure dislike. All the other members of the committee knew Hope had it in for Ellen. It was mutual. Ellen riled Hope, did it on

9

purpose. Perhaps Mrs Bryant's slim elegance was enough to upset Ms Mapple. Zoë wondered, not for the first time, about Mr Bryant. Ellen never mentioned him and no one had ever seen him. But she wore her wedding ring all the time, a great broad gold band of a thing, 'Ellen's knuckleduster', Robin called it.

'Hope has!' Robin said now unexpectedly. 'You have got a plan, haven't you, Hope? Come on, spit it out!'

Ms Mapple rose to her feet to make some momentous pronouncement.The atmosphere became electric. But the contrast between Hope and Mrs Bryant couldn't have been underlined more. It was unwise of Hope to wear those baggy floral pants, thought Zoë. And the shocking pink jersey halter top didn't help. Someone ought to have a word with Hope about brassières. It was downright embarrassing.

Robin, also eyeing Hope's top-heavy form, muttered, 'That woman needs scaffolding!'

'Shut up!' Zoë hissed.

They were after all in Hope's tiny flat, drinking Hope's abysmal tea, and one oughtn't to insult one's hostess. Also sharing the room were Hope's three pekinese dogs. Their odour hung in the air and their hair got on everyone's clothes. Ellen Bryant had already ostentatiously picked some from her scarlet sweater. One of the dogs was wedged on the sofa between Charles Grimsby and the arm-rest. He didn't dare try to move it because it was a snappy little beast and for some reason all three pekes snapped more at Grimsby than at anyone else.

Ms Mapple threw out her hand towards her television set. On the top of it was a photo of the three dogs. 'They will be there on Saturday!' she announced dramatically.

'Not the dratted pekes!' Grimsby exclaimed unwarily.

'No, not my poor boys! They'd be terrified by all those strangers! Really, Charles. No, I mean the television people. Schuhmacher and the forces of mammon may have won in a sense, but they haven't heard the last of us! We shall go out in a blaze of glory, not abjectly, not beaten by base commercial interest! We'll show 'em! We'll demonstrate! On their opening day with the TV cameras to show our protest to the nation!'

'All right!' said Grimsby, sitting up straight and inadvertently nudging the pekinese which growled. 'And a real bunch of twerps we'll look! Ten to one security will be laid on with all those celebs there. Some thugs with no necks and wall-to-wall shoulders will grab us before you can say knife! Certainly before we can get our banner unfurled! We'll never get it or a placard into the grounds so how will the TV viewers know what we're demonstrating about?'

'Thought of that. I'll smuggle the banner in,' said Ms Mapple. 'I'll wind it round my midriff beneath my Batik shift.'

Stunned silence fell on the committee.

'Would that be practical, Hope?' Zoë ventured. 'I mean, how would you get it out?' Robin began to shake in a silent mirth but Zoë went on, determinedly ignoring him, 'You can't undress on the lawn and unwind the banner from your middle.'

There was another silence. Robin's shoulders stopped heaving and he looked up, his face appalled. 'Gawd, Hope! You wouldn't?'

'Oh yes I would!' cried Ms Mapple in ringing tones. 'What's more, I intend to go the whole hog!'

'Hope!' they yelled in unison.

'I shall streak!' cried their leader.

11

Sensitive perhaps to the sheer power of emotion in the room, all three pekes awoke and began to yap frantically.

'Well, I think you've been slighted!' said Laura Danby fiercely.

Her husband, placidly making mayonnaise at the kitchen table, looked up and smiled affectionately at her as she stood arms akimbo in the doorway. She'd departed for her office that morning a picture of legal efficiency, but a long busy day and supervision of the younger children's bath-time had taken its toll. Her blonde hair had fallen out of its neat pleat and tumbled round her flushed face. She'd changed out of her solicitor's severe tailored costume into shorts and a striped French matelot's shirt.

'You look very sexy,' Paul said.

'Denis Fulton!' She wasn't to be distracted. 'What does he know about cooking? He pinched your recipe.'

'He asked my permission and I was happy to give it. After all, once you've given out a recipe it's common domain. You're a solicitor, I'm surprised at you throwing wild accusations around.'

'Wild, my eye! Not illegal perhaps, but shifty. He picked your brains. He ought at least to have given you credit. A man who doesn't own up to a thing like that is likely not to own up to other things!' She nodded vigorously.

'He's pretty good, actually, knowledgeable and a big name.'

'You're as good! If he's such a whizz, let him think up his own recipes!'

He knew better than to waste time in confrontational argument when she was off in full cry like this. Diversion was the best option. Paul tapped his mayonnaise spoon against the side of the bowl.

'Tell you who's better than either of us. That chef of Eric's, Ulli Richter. I for one am looking forward to Saturday night even if it will be a bit of a busman's holiday! I hear Eric's made a wonderful job of the interior of the house. He had Victor Merle, the art historian, to advise him, you know. Nothing but the best in every department! It'll be a memorable evening! Yodel-ay-i-dee!'

'How can you talk like that? How can you joke about it?'

The cry came not from Laura but from behind her. Emma Danby burst into the kitchen with all the passionate fury of eleven years old. She was wearing muddy jodhpurs and a sweatshirt with a horse's head depicted on it. Her freckled face was red with emotion and the faint odour of horses which had entered with her suggested she had just come from her stint at the Alice Batt Rest Home. Both her parents stared at her in consternation.

'We're not laughing about it, darling,' said Laura hurriedly. 'Dad and I know how you feel . . .'

'No, you don't! All you talk about is food!' Emma invested the word with a power of scorn which made her father wince. 'That horrid man is closing down the rest home!' Tears began to flow copiously down Emma's cheeks. 'All the animals will have to be put down because no one wants them! They're too old and ugly and can't work! You just wait till you're old and ugly and no one wants you and you can't work! I hate Eric Schuhmacher and the art person, all of them! I hope something dreadful happens on Saturday to spoil their whole rotten opening night! I hope someone drops dead and they blame it on the cooking!'

Chapter Two

'Can I have a word, sir?'

'Is it urgent?' Chief Inspector Alan Markby kept going towards the staircase to his office.

Wpc Jones was tenacious. 'Yes, sir, I think it is!'

He halted. She was an officer for whose judgement he had a healthy respect. 'Go on, then. Only make it snappy.'

'He's back,' said Jones calmly. 'That creep who was hanging round the schools last year, trying to pick up the children.'

'Oh, is he?' Markby said grimly. 'Yes, quite right, Jones. It is important!'

Perverts of all kinds appeared on charge sheets or were the subject of enquiry more or less every day of the week in most police stations. They ranged from the fantasisers, flashers and whisperers on the telephone – pathetic, inadequate or plain mentally ill – to hard-core vice circles of sickening depravity.

Particularly dangerous were those who preyed on children. They were often present in an area for some time before anyone reported their activities. These were the ones who lurked around school gates and playing fields, watching for the child alone. Or who prowled the streets in cars, offering children lifts or even attempting to drag them into the vehicles, and they were every policeman's nightmare. Only too often, such things ended with a battered little corpse and a family devastated.

The previous year worried parents had reported a man seen waiting near school entrances and watching children at play in parks. No sophisticate in a car, this one. He was on foot and had been described as scruffy, in his late forties with thinning hair, wearing a navy nylon bomber jacket with red and white stripes on the sleeve, and jeans. Twice, witnesses said he had an old haversack with him of the type bought in army surplus stores and the inference was that he was sleeping rough.

Despite a diligent search following up all reported sightings, they had failed to find him. But they had, it seemed, frightened him off because he hadn't been seen for some time. They'd passed on his description to neighbouring police forces and assumed they'd seen the last of him. Apparently, not so.

'The headmaster of King Charles the Martyr school phoned about it.' Jones waved a notepad. 'It's the same man, he thinks. He's still wearing that navy jacket with the stripes, although it's even dirtier. He's also got a flat cap now. He did speak to some children – the old tale about going to see some puppies, but a parent hove into view and he ran off. The parent, a Mrs Mayhew, told a teacher at the school about it. Also . . .'

Jones turned over a sheet of her notebook. 'One of the local farmers called in this morning and said he's found a rough shelter, a sort of hide, built on his land. Someone had been living there recently. He wouldn't have thought much of it – there are a lot of people wandering about the country sleeping rough. But a man came begging at the door and the farmer's wife, who saw him, didn't like the look of him at all. She fancied he was actually looking to see what he could pinch and when she appeared, he quickly pretended to be a beggar. The thing is, she described him as middle-aged and scruffy, unshaven, wearing a very dirty and greasy dark blue jacket with stripes on the sleeves. Sounds like the same man, sir.'

'Damn!' said Markby forcefully. 'All right. All officers on the beat are to look out for him and to report anything which might seem relevant. You're in charge of co-ordinating all that, Jones. Tell Sergeant Harris I want an officer at the gates of all primary schools at going home time. And we'd better run that school exercise again, send someone round to talk to the children, warning them about strangers. Someone had better go out to that farm and take a look at this shelter or hide or whatever it is. Phone round the other farms and ask them to keep an eye open. And get on to divisional headquarters and ask them to check known sex offenders to see if anyone of that description has been active elsewhere in the area.'

'Hope we pick up the pervert this time!' muttered Jones. 'Pity we couldn't have found him last time!'

'So long as we get to him before there's trouble. On the other hand, we don't want him frightened off out of the district before we can nab him, like last time. This time I want him!'

He sprinted up the stairs and burst into his office where he discovered Sergeant Pearce studying the football pages of the local paper.

'Time on your hands?' Markby asked politely.

Pearce jumped to his feet, hastily folding up the tabloid sheets. 'No, sir . . . well, just at the minute it is a bit quiet.'

'Let's hope it remains so. I've just seen Jones downstairs and she tells me our child molester is back in the area! Too much to hope for a quiet weekend, I suppose!' Markby went to the window and peered out at the sky.

'Doing a spot of gardening, sir?'

'No, I'm going along to the opening of the Springwood Hall Hotel. Best bib and tucker job.'

'Wish I was,' said Pearce wistfully.

'Actually, that kind of thing isn't really my scene. However, I ran into Schuhmacher in town a week or two back. I had met him briefly years ago, but I assumed he would have forgotten me and I doubt I'd have bothered to remind him. But he greeted me like a long lost brother and pressed two invitations to his gala opening into my hand.'

'Two . . .' muttered Pearce.

'One for me and one for the lady of my choice, Pearce. By no stretch of imagination does that qualify you.'

'No, sir.' Pearce grinned. 'Is the Foreign Office lady, Miss Mitchell, coming down from London for this shindig, then?'

'Yes, she is.'

Truth to tell he was feeling a little guilty. He had not been entirely frank with Meredith over the phone. Inviting her down for the Springwood Hall gala opening had been easy. It was the other problem he had on his plate which wasn't easy to discuss on the phone, and he wanted to talk it over with her when she arrived. Not on Saturday, though. That would be eat, drink and be merry day at Eric's expense. No, on the Sunday, when things were quiet again, police business permitting, as always!

Pearce, still continuing their conversation, now said, 'I hear the old Hall's been changed beyond belief!'

'Eric's had advice from that fellow Merle, the art historian. He had a TV series, Channel 4, if you saw it.'

'Don't watch Channel 4 much,' Pearce confessed. 'I

18

remember how the Hall used to look. Like something out of the Hammer House of Horrors it always seemed to me. All those turrets and stone heads.' He frowned. 'There was something in the local rag about it, the alterations I mean. A local society kicking up a fuss . . .'

'The Society for the Preservation of Historic Bamford,' Markby supplied.

'Never thought of Bamford as being historic,' Pearce observed.

Well, it wasn't, Markby thought. Not in an obvious way. It wasn't on the tourist maps at least and for that he was thankful. But it had its old buildings and its High Street might qualify as quaint if one ignored modern shop fronts and fixed one's eyes on the upper storeys of its Queen Anne buildings. He liked Bamford. That was why he'd steadfastly resisted all attempts to prise him away from it, although by virtue of seniority he ought to be stationed somewhere bigger and busier.

Aye, there's the rub . . . That's what he wanted to talk over with Meredith, anxious to hear what she had to say.

Though what many people would call a career woman, Meredith still appreciated the important if little things which made up personal satisfaction in a job. She combined the rare double of being both sensible and sensitive, and she knew how he felt about Bamford. He wished she also felt that way about this quiet country town and would move back to live here. But he supposed there was no way of dislodging her from that flat in London. It was, after all, so much more convenient for her, going daily to Whitehall as she did.

The pressure was on to move him from his familiar patch at Bamford and pitchfork him, suitably promoted, into some larger and busier theatre of operations and possibly, eventually, to glory at divisional headquarters. He had done too well: he was too senior. Upward and onward, was the cry: from others, not from him. He was resisting fiercely.

It was all a deadly secret. As far as he could tell no hint of this possible cataclysmic change in his life had leaked out. There had been no knowing glances in Bamford station when he hove into view. Wpc Jones, indefatigable passer of the hat, was not, as far as he could tell, furtively organising any whipround for a goodbye presentation. Pearce, surreptitiously perusing his sports pages again, was looking deceptively innocent and slightly thick . . . which was a pity because Pearce was an exceptionally bright young man. The vacant expression which often glazed over the sergeant's face had its uses, however, and had in the past lulled unsuspecting villains into a fatal confidence. Pearce wanted promotion. Pearce, no doubt one day soon, would be given it. But he, Markby, just liked being what he was, Detective Chief Inspector and in charge of his own little subdivision in this old but unromantic country town. He didn't want a change. Not in that area of his life, anyway.

The only change he really wanted to see concerned his relationship with Meredith and that, perversely, was not on the cards. Sod's law at work again.

'I always thought,' said Pearce, 'that the old house looked downright creepy. The sort of place where if you opened a cupboard, a body might fall out.'

Markby turned from the window and fixed him with a steely eye. 'Thank you, that's the last thing I want to happen, especially if I'm standing by dressed like a penguin with a glass in my hand.'

'Should be a bloomin' good bash!' said Pearce – who wasn't a reader of the society columns but recognised the signs of a good party about to start.

'Yes, it should be an evening to remember.'

'Denis, darling?'

The man hunched scowling at the word processor which had been absorbing his entire concentration looked up, blinked and seemed to locate and identify his wife after a perceptible delay. 'Sorry, Leah, didn't hear you come in.'

'How are you getting on with the new toy?' Leah Fulton stooped to plant a light kiss on her husband's forehead.

He put out a hand and patted her backside absentmindedly. 'Bloody thing keeps going down. I don't know what I'm doing wrong. I've read the handbook any number of times but it seems to have been written by one of these machines in the first place. You need the services of an MI5 cipher clerk to make head or tail of it. I read a paragraph of instruction and it sounds all right. Then I read it again and it seems to be complete mumbo-jumbo, utterly meaningless. I don't know why I bought this damn contraption. I was all right with the old sit-up-and-beg typewriter.'

'Your accountant advised it, sweetie. Wish I could help but I don't know a thing about it. You'll get used to it.'

'I doubt it!' Denis stood up, pushing back his chair. 'I know every five-year-old child in the country can use a computer nowadays but I'm obviously too far over the hill to learn. I could use a drink. So could you, I dare say? Good lunch with Elizabeth?'

He shot a sideways glance at his wife. She was looking relaxed and happy and fiddling about with the papers on his desk, setting them all straight. His habitual untidiness was anathema to her. Leah was an organised soul and not bad at organising other people. Why was she looking so damn pleased with life? Why not? Why was that little smile playing round her mouth? Was it a smile? Was he imagining it? But for God's sake, the poor woman could smile, couldn't she? What kind of a monster of a husband was he?

He waited for her reply, forcing down the unworthy suspicions, trying to look unconcerned, hoping he'd sounded normal. Getting himself into his usual stewed-up mess, in other words.

'The lunch was fine. Lizzie was – Lizzie. I'm devoted to her, naturally, but even when she was a little thing she wasn't the sort of daughter anyone could make a fuss of. Now I look at her and listen to her and think, is it possible she's only nineteen? She looks like a woman of thirty, talks like one of forty and frankly, frightens me. However, duty is done. We parted affectionately and with mutual relief. I don't have to get in touch with Lizzie nor she with me for at least another month.'

As she spoke she led the way out of his study and set off towards the drawing room. Denis, following, took a surreptitious glance in a mirror and straightened his tie. Leah, with every hair in place, was, as usual, immaculately groomed from tip to toe. Presumably the late Marcus Keller had liked it that way. From wherever Keller was now, his shade probably watched balefully over his once wife and her new husband, waiting for the signs of disintegration in her well-being which must surely come about now he wasn't around to take care of her and it was left to a prize idiot like Denis.

That Leah had married him when she could have had anyone remained one of life's insoluble mysteries not only to him, Denis, but to their entire joint acquaintance.

Sometimes, about a dozen times a day in fact, Denis wondered why Leah *had* married him. It wasn't for money because she had plenty of that. Or rather she had a good part of Marcus Keller's. She certainly had more than he had, or ever would have. Being a food expert didn't pay the kind of money some people imagined and the late Mr Keller still paid their household bills from the afterlife, as it were.

It wasn't because Denis was young (he was fifty-two) or handsome (he was losing his hair and his chest seemed inexplicably to be located where his waist used to be) or indeed because he was particularly anything. He was of course modestly successful in his own way, which was writing about food and wine, and the TV series had made him a household name. But that wasn't the sort of professional line he would have expected to attract the widow of a multi-millionaire who had dominated the financial world in his lifetime and whose portrait graced the boardrooms of half the financial institutions in the city, as far as Denis could make out.

They had reached the drawing room. It was Leah's house and all the beautiful furnishings had been chosen by her and paid for with Keller money. Everything was done in Leah's taste. She had a liking for pearl greys, misty blues and salmon pinks. Denis, who liked stark contrasts, black and white, splashes of scarlet and tropical greens, found these dawn hues muffling and soporific. He couldn't tune in to them and frequently felt like a sort of lodger in superior digs. Even worse, among the mauve-pinks and gilded rococo furniture of their marital bedchamber he sometimes felt he'd strayed into some upmarket brothel he couldn't afford.

Leah had sunk down in a chair and crossed her beautiful legs. She tossed back long shining chestnut hair and said mellifluously, 'G and T for me, sweetie.'

Denis, the booze expert after all, always poured the

drinks. He busied himself at the cabinet now and wished he felt more like a man relaxing in his own home and less like a barman. It wasn't Leah's fault. It was a stupid neurosis of his own. Putting it bluntly, he couldn't manage to come to terms with his amazing good fortune in capturing Leah – and all the Keller millions with her. He kept thinking he'd wake up, and Leah, everything, would be gone. Or that something would happen to destroy it all. And something might, yet . . . Or already had. God, he felt so guilty.

'Denis? You've gone off into a brown study again!' Laughter gurgled attractively in his wife's voice.

'Um, sorry . . . one drink coming up!'

He crossed the room to hand it to her and went back to pour himself a scotch. When he was seated opposite her, nursing his tumbler and wishing he had a cigarette (he'd given up six months before, on marrying Leah), she said:

'Are you worried about anything, Denis? I mean, apart from the wretched word processor?'

'No – do I look it?'

'Frankly, yes. And you've taken to mumbling in your sleep.'

'Sorry . . .'

'And you keep apologising to me, which makes *me* nervous!'

'Sor— I mean, I hadn't realised I was doing it.'

'Is it the party on Saturday at Eric Schuhmacher's new place?'

The scotch splashed out of Denis's tumbler and he dragged out his handkerchief and scrubbed at his knee where a damp patch stained it. 'Lord, no, why should it be? I mean, it's straightforward. Eric wants me to give him a decent write-up and unless something really horrendous goes wrong, I shall.' He fell silent, chewing his lip. Something really horrendous . . . For whom? For Eric?

'Denis . . .' Now Leah was beginning to sound less concerned than cross. 'Honestly, you're going to have to see a doctor.'

'Whaffor?' he demanded defiantly.

'Because you're a nervous wreck!' Leah paused. 'It isn't anything to do with me, is it?'

'No!' he almost shouted.

'I keep forgetting it's a first-time-round marriage for you. I'm sort of used to being married, first to Bernie, then Marcus and now to you. But to you, well, being married must be like having a permanent intruder in your life.'

'I'm very happy!' Denis leaned forward, clasping the tumbler tightly. 'I swear, Leah. I was never so happy in my life.'

'Well, look it, for heaven's sake! Or sound it! One or the other – preferably both!'

'It's just that I'm not like Bernie or Marcus, I'm not a financial wizard, a go-getter, possessor of a rapier brain at whose approach lesser mortals tremble. I'm just a scribbler about nosh who can't master his own word processor and I feel—'

Leah leapt up and came over to him. She put her hands on his shoulders and, bending down, kissed him, her long chestnut hair brushing his cheek, her perfume filling his nostrils and the warmth from her body seeping into his skin. As always, when she touched him like this, he felt he trembled from top to toe. He set down the glass and grabbed her, pulling her down on his lap.

'I love you,' she whispered, twisting her arms round his neck.

He said desperately, 'I love you too, Leah. I love you so much I ache.'

* * *

'Margery?' Ellen Bryant paused by a display stand to straighten up a stack of expensive angora wools. 'I'm taking this Saturday afternoon off. You can manage in the shop, can't you? This hot weather makes it a slow time. No one thinks about sitting home and knitting when the sun is beating down.'

'Needles' was the name of the shop Ellen ran in Bamford High Street. It catered for home knitters, needlecraft workers and dressmakers and Ellen aimed for the best. Nothing in Needles was cheap, but people came from miles around to buy their wool, patterns, trimmings, embroidery silks and all the other bits and pieces associated with nimble fingers.

Ellen looked complacently around the shop now, a wonderful treasure house glowing with the jewel-like colours of the wools and silks. Just in front of her was a special display in shades of mauves and purples of which she was particularly proud. She was clever at showing things off to their best advantage. She knew how to make the best of her own natural advantages too. Unthinkingly, she straightened her sweater and pushed up its sleeves. Her bangles jingled musically.

'Oh, yes, Ellen,' said Margery Collins quickly. She brushed away a wisp of untidy hair and blinked eagerly at her employer through her large round steel-rimmed spectacles.

The blatant heroine-worship in Margery's brown eyes would have embarrassed most people but Ellen usually accepted it with amusement and, frankly, as no more than her due. Margery was such a mouse but at least she had the sense to recognise it. Unlike Hope; what a mess that woman was! Hope's reaction towards Ellen had been one of jealousy from the start and it was only to be expected, thought Ellen serenely. However, something about Margery's admiration just now irritated, and those devoted brown eyes reminded her of a spaniel.

'Just lock up as usual – and I'll see you on Monday morning!' she said a little sharply.

'Right you are!' breathed Margery, adding daringly, 'I hope you'll have a nice time – wherever it is you're going.'

'I doubt it!' said Ellen brusquely and poor little Margery looked appalled at her own temerity at asking in the first place.

Ellen lived over the shop. It was a comfortable flat and opening the door to it gave her the same kind of satisfied glow that gazing round her business did. She reflected on her good fortune as she climbed the spiral stair. The building was unusual for this area where so much was built in stone. It was timber-framed, black and white, with a jutting upper storey supported by carved corbel heads which grimaced down at passers-by. It was known locally as 'the Tudor house'. Apart from the church, it was the oldest building in Bamford to survive in anything like its original form and its appearance certainly helped to entice people into the shop.

She made a decent living from Needles and didn't pay Margie a vastly generous wage. Let's face it, no one else would have employed Margie, so dowdy and without interests in life except the shop and some sort of ultra-strict religious sect she attended on Sundays. Ellen knew she terrorised and exploited her assistant but she salved her conscience with the knowledge that it would all be made up to Margie one day. Not that Margie knew this. It would be a big surprise. But not for a long time yet, let's hope! thought Ellen as she closed the door of her living room.

She dismissed all thought of Margery Collins. She had, goodness only knew, enough other things to think about. For Ellen was by no means as pleased with life as it appeared, nor as she had been a year ago. Dissatisfaction had crept in, a tiny worm in the centre of the apple, gnawing away at her peace of mind. She wasn't a woman to do nothing, and so she'd done something . . . convinced at the time it was right and proper and her due. But then it hadn't quite gone as she'd envisaged. Perhaps she ought to have planned things better. The whole business was a damn nuisance. In a way she wished she hadn't started any of it. And there was Hope and her wretched determination to make a scene at Springwood Hall. But Ellen was going to turn up all right that Saturday. However she had her own reasons for it and they had nothing to do with preserving mausoleums of old houses.

She took the envelope from the letter-rack on the desk and pulled out the slim sheet of paper. She'd read it through so many times it was beginning to get quite grimy. The typewritten message was disagreeably blunt and it was unsigned.

'We can discuss this better face to face,' it read. 'It should be possible on Sat at SH. I'll see you there and let you know when there's a chance to slip away for a private chat. I am assuming you'll be there. I really think this opportunity ought not to be missed.'

The tone of the note was a mixture of the informal and the peremptory. 'What a nerve!' she muttered. 'Ordering me to turn up!'

However, the writer was keen to maintain a façade of civility. Even so, Ellen wasn't used to people taking that kind of line with her. She always took care to make the running, took pride in doing so. Meeting opposition of any kind had come as quite a shock. Not that she couldn't deal with it.

'I'll go,' muttered Ellen. 'Why not?' She crushed the note in her hands and tossed it carelessly towards the wastepaper basket in the corner. It bounced off the rim and, unobserved, rolled under the unit housing her music centre. 'I'm not scared to spell it out, face to face. I hold all the cards, when all's said and done!'

Chapter Three

Meredith Mitchell shifted her weight cautiously from one foot to the other. Wearing stiletto heels for drinks on a lawn had perhaps been unwise. Wherever she went, she left a trail of little holes in the soft turf. Not that she wasn't enjoying the occasion. So far she'd enjoyed the day very much. She hoped Alan was enjoying it too, although she fancied that from time to time he looked a little abstracted, as if he had something on his mind. He'd tell her about it when he was ready, no doubt. One of the blessings of their relationship was that each respected the other's essential privacy.

She lifted her face to let the still-warm rays of early evening sun play on it and the breeze flutter escaping tendrils of her hair. Before her, Springwood Hall's honey-coloured stone glowed in the mellow light and in its setting of manicured lawns and clipped hedges it looked near perfection. She raised her glass in the direction of the old house and said aloud, 'Cheers!'

Laura Danby said, 'I just want to sit down.'

They had been shown over the entire place by a proud and indefatigable Eric Schuhmacher. They'd opened closets and taken due heed of colour schemes. They'd admired the sauna and the indoor swimming pool housed in the converted coachhouse. They'd been led in a respectful crocodile round the kitchens where the staff had hovered in spotless aprons and hats, obviously anxious to get on with their interrupted work. They'd descended with cries of awe into the wine cellar. Actually, thought Meredith, she hadn't much enjoyed that bit. She'd found the cellars rather chilly.

Afterwards they had been served tea. Then they had all retired to the various rooms allotted to them and changed into their evening finery. And here they all were, holding glasses and chatting against a background of trees and flowerbeds, with the promise of a marvellous dinner ahead of them.

'It is,' she said, 'a bit like Glyndebourne. All this standing around in gardens in full evening fig at far too early an hour of the day. That was a quartet I saw lugging their instruments in just now, wasn't it?'

'Eric's pulled no punches,' Alan admitted.

'There's a right old mixture of people here,' she went on. 'That distinguished looking chap is Victor Merle, I know, because I once went to a lecture he gave. I did get a chance to have a word with him when we were being shown round. That balding chap with the expanding tum is, I understand, Denis Fulton. He looks as if he's had a few gourmet meals all right, a few too many!'

'He pinched Paul's recipe!' said Laura firmly.

'Don't start that again,' Paul said wearily. 'He didn't. He borrowed it. And he wrote and asked first if he might. He didn't have to do that. I kept his letter and when we get home I'll hunt it out and show you and perhaps then you'll stop harping on about it.'

'He wrote and asked you but he knew you wouldn't refuse, couldn't really.'

'It's Mrs Fulton that takes my eye,' said Alan Markby, breaking into this beginning of a domestic tiff between his sister and her husband. 'I am informed by those who follow the social scene that she was the relict of Marcus Keller, the millionaire. Rather a stunning lady, wouldn't you say?'

'Marcus Keller to Denis Fulton!' said Laura in tones which implied a dreadful fall from grace. 'Denis won't have to sing for his supper nowadays! All right, he may be a frightfully nice chap as Paul insists and I doubt, but frankly, I wouldn't have thought he was her type.'

'Who is ever whose type?' asked her brother mildly.

Meredith, knowing he was looking at her and the question directed at her, turned away. She studied the glamorous Mrs Fulton, formerly Keller and before that hadn't there been a first husband? Meredith was apt to get confused about this sort of social tittle-tattle in which she had basically little interest. Anyhow, there Leah Keller Fulton was, slim, elegant and turning all heads.

Beside his wife Denis looked flustered. Meredith began to concentrate on Mr Fulton, forgetting Leah. He looked unhappy, even hunted. Was he worrying what to put in his review? He was doing his best to behave as if he were at ease, but he was no actor.

Leah Fulton, Meredith now noticed, began to move away from the group including her husband to the other side of the lawn where Victor Merle greeted her. She saw the art historian incline his head of beautifully waved silver hair, take Leah's hand and raise it briefly to his lips. To do that kind of thing a man needed real style and assurance and Merle had both. Denis, as if aware that just at the moment he didn't give the impression of having either, looked miserable, observed Meredith. He shuffled about, straightened his bow tie, scrubbed furiously at the sleeve of his jacket as if some mark had appeared on it and glanced doubtfully at his wife and balefully at Merle, as if he would have liked to have followed and listened to their conversation but didn't dare. Eventually he excused himself from his companions and trailed away to join others, still casting occasional unhappy glances at his wife. Meredith wondered what worried him. Leah was presumably circulating in a well-trained way and before long the social Paul Jones executed another change of partners, this time Merle himself crossing the short patch of lawn to join Meredith's group.

'The house looks remarkably improved,' Markby said to him. 'I'm impressed by what's been done and I understand you advised Eric on most of the changes. I remember this place as a near ruin.'

'Yes, it's a pleasant old house of its type,' Merle replied in his slightly professorial manner. He was no different standing here on a lawn with a drink in his hand to how Meredith remembered him, lecturing to a room full of students. Although viewed closer to hand he was perhaps even more of an impressive figure. 'But it's not important,' the art historian went on. 'The architecture is a mishmash of fashionable styles of the time and the architect unknown. I suspect he was a local builder with some knowledge of design and he looked in books for ideas. To see it as an important Victorian residence and wish to preserve it, every brick and stone, as did the Society for Preserving old Bamford or whatever it's called – that was sheer nonsense.'

'Did the society give you a lot of trouble?' Meredith asked.

'My dear Miss Mitchell, they made a lot of fuss but they never had a case. They wanted a public inquiry but they didn't get one! We had more trouble with the fire service which worried about the open staircase and so forth. They were extraordinarily particular about the safety arrangements but I think we managed to satisfy them in the end. But the historical society? No.' Merle's tone became one of contempt. 'A bunch of cranks! I just hope that now they've found some other cause to campaign about. I don't care what it is, so long as I don't receive any more correspondence from them!'

Meredith glanced across the lawn. Neither of the Fultons was now to be seen nor, come to that, was Schuhmacher, and she wondered if he'd gone to check on his kitchens.

At this point she became aware of some disturbance. A little way away a small crowd of local sightseers had gathered, kept back behind a barrier. Not much went on around Bamford apart from the occasional fête or jumble sale, and the opening of the hotel and on such a fine day had provided an obvious and popular outing. They'd been there all afternoon, snapping away with their cameras, ooh-ing and ah-ing, but now some new happening had taken their attention. The crowd parted and Meredith saw that the TV camera crew had arrived. As one, the assembled special guests straightened up and surreptitiously tidied hair and fixed smiles.

Zoë Foster and Ellen Bryant, standing together at the back of the crowd, also observed the arrival of the TV crew.

'This,' Ellen said in a low voice, 'is where I slip away. And if you've got any sense, Zoë, you'll do the same!'

'You don't think Hope really will – will do what she said?'

'Why not? She's crazy enough. But I can do without that kind of publicity for Needles. I don't suppose it's really what you want for your old nags' home. I'm just not going to be around when the cameras start turning and Hope starts streaking!'

'But we ought to stop her!' exclaimed Zoë anxiously.

'A tank couldn't stop her.'

Zoë hesitated then took her stand. 'I can't leave – it would be like, well, deserting Hope.'

'Rubbish. You've turned up and shown your face, haven't you? As I have? We've done our bit, we're excused. So long – see you around!'

And Ellen slipped between the nearer bystanders and vanished from sight. Robin Harding appeared in her place.

'Ellen deserted?'

'Sort of. I can't blame her. She's worried about bad publicity for her shop. I mean, Needles is a posh sort of shop. Hope won't really do it, will she?'

He shrugged. 'We'll have to wait and see. I haven't seen her for the past ten minutes. Your animals have been quiet this afternoon. Have you got them all doped?'

'Emma Danby is with them. I've shut the noisiest ones in the barn. Robin, I'm worried sick about it all. I don't mean Hope's protest stunt, I mean the rest home, I know it's nothing to do with you—'

He seized her hand. 'See here, we're friends, aren't we? If you've got troubles, we'll share them. Something will turn up, never fear. Old Schuhmacher will relent.'

'Not a chance,' said Zoë dismally.

'Well, in the meantime Ellen isn't going to quit on us! We're all in this together. If my ugly mug and your fair countenance are going to be put before the nation's viewers, to say nothing of a great deal more of our chairperson than most people would care to set eyes on – Ellen is going to be there too. I'm going to find her and drag her back!'

Robin disappeared into the crowd and Zoë found herself

alone again. She could see Charles Grimsby mooching
about with scowling visage a few yards away and now he
came over.

'Seen Hope?'

'No, neither has Robin.'

'I've been looking for her for a quarter of an hour by
my watch.'

'Perhaps she's gone home?' suggested Zoë forlornly.

'We should be so lucky. I'll keep looking and you keep
your eyes peeled. It's up to us.' He stalked grimly away.

As for Hope . . . where was she? Zoë looked round frantically and thought she caught a glimpse of the batik print
between some shrub conifers. She made her way as unob-
trusively as possible in that direction and saw the coloured
cloth more clearly. Hope was behind the screen of trees,
moving energetically about. Quite possibly she was taking
off her clothes and unwrapping the banner. Zoë's heart sank
and a paralysis of horror seized her. Hope really was going
to do it.

Zoë snapped back into life. 'No, she's not!' she muttered.
'I'm going to stop her!'

She began to walk briskly towards the conifers which
were providing Hope Mapple with an *al fresco* changing
room but she was too late. The greenery parted and their
chairperson emerged, flushed of face and stark naked but
for a pair of plimsoles.

The awful thing was, as far as Zoë was concerned, that
Hope just looked so funny. Not shocking, not sexy, not even
rude. Just vulgarly comic, like one of those seaside post-
cards. Even so she began to run towards her, holding her
arms outstretched to either side in a vain attempt to shield
others from the view and trying to call just loud enough
for Hope alone to hear it, 'Go back! Don't do it!'

* * *

The first thing to attract Meredith's attention was the shriek, a sort of ululating war-whoop which made everyone's head turn, not only hers. A united gasp went up from the onlookers.

A grotesque figure had emerged from the spectators who, astounded, had fallen back like the parting waves of the Red Sea to let her through their midst. The figure was undeniably female; the evidence for that was startlingly displayed. She was a very large lady, shaped like one of those primitive earth-mother figurines, ample charms flaunted in a wonderful free and proud manner. In her way she was awesome, not beautiful, but to Meredith's eye, magnificent if flawed. She had a great deal of black hair falling about her shoulders and very little else to disguise anything. Nothing else, as far as Meredith could make out.

The apparition looked round as if to make sure she had everyone's attention. She raised a banner with an indecipherable legend and set off at a lumbering run towards the crowd and the lawn with its invited guests, heading, so it seemed to Meredith, straight towards her.

Reactions were initially slow. Only one man from the crowd was racing around the edge, perhaps intending to cut the streaker off. But she was too quick for him and others had not yet organised themselves to intervene. The naked woman was moving deceptively fast and she'd reached the barrier.

For a dreadful moment Meredith feared she meant to try and hurdle it. But she just swept it aside and, whooping, raced on, brandishing her flowing banner. She'd reached the edge of the lawn and the gala guests, attracted by the rumpus, had all seen her now. Their faces, frozen and disbelieving, gazed at the sight and their hands remained clasping their drinks half raised to their lips. In the surrounding crowd faces were equally dazed and only one person was pointing and saying something to a companion.

But the TV crew had spotted the cause of the commotion all right and their reporter, who had been trying to inject some enthusiasm into what he privately considered a dreary society shindig, had the look on his face of a man whose pools coupon had come up.

Then one of the security guards hired by Schuhmacher to watch over his special guests, his face white with shock, shouted a warning and began to pound heavy-footed towards the demonstrator. Schuhmacher himself was back, his face as red as the guard's was white. Beside Meredith, Alan Markby swore softly and began to run, dragging off his jacket with great presence of mind as he raced forward, intent on veiling this unexpected and undesirable display of flesh.

The streaker avoided them all. She ducked and dived under the guard's outstretched hand, hurled the banner over Schuhmacher's head and raced round the corner of the building. Behind her came the security men, Schuhmacher still entangled in the banner, Markby, Laura and Paul Danby and even Victor Merle. After them came the TV camera crew, all baying like hounds in full cry. Meredith was caught up in the crazy chase, picking up her long skirts clear of the grass and bounding along as if headed for the tape on some far-off school sports day. 'This is madness!' she thought, but couldn't stop. Her legs had taken on an impetus of their own and any attempt to stop or even slow down would have caused a disastrous pile-up all around her.

The crowd of sightseers, who'd never expected a show half as good, had entered into the spirit of the thing. They whistled and cheered and roared on the competitors in the impromptu fancy-dress race presented. Several of the younger ones surged through the destroyed barrier and joined the pack.

The front runners vanished round the side of the building to the back. Meredith, in company with everyone around her, followed them. They were all mingled together now, invited and mere onlookers. Social and technical barriers had broken down. Dinner jackets and long gowns jostled among blue jeans and sweat-shirts, diamonds glittered next door to chainstore plastic earrings. Cameras of all kinds from the TV company's to humble snapshot varieties were waved. Expensive hairdos were wrecked. The man from the television was shouting himself hoarse. It was bedlam.

Their quarry had been cornered at the back of the house. But she still tried to avoid capture. She turned and dived into the entrance to the kitchens but seeing an array of startled cooks in front of her, stopped, pinned against the side wall of the narrow corridor. Her hand groped vaguely at the wall behind her and connected with a door handle. Desperately she tugged at it and miraculously it opened.

She vanished backwards through it with the suddenness of the demon king in panto. Meredith wouldn't have been surprised to see a puff of smoke. But an empty doorway was explained by the fact that following some instinct, she must have run down steps inside. The pack, in considerable disarray, tried to follow her. They piled up in the cramped vestibule, getting squashed in the narrow doorway, howling contradictory instructions at one another and uttering squawks of pain as elbows encountered ribs.

The steps down which the streaker had vanished led, Meredith knew from their earlier tour, to the wine cellars.

There was no other way in or out and they had the streaker trapped. Meredith didn't really want to go down after her, but caught up in the crowd she found herself pushed through the door and down the stone staircase underground.

At the bottom the woman stood at bay, panting but triumphant. Her modesty had been restored, more or less, in haphazard fashion. She wore Alan Markby's jacket and round her lower half was swathed a silver lamé evening shawl donated by one of the lady celebrities.

As Meredith arrived, Eric Schuhmacher erupted from the crowd and shook his fist under the miscreant's nose. He was nearly incoherent with rage, his eyes, bloodshot and rolling, protruded from his head and sweat poured from his brow.

'Bloody stupid woman! You've ruined my entire opening! Ruined! So much work! The preparation, have you any idea? No, no, you are too stupid! All these people! My God, I kill you!' He stretched out his hands as if to grab the dishevelled woman's throat.

'Steady, Eric!' snapped Markby, putting up an arm to deflect him. 'The TV people . . .'

Schuhmacher groaned and turned away, clasping his head.

Meredith, still panting, made an effort to extricate herself from the mob at last. Both embarrassed at having joined in the hunt and oppressed by the squash of bodies in such a small area, she edged her way out of the throng into the further recesses of the cellars.

They were surprisingly extensive. As she knew from her earlier visit they consisted of a number of parallel galleries linked by rounded stone arches. It was a sort of catacomb, white-washed and with a thick black cable running along the ceiling to link the electric light bulbs which lit the place. The rows of bottle racks filled much of the space but the effect was still eerie and the temperature was several degrees cooler than outside. Cautiously, Meredith found her way into the furthest gallery. Here a worn flight of steps led up to a blank wall: the old entrance connecting the cellars to the kitchens, now blocked up. It reinforced the feeling of being trapped, of being bricked up alive.

Meredith shivered. There was a story by Edgar Allan Poe about a man who lured his enemy into his wine cellar in order to brick him up in it. No, sherry – that was it. She contemplated the rows of wine bottles and wondered vaguely as to their joint worth. She wasn't a wine buff. The man in the story lured his enemy down to try a rare Amontillado. What nonsense. Why, then, did these rows of bottles lying on their sides in their cradles look so sinister, like so many cannons pointed at her? She sniffed. The air wasn't as fresh as it could be. That might be because of all the people who had traipsed in and out of the cellars today, to say nothing of the arguing mob round the corner in the further aisle. An odd smell, a bit winy, a bit dusty, a bit flowery or fruity. She sniffed the air again. Surprisingly flowery. Not a wine smell at all.

She turned to go back and her eye caught a glimmer of white at the far end of the gallery where the wine racks finished and there was a gap between them and the wall. Meredith squinted. It was a white glove, lying on the stone-flagged floor. Someone, a guest earlier or perhaps a waiter, had dropped it. She began to walk towards it and then she saw that it wasn't a glove. It was a hand.

Meredith stopped, feeling suddenly sick. She could have turned and called for help, but a babble of voices indicated everyone was concerned with getting the streaker out of the cellars and fending off the camera crew. She made herself walk forward, one step at a time, one step nearer.

The hand was turned palm uppermost and now she could see the arm, and the body of the woman curled up in the recess.

A mixture of thoughts jostled for supremacy in Meredith's head. Her first was that this person hadn't been crouched in the gap earlier when they'd all been shown over the cellars. The second was a fervent wish that this same person, whoever it was, was merely drunk or playing some stupid game rather in the way the streaker had done. Perhaps this was another of someone's nonsensical ideas for disrupting the gala. But behind all these random speculations loomed a greater truth and a more terrifying one.

Meredith stooped over the huddled form. She could now see it was a woman of perhaps forty, dark hair trimmed into a straight bob. She was – or had been – good-looking with high cheekbones which were faintly Slavic. Her lipsticked mouth was slightly open, as were her eyes. She looked surprised, as if she'd been stopped in mid-speech. Meredith wondered what she had been saying. She saw that the woman wore a scarlet hand-knitted sweater.

Protruding from the indentation above her collar bone was the handle of a knife, and a rivulet of blood, unnoticed at first because it was so uncannily alike to the sweater in hue, ran down and soaked the knitted neck of the garment.

Meredith fought back nausea. She straightened up and looked quickly round her and in doing so, caught a movement on the other side of a free-standing open rack of bottles to her left.

'Who's there?' she called sharply. 'Come out!'

As the words left her mouth she realised that the invitation was both stupid and dangerous. It could.well be the killer who lurked there. But it was too late to run. She steeled herself.

Her words were answered with a gasp, the scrape of a foot on the brick floor, and a figure emerged unwillingly to stand before her.

It was a young woman, in her early twenties. She wore jeans and trainers and her hair had been chopped off in a ragged urchin cut so uneven she must surely have attempted her own hair-dressing. She was weather-tanned, like a much more elderly person, but nonetheless pretty, although her face was now distorted into a picture of terror, the mouth working but no sound coming out, her rounded pale blue eyes starting from their sockets.

Meredith, recognising incipient hysteria, said quickly, 'It's all right, don't panic!'

The words were nonsensical, but did the trick. The other looked up at her and whispered. 'She – she is dead, isn't she?'

'Yes. I think so. We mustn't touch her.' Meredith hesitated. The girl hardly looked like a murderer but was certainly an important witness. The choice was between sending her off to find help and risking her disappearing – or leaving her here while Meredith fetched help, and risking her tampering with the evidence in some way. If they went together, it might be difficult in the crowd to attract Markby and keep an eye on the girl. And someone had to stop anyone else wandering into this bay and raising a further hullaballoo. She made her decision.

'I'll go and ask Chief Inspector Markby to come. He's only just over by the entrance. You must stay here—'

'Oh no, I can't!' The voice emerged in a strangled cry.

'It will only be for a few minutes. He's in the first bay with the crowd. What's your name?'

'Zoë – Zoë Foster.' The girl blinked. 'That – that's . . .' Her eyes rolled whitely towards the body.

'Yes? Do you know her?' Meredith frowned.

'Y-yes. It's Ellen . . . Ellen Bryant. She's – she's a member of our society.'

'Society?' For a moment Meredith didn't make the connection.

'For the Preservation of Historic Bamford. She – I – all of us, we came here to protest. The – the streaking was Hope's idea. Ellen didn't want to be there . . . she went away. We only came to protest . . .'

The girl's voice died and she gulped, turning her face away from the dead woman.

Meredith hoped the girl wasn't going to be sick. As much to distract her as in the hope of securing information, she asked quickly, 'And, er, Ellen, she didn't want to join the protest?'

'No – because of her shop, the bad publicity. I was only worried about Hope. I wanted to s-stop her.' The speaker rubbed her hand over her mouth. Hand and voice were shaking. 'I followed the crowd down here, but when I saw Hope with all those people around her, I was so ashamed – embarrassed – I don't know! I wanted to get away and I couldn't get back up the stairs so I came through here and – and I found—'

She raised a trembling hand and indicated the collapsed form. 'And then I heard someone coming. It was you, but I didn't know that. I hid quickly, over there. I was frightened.'

'Yes, of course you were.' Meredith eyed her thoughtfully. 'But you don't need to be afraid now. The – your friend, can't hurt you. I must go and fetch the chief inspector and you must stay here and stop anyone else coming

45

into this bay. Be brave, just for a few minutes more.'

The girl nodded and made a visible effort to pull herself together.

Meredith gave her a reassuring smile and hurried past the ranked muzzles of the wine bottles to find Markby.

Chapter Four

The change which came over the scene at Springwood Hall once the gala occasion became a police investigation seemed even to extend to the weather. The late afternoon sun disappeared. Everything was now suffused by the mournful tone of the cool, dull grey light which replaced it. The bright colours seeped out of the flowers, making them look tired, and out of the women's high-fashion gowns which now just seemed garish. The green lawns took on an olive tinge. The faces of the prestige guests looked all at once older and unglamorous. The local people who had come to be entertained now looked frightened and awkward, huddling in whispering groups. The identity of the murder victim was not yet generally known but it was enough that 'they' had found 'a dead body'.

Shivering in the fresh breeze and with the addition to their company of the members of the Society for the Preservation of Historic Bamford, those invited to the gala were disentangled from the *hoi polloi* and herded into the restaurant to await police attentions.

'Sheep from the goats!' said Meredith to Laura. Of the two groups theirs, she had a nasty feeling, was to be sacrificed. The common bond of party-goers was broken. Murder had come among them and with it distrust, suspicion and fear.

47

The restaurant, its tablecloths so crisply white, its glass-ware shining and cutlery gleaming, now looked less set out for a festive gathering than for a funeral wake. The profusion of fresh flowers Eric had ordered arranged all round the room only enhanced this impression. An air of sadness had entered it and Meredith felt a pang of pity for Schuhmacher who, with his staff, had worked so hard for this occasion. She wondered what the scene in the kitchens was like, where Ulli Richter now presided over a wonderful meal, spoiling as it waited indefinitely with the strong possibility it would never be served. She doubted anyone here felt like eating.

They were standing in subdued groups, nervously avoiding one another's eye, few people attempting conversation. Paul Danby, to his wife's obvious annoyance, was lost in frowning study of a menu card. Markby was appearing and disappearing again with disconcerting suddenness, having taken charge of the emergency on an *ad hoc* basis. Victor Merle stood alone before an oil painting, inspecting it closely, his back to the rest of them. His disapproval at the turn of events was registered in every line of his body. He had simply opted out of the gathering, present in body but not in spirit.

Meredith still felt cold, probably, she realised, as a result of shock. She made her way to the exit into the main hall with the intention of going upstairs and collecting her coat, only to find her way barred by Sergeant Pearce who had arrived with the first siren-sounding posse of police vehicles.

'Good evening, Miss Mitchell!' he greeted her amiably. 'Nice to see you again. Pity about all this.'

'Yes,' said Meredith glumly, hugging her bare arms. 'Can I go and get my coat?'

'Everyone's supposed to stay down here where we can see 'em until we've got statements,' he pointed out, more in sorrow than reproach. 'I'll have to get his nibs' – sorry, I mean the chief inspector's say-so.' Pearce looked across the room. 'He's pretty tied up just at the minute and I'm supposed to keep my eye on this door until he's sorted out what he wants everyone to do. If you could hang on for a bit, one of the constables will come over here to stand guard and I'll be free to collect statements. I'll ask the chief inspector about you going upstairs.'

'I don't like to bother him.' Meredith sighed. 'I could try mind over matter! Tell myself the place is like a hothouse.'

Pearce grinned sympathetically and then, without warning, acquired a conspiratorial manner. 'Just between the two of us, Miss Mitchell . . .' He looked furtively across the room. 'He's not said anything to you about leaving us?'

'Chief Inspector Markby?' Meredith stared at him. 'How do you mean, leaving?'

'I mean, getting promotion and shoved upstairs, you know.'

'No, not a word!' Meredith tried to digest the idea. 'Is this certain?'

'I don't know for sure, none of us does! He hasn't said a word to anyone. Don't tell him I was asking, will you? It's just that a rumour's been going round. I mean, we all think he's earned his promotion, but we'll all be sorry to see him go from Bamford.'

'Go from Bamford?' This was so incredible a notion that even Meredith's fertile imagination had difficulty absorbing it. 'Alan – not in Bamford?'

'People move about,' said Pearce argumentatively. 'I would have thought you'd know that, in your line of work.'

'Well, yes, I certainly do. But he hasn't said anything of the sort to me and in any case—' She paused. 'Maybe it's only a rumour.'

'Perhaps.' Pearce eyed her doubtfully. 'I thought he would have told you, you being friendly with him, as it were. I didn't mean to put my foot in it!' he added with a wry grimace.

'No, of course not.'

The brief discussion was over but it left Meredith thinking furiously and feeling a niggle of annoyance. Perhaps it wasn't true, only a rumour. On the other hand, there was no smoke without fire, according to the old saying. In any large organisation word of change, promotions and the like, tended to precede official announcement. If it were true, Alan might have mentioned it. They were close enough, surely?

She looked across the room. 'I'll go and ask him myself if I can go upstairs. It won't take a second or two.'

Meredith retraced her steps to where she'd last spotted Alan and found him surrounded by a small but agitated crowd consisting of Eric Schuhmacher, two police officers (male), one police officer (female, Wpc Jones) and a man she recognised vaguely as being the one who had raced vainly to cut off the streaker at the outset. She couldn't see Zoë Foster there and supposed that the girl had been isolated somewhere to be dealt with separately. Meredith, remembering Zoë's pale frightened face, felt a pang of sympathy.

As for the streaker, now identified as Hope Mapple, her limelight had been abruptly switched to another and more sinister subject. Silenced, yet still able to display in her manner a trace of her former bold defiance, Ms Mapple had been reunited with her clothes and whisked away in a police car to make her statement at the station.

It took a minute or two to catch Markby's eye and engage in a pantomime indicating she was freezing to death and could she go upstairs to get her coat. He nodded and signalled across the room to Pearce.

However, before Meredith could gain the staircase she was intercepted by Denis Fulton. He looked dreadful, grey-faced and sweating. Really, she thought, quite ill.

'I say,' he said hurriedly, 'all that charade-type miming you were doing over there, I take it you're going upstairs for some warm clothing?'

'Yes, my coat.'

'You couldn't nip along to our room, number fourteen, and fetch down Leah's stole? She's very upset and feeling cold and it would mean interrupting that fellow Markby again . . .'

'Certainly,' Meredith said. She glanced across the room. Leah was sitting alone on a chair staring fixedly into space, her face quite expressionless. Meredith would not have said that she gave any sign of being more upset than Denis. On the other hand, Denis presumably knew how to interpret his wife's mood.

'I don't want,' said Denis, again in a hoarse undertone, 'to interrupt him, Markby.'

'He's very understanding,' she heard herself say in defence of Alan, whom Denis seemed to view as some kind of ogre. 'But yes, he is rather busy.'

'Don't want to talk to him!' said Denis, now showing a tendency to develop an alarming twitch at the corner of his left eye. 'Have to talk to him, one of them, soon. But what for? We don't know anything about it!' His voice rose on a querulous note. 'I don't see why we have to be kept hanging around here. We're not suspects, for pity's sake! Why couldn't Eric keep an eye on his blasted cellar? He's got no business letting bodies be found in it. It's Eric's hotel! I can understand why the plods want to talk to him! Why have we got to be grilled?'

'Routine, I suppose. I'll get the coats.'

Upstairs the hotel was empty and her footsteps echoed, muffled on the new carpeting. She found her coat and went along to room fourteen to find the stole. In the Fultons' room the subtle scent of expensive perfume lingered on the air. Leah's make-up items were on the dressing table and the dress she had worn earlier in the day was on a hanger hooked over the open bathroom door. Meredith, who had employed the same trick to remove creases by means of bathroom steam on many occasions, smiled. All the same, it was embarrassing to ferret about in someone else's room. Although there was no one on this floor but herself, she still felt that someone, a staff member or a police officer, might come in and ask what she was doing. She grabbed the stole and hurried back downstairs.

During her absence someone had organised cups of tea which were being served by an immaculate and admirably unflustered waiter from a trolley, incongruous in the circumstances. Eric clearly meant to look after his guests, no matter what. Meredith took the stole to where Leah sat and bent over her.

'Your husband asked me to bring this down for you.'

Leah Fulton looked up and smiled. It was such a radiantly beautiful smile that Meredith experienced quite a feeling of shock. The same perfume as had left its traces in the bedroom made its discreet presence known and Leah's pose seemed perfect, not a hair out of place, no obvious sign of being upset. It would be difficult to imagine a greater contrast between her manner and that of her agitated spouse and no one could have looked more unsuited to be on the scene of a murder. Years on the social treadmill, however, might explain her composure. Society hostesses and humble consular staff alike have to be able to cope with anything.

'Thank you!' Pearly-pink varnished nails closed on the stole. 'Denis is very thoughtful. And it's so kind of you to bother.'

'No trouble. It seemed easier than asking permission to leave the room twice.'

'I shall have to ask permission to leave the room in a minute,' said Leah unexpectedly. 'I need to go to the loo.' She pulled the stole round her shoulders with a sudden irritable movement and Meredith began to suspect that beneath the serene exterior Leah was very distressed, after all. Denis was right. 'I suppose,' Leah said drily, 'that if and when we go, that woman police officer will accompany us. It's degrading.'

'I suppose she will,' Meredith looked at Wpc Jones. 'Not much fun for her, either.'

'Yes, well, we're not camels!' Leah wriggled. 'And the last thing I need is to be plied with wretched cups of tea!'

This last was a response to the arrival of the waiter. Meredith took two cups of tea from him nevertheless and put them on the pristine damask cloth of the nearest table. 'You ought to drink something hot. It's good for shock.'

'A brandy would be better but I suppose we wouldn't be allowed that!' Leah sighed and added in a resigned voice. 'Denis didn't want to come today but he felt he owed it to Eric. I should have been firm and called it off. After all, there are plenty of food writers. Eric could have got someone else.'

'Why didn't Denis want to come?' Meredith asked curiously. 'I would have thought he'd have been keen to see the new restaurant.'

'Well, to begin with, Denis said the restaurant couldn't be judged by a gala evening. What's needed is for someone to turn up on an ordinary evening and see how the food and service is then.'

That seemed a fair point and reason enough, but Leah went on after a pause. 'And Denis has been under a lot of strain recently. He's got a new computer, word processor, I suppose you call the thing. He can't get the hang of it. And then there's . . .'

She fell silent. Meredith picked up her cup and sipped at the tea, grateful for the warming brew. Over the rim she could see that Denis had now been cornered by Paul, who was no doubt talking shop. She supposed that was Paul's way of coping with any upset, but it made him appear unfavourably thick-skinned. Denis did not appear to think this was the time or the place either. He was answering in irritable monosyllables, fidgeting about, in turn shooting glances towards his wife, Meredith and the policemen.

'We haven't been married very long,' Leah went on. 'Less than a year. Are you married or cohabiting or anything? Sorry, I've forgotten your name.'

'Meredith. No. I'm a singleton in every way.' She wrenched her gaze from the two professional cookery experts.

'I thought you were with the police chap – the one who's taken charge?'

'Yes – he's a friend.'

'Bit of luck, his being on the spot, I suppose. Or not, depending how you view it. I don't suppose he's feeling very chipper about it.'

Meredith looked across at Markby. He was looking distinctly harassed and was engaged in some argument with the man she didn't know. The one who had tried to head off the streaker.

Leah had picked up her cup but put it down again with a rapid movement which splashed the tea into the saucer. 'Look,' she said, leaning forward urgently. 'You'll think I've got a frightful nerve, but I'd like to ask you something. It's personal.'

'Fire away. I suppose I can always refuse to answer,' said Meredith, wondering what on earth was coming and if it was anything to do with Alan.

'You said you're a singleton. Have you ever been married or lived with anyone?'

'No, not really. I'm in the Foreign Service. I'm posted in London these days, but I've spent a lot of time travelling about on my own. I've got used to it.'

'That's it!' Leah said eagerly. 'You've got used to it! That's how Denis was till he met me. Used to being on his own. I've been married before. The first time I married I was only eighteen and I married from my parents' home. I've never lived alone, you see. When my first marriage broke up, I remarried almost at once. When Marcus died, I met Denis quite soon after. I suppose it was quite indecent, in a way, marrying Denis so soon after Marcus passed on. But I wasn't being heartless. I loved Marcus and was very happy with him. But I wasn't used to being alone. I've never had a career. I – I need someone there. I need to be married. And I do love Denis.' She paused. 'I have to have someone to love, you see.'

'Have you got any children?' Meredith put the question cautiously. As she had noticed before, shock acted on some people as too much alcohol did on others: it made them talkative, unburdening their troubled minds of personal problems with an often embarrassing degree of intimate detail to complete strangers.

'Yes, a daughter. But she's like all youngsters now, very independent with her own flat, own friends, own life . . . We really have nothing in common. We get along all right – but don't see too much of each other.' Leah sighed. 'It's difficult for poor Denis, trying to adjust to having me around. Have you and that police boyfriend of yours ever contemplated moving in together? He seems a nice man. Good-looking, too.'

Meredith smiled apologetically. 'It wouldn't work!' she said more bleakly than she'd meant to. 'I suppose, refer-ring back to what you were saying, I'm used to being on my own. Alan was married once. It didn't work out and it's left him wary. I think he'd – well, he'd like it if we were together on some permanent basis. But I'm not good at sharing my life with anyone else all the time. It sounds selfish but I don't think I'm selfish. I think I'm realistic. I think whatever relationship Alan and I have, it will last longer if we're not under one another's feet. I might be wrong, of course.'

Confidences had a way of inspiring other confidences, she thought wrily. Why was she telling her all this?

'Is he ever jealous?' Leah asked.

Meredith thought that one over. 'I've never really – well, he might be. He's never said anything. Not that he's got any reason to be jealous. I haven't got another lover hidden away in London.'

'They never do say anything,' Leah muttered. 'That's the trouble. They brood. They build things up in their imagi-nation. Then when you ask them outright, they deny it. You can always tell because they start to act shifty. I mean, I might not know much in general but I do know something about men! It's the devil's own job trying to get them to talk about what they really feel. They think it isn't macho, or something. Men, frankly, can be extremely difficult!'

There was a disturbance. Alan Markby had come into the middle of the room. Everyone fell silent and looked at him expectantly.

'Ladies and Gentlemen, I'm sure you'll all agree with me that this is a most unfortunate occurrence. We have the names and addresses of everyone here and, if anyone would now like to leave, you are free to do so. I'm afraid the activities of the police both inside and outside the building mean that the dinner has had to be cancelled. Mr. Schuhmacher asks me to make his apologies and I apologise on behalf of the police. It can't be helped!'

Markby's voice rose on the last phrase to drown the groan from the hungry crowd in the dining room.

'There are two other hotels in Bamford and several pubs which do food in the immediate area so if you'd all be so good, perhaps I could ask you to make your own arrangements. We're all sorry for the inconvenience!'

Markby's brisk words met with mutinous silence.

'I shall go back to London at once!' said Merle in a loud voice.

'Find ourselves a pub meal!' Leah gave a short laugh. 'And all of us dressed to kill!' She broke off and pulled a face. 'Oh dear, wrong expression in the circumstances!'

'Miss Foster?' Markby asked courteously.

The girl was huddled in an armchair in the hotel lounge. She looked ill, her face grey and twitching, unshed tears glistening in her eyes. His question may or may not have registered with her.

'I'm Chief Inspector Markby,' he introduced himself as he took a seat by her. 'I doubt I'll be in charge of this case but as I'm on the spot and until someone else is put in charge, I'm co-ordinating the early work. Do you understand?'

This time she reacted, nodding. 'Yes.' It was a whisper.

'I'm sorry to ask you questions now. I realise you're shocked. But I understand you discovered the body.'

'Yes.' She seemed to realise she must be almost inaudible, cleared her throat and repeated more loudly and firmly, 'Yes, I did.'

'And . . .' he glanced briefly at his scribbled notes taken down on the first thing to hand, a menu card. 'You are a member of the historical society and came here today to help mount a protest. Isn't it a bit late for all that? The hotel is now a fact of life.'

She shook her head violently. 'No, no! It wasn't like that! We weren't all here to protest. It was only Hope who wanted to do something so that our campaign shouldn't just come to a sort of soggy end. We know we're beaten – or at least, the rest of us do. But Hope still wanted to make some kind of statement. The rest of us came rather hoping we could put her off, but we didn't.'

'No, quite. Are you the young lady who runs the animal sanctuary, by the way? My niece helps out there occasionally, I believe. She's talked about you. I dare say she gets under your feet.'

The girl perked up. 'You mean Emma, don't you? Yes, and she's really a great help. It's the Alice Batt Rest Home for Horses and Donkeys.' Her manner became dejected again. 'Only Schuhmacher wants to throw us off the land. He's our landlord and the lease is up. The animals make a disturbance, he says, and our old barn spoils the view.'

'I see.' Markby eyed her thoughtfully. 'Was that your

reason for joining the campaign against turning the Hall into a hotel?'

'Yes,' she said frankly. 'But it didn't work and I suppose we'll have to go.' She looked at him, her eyes filled with misery. 'But we don't have anywhere to go.'

Markby doodled on the back of his menu card for a moment. 'May I ask your age?'

'Twenty-four.'

'And do you live out there at the rest home alone?'

She flushed deeply and her eyes sparkled defiance at him. 'Yes! I can run the place! I'm not incapable!'

'I wasn't suggesting—' he began but she swept on in a burst of indignation which, just for the moment, wiped the murder from her mind. He let her run on, hoping the outburst of emotion might act as a safety valve and help her come to terms with the recent horror.

'I know the place is as much a mess as Schuhmacher says. But the animals are all of them looked after properly! I do have some help, not just Emma. There's Rob, too. Robin Harding, I mean. He's a clerk at the estate agents' in the High Street and he belongs to the historical society. He's been a great support to the Horses' Home in lots of practical ways. Perhaps he's at a loose end, I don't know. I don't think he has much family, if any. Maybe he's just filling time. But he's always willing to come out and do the heavy jobs I can't manage. So you see, I cope very well, thank you!'

Markby, overwhelmed, retreated to the real matter. 'I see. So tell me how you came to be in the cellar.'

Her lively manner evaporated at the reminder and the pinched look returned to her face. 'I ran after Hope, trying to catch up and stop her. But then everyone else started running and I just followed. She was making a fool of herself and looked so – so silly! When we all piled down the cellar steps and I saw you and someone else trying to cover her up, and you gave her your jacket, it was so embarrassing. I wanted to get away. I was afraid Hope might call out to me and I'd be dragged into the row. That cameraman was there.'

'Yes, he was!' said Markby sourly. Getting rid of the TV crew once they'd realised they were on the scene of a murder hadn't been easy.

'I couldn't get back up the cellar steps so I retreated into the back and as I thought, empty, part of the cellars. It wasn't empty, Ellen was there – dead.'

Her voice came to a clipped halt. What she was saying tied in with what Meredith had just had time to gabble in his ear. The story raised one immediate question.

'The person to arrive next on the scene saw you emerge from behind a wine rack where you'd apparently been hiding.'

She nodded. 'I realised someone was coming and I thought the murderer might be coming back. I was scared and crouched down behind the rack because it was the nearest thing.'

'All right. Now think carefully, did you see or hear any sign of anyone else before that person, Miss Mitchell, came round the corner?'

'No. I was alone with Ellen. There was a commotion from the cellar steps, of course, and the people round Hope. But I think I would have seen or heard anyone else there by Ellen.'

'You didn't glimpse even a shadow or get an impression of another presence?' he persisted gently. 'You are quite sure you were alone with the body?'

Her eyes widened in horrified comprehension. 'I didn't kill her!'

'Now take it easy,' he soothed. 'I'm only trying to get a picture in my own mind. Did you touch the body or the weapon?'

She shuddered and shook her head.

'All right, that will do for now. Sergeant Pearce will be along in a moment to take a proper statement from you. You won't be leaving the Bamford area, going on holiday or anything like that?'

'I don't go on holiday,' she said flatly. 'Ever. I've got to look after the animals. There's no one else.' With a burst of energy and a return of that defiant look, she added, 'I don't mind! They *are* my whole life, after all!'

At twenty-four years of age, Markby thought, what a very sad little statement that was.

'That was awful,' said Laura later, summing it all up.

Three of them were collapsed in various attitudes in the Danbys' drawing room. It was after midnight and the quiet of the world outside seemed to underline the chaotic and macabre experiences of the day. Paul was slumped in an armchair. His untied black tie hung round his neck like a piece of misshapen ribbon. Laura had taken off her high-heeled shoes and propped her stockinged feet up on a coffee table. Meredith sat with feet curled under her on the sofa. Mugs which had contained coffee stood on the floor. They were waiting for Alan.

'He could be ages yet,' Meredith said. 'He mightn't come.'

'He said he'd come. If Alan says he'll come, he'll turn up – even if it's at three in the morning.'

'Hope bloody not,' said Paul gloomily.

'Go to bed, then!' snapped his wife.

'It's no use getting narked with me! I didn't bung a

corpse down in poor old Schuhmacher's cellars!'

'You didn't find it, either!' said Meredith bitterly.

The Danbys regarded her with commiseration. 'Bad luck,' said Laura.

'Teach me to go wandering off. I should have stayed with the mob.'

'That woman . . .' said Paul in an awe-struck voice. 'The streaker, what a sight.'

'I thought she looked rather splendid,' Meredith opined.

'I thought she looked ghastly!' said Laura firmly. 'And it was Hope Mapple, too. I suppose that banner was something to do with her society but I'm still surprised.' Laura turned in explanation to Meredith. 'Hope gives art lessons at adult classes and special groups and so on. Despite what happened today, I've always thought her quite reasonable, just a bit colourful. I can't think what possessed her.'

The doorbell rang. 'Alan. I'll let him in.' Paul hauled himself to his feet.

'Sorry to keep you so late,' said Markby, coming in. 'If there's any coffee left, I could do with a cup – black, please. I should have told you to go on to bed and not wait for me.'

'As if we could!' said his sister.

'I can't tell you anything. Anyway, the whole thing's probably out of my hands now. It's extremely unlikely I'll be in charge of the investigation, given that I was a guest of Eric's.'

'You can tell us if you've cast poor Hope into gaol.'

'No, good Lord! She'll be up before the magistrates in the morning. She'll probably be bound over to keep the peace. I gave her a lecture and sent her home. Serve her right if she catches cold after her escapade,' said Markby sententiously.

Paul had gone into the kitchen to make more coffee. Laura got up. 'I might as well go on to bed, then. See you in the morning.'

Alone with Meredith, Markby gave her a hunted look. 'Sorry – I thought the weekend would be fun.'

'Can't be helped.'

'I shall be busy tomorrow, too. I'm in the unenviable position of being a copper who chanced to be at the scene of a crime and so everyone assumes I must have a photographic memory – which I haven't! And on top of that we have a child molester who's been seen hanging around. So we're already stretched to breaking point.' He sighed. 'I had hoped we'd be able to go for a nice long country walk and talk about things.'

Meredith untangled her feet and stretched. 'Oh? What things?'

'Um, well . . .' He leaned forward, hands clasped, hair falling untidily over his forehead. 'This and that.'

'Alan – you're not planning to move from Bamford, are you?'

He gave her a suspicious look. 'No. I'm not. Has someone been talking to you? Where did you get the idea?'

'Nowhere in particular. I just wondered. You've been here a few years, haven't you?'

'Yes. I like it here.'

'If you got promoted—'

'Promoted? I don't want promotion!' He glared at her. 'You sound just like my ex-wife!'

'Hey! That's unfair!'

'It's true!' He threw himself back in the chair and folded his arms grimly. 'I don't want promotion and I don't want to leave here.'

'Which means, I take it, that both things have been

suggested? Is that what you wanted to talk over with me?'

'I was . . . yes, it's been suggested. I'd still like to know who put the idea in your noddle!' He scowled. 'I've got a feeling I'm entering some rotten star-sign or whatever. Not that I go in for that sort of guff. But just recently, everything is going wrong.' He leaned across impulsively. 'But we can forget it for what's left of tonight, can't we? Why don't—'

'Coffee!' said Paul cheerfully, kicking the door open and marching in with a tray. 'And I've brought my special cognac. I thought you needed cheering up, Alan, old son!' He sat down and began to busy himself pouring coffee and brandy. He'd brought three glasses.

'See what I mean?' Markby muttered to Meredith. 'Everything is jinxed!'

Chapter Five

Superintendent McVeigh slapped his broad hands with their spatulate fingers on the desk and made a hissing noise reminiscent of a steam engine coming to a halt.

'It's a tricky situation. I ought, of course, to take you off the case immediately. You're far too close to it. But on the other hand, that party was like Noah's ark, something of everything there, and no one could argue that you're not the person best placed to deal with such a variety of people.' He looked meaningfully at Markby. 'You understand the local viewpoint, which could turn out to be significant. The dead woman belonged to that protest group. You get along with these celebrity types who were all over the place at the time. You know the owner, Schuhmacher. And that's our real problem. How well do you know him?' McVeigh's sharp grey eyes rested on Markby's face.

'Hardly at all!' returned Markby promptly. 'I met him a few times literally years ago and hadn't seen him again since until the other day. I was still married when I first met him. Rachel liked going out and having fun. She also collected acquaintances. Schuhmacher at that time had a small riverside restaurant with a fast-growing reputation, and Rachel took it into her head it was her favourite place. We were all younger then. Schuhmacher used to appear on the party circuit himself, probably doing what Rachel was doing, collecting useful names. He'd played ice hockey professionally, either in the States or in Canada, but I can't swear to which. Some of that sport-star aura still clung to him and he hadn't altogether given up the lifestyle. Nowadays, as far as I can judge, he's sobered down completely and it's business first, foremost and all the time with him.'

McVeigh grunted. 'He seems to have made money.' His fingers thudded a tattoo on the desk. 'There's nothing on record known against him. Have you knowledge of any scandal in those far-off days you're talking about?'

'No, none. But I repeat I hardly knew him. Rachel would have known if there were any spicy stories and she never spoke of anything. She would have done! I honestly hadn't expected him to remember me,' Markby went on doggedly. 'I ran into him by chance and he acted as pleased as punch and invited me along to this party to inaugurate the new business venture. I knew about the hotel because of the fuss locally about it. As to his character, as I recall it, even years ago he was basically a bit dour. The strong, silent type but with a shrewd business brain. I don't mean he wasn't like-able enough, always very polite, very professional. But some might find him cold.'

'Would he,' McVeigh asked slowly, 'be more likely to talk freely to you than to an investigating officer he didn't know personally?'

'The honest answer to that is, yes, he would,' Markby returned.

'And the same goes for these others, these celebrity guests, Merle, the Fultons and the others?'

'It's possible.'

'More to the point,' went on McVeigh gloomily, 'the area

major investigation group hasn't anyone else available, or no one as suitable, to put in charge at the moment. One man is on leave, touring Europe with a caravan, can't even find him at short notice. Two people are sick. Two have gone up North on that lorry-driver case. That's about to break and I can't call them back. Several others are looking into the sub-post office robbery. And I don't want to ask for anyone to come in from outside because I feel local knowledge may be very important.' McVeigh stared out of the window.

'How busy are you with that child molester business? Any more sightings?'

'No, none. He may have moved on out of the district or he may be lying low. I've got a good man in charge of it, Harris. I'm not involved myself.'

'Good. You're reasonably free, then. I shall oversee the Springwood Hall murder inquiry myself. But I've too much on my plate to go foot-slogging round, interviewing witnesses and all the rest of it. You'll have to carry on for the time being, Alan. Report everything to me and don't initiate any action without my say-so, all right?'

Markby nodded glumly. Just great. All the work and none of the freedom to do things his way.

'Of course, if you feel the clash of interests is too great . . .'

'It's all right, I can manage. What about the film the TV crew took?'

'We've obtained a copy. It's currently being blown up and studied frame by frame but so far it's disappointing. You can nip over and take a look at it before you leave. There was always doubt whether the television company would use any of the footage because it was assumed the occasion wasn't really interesting enough apart from a few known names being there. They covered it in case they were short of material and could use it to fill in. Once they realised a body had been discovered they were keen to film everything, of course. Prior to that, they'd only filmed views of the house and a clip of guests arriving – until the streak. They got a good shot or two of her and it's still possible there might be something in the background. Don't count on it.'

McVeigh pushed all the papers back in the cardboard folder from which they'd spilled. 'See what you can do. If Morton gets back from Yorkshire ahead of time, he can take over if necessary.'

'Some people,' said Markby mildly, 'might interpret such an action in mid-investigation as a declaration of lack of confidence in my progress.'

The superintendent's bushy eyebrows shot up alarmingly.

'Nonsense! You know we've all got every confidence in you! That's why everyone thinks it's time your career moved on and up.'

'Can we discuss that some other time?' Markby asked brusquely. 'About this case. If I take this on, I'll do it on the strict understanding that I'll be left on it. Unless, needless to say, I feel the slightest tug of loyalties, at which point I'll ask myself to be taken off. Of course you're overseeing it and I'll keep you informed. I won't do anything unusual without checking it out with you first. But otherwise I must be able to do things in my own way.'

There was a silence. McVeigh wasn't used to having terms dictated to him but for once he conceded defeat gracefully. 'All right!' he acknowledged. 'But just remember that technically I'm directing this and if the balloon goes up, my name will be attached to it!'

* * *

'I'm not sure,' said Finlay Ross, 'but that I should report you for employing child labour!' He twitched a bushy eyebrow and nodded in the direction of the ramshackle buildings which constituted the Alice Batt Rest Home for Horses and Donkeys.

'Oh, Emma!' exclaimed Zoë, glancing towards the scene which had met the vet's eye.

Emma Danby was engaged in the energetic grooming of an aged donkey. It was large as donkeys went and to reach over its back Emma had to stand insecurely on an upturned bucket. Both the animal's forelegs were distorted by swollen knee joints. It was also possessed of a very large head at the end of a ewe-neck and ears which flopped to either side. No one could have called it an endearing animal or supposed that any amount of currying and brushing could improve its moth-eaten coat. But Emma worked with dedicated ferocity, a small whirlwind of activity in jeans and gumboots.

'I only wish I could afford to pay her something, poor kid! Even pocket money. But she does it all for love, works herself into a frazzle if I don't stop her. I have to physically pull her away. Mind you, she's a great help and the animals behave wonderfully with her. Horses and children, you know, operate on much the same wave-length. And I do give Emma her lunch when she's here all day. Anyway, her mum is a lawyer and wouldn't let me exploit her if I wanted to.'

'And her uncle is in charge of the local cop-shop, as I understand it.'

'Chief Inspector Markby, yes.'

There was an awkward silence. Forty-eight hours had passed since the murder but the feeling of tension which hung over the whole district had not faded.

'In charge of investigations into the death of your fellow

history-buff, isn't he?' Finlay Ross laid the ghost firmly by naming it aloud.

'Yes, poor Ellen. I can't bear to think of her. So – so dreadful. There are no words to describe it. Obscene, somehow. I keep seeing her, crouched in that gap between the wall and the wine racks . . . and the knife sticking out of her neck. She was all curled up like a foetus in the womb.'

'I'm an animal doctor not a human one,' Finlay growled. 'But my advice to you is go and see your medical man and get him to give you something for your nerves. You look, my dear, very stressed.'

'No thanks, I'm not a pill-taker. I know I'm stressed. Pills won't help.'

'Fine. Then try a tot of whisky.'

'Don't like that either. It smells horrid.'

Finlay looked shocked to the depths of his Scots soul. 'My dear girl! The water of life! Smells horrid? Whatever next? Anyway, a word of caution: don't describe details of the appearance of the deceased to others. I realise I invited it and shouldn't have done. The police might not like it. Careless revelations can prejudice trials, inspire cranks, tip off murderers to cover their tracks or Lord knows what else. Or so I've been informed. Now then, let's look at the patient, shall we?'

They walked together across the yard. Emma stopped her manic brushing of the donkey and stood back, purple-faced, sweating and dishevelled. She rubbed a grimy palm over her freckled face leaving it liberally streaked with grease. 'Hullo, Mr Ross,' she said doubtfully.

'Hullo, Emma! You look about to succumb to spontaneous combustion. Why don't you go and sit down for a bit while I take a look at Maud here?'

The donkey turned her ugly hammer head and leered malevolently at the vet, rolling her heavy top lip back to reveal discoloured teeth.

'Yes, Emma, go over to my trailer and help yourself to some orange squash,' Zoë urged.

'I want to know what's wrong with Maud!' Emma stood her ground defiantly.

'And you shall. I'll tell you what Mr Ross has to say just as soon as he's had a chance to look Maud over.'

'You're not going to put her down?'

'Guid grief, no,' said the vet cheerfully. 'Go on, Emma, scram!'

Emma returned him an uncertain smile and wandered away in the general direction of the rickety caravan which was Zoë's home. She cast many a mistrustful glance back at them as she went.

'Move over, old lady!' ordered Finlay. Maud gave a deep groan and shifted about six inches. He ran practised hands over her, looked at her teeth which she allowed him to do with surprising cooperation, pulled affectionately at one of her long drooping ears and returned to the anxiously waiting Zoë. 'Just walk her round in a small circle.'

Zoë took the halter and urged Maud to accompany her. The donkey lurched forward in ungainly fashion, the distorted knees now more obvious, her forelegs permanently crooked.

'How's she eating?'

'Some things she can't digest but on the whole she eats well.'

'Has she any trouble getting up if she lies down?'

'Sometimes. She doesn't lie down much. I think she knows. But actually, I think that's what caused the present

71

aggravation in her knees. She lay down, struggled to get up and knocked her legs against the wall of her stall.'

'Quite possible.' Finlay scratched Maud's mealy muzzle. 'I'll be frank. She's a very old lady in donkey terms and I don't know how she'll cope with the coming winter. At least,' he indicated the ramshackle stabling with an apologetic gesture, 'not in present conditions. She needs a proper, warm, draught-free loose-box.'

'We're not likely to be in our present conditions much longer, much less improved ones!' said Zoë gloomily. 'We'll be camping out at the roadside, me and the animals all, if Schuhmacher has his way.'

'Well, if you are still here come winter and nothing's changed, I'll have to recommend the old girl is put out of her misery.'

'She's not miserable!' Zoë glared at him.

'No, my dear,' Finlay said gently, thinking how much this young woman resembled the child Emma in her devotion to these infirm beasts. 'Not now, not today with the sun shining on her poor old back. But come wet damp weather and given her rheumaticky knees . . .' He shook his head. 'She'll be in pain. She'll very likely go down and not be able to get up – get pneumonia quite likely. If she's not in a good, warm, dry stable, it just wouldn't be right, lassie. Not all your loving care can prevent her suffering. You know me. I'll never put down an animal I can save. But I won't agree to Maud seeing winter out in these stables. They just aren't adequate.'

'I'll find us all somewhere! Something will turn up!' Zoë said desperately.

'I hope it does, Zoë. I hope it does. Well, I must be on my way.'

'Thanks, Finlay.' Zoë put her hand on his arm. 'You've

been a tower of strength ever since I took over from Miss
Batt.'

'Pshaw! Only too happy . . . Wish I could help, finan-
cially, I mean. Can't, I'm afraid.'

'You do more than enough, Finlay. We couldn't have
kept going at all if it wasn't for you.'

They walked together across the yard to where the vet's
hatchback was parked by the gate. Deep in their conversation, neither of them saw Emma creep out from behind
the horsetrough where she had been crouched, listening,
nor did they see her put both arms round Maud's scrawny
neck and press her face against the rough hair.

Maud hitched up one hind hoof and to the child's snuffles added a long deep sigh of sad acceptance.

Markby at his desk that same Monday was already regret-
ting his assurance to McVeigh that he could manage this
case despite his nearness to it. A help or a hindrance in the
investigation? Time would tell. In one respect however, it
had already disrupted his private life. Hadn't police work
always done that? Years ago, when he and Rachel had had
so many bitter rows, he had tended to blame his wife for
what he had considered her lack of understanding. Since
then, however, with the passage of time he had grown
more and more sympathetic to her view of things. All
those broken dinner dates he had thought of trifling impor-
tance, those lost weekends and midnight calls out to her
had meant her life was no life. It had not been a good
marriage. They would have divorced sooner or later anyway.
But the faults had been split pretty evenly between them.

He reached out a hand and touched the sheet of typed
paper which was signed in a bold hand 'Meredith Mitchell'.
Her statement. The only time they'd had together on Sunday

had been spent here in the station, waiting for it to be typed up. She had read it, signed it and then it had been 'Thank you very much, we'll be in touch.' Now it was his relationship with Meredith which was called upon to pay the price. She, at least, understood. That was cold comfort to him as she returned to the bosom of Whitehall and this scrap of paper remained alone behind as an epitaph on a dead weekend.

Dead as Ellen Bryant. Markby picked up another report, the pathologist's. Since his life did not normally include such matters as needlepoint cushion covers and crocheted waistcoats, he had never encountered Mrs Bryant alive nor been in her shop. He knew nothing about her before her death – and despite the unspeakable intimate intrusion of the autopsy, precious little about her now.

She'd been in good health at the time of her death. She'd died quite quickly. Either the murderer had known just how to strike or the blow had been lucky. A slight deviation would have led the blade to be deflected by the collar bone. As it was, it had driven straight in, severing a jugular. A messy business. The woman's sweater had been sodden with blood and only the scarlet colour of the wool had disguised it. She had good teeth but no dental records in Bamford. She was registered as a patient at the local medical centre, but had never been there to complain of the slightest ache or pain. She wasn't a virgin; not unexpected as she had been forty-one years old and a married woman by the evidence of her ring and title. But there again, there was no sign of recent sexual activity. Everything about Ellen was negative.

Another problem was that there was no next of kin to inform. Everyone has someone. But not Ellen. They'd been reduced to informing her shop assistant, Margery

Collins. Wpc Jones had done that. Jones reported that Margery received the news with floods of tears, but her only voluntary comment had been that God would punish the evil-doer.

In the meantime, Markby had to find the perpetrator of the crime and deliver that person up for punishment here on earth.

Questioned, Miss Collins said that Ellen had told her she would be taking the Saturday afternoon off. She had not said where she was going. She did not normally confide in Margery. Margery had the keys to the shop and Ellen lived in the flat above it.

One piece of firm evidence they did have was the weapon itself. It was a cook's knife and it came from the kitchens of the hotel. It was identified and claimed by the chef, Richter, who declared that knives and other pieces of small equipment wandered frequently. Eric Schuhmacher had confirmed this. Richter had complained to him about it. In the circumstances, the setting up of new kitchens and a certain degree of chaos, Markby supposed it would be a mistake to make too much of that.

Richter did say, however, that the particular knife in question had been used by him on the Saturday morning. It would have been lying about in the kitchen after that. Almost anyone could have picked it up and when one considered how many people had been in the vicinity on that Saturday, the day of the gala opening, the list of people who could have got to that knife was long. The handle of the blade had been clean, no fingerprints. Either the murderer had worn a glove or wrapped the handle in something or had leaned over the victim and carefully wiped the handle clean without removing it from the wound. That, if so, showed iron nerve and a high degree of callousness.

'Come on, Pearce,' said the chief inspector. 'We'll take a look at the deceased's flat.'

He picked up the bunch of keys found in Ellen's handbag. It had been the shoulder-strap variety and had still been wound round the dead woman's arm in the cellar. The motive for her death hadn't been theft. She still wore her wedding ring and an expensive wristwatch and, although the shoulder bag had been unfastened, her purse and twenty pounds in fivers had still been in it. She may simply have left it unfastened herself, careless.

Apart from purse and money, the bag had held a driving licence, a powder compact, lipstick and a shopping list of groceries scrawled on a scrap of paper. The driving licence had supplied Ellen's date of birth, further corroborated by Margery Collins who mournfully recalled that Ellen had celebrated her birthday every year by bringing two sticky cakes into the shop for her own and Margery's 'elevenses'. Some celebration, thought Markby sadly. Nothing in the bag gave a clue to her private life. Ellen, alive or dead, had given nothing away.

'One of these,' he said, jangling the keys, 'must fit the shop door.'

Bamford on a Monday was a quiet place. Only now, thought Markby grimly as he and Pearce got out of the car, in addition to a murderer there was a child molester roaming round. One reason why he was loath even to contemplate handing over to someone else was that he had proprietorial emotions about Bamford. It was his patch and, just as he kept his garden carefully tended and free of weeds, he felt it was his duty to keep Bamford free of contamination, to dig out any evil that took root there.

The two CID men attracted little curiosity as they stopped

before the Tudor house and peered through the window at the stacked wools and array of tapestry canvases. A sign in the glass door read 'Closed'. Markby tried the keys and struck lucky at the second attempt. He and Pearce closed the door behind them, made their way across the shop and began to climb the narrow staircase at the back.

'Quaint old place,' said Pearce. 'I suppose she was interested in history since she belonged to that society.'

'We'll have to question the members of the society again. They seem to have been her only friends, if friends is the right word.' So speaking, Markby opened the door at the top of the stair.

He was encouraged to find the flat so neat. It should make it easier to find anything relevant. The desk was locked but another key on the ring opened it up. It contained account books and business correspondence, all neatly clipped together or filed. There were no personal letters in the letter rack and no diary. He was especially sorry about the last. Diaries often provided vital clues.

'Photo here,' said Pearce, walking across with a frame in his hand. 'Only one there is. No family snaps anywhere.'

The photograph showed Ellen standing outside Needles. Markby slipped it out of its frame to see if anything were written on the back and a newspaper cutting fell out. Any hopes this raised were quickly dashed. The cutting was a report on the opening of Needles and the photo was a print of one taken by the *Bamford Gazette's* photographer. The one interesting comment was in the report which spoke of Ellen being 'a newcomer to Bamford'. There was no date to say when this report had appeared in the *Gazette*, but the newspaper offices would be able to supply that.

'If they'd only said where she came here from!' Markby growled, handing the photo and frame back to Pearce. He returned to the desk and rummaged further in the pigeon holes. 'Hullo! What's this? Now, then . . . now we're getting somewhere!'

He withdrew a small booklet with a folded paper tucked into it. 'A passport and what's more, an Australian one!' He opened it. 'Ellen Marie Novak, born 6 June 1951 in Melbourne. And this?' He opened out the folded paper. 'It looks like a graduation certificate of some kind. "School of Classical and Modern Dance". What's the date on this? Hm, she would have been just sixteen. So she wanted to be a dancer! Perhaps she did work as one for a while. She carried her certificate around in her passport so that may mean she went after dance work around the world.' Markby looked up. 'We'll get on to Australia House. This passport was renewed by them last year and so they must have a record of her, though I doubt it's more than a name on a computer. A former dancer . . . no wonder she was fit and healthy.'

He closed the passport and tapped it thoughtfully. 'Perhaps she came here with a dance troupe and stayed on? Ballet? Chorus line? TV work? Night clubs? We'll try the theatrical agencies and the stage publications.'

'She mightn't have worked as a dancer for years,' said Pearce pessimistically. 'And not at all in this country. She'd been quite a while here in Bamford and there's not much call for dancers in this town!' He looked slightly depressed at this thought.

'Dancers' professional lives can be short. She may have got out while the going was good. Saved her money and bought this place. She had a business brain.' Markby indicated the neat records in the desk.

'So who,' asked Pearce, 'is Mr Bryant? Or did she just choose that name and call herself Mrs? She never got her passport changed.'

'Quite a lot of modern women find it easier to keep things in their maiden names. Or the marriage may have been very brief, some six-month teenage fling. He might be in Australia, probably remarried with kids, and the chances of finding him are probably nil.'

They searched on in silence for some minutes. The wastepaper basket and the kitchen bin yielded nothing of interest.

'You know what?' said Pearce, after a hunt through the kitchen cupboards and the fridge. 'She was a veggie. There's nothing but dried beans and wholemeal flour here, except for a load of fruit in a bowl.'

Markby crinkled his brow as he tried to recollect the items on the shopping list in Ellen's bag. It was like one of those party games, how many objects can you remember? Cheese, yes. Cereals, yes. Fruit, yes. No meat, bacon or lard. He was pretty sure.

'Well done,' he said to Pearce. 'Where do you shop in Bamford if you're a vegetarian?'

'There's a health food place in the High Street.'

'Then it might be worth your while to nip along there when we've finished here and ask if they knew anything about her. They might have got chatting over the lentils.'

They took the paper bag out of the vacuum cleaner and emptied it carefully on to a sheet of newspaper. Pearce sneezed. 'Nothing.'

Markby went back to the living room and stuck his hands in his pockets and sighed. This was going to be one of those frustrating cases where you had to fight for every snippet of information. He looked round the room again. She liked music – that was quite an expensive set of equipment over there. But then, she'd been a dancer.

He walked across and bent down to examine the music

79

centre. Then he frowned and got down on his hands and knees. A glimpse of something white had caught his eye. He reached out and withdrew a crumpled scrap of paper.

'*Eureka!*' he murmured, unfolding it carefully.

'Found something, sir?' Pearce asked, coming up to peer over his shoulder.

'I fancy I have.' Markby began to read aloud. '"We can discuss this better face to face. It should be possible on Sat at SH. I'll see you there and let you know when there's a chance to slip away for a private chat. I really think this opportunity ought not to be missed."'

He turned the crumpled sheet of paper over. 'Regular A5 typing paper. No signature. Typed message. SH I think we can presume to be Springwood Hall. Come on, Pearce. We've got to find the envelope.'

They searched desk, wastepaper basket, kitchen bin and vacuum-cleaner bag again. Pearce went downstairs and found a dustbin in the back yard. After a frustrating hunt through odds and ends of wrapping paper and teabags he came back to report no success.

'Might have been hand delivered?' he suggested half-heartedly.

'Unlikely. No, she must have destroyed the envelope. But how? It's not thrown away here.'

'Some people use envelopes as jotting paper – you know, write things down on them, telephone messages or—'

'Or shopping lists!' Markby interrupted. 'We're a pair of idiots. What's the betting that part of the envelope is back at the station – taken from her handbag with that shopping list on it! Come on—'

He stopped. From below came a clatter and a faint gasp of breath.

'Someone in the shop!' hissed Pearce. 'I closed the front door! How—?'

Markby signalled him to silence and they waited as the footsteps began to climb the staircase to the flat.

painfully thin, arms and legs sticklike almost to the extent

Chapter Six

The door creaked open a couple of inches. 'Who's in there?' asked a tremulous voice.

'The police, madam,' returned Markby in best avuncular manner. Pearce grinned.

There was a sigh of relief. The door was pushed right open and Margery Collins appeared. 'I thought I'd just look in on the shop to see everything was all right,' she gabbled. 'I mean, I've still got the keys. Perhaps I ought not to have. But I came in and then I heard your voices up here. I couldn't think who it was. I was scared stiff but I felt responsible, if you see what I mean . . . I wondered if I ought to call the police, but then, you are the police . . . so it's a good thing I didn't, isn't it?' Margery was panting slightly by the time she reached the end of her speech.

Markby eyed her thoughtfully. He supposed she must be in her mid to late twenties. She was quite tall but painfully thin, arms and legs sticklike almost to the extent that a casual observer might have thought her prey to some wasting disease. Eyes and nose seemed too large for her pointed face and her complexion was drained of all colour. This last was not because of fear but because Margery had one of those matt white skins admired a hundred years ago but in today's world, where golden tans and beaming health were considered desirable, looking unhealthy. Yet for all that it was a fine, unblemished skin and she had thick reddish-brown hair with a tendency to natural curl. It was very badly cut, but cut well and with better clothes and a dash of make-up and a few pounds' extra weight she would have been quite attractive. She was wearing black, presumably as a mark of respect for her late employer.

'What are you looking for?' Margery glanced round the room and her expression became mistrustful again when she saw the open desk and disturbed papers.

'Clues, I suppose you'd call it!' Markby said humorously. Serious again, he went on, 'We're trying to establish a motive for Mrs Bryant's murder.' He held up the letter. 'She seems to have received this shortly before her death. Would you happen to know where the envelope might be? Did she discuss the contents with you?'

'No – she didn't, she wouldn't have – I don't know about the envelope!' He might just as well have accused Margery of some horrendous crime. Her eyes fixed him, saucer-like. 'I don't know anything about her correspondence. She was a very private person.'

'What time does the day's post arrive at the shop?'

'About nine-thirty. The postman brings it in and Ellen takes – took – charge of it. I never saw any of it, either business or personal. Unless you count an occasional invoice when we had a delivery. Ellen was like that. I don't mean secretive exactly. Just private, as I said. She would never have discussed anything with me she didn't consider strictly within my sphere of activity. She'd talk about new stock or a display for the window or whether some item was slow moving and could be offered at reduced price. But Ellen didn't go in much for sales. She bought very carefully. She always said too many sale tickets take a shop downmarket.

It looks as if you can't sell the stuff and customers begin to think there must be something wrong with it.'

Markby drew the conversation firmly back to the letter. 'So she didn't discuss this or any other letter with you? You never overheard a telephone conversation? It's quite all right to say so, if you did. No one will think you were eavesdropping. All information is very important, even little things.'

She shook her head but was staring curiously at the crumpled sheet of paper in his hand. 'What does it say?'

'Well, it—' Markby hesitated. 'It's an arrangement between the writer and Ellen to meet, probably for the day of her death, although the letter isn't dated. Can you think of anyone likely to write and make an arrangement like that? A friend of Ellen's?'

'I don't know about her friends. Anyway, most people phone, don't they? If they want to arrange something.'

Markby nodded. True enough. But this person hadn't, fearful perhaps that the wrong person might answer the call – Margery here, for example.

'It might have been someone in the historical society!' Margery said suddenly, with the anxious air of someone trying desperately to be helpful.

'Why one of them?'

'Because that's where she was going on Saturday, to Springwood Hall with the rest of the society to protest.' Margery's mouth set primly. 'I was amazed that Hope Mapple could behave so disgustingly and I'm really astonished that Ellen could be a party to it.'

'As far as we know she didn't approve of it and she left the scene to avoid witnessing Miss Mapple's, er, demonstration. In the light of subsequent events, it seems she left to keep an appointment with her killer. Perhaps she would have been wiser to have stayed.'

This presented Margery with a moral conundrum. Her brow furrowed. 'But she didn't know, did she, that she was going to – to meet a lunatic with a knife?'

'That's who you think did this? A deranged person?'

'Don't you?' asked Margery simply. 'Normal people don't behave like that. Unless, of course, they're wicked. That's possible, too. The devil is real and among us, Mr Markby.'

'I've never doubted it, Miss Collins. Now then, you said "because that's where she was going", but I believe in your statement to Wpc Jones you said Ellen didn't tell you where she was going.'

'No, she didn't. But we all know now she went to Springwood Hall, don't we?'

Markby sighed. Margery Collins was a nice girl, but she couldn't help. 'I'd be obliged, Miss Collins, if nothing were disturbed in the shop or up here in the flat. You weren't contemplating opening up for business, were you?'

'Oh no! That would be really tasteless!' Margery looked at him in horror. 'Anyway, I don't know who owns Needles now or whether I'm still employed here.' She ran a nervous hand over her untidy hair. 'I suppose Mrs Danby will be able to tell me.'

'Laura? I mean, Mrs Danby the solicitor?' Markby asked, startled to hear his sister's name brought into this.

'Yes. That's actually where I'm going. I just passed the shop on my way and thought I'd look in. Mrs Danby's secretary rang me this morning and asked me to call as soon as possible. Something to do with Ellen's will.'

'Her will!'

'That's helpful . . .' muttered Pearce.

'Quite.' Markby shot his subordinate a warning look.

'Perhaps you had better run along then, Miss Collins. I'll lock up.'

'All right.' But Margery still hovered. 'It is all right, your being here, I suppose? You aren't going to remove anything, are you?' Scarlet-faced she added in haste, 'I didn't mean steal anything.' Markby raised his eyebrows. 'I meant, evidence . . .'

'Don't worry, Miss Collins. Our investigations are always conducted with every regard for the rules.' Pearce stared up at the ceiling. 'We may have to take a few things away, but we always take the greatest possible care of such items and everything will be returned in due course. I dare say I shall be having a word with Mrs Danby and, if she's the victim's solicitor, I'll keep her posted.'

Margery smiled unhappily and fled, her footsteps pattering down the stairs like a large mouse. The front door clicked shut.

'Turn up for the books!' said Pearce enthusiastically. 'Bit of luck, Mrs Danby being her solicitor. At least we know she'll cooperate, being your sister.'

'Not necessarily,' said Markby in dampening tones. 'Put all those ledgers and business letters into a box, we'll examine them in the office.'

'There, there,' said Laura, hoping it would have the desired effect. 'Would you like another hankie?'

She put her hand out to take one from the box on her desk and then decided it would be easier simply to hand over the entire box of tissues. The girl was gushing like a fountain.

'But I didn't know!' Margery wailed. 'I had no idea! Honestly, I didn't, Mrs Danby.' She fumbled with the

Kleenex box and dragged out a bunch of multi-hued paper sheets.

'Yes, I know, quite a shock for you. We have a bottle of brandy for emergencies in the office. Would you like a drop?'

'We don't drink in my church.' Margery snuffled into the tissues, rubbing at her pointed nose until it shone scarlet.

'I see. Well, a cup of tea or coffee?'

'We don't take stimulants.'

'Right. How about a glass of water? I've a bottle of Evian.'

'Y-yes, please.'

Laura fetched the water and took her seat again. Margery made an effort to pull herself together and leaned forward.

'It seems wrong, Mrs Danby!' she said emphatically.

'Oh? Why so? It was obviously Mrs Bryant's express wish.'

'But there must be someone else with a better claim than I have, surely? Her family? Not that she ever talked about them.'

'Perhaps she had none? Or they'd quarrelled. That does happen. She would certainly have named relatives if she had any to whom she wanted to make bequests. Had you worked for her for a long time?'

'Four years, ever since the first day she opened Needles.'

'There you are, then,' said Laura firmly. 'Mrs Bryant obviously appreciated that you helped her build the business and wanted to show her gratitude.'

She was dreadfully afraid the girl was going to start weeping again. Instead, Miss Collins sat up with a jerk.

'But she wasn't like that, Mrs Danby!' She blinked her red-rimmed eyes earnestly. 'Ellen hardly ever said thank you for anything. She could be quite brusque, even hurtful.

One doesn't want to speak ill of the departed, especially since she – she—' Margery made a distressed gesture towards the papers on Laura's desk. 'But she wasn't a friendly person in any way. Mr Markby was asking about her friends but I don't think she had anyone, except in the historical society. Oh, Mrs Danby, it would be too awful if the only person Ellen had in the whole world was me!'

Laura tried and failed to find a suitable response. She took refuge in facts and figures. 'Apart from the shop of which Mrs Bryant owned the freehold, there is a bank account, a deposit box in the bank and shares in British Telecom and British Gas. Also a high interest account in a building society.' Laura looked up. 'I think you'll find it will add up to quite a lot of money, Miss Collins. Miss Collins!'

Margery swayed on her chair, clutched at the edge of the desk and sent the glass which held the water flying. Rivulets of Evian ran across the papers as Laura snatched them up for safety and dripped down on to the carpet. Margery gazed despairingly at the mess she had made and burst into tears again.

'All I'm saying,' said Markby patiently, 'is that you might have mentioned the fact that you were, are, Ellen's solicitor as soon as her body was officially identified. Superintendent McVeigh isn't going to like this!'

And he didn't like it either. If Margery benefited by her employer's death her movements for Saturday afternoon must be checked, despite the fact that she had been in sole charge of the shop and there really was no way she could have left it long enough to get over to Springwood Hall and back again.

'And I keep telling you,' Laura retorted crossly, 'that until this morning I didn't realise I was! Ellen was a client of the firm. All her business, including drawing up her will, was handled by one of the other partners. Jimmie, who died recently, you remember him. Jimmie's files, his clients, were farmed out round the rest of us and I inherited Ellen, if you like to put it like that. Of course a letter was sent out telling the people concerned in case they wanted to make other arrangements, but I suppose Ellen didn't, because she didn't object. She had no cause to consult me during the period between becoming my client and her death. It wasn't until this morning that someone said, "Oh, Ellen Bryant, wasn't she one of Jimmie's clients?" Then we checked and found we held a will. So I opened it up, since presumably I am handling the estate. She named the law firm as her executors.'

'So why did you want to see Margery?'

Laura hesitated and then gave a hiss of annoyance. 'Well, Margery's been informed so I suppose there's no reason why I shouldn't tell the police. Ellen left Needles to her.'

'To Margery!' Markby shouted.

'Alan!' Laura put her hands over her ears. 'Yes, left everything to Margery, in fact. Estate *in toto*. Don't ask me why. Perhaps she had no one else to leave it to? Margery appeared to know nothing about it and had hysterics in my office. I've had a very trying day, Alan, and I'd appreciate being spared police third degree.'

Her husband put his head round the door. 'Those kids have hollow legs. All the apples have gone. I was going to make a pud with them and the bowl's empty. Emma's not been pinching them to feed those old nags again?'

'You should have said you wanted them!' said his wife tersely.

'Food flies out of the store cupboard. I went for a tin of baked beans lunchtime and there's not one!'

'Then you forgot to buy any! Why should the children steal baked beans?'

'I didn't forget. I bought—'

'Look, I've got to be going!' Markby interrupted. 'I'd be obliged if you'd ask round your professional colleagues, Laura, and find out if anyone knows anything at all about Ellen. I am trying to find her murderer! Oh, and Laura – that fellow who was hanging round last year trying to pick up children seems to be back in the area. Warn Matthew and Emma and don't let Vicky play outside if no one can see her.'

'Oh no . . .' Laura looked harassed. 'Paul, do you think Emma ought to spend so much of her free time down at that horses' home? It's quite lonely out there.'

'Try and stop her!' said Paul. 'Emma's sensible, she wouldn't go with a stranger.'

'Sensible but only possessed of a child's strength!' said Markby.

He took himself home in low spirits. To console himself he went out into his new greenhouse and inspected the fuchsias for white fly. After a while he felt better. No white fly. No red spider. But he did not feel happier about his case. They had hotfooted it back to the station to find Ellen's shopping list had indeed been written on part of an envelope, but the stamp and postmark had been torn off except for a small smudged section. Close inspection through a microscope hadn't revealed the origin and the help of the post office had been enlisted.

'Probably a London postmark,' said the man at the main sorting office. 'But there's not enough to go on. I couldn't swear to it.'

Yet another blind alley. Ellen Bryant had passed out of this world leaving no trace, unmissed and it seemed unmourned – except possibly by an employee to whom she had willed her earthly goods 'because she had no one else'.

'I care for nobody, no not I, and nobody cares for me!' Markby sang the nursery rhyme softly to himself.

Why then, should anyone want to kill her?

Meredith was feeling cheated. She decided, after much trawling through her vocabulary, that was the best way to describe her present dissatisfied mood. She had gone down to Bamford to see Alan and attend the party at the new hotel, a prospect full of delights, and how had it ended? With a dead body, a spoiled dinner no one fancied and making a statement to the police.

If she were to be honest, unpleasant though all these events had been, the thing which frustrated her most was that she was stuck here in London, cut off from all the excitement with no way of knowing how or if Alan's investigations were progressing. Not, of course, that he'd discuss them with her. A brief call to her from him had merely confirmed that he had, contrary to his expectations, been put in charge of the case. It made it all the more annoying not to be there, sharing in the buzz of the activity. Ghoulish, perhaps, but a human desire.

Meredith prowled round the flat, making coffee, switching the TV on and off, picking up and putting down books and newspapers. The press had had a field day over the crime. There were pictures of the hotel, of Eric scowling and of Alan looking purposeful. Hope Mapple appeared in various stages of undress. (The local photographer of the *Bamford Gazette* had snapped a beauty of Hope unveiled and the nation's press had obtained it from him.)

Always looking for a fresh angle, one indefatigable reporter had even dug up the story of the equine Rest Home and the sword which Eric held poised over it. The nation loved an animal story. 'Pretty, plucky Zoë Foster' was pictured together with a Shetland pony 'once destined for the continental meatmarket'. Zoë, claimed the paper, had been the murdered woman's 'best friend'. What's more, Zoë had found the body in company with one of the hotel's 'wealthy society guests'. And lo and behold, there was a lop-sided snap of Meredith in her best party dress, gripping a glass of sherry and with her high heels sinking into the lawn, taken by one of the camera-waving sight-seers and enterprisingly sold on to the newspaper.

'Silly idiots!' muttered Meredith, appalled. The rag had it wrong too, naturally. She and Zoë hadn't been in one another's company when the body was discovered. Zoë had done that alone. Meredith wrinkled her brow. And was the newspaper correct in declaring Ellen to have been Zoë's best friend, since Zoë had simply said Ellen was a fellow member of the historical society? Or had the relationship between the two women been closer?

Meredith studied the picture of pretty, plucky Zoë Foster again. She took another disgusted look at that of Meredith Mitchell, the society belle. Then she threw the newspaper in the wastepaper basket.

Some activity was called for to counter her thumb-twiddling. She went into the kitchen.

This was not her own flat. It was borrowed from an FO colleague currently abroad. The awareness that it was Toby's flat made it difficult to settle in it. Recently things had been made worse by a string of telephone calls from his friends, male and female, who seemed not to be aware that he was out of the country. As he'd been gone some

93

time, it made one wonder how long an interval Toby's
friends left before trying to get in touch with him or why
he never seemed to send them so much as a postcard. Or,
come to that, why this past two weeks all of them seemed
intent on getting in touch with him at once. Also intrigu-
ing was that none of them, whilst fully expecting Toby to
be in residence, expressed any surprise at hearing a female
voice at the end of the line. Toby's social life when in
London had become the object of much idle speculation
on Meredith's part. She wondered how he was getting on
in South America.

Cutting a length from a stick of French bread, she split
it, scraped butter on both pieces and amused herself deco-
rating one with ham and sliced tomato and the other with
crumbly Caerphilly cheese pressed into the butter and
artistically studded with olives. She took these and a glass
of white wine into the sitting room and prepared to make
an early supper of them. But before she could take a mouth-
ful the telephone rang again. Meredith approached the
instrument, glass of wine in hand, and picked it up, praying
that this time it would be for her.

'Meredith? It's Leah Fulton.'

'Leah?' Meredith realised she sounded puzzled and just
a little disappointed because she had hoped the caller would
turn out to be Alan. She promptly said more cheerfully,
'Leah, how nice to hear you.'

'I realise it's a bit of a shock!' came Leah's voice. 'Are
you busy this evening, Meredith? Could you come over
to dinner? Nothing formal or very exciting, just a small
party, four of us. Denis has been rather low and I think
that business at Springwood Hall is preying on his mind.
The trouble is he won't discuss it with me. I thought if we
got together and chatted about it, it might clear the air. I've

asked Victor to join us, Victor Merle.'

'Yes, I'd also like to talk about it!' Meredith said. 'I can't think about anything else, either. You're quite right, Leah. If we talk about it freely, it will help us all.'

Someone else is as uneasy as I am about it all! she thought as she took her all-purpose little black dress from the wardrobe. Her sense of frustrated impotence was gone, replaced by tingling excitement. Events were moving, she felt it in her bones. Something was about to happen.

Chapter Seven

The Fultons lived in Chelsea in a quiet street of early Victorian terraced houses. The graceful arched doorways and whitened steps flanked by black-lacquered iron railings ran away from the eye in pleasing symmetry. Meredith found a free space and parked near the house. When she had locked the car carefully she walked the few steps to the Fultons' front door and stood looking up at it.

On either side heavy velvet curtains doubled with almost as heavy cream lining shut out any view of the rooms behind them. But a little light shone round the edges and on one windowsill glowed a lamp with a silk shade. Meredith climbed the steps and looked down into the basement area. A stone stair ran down to a door. Another window, curtains open, seemed to be that of a staff flat, affording a glimpse of a homely living room cluttered with cushions and religious statuettes. There was a cat down in the stairwell, a black and white gentleman of the tiles with spotless bib and socks. He looked up at Meredith and miaowed, bristling his handlebar whiskers before disappearing into some recess which doubtless harboured the rubbish bin. She smiled and lifted her hand to the heavy brass door knocker. The sound echoed within the house.

The door was opened by a Filipina maid but her hostess

appeared at the sound of Meredith's voice to greet her. As before, Meredith found the initial sight of Leah impressive. She wore royal blue, her long hair coiled on top of her head to show off her large gold and pearl earrings. These and her wedding ring constituted her only jewellery.

'Nice house!' said Meredith, meaning it, and thinking how well Leah's discreetly perfumed elegance complemented the tastefully designed surroundings.

'Marcus and I bought it,' Leah confided as she guided her through the hall. 'I often think we ought to sell it and buy a new house, somewhere to make a home which would be Denis's and mine, no memories of anyone else. Denis says nonsense, this is my home and he wouldn't think of making me leave it. At the same time, I think he really doesn't like it. He can't relax here somehow. I'm sorry to pour my domestic problems into your ears. I don't mean this to turn out a dreary evening for anyone. I can promise you a decent dinner and Victor is always good company.'

Before Meredith could answer, Leah threw open the drawing room door and called, 'Denis darling, here's Meredith!'

'Hullo,' said Denis, taking her hand. 'Good of you to come over at short notice. Drink?'

The poor man certainly didn't look relaxed, thought Meredith, but just as harassed here at home as at the hotel. She said, 'Just a glass of sherry, please, would be fine.'

Leah murmured, 'Excuse me for a minute, will you?' and disappeared. This was a signal, Meredith suspected, that she, Meredith, was supposed in some way to broach the subject which vexed all their imaginations and persuade Denis to open his heart and mind while they were a cosy twosome. She did not altogether fancy the role of confessor and had no idea how to introduce the subject. As it was, however, Denis began unprompted.

'I really do mean it's good of you to bother.' He handed her a sherry glass and perched himself on the edge of a chair, gripping a half-emptied whisky tumbler. 'Leah's been upset, you know, ever since that wretched affair at Eric's place. I think it will help her to talk about it with you, since you were there.'

'Oh?' Meredith sipped her sherry and reflected that acting as confidante to both Fultons was tricky. She felt a little like Alice faced with Tweedledee and Tweedledum. Either the Fultons shared unspoken emotions or one of them – there was no way of telling which one – was imputing emotions felt to the other.

'You, you found her, didn't you, the dead woman, I mean.' Denis fixed anxious eyes on Meredith's face. 'That was a rotten business, rotten for you. Hell of a nasty shock.'

'Yes, it was. I was so sorry for Schuhmacher and his staff. All their hard work more or less for nothing. But I didn't actually find her first.'

'Oh yes, quite. As to Eric, he's pretty durable. He was a first-class ice-hockey player once, you know, and a fine winter sportsman still. Businesswise he's hard to beat and altogether Eric's a tough nut to crack. He'll recover.' Denis sounded envious as he catalogued Schuhmacher's virtues, perhaps comparing the Swiss with himself.

'I thought he seemed a nice man. I hadn't met him before.'

'I've known him for years because of his association with the restaurant business and my own interest in food and wine. I like Eric too, of course, and I'm sorry his grand opening was ruined. I didn't mean to sound unsympathetic.' Denis rolled his now empty whisky tumbler between his hands. 'You're a friend of the investigating officer, aren't you? Markby, he's a good chap, I suppose? Efficient and all that?'

'Very. He'll get to the bottom of it.'

'His being there on the spot, fortuitous.'

'Not good fortune for him, he was meant to be a guest and enjoying himself!' Meredith said wrily.

'Quite. Has he any idea who did it?'

'It's early yet. Anyway, he doesn't confide in me,' Meredith said with a touch of asperity.

Denis gave her a dubious look. Obviously he didn't believe this. He seemed disappointed. But that was the worst of being friendly with a police officer. Denis and others probably assumed she must be in the know. She hoped she hadn't been invited along here in the hope that she'd entertain the company with titbits of inside information.

'Thought you were pretty friendly with Markby!' Denis said.

'Yes, but we don't talk shop when we're together!'

Denis looked suitably rebuffed and went on to another tack. 'You know Merle too, don't you?'

This took her by surprise. 'Not exactly. I attended one of his lectures once. He remembered me, which I hadn't expected.'

'You're an attractive woman,' said Denis unexpectedly. 'You can bet your life Victor remembered you!' He got up and splashed a refill of whisky into his glass. Glancing over his shoulder, he asked, 'Sherry okay? I should have asked you first.'

'Fine, thanks, I'm not much of a drinker.'

'I hope you like a glass of wine. I've got a Russian wine for us this evening. I'm anxious to get opinions on it.'

'That's what we should be buying now, is it?'

'Well, they produce a heck of a lot, variable quality. Truly awful version of champagne-type. But some of their better table wines are very acceptable and now, with opening up to the West and profit no longer a dirty word over there, their producers are very anxious to find export markets. The Georgians are particularly bullish about their prospects. Of course they'll have to settle down and get themselves organised first. I'd say they were worth trying and yes, I'd recommend laying in a few bottles.'

'You'll have to tell me which ones.' It was remarkable how his manner had changed now he was talking on his own subject, suddenly at ease, affable, humorous. A different man altogether, she thought.

'I say,' said Denis now, confidentially. 'You don't know anything about computers, do you?'

'A little, not much.'

'This word processor I've got. I'm assured it's a state of the art machine and can do just about everything. It's obviously my fault I can't make it do anything. Perhaps I can lure you to my study to take a look at it later. If you could decipher the handbook you'd earn my eternal gratitude.'

'I honestly doubt I could help.'

Voices were heard again outside including a man's. Denis's cheerful manner disappeared and he scowled. 'Merle!' he said dourly.

The door opened. 'Here's Victor!' said Leah, appearing with an armful of flowers. 'He's brought me these, aren't they gorgeous? Meredith, you and Victor have met before, haven't you?'

'Of course, and the last time at that débâcle which marked the opening of the new hotel. None of us is likely to forget that day! My dear Miss Mitchell!' Merle executed

101

his elegant bow- and kiss-hands routine. 'I'll have a small whisky, Denis.'

Denis grunted and shambled to the drinks cabinet where he began to make a great clatter among bottles and glasses, his back turned to them.

'You've no news concerning the progress of investigations, I suppose?' Merle asked Meredith, setting himself in a chair next to her, smoothing his leonine silver mane and adjusting his cuffs. He was a man who still wore cufflinks, gold ones with diamond chips in them.

'No, but I'm thinking about taking a few days off and going down to Bamford. I have friends there, after all.'

There was an almighty crash. 'Sorry!' called Denis. 'I've broken a glass. Careless of me. It's all right.'

'My dear fellow!' Merle rose to his feet in concern. 'You've cut yourself, you're bleeding!'

'It's all right, I tell you!' Denis snapped, warding off help and sympathy. He dragged out his handkerchief and wrapped it round his thumb before realising this would hamper the use of his hand. 'Excuse me, I'll just go and get a plaster—' He bolted out of the room.

'Poor Denis,' said Merle majestically. 'He lives on his nerves. Very trying for Leah. I suppose I must get my own drink!'

Dinner wasn't a success. Merle lectured them at length about the architectural alterations he had supervised at Springwood Hall. Denis, his thumb bound up in pink sticking plaster, drank the greater part of the wine they were all supposed to be sampling. He grew moodier by the minute and finally fell out with Merle's opinion on the wine when it was given.

'Well, I don't think it's bad and I've drunk enough

bloody wine in my time!' he said truculently.

Merle twitched an eyebrow. 'So we see. However, I didn't say it was bad. You're putting words in my mouth. I'm just not a great fancier of these East European wines. How about you, Meredith?'

'I rather like them. But then I'm sort of used to them, Hungarian ones like Badacsonyi, Egri Bikaver and Tokay and so on,' Meredith confessed.

'Ah yes, you're a much travelled lady, of course!' Merle acknowledged this with a bow over his glass.

'I shall be recommending this one!' said Denis fiercely, grasping the bottle in question by the neck in a manner which suggested he would have preferred it to be Merle he had by the throat.

'You're the connoisseur, Denis!'

'You needn't sound so patronising about it! I don't know much about art or architecture but I know something about food and drink!'

'Denis, darling—'

'My dear fellow—'

'My thumb's throbbing! I should have nipped out to the hospital for a tetanus jab. Probably get lockjaw!' Denis's resentment, fuelled by alcohol, was settling on any grievance.

'Isn't that necessary only if the cut is caused by a metal blade or got when doing gardening or woodwork?' pontificated Merle genially. 'I once injured myself quite severely on rosethorns—'

'Who cares about your blasted gardening accidents? I suppose you're an expert on gardening as well as on art and wine?' yelled Denis.

'I'm awfully sorry,' interrupted Leah with a placatory smile, 'I'm afraid Denis has had a drop too much to drink.

Hazard of his profession, I expect. We'll go into the drawing room, shall we, and let Dolores clear away here? Coffee will be ready directly.'

'I'm not drunk!' growled Denis as he was bundled along by his wife. 'What hazard of profession? I can hold my drink! When have I been found drunk? You tell me—'

'No, darling, of course you're not drunk. But you are just a teeny bit tiddly. You're being awfully rude to Victor.'

'That's it! Take his side!' Denis came to an abrupt halt and jerked his arm free with a wild gesture. 'I might have expected that!'

'Now see here, old chap—' Merle began disastrously.

'Don't you old-chap me, you – you silver-rinsed philanderer!'

'What's that supposed to mean?' Merle snapped without it being clear whether it was the slur on his hair-colour or his morals he resented.

'Think I'm blind? Think I don't know what's been going on? You sit there, ogling my wife—'

'Stop it, Denis!' ordered Leah sharply.

He rounded on her. 'No, why should I? Afraid Meredith might find out what a two-timer I married? Afraid I might find out? Unless Meredith is blind she'll already have sussed it out for herself, nor am I stupid! Lunches with Lizzie? Lunches with him!' Denis threw out a hand and pointed accusingly at Merle, the gesture somewhat spoiled by the sticky plaster on his injured thumb.

'You're drunk!' said his wife coldly.

Meredith's heart sank. She was to be obliged to witness a domestic spat and all indications were it was going to be one with embarrassing revelations. Why couldn't they keep it till later?

'Oh, am I?' snarled Denis. 'How's this for a bit of

drunken logic? It just so happens I met Lizzie in the street the other day and she hasn't had lunch with you since last March! The most she's shared with you is half an hour and a cup of tea at Heal's! Any lunches you've had you've had with him!'

'Rubbish!' Leah's eyes blazed.

'Of course she wasn't with me, hasn't been with me!' Merle declared vigorously. 'If you seriously mean to suggest such a thing, you're a fool!'

'Yes, yes, I am a fool, aren't I?' Denis was getting more and more agitated, purple-faced and sweating. 'And you've both played me for one! But I'm not quite so thick as you imagined. Okay, Leah, if you weren't with him, where were you and with whom?'

'I'm not going to discuss this now, Denis! Meredith, I'm so sorry about this little scene—'

'Stop apologising for me!' Denis bellowed. 'Stop acting the injured innocent! I'm the injured party, dammit!'

'Indeed yes,' observed Merle. 'But only in so far as you've cut your thumb, Denis. Otherwise I'm afraid it's all in your imagination! Have you thought of having a word with your doctor about these delusions of yours?'

'That does it!'

As bad luck would have it, Denis had fetched up standing by a pair of ceremonial daggers fixed in a wall display. Without warning he whirled round, seized one of them and lunged at the astonished Merle.

'I'll bloody injure you! Go on, get out of my house!' The blade glittered in the bright electric light as it swished through the air. 'Go on,' yelled Denis, jumping back and forth in a clumsy parody of fencing steps. 'Or I'll slice you into ribbons!'

'As it happens, this is my house!' Leah said loudly.

'Victor, stay right where you are. Denis, you're just being childish. I think perhaps you ought to go upstairs and lie down. Your behaviour is inexcusable. I can only suppose you're ill.'

'My – my behaviour!' Denis appeared about to choke. He spun round to face his wife and the dagger flashed dangerously near to her. She stepped back with an alarmed cry, throwing up her hands.

'Watch out, you idiot!' cried Merle.

Shouting wasn't going to do much good! thought Meredith in exasperation at it all. Denis was going to do some damage with that dagger at any moment, if only to himself. She looked round. Someone, presumably the late Marcus, had been quite a collector of militaria. Also on the wall was a silver-topped swagger stick.

Meredith snatched it off, raised it on high and brought it down with a crack on Denis's forearm.

'Ow!' Denis shrieked and the knife dropped from his fingers to the floor. Meredith stooped and grabbed it.

Silence fell. Denis nursed his arm and glowered at her. 'You've probably broken my wrist! Maniac!'

'I'm sorry, but this dagger is very sharp and you wouldn't want to hurt anyone, would you?' Meredith returned reasonably.

Denis's fury and belligerence evaporated. 'No – oh – oh, shit!' He turned and stumbled out of the room.

'Thank you, Meredith,' said Leah, breathing heavily. 'I am sorry, I apologise to both of you. I can't think what's come over Denis. He really isn't a violent man. Victor, you know him. He's been under a lot of stress.'

'Quite, quite, Leah my dear. These things happen. But are you sure you can manage now? Who is in the house besides the maid?'

'Dolores' husband, Raul. our cook. But I can manage.
He won't make any more fuss. You saw him . . .' She smiled
sadly. 'Denis isn't good at standing up for himself. What
– what you saw just now, that was just a flash in the pan.
Over and done.'

'Then I think I should be going now. It really is quite
late.' Merle managed to make it sound as if almost nothing
had happened. 'But try and get him to see a doctor or to
take a little holiday.'

Outside on the steps when the door had closed behind
them Merle paused and asked, 'May I give you a lift home,
Meredith?'

He actually wore a cloak, a black one which he threw
dramatically round his shoulders as he spoke. Standing on
the bottom white-washed step, one hand resting on the
wrought iron balustrade and light from a street lamp gleaming on his silver hair, he presented a quite extraordinary
sight. He was, Meredith realised, quite well aware of it.

Denis really did get it all wrong, she thought in a burst
of insight. Leah hasn't been seeing Merle. Victor amused
himself with that kiss-hand routine but it was just empty
gallantry. He would never compromise himself. Really
Victor wasn't interested in women, nor in men either come
to that. Only in himself and in things, beautiful things.
Houses, paintings or sculpture had meaning for him. People
had none.

She shivered, possibly because of the cool evening air
and said aloud, 'I've got my car, thanks.'

Merle had noticed the shiver. 'Well, we mustn't stand
here while you catch cold!' He glanced up at the first-floor
windows of the house they had just quit and an extraordinary expression crossed his face. There was a new

sharpness in his eyes and the silver wings of his waved hair stuck up like pointed ears. Just for a moment, in his dark cloak, he looked like a great black bat.

'Denis really isn't a bad chap,' Merle said. 'But not good at coping. Such people often go to extremes. It was interesting, don't you think, that he automatically reached for that knife? It really makes one wonder if he hasn't done something similar before?'

Chapter Eight

'There's something wrong with these figures!' said Markby firmly.

'But I don't understand!' protested Margery Collins.

It was Monday afternoon and it was raining, a steady drizzle which beat against the windowpanes of the upstairs flat which had been Ellen's and where Markby sat with Margery at Ellen's dining table. It was chilly in there. Margery, after some hesitation, had made them both coffee in Ellen's kitchen. But she hadn't drunk hers and the steam from it curled into the cold air, growing gradually fainter as the coffee cooled and an unpleasing thick skin formed on it. 'It's like sitting at table with the dead!' Margery had said.

Markby had replied he hoped she didn't mean him, which had roused a brief weak smile. But he was inclined to agree with her. The flat resounded with that echoing emptiness which said the owner had gone away for good. A faint smell of damp had invaded it. Dust had settled on the furniture. The welter of papers scattered across the table top only emphasised that this had ceased to be anyone's private home and sanctum. It was now the scene of a post-mortem on a business.

Markby reached out and picked up several bank statements, clipped together.

'Now look, according to these statements Ellen banked increased takings from the shop on several dates during the past eight months. Roughly these dates are every six weeks. The spacing isn't exact but it's near enough to suggest a regular pattern of sorts. The leap in the amount on those dates suggests that the shop wasn't just doing well but doing outstandingly well – once every six weeks. Why is the increase in turnover not more evenly spaced out?'

He tapped one entry and Margery peered at it from beneath her untidy fringe. 'This is an increase here of one thousand pounds over the equivalent date last year. And we're supposed to be in the middle of a recession!' Markby stretched out his hand and indicated another stack of papers. 'But looking at the corresponding invoices for goods delivered in the period and checking the stock held in the shop as you have so kindly done, well, you can see for yourself that the two sets of figures don't tally.

'According to goods ordered and stock held, the shop was doing no better or worse than average for the time of year. Was it your impression, Margery, that Needles was doing exceptionally well over the past six to eight months? Sales up? Bumper demand for any particular item?'

She shook her head. 'No. Summer is a slow time for wools. People start buying in August, looking ahead to the long winter evenings. They think they'll start a tapestry or embroider something or knit a cardigan, you know, looking for a winter hobby. We are expecting a new delivery soon to anticipate that. Or at least, we were. I wrote and asked the suppliers if they could hold off for a bit. I didn't want to cancel it – but I didn't want boxes of stuff arriving just at the moment. I mean, the will's not yet been granted probate and I don't know how I'd pay for it.'

'Yes. But going back to the past year. Where did all the

extra money Ellen was banking in the name of the shop come from?'

'I don't know, Mr Markby!' She was becoming agitated. The rain beat more insistently at the window and she threw a hunted glance in that direction. 'I had nothing to do with that side of things. I never went to the bank. Ellen took the money there. She banked every day. She didn't believe in keeping money on the premises. She said, word would get round. I keep telling you she didn't discuss it with me!'

Markby sighed and began to put all the papers together again. 'I'll have to get an expert to cast an eye over them, someone who knows more about business accounts than I do.' He meant someone in the regional Fraud Squad, but he didn't want to alarm her even more. 'Did Ellen never use the professional services of an accountant?'

'She did it all herself. She did have a firm in Bamford do it for her the first year we were here, but after that she said she'd got the hang of it and didn't see why she should pay anyone else.' Biting her lip, Margery watched as Markby shoved papers and ledgers into a document case. 'Mr Markby, I know Ellen was – was horribly murdered and you have to find her killer. But all this, this poking and prying into her private affairs, is it really necessary? Ellen would have hated it so. I feel, sitting here in her room, as if she were here and could see us. I feel so guilty.'

'There's no need for that. I dare say Ellen wouldn't have liked it if she were alive – but she's dead and if her shade is watching over us I'm sure it wants us to do justice by her!' Markby smiled, he hoped encouragingly. 'If it weren't necessary, I shouldn't do it. I am a busy man with other things demanding my attention.'

'Yes, I appreciate that,' she mumbled. 'But what exactly are you looking for? All those numbers, they might be slightly out here and there but there's probably some reason for it and it doesn't matter, does it?' Margery's eyes, exaggerated by her round spectacles, looked enormous in her pale, triangular face.

She reminded Markby vaguely of Minnie Mouse. He wondered whether she was really so naive that she believed it didn't matter that the books didn't balance – or whether in her obscurely loyal way she was trying to protect Ellen's reputation. What a strange creature she was. Despite himself he couldn't help but find her slightly repulsive.

'I am looking for a motive,' he said gently.

Her slight form seemed, if possible, to wither and wilt even more, subsiding on to her chair, hunched and miserable. 'Money is the root of evil!' she said in a sullen, resigned way.

'And yet, Margery, people so often kill for other reasons, not money. Love, jealousy, envy—'

Almost inaudibly she whispered. 'I don't know anything about any of those things . . .'

'Some people,' Markby returned almost as quietly, 'would say you were fortunate.'

A gust of wind scooped up a flurry of rain and tossed it noisily at the pane, rattling at the latch as if impatient fingers tried it. Ellen's shade after all, he thought, wrily, trying to get in here and prevent me. Too bad. He was in charge now.

'I was looking for a motive,' he said later to Pearce in his office. 'And I fancy I may just have found one.' He tapped the wet document case he had put on top of his desk and pulled off his green waterproof, sending a spray of raindrops across the room. 'That shop, Pearce,' came his voice, muffled as he hung the Barbour up on a hook and attempted to smooth his hair, 'was being used not only as an arts and crafts centre but as a laundry!'

He turned and saw Pearce's eyebrows had rocketed up to his hairline and added, 'Not for dirty linen: for dirty money! Although dirty linen and dirty money do often go together!'

'Blimey,' said Pearce after a moment. 'You think she was into blackmail?'

'Unexplained sums of money paid into her account at roughly equal intervals starting eight months ago? Purporting to be part of the shop profits but untraceable in the day-to-day running of the business? What else?'

'But she didn't need the money, exactly, did she? The shop did pretty well.'

'Financial gain isn't the only motive of blackmailers.'

'Think the girl, Miss Collins, knows about it?'

'Doubt it. Painfully honest. Might have had a suspicion something was wrong though. She's fighting a rearguard action to stop me asking any more questions. Odd sort of relationship, that. Ellen was never very nice to Margery, but left her a tidy amount plus the shop. Bad conscience? Warped sense of humour? Just didn't care who had the money? We'll never know. Margery seems to have admired Ellen but not exactly liked her. Now, I think, she's burdened with what she feels ought to be gratitude. Poor kid's in a complete muddle about it all.'

'Blackmail . . .' repeated Pearce. 'The victim won't come forward, that's for sure.'

'Perhaps the victim did come forward . . . came forward holding a knife and put an end to the sorry business.' Markby's gaze settled on the document case. 'Ellen Bryant was playing with fire. How very, very foolish.'

* * *

'I have no regrets!'

Although Ms Mapple echoed the words of the late Edith Piaf she hardly resembled her. Fully dressed and seated in her own living room Markby found her twice as alarming as when she had been unclothed out in the open. She wore a sort of pleated tent which fell from a round yoke and was coloured in shades of violet. Her abundant black hair was brushed out in a wild halo and long earrings dangled to her shoulders. They were the sort of earrings made by hobby-ists, beads threaded on silver wire. He was sure she had made them herself.

Other examples of her artistic talent abounded in the room, paintings, clay mugs and vases and an abstract collage made of buttons and scraps of brightly coloured material.

'Ah, you've spotted that,' said Hope, seeing his eyes rest on this last creation. 'My students made that.'

'Oh, at the polytechnic?'

'No, in the psychiatric wing at the hospital. When the mind is closed in some areas, Chief Inspector, windows open in it in others. I have seen the most wonderful artistic work done by those whom society would view as mentally impaired or ill. You are acquainted with the work of the nineteenth-century artist, Richard Dadd?'

'Yes, I am. Unforgettable, fantastic stuff.'

'He was a homicidal maniac.'

'Speaking of homicide,' he began but she interrupted.

'I know absolutely nothing about that. I suppose you want to talk about Ellen's murder again. I've already told you I know nothing whatsoever about it! I saw Ellen earlier, as I'd expected to. She was a committee member and I expected her support. When I demonstrated at the opening of the hotel, it was in the cause of the environment, our history, our heritage! Preserving things, Chief Inspector, not destroying them! And I repeat, I have no regrets!' She tossed her mane of black curls. 'I dare say you think I'm a crank. No!'

She held up a beringed hand on the assumption, he felt somewhat premature, that he was going to disagree. 'Say so, if that is what you think. However, I am not. I have lived in Bamford all my life. As for other long-time residents, Springwood Hall was a part of my childhood. I know that no family has lived there for years, but it was put to other uses. It was a school for a while, if you remember, and then a holiday centre for the handicapped – only of course it was a little too remote and it didn't have the facilities so they had to give it up. I visited it myself when it was a holiday centre for the disadvantaged and gave some art classes. They were great fun. We held a little exhibition of our creative work afterwards in the church hall and everyone who came along to see it was amazed and impressed.

'I know that the Hall was left without a use over the past few years, but a new use could and should have been found for it. Something which would have left it accessible to the people of Bamford and the surrounds.' She pulled a face. 'I don't think many Bamford people will be dining in the new restaurant! It will be an island of wealthy strangers, visitors, birds of passage and worst of all, it will be "off bounds" to local people!'

Markby wondered if she knew she had found his Achilles' heel. 'That's all very well and I can't argue with your basic principles,' he wanted to say, 'I agree with you that in a perfect world some use would have been found for the place so that it could serve the community. But the plain fact was no one wanted it. It wasn't suitable, as both the school and the disabled charity had already discovered. And with no one offering to take it on, it was falling down in the meantime and repairs were going to cost a small fortune.' But getting into an argument with Hope was not why he had come here so he said none of this aloud.

'Mrs Bryant was a member of your committee.' He dragged the conversation firmly back to police matters. 'I'm trying to find out as much as I can about her. She doesn't seem to have had many friends and so her contacts with your committee become very important.'

The word important appealed to Hope. She rustled the tent and gave a sort of satisfied chirrup. One of the three dogs slumbering about the room looked up and yapped. Markby eyed them with some misgiving and surreptitiously picked pekinese hairs from his jacket sleeve.

'She was not,' said Hope curtly, 'a friendly person. Ellen was really a problem.'

'Oh, to the society?'

'No, to herself. One can always tell an unhappy person, Chief Inspector. They spread their misery. They push it on to other people. She was bitter.'

'About what?'

'How should I know?' Hope's ample shoulders quivered. 'I tried to be friendly, goodness knows I tried. I even asked her if she'd like to join one of my craft classes at the poly. I mean, she was artistic – in a way. A commercial sort of way.'

No one had said the word commercial like that, thought Markby, amused, since the word 'trade' had been unacceptable in a gentleman's drawing room. 'And what did Ellen reply?' he asked.

The violet tent heaved. 'She was very rude! She said she had no interest in painting daubs and stringing beads! She could be very coarse. I'm not surprised she had no friends!'

'No one in particular in the society?'

'No. Well—' Hope paused. 'No. Not really.'

He let that go for the time being. 'Can you think of any reason why she was killed?'

'Chief Inspector!' Hope leaned forward. 'You should not be wondering about why, you should be wondering about where! You should be at that hotel asking questions, not here!'

'In what way could her death be linked directly with the hotel, other than it taking place there on a very public occasion?'

'You really are a very tiresome man. I should have thought it was obvious. She found out something sinister about that place and she was killed to prevent her telling!''

'Found out what?'

'That's your job to establish,' said Ms Mapple, throwing herself back on her divan. 'Not mine. Go and talk to Schuhmacher.'

'Well, I dare say I shall,' Markby said, rising to take his leave. 'Oh, in the meantime, if you should think of anything you may have forgotten to mention, you can just pick up the phone and give me a call or leave a message, you know. In the utmost confidence.'

She stared at him resentfully.

The rain had stopped when he left Hope's flat to drive to Springwood Hall. The countryside looked freshly washed and green. It had been a pleasant summer and it was hard to think that in only a few weeks' time the leaves would change colour and flutter from the trees in showers of red and gold.

The harvest was in, fields shaved to ground level and here and there black patches marked where a few farmers still burned stubble, something they wouldn't be allowed to do much longer. Markby was pleased about the recent ban, only too aware that the drifting smoke from burning fields had been known to cause traffic accidents or to flare up into conflagrations requiring the fire brigade. Moreover he had walked over fields scorched by the flame and mourned the charred bodies of fieldmice. Dotted about the field he passed at the moment pheasants roamed, both handsome and incongruous in their bronze, purple and sea-green plumage. They had left the cover of nearby woods, perhaps knowing by some instinct that the open season for them was still some weeks away.

Eric greeted him with a kind of gloomy enthusiasm. 'You have made no progress. I see it in your face. But you've come to tell me so in person and I appreciate that. Make yourself comfortable. I will open up a bottle of good wine – or perhaps you would prefer a beer?'

'Sadly, I'm driving myself so I'll have to refuse both. But a cup of coffee would be much appreciated.'

'Of course.' Schuhmacher reached for the phone and spoke on some internal link to the kitchens. Then he put down the receiver and sat back in the comfortable leather-covered armchair in his private sitting room. 'Well, then? She remains a mystery, this lady in my wine cellars?'

'Afraid so. Very much a lady of secrets. I've – I've just been to see Miss Mapple of the historical society—'

Eric's face had changed, working alarmingly. 'That woman! She should be in an asylum! Locked away! Locked away for everyone's sake!'

'I'd rather not become personally involved in that argument, Eric. The puzzle for me is this. Ellen Bryant was killed here. Therefore her killer was also here. But Ellen came here to demonstrate or lend her support to Miss Mapple's demonstration. So why did her killer come here? Only following Ellen? Did he or she know about the planned disruption of the opening? Or was the killer here already in some other capacity?'

'I hope you do not accuse my staff. That would be nonsense. He or she probably came for the same reason as the Mapple woman and belongs to the same crazy society! They would stop at nothing, that bunch of lunatics!'

The door opened and coffee was brought in by a young man in waiter's black trousers, shirtsleeves and waistcoat, with a bow tie. When he had left them and Eric had poured coffee for them both, Markby said in reasonable tones, 'However strongly the society felt about your use of the Hall, I don't think they would go so far as literally to sacrifice one of their members to disrupt the opening.'

'They would do anything!' said Schuhmacher ominously.

'Come off it, Eric, not murder.'

'As it happens, I have made inquiries of my own. I am told that the dead woman and Miss Mapple were not friends. They had some quarrel. If you wish to know who told me, it was one of the chambermaids here, a local girl. She worked for a week or two as a cleaner for Miss Mapple but gave it up because, it seems, the woman Mapple's flat is infested with dogs and the furniture covered in hair.'

That was true enough. 'What is this chambermaid's name?'

'Ah – Pollock, I think. Denise, I believe she is called, or Deirdre. I am not sure which. You wish to see her?'

'Not right now but I'll send my sergeant over to have a word with her, if that's all right.' Markby sipped his coffee. 'This is excellent coffee.'

'Of course,' said Schuhmacher testily. 'Everything here is of the best. And to what purpose? To get lurid stories in the tabloid press! Do you know I am also now a persecutor of aged horses?'

'I do assume you haven't been accused of serving up horsemeat steaks.'

'If that is a joke, it is a very bad one!' said Eric fiercely. 'No! Of course not! I mean, because I don't want smelly animals under the noses of my guests, I am some kind of monster!'

'Ah, the Horse and Donkey Rest Home.'

'The girl who runs it, her name is Foster, she is also a member of the Society for the Preservation of Historic Bamford! Historic, pah! We have historic towns in Switzerland. They have beautiful, interesting buildings. They are surrounded by stupendous scenery! Bamford – some of it is old, I suppose – but it is very modest. It has few interesting buildings except for its church and its market cross. Its old houses have not been respected. They have modern aluminium frame windows put in them and do I hear the society for preserving the place protest about that? As for the countryside here, it is very pleasant, but its hills are not the Alps.'

'I like Bamford myself!' Markby heard himself say more sharply than he had intended. 'And my family has long associations with the surrounding country area.'

Eric's face showed consternation followed by contrition. 'Forgive me. I must have sounded both arrogant and discourteous. That was not my intention. What I meant to say was that I have not destroyed any of the amenities on offer in the area by renovating the Hall and putting it to a new use. I believe I have added to them. I have saved the Hall, for a start. Without me, this grand old house—' Schuhmacher indicated the building in which they sat, 'it would have tumbled down. Who today can afford to live

privately in such a place? To be a lord of the manor, as you say. No, no, it must be found a commercial use if it is to be saved.'

'Had you ever met either Ellen Bryant or any member of the society before the Saturday of the opening?'

'Yes, I had met one of the men, a fellow called Grimsby. He came to see me in London. I was polite. He was not. We had nothing to say to one another. That is the only one of them I met face to face and it was obvious that there was little purpose in my seeing any of the others. We corresponded – or my lawyers did with them.'

'You haven't spoken personally to Miss Foster about the horses' home?'

'No – I have seen her from a distance. I drove to a place near the stables where I could observe through binoculars. I saw clearly that reports I had received were not exaggerated. It is an eyesore. Moreover, the wind blew from it to me and smelled very bad of manure. Also there was a noise. Some days you can hear it even here at the hotel. Like something being slaughtered or a cry of the damned. It is caused by a donkey, I understand. Are my guests to suffer that?'

He leaned forward, his square capable hands gripping the arms of his chair. He looked large, solid and dangerous, far more the ice-hockey player than the hotelier. 'This place, Alan, it is the summit of my career. Everything I have dreamed of, worked for, planned – for years! And is it all to be ruined because a woman I have never met is murdered in my cellar by some lunatic for a reason which has nothing to do with me? It is intolerable! You must find this criminal quickly!'

'We are going as fast as we can but it's a curious case. I suppose you aren't doing the kind of business you anticipated with this hanging over you and the press reports.'

'What do you imagine? Even worse, the prurient come here, the voyeurs, those who get a kick from being on the scene of a murder! They ask, can you imagine it, to be shown the cellars! We have learned to spot them, these psychos, and refuse them. Is my hotel to be a waxworks' museum, a chamber of horrors? I will not,' Schuhmacher's huge fist balled and struck the arm of his chair, 'I will not have my entire life's work and financial investment together with the careers of my staff brought to nothing because of this! I will not allow it!'

'It'll prove a nine-day wonder, these things do,' Markby soothed him without great success. 'And then you'll be able to get on with the business without either us or the press bothering you.'

Schuhmacher growled.

Markby glanced at his watch as he left the hotel. He ought to finish his round of visits with another talk to Zoë Foster. The Alice Batt Rest Home was only a few minutes away, as Eric had forcefully pointed out. What was more, should Markby's niece, Emma, be helping out there this afternoon, she'd be thinking about setting off for home about now and he could take her back to Bamford by car.

There was a temptation when one had no children oneself to develop strong ideas about how other people should bring up theirs. Markby was well aware of this trap and tried to avoid expressing anything like criticism or helpful advice either to his sister or to her husband. The warning about the prowler in the district had been different. That had been his duty as a police officer.

Generally the problem didn't arise, although he did feel they nagged at Matthew too much about his schoolwork and that they could, surely, have taught Vicky not to break everything she touched. Vicky in a greenhouse was a gardener's nightmare. But he was fond of the kids. He was Emma's godfather as well as her uncle and he sometimes felt Paul and Laura should keep a better eye on her. Emma spent every Saturday and all her free holiday-time at the horses' home, fine. But the lane leading down to it was lonely and even to get that far Emma had to travel alone by country bus to descend at a remote wayside bus-stop surrounded by fields. He had mentioned this to Paul before. Paul had replied, rather tersely, that if it was raining he drove over and fetched his daughter home. 'What's she supposed to do if it's not raining?' Markby had been tempted to retort. But knowing the answer would have been on the lines of 'She gets on the bus and mind your own business!' he had with difficulty kept silent.

Perhaps, as a policeman, he was over-sensitive to danger. But as he passed the bus-stop where his niece would have been waiting, he scrutinised the deserted grass verge intently and when he turned off the main road to drive down the lane, he kept a sharp eye open for her sturdy little form in gumboots and old anorak, stomping along the roadside. She was not to be seen. Perhaps, as it had been raining, Paul had driven over today and fetched her.

Markby pulled the car over to the verge by the gate and stopped. He got out and surveyed the ramshackle stable-yard. The horsy odour of which Eric had complained immediately made itself known, a good country pong. He opened the gate, refastening it carefully. There were some animals grazing in a paddock to his right, ponies and a large and very ugly donkey with something wrong with its front legs. As he watched, it lurched forward to find a fresh patch of grass. In a spirit of goodwill Markby paused to lean on the fence and whistle at the beast. It looked up and rolled back its upper lip showing fierce yellow teeth and its lop ears flattened. He was rather glad it was slow on its feet. He suspected that if it could have charged him down, it would have done.

He resumed his way to the yard where Zoë was talking to a stocky, shock-haired young man in a motor cyclist's leather jacket, holding a crash helmet by its straps. Markby recognised him as another of the committee members, Robin Harding. The machine over there was presumably his motorbike. He recalled that Zoë had spoken of Harding's help. He wondered whether the young man was attracted here by the notion of good works or the opportunity to impress a pretty girl.

'Good afternoon!' he hailed them. 'My niece around anywhere?'

They broke off their earnest conversation and faced him. 'Oh, hullo, Mr Markby!' said Zoë. 'Emma? No, sorry. I haven't seen her today. I expect the rain earlier kept her away.'

'Right,' said Markby, relieved. 'As you may know, I'm investigating Mrs Bryant's death, after all. Since you're both here perhaps I could have a word with both of you?'

'Kill two birds with one stone?' said Robin drily.

'Something like that. I've just called on your landlord, Miss Foster.'

The expression on her freckled face clouded. 'What did he say?'

'About this place? Not much. This is a difficult time for him, of course. For all of you, I dare say.'

'I should think so!' Robin burst out before Zoë could reply. 'Zoë's worried sick! Don't ask either of us to feel sorry for Schuhmacher! I only hope you're not going to

badger Zoë every other day just because she had the bad luck to find Ellen's body!'

Markby let that go but he saw the girl wince. 'I saw Miss Mapple earlier so I'm particularly pleased to see you two. It enables me to tick the historical society off my visiting list, apart from Mr Grimsby. I hope to see him later.'

'He runs Grimsby's Stationers and Bookstore,' Zoë said. 'But I suppose you know that. You could find him there.'

'Ellen Bryant also ran a shop,' Markby got to his subject rather neatly, he felt. 'So she and Mr Grimsby had something in common.'

'If you're suggesting Ellen and Grimsby were having an affair,' said Robin scornfully, 'forget it! If you said "sex" to Grimsby, he'd take you to the appropriate shelf in his shop and sell you a book on it. If his shop has any such books, which I don't suppose it has. He's an old pedant and his mind works like a cash register.'

'I've always found him very pleasant,' said Zoë, looking slightly surprised at this condemnation. 'He isn't that old. I'd say about forty-five.'

'He's all right. I didn't say he wasn't. But the chief inspector here was suggesting he and Ellen indulged in bouts of purple passion and I'm just saying, no way.'

'Actually,' said Markby, 'I suggested no such thing.'

'It's what you meant.'

'What about Ellen's relations with the rest of you? I understand Miss Mapple and Mrs Bryant didn't get along well, but were either of you friendly with Mrs Bryant?'

'Who told you Hope and Ellen didn't like each other?' Robin returned pugnaciously. 'They weren't best buddies but they served on the same committee and got along as well as was necessary.'

'I think Ellen niggled Hope on purpose sometimes,'

Zoë confessed. 'Actually—' she flushed. 'I got on quite well with Ellen. I thought she was probably nice underneath but a bit outspoken and didn't tolerate fools gladly. She was clever herself. Look how well she ran that shop. She could be a little cryptic in her remarks. Sometimes it was difficult to know just what she did mean. Perhaps Hope misunderstood Ellen and of course Hope does – oh dear, this is awful, talking about people. But Hope does sometimes sort of invite people to make fun of her.'

'And Ellen did that? Make fun of Hope?'

'Yes, but who doesn't?' Robin said firmly.

'I don't!' Zoë protested.

'No, you don't, sorry! I didn't mean you!' Robin gazed down at his companion.

Love's young dream! thought Markby unkindly. That complicated matters. He wondered if the girl realised he was smitten. Probably not. No doubt she thought about her old nags and nothing else.

'Miss Foster, when you say people might have misunderstood Ellen, could you give me an example?'

She fidgeted about, redder in the face than ever. 'I can't talk about other people, that wouldn't be right. Anyway, it would be what do you call it? Hearsay, that's it.'

'In a court of law, but we're not in a courtroom, are we?' Markby prompted gently.

'Funny old job you've got, haven't you?' Robin interrupted.'Collecting gossip like this and always trying to prise out people's secrets.'

'Have you got any secrets you'd rather I didn't know?' Markby eyed him coolly. This young man was beginning to annoy him. Someone ought to take him down a peg or two.

Robin had flushed. 'No, of course not! And why don't

you mind your own business!'

'Right, Miss Foster?'

'Secrets? I have got a sort of one. Actually, I'd quite like to tell you and get it all off my chest. It's such a silly thing, but I keep thinking about it and it makes me ashamed of myself because it doesn't show me in a very good light.'

'Zoë?' Harding was beginning to look both surprised and alarmed. 'What are you on about? You don't have to tell him anything, you know! He's fishing. Let him fish.'

'I feel I should like to tell someone and sort of expiate it. It makes me look a bit of a fool and mercenary as well.'

'For goodness sake, Zoë!'

'Mr Harding!' said Markby crisply. 'Would you mind keeping quiet and letting Miss Foster speak?'

'I told you I got along quite well with Ellen!' Zoë began quickly before the irate Robin Harding could explode. 'On several occasions she came out here on a Sunday afternoon and we went for a walk over the fields. We talked mostly about the campaign to save Springwood Hall and things which were in the news around Bamford. I talked about my problems here at the Rest Home and how difficult it is to raise money.'

Zoë paused. 'As a matter of fact, I've had some quite generous donations recently from readers of that newspaper which published the story about how we're threatened with eviction here at the home.'

Oh no, prayed Markby. Don't get off the subject, not just when you were beginning to prattle along so nicely! Aloud, he prompted, 'You didn't talk about yourselves, you and Mrs Bryant? I mean, did she tell you where she lived before she came to Bamford?'

'I'm not sure. She was from Australia originally but came

127

over here a long time ago. She said she might go back there one day for a holiday. That's all I remember her saying. But what I wanted to tell you was this – one Sunday as we were walking and I was describing how chronically hard up we were, she started saying how well the shop was doing. She'd been surprised at her success. She made a joke about it, morbid, really. "At this rate," she said, "I'll die a wealthy woman." Then she said, she'd had to find someone to leave it all to in her will. She said, "No family, no friends, that's me! But I haven't forgotten people who've been decent by me." I understood her to mean she had made a will and I thought—' Zoë was by now crimson. 'I thought she meant me, that I'd been decent to her and I wasn't forgotten! I know it's awful, but I really thought she meant she'd put me in her will, or not me exactly, but the Rest Home—'

'Zoë!' yelled Harding.

'Shut up!' Markby ordered him unceremoniously. 'But she hadn't, Miss Foster, as it turned out, had she?'

'No. I wish she had remembered us. I don't mean I wanted Ellen's money for myself. It just would have been nice if she'd only left the home a couple of hundred pounds. We really need it.'

'Please, Zoë!' Harding pleaded.

'Will you be quiet, Mr Harding!' thundered Markby.

'And of course I didn't want her to die. I wouldn't want anyone dead. It's just that apparently she left the lot to Margery Collins. All of it, the shop as well. I do think she might have been kind enough to remember the horses. But then, thinking it over now, perhaps she thought that by telling her how much I needed money, I was sort of begging or trying to put the idea in her head, and that's why she didn't leave us anything. Still, it was a shock to hear Margery had everything. I really thought Ellen had made a bequest to us.'

This time Harding wouldn't be silenced. 'For God's sake, Zoë! Don't say another word! Don't you realise you're telling this nosy copper that you've got a motive for murder?'

Chapter Nine

Deirdre the chambermaid smiled provocatively at Sergeant Pearce. She had dimples in her plump cheeks, curly fair hair, a pink and white complexion and a remarkable figure. In a very few years' time she would no doubt be a fat, untidy slattern, but right now she looked like the milkmaid from a child's nursery rhyme picture-book.

'She's a right old cow,' said Deirdre, tailoring her vocabulary to suit her appearance. 'If you want to know about Hope Mapple, you ask me. I'll tell you!'

'I am asking you,' said Pearce, eyeing her with some unease. For the past five minutes she had been shifting steadily nearer to him, inch by inch, and the gleam in her round blue eyes was positively predatory.

'She said she wanted someone to do light cleaning. She put a card up down the job centre. I didn't fancy it really but they kept on at me down there to go after a job and grumbling about my unemployment benefit so I went and took it on. Just to keep them quiet at the job centre. I didn't like the place as soon as I saw it, and I didn't like the look of her, either! Snoopy sort, creeps up behind you. Now here, at the hotel, it's really lovely. All the furniture new and smelling nice, lovely curtains and that. I wouldn't half like to be able to stay here. I took the job on here like a shot.'

'But you took the job at Hope Mapple's . . .' prompted Pearce.

'Yes. Light cleaning!' Deirdre snorted. 'You want to see that place of hers. Full of smelly little dogs, it is, and a lot of old arty junk. The dogs leave their fur all over the furniture and if you so much as brush against one of the weird paintings or clay pot things, she lets out a shriek like you'd tried to murder her.' Deirdre paused. 'As a matter of fact, if anyone had tried murdering old Mapple, I wouldn't have been a bit surprised. She gives art classes over at the loony-bin and I reckon they ought to keep her in there. Don't know how they tell her from the patients! I was sorry about Mrs Bryant from the wool shop. I thought she was a really smashing looker. I never understood why she didn't have no man in tow.' Here Deirdre's eyelashes drooped suggestively. 'I mean, it's natural, isn't it? A woman likes to have a man around and men like it, don't they?'

Cripes . . . thought Pearce, quickly judging the distance between himself and the door. 'You told Mr Schuhmacher that Miss Mapple and Mrs Bryant quarrelled.'

'You bet they did!' said Deirdre sapiently. 'You should have heard it.'

'But you heard it?' Pearce persisted.

Deirdre's assurance faltered a little. 'I heard her side of it. It was all on the phone. But I didn't need to hear the other side. Calling each other names, they were. Well, I only heard old Hope. But she kept squawking "How dare you?" so I reckon Mrs Bryant was giving as good as she got. And good luck to her. I had a few things to say myself to old Mapple when I left. You know what she did? She said I ate her rotten chocolates! I never touched them! I'm on a diet . . .' Deirdre paused and simpered. 'Well, I was then . . . but I mean, I didn't want to end up like a matchstick, did I?' She preened herself, her pneumatic breasts thrusting against her overall.

Pearce thought that it was unlikely Deirdre could ever be reduced to matchstick proportions. 'No . . .' he said weakly.

'Like plump girls, do you?' asked Deirdre archly.

'That's not what I'm here to talk about!' retorted Pearce, scarlet and sweating.

'I get off at four. I'm free this evening. You free?'

'No, I'm working late – all week!' said Pearce firmly.

Deirdre sighed. Then she remembered where she had reached in her narrative and her air of offended innocence returned. 'Never touched her sweets. It was them dogs! Horrid little things, all small and yappy and bite you if you tried to pat them! They had those chocs. All I did was to pick the box up from the floor, empty it was by then, and old Mapple came in and found me with it in my hand. So, of course, she started yelling at me and saying I'd eaten them! Blooming cheek. That's when we fell out good and proper and I walked out. Threw down me duster and tin of polish and told her she could do it herself. Not,' added Deirdre, 'that I suppose she did because before I went there the place hadn't been touched in weeks. Thick with dust and the kitchen – gawd, you should have seen it! Fridge full of tins of dogfood, stinking to high heaven, and you couldn't get in the bathroom to clean it! Full of old Hope's knickers hanging on a line. Here—' she grinned. 'You ought to see them! Like barrage balloons. I mean, I'm not slim, but she's well, like a blooming elephant. I wish I'd seen her running about in the altogether. It must have been a sight!'

'Yes,' said Pearce. 'I didn't see her myself. So that's all you can tell me?'

'You wouldn't think . . .' said Deirdre dreamily, ignoring his question, 'that any bloke would fancy old Hope, would you?'

'I'm sure I don't—'

'But one must've because he gave her the chocs . . .'

Pearce, who had risen to leave, sat down again. 'Who did? How do you know?'

'Because there was one of them little white cards on the box. I was just dusting the table when the box was new, still all wrapped up in cellophane, and sitting on it. That was the day before I found it empty on the floor like I told you. There it was with the little card stuck on it and I thought, blimey, old Hope's got an admirer, must be one of her students from the loony-bin! Naturally I just took a quick look while I dusted it, you understand.'

'Yes, yes!' said Pearce crossly. 'What did it say?'

'It said, "With kindest regards, Charles". I call that a pretty crappy message. You'd have thought he'd have written something a bit more passionate, wouldn't you? I mean, if he'd gone to the trouble to buy the chocs in the first place. Milk Tray they were. I like Milk Tray myself. I like the orange creme ones.'

Grimsby, thought Pearce. 'You're sure about this now?'

'Course I'm sure.' Deirdre eyed him. 'If you're working late all week, they got to give you some time off next week . . .'

Emma scrambled out of bed and stood in her pyjamas, listening intently. Her toes curled up with tension, sinking into the deep nylon pile of her bedside rug which was imprinted with a pattern of a prancing pony. It was spookily dark and she would have liked to switch on at least her bedside lamp. But a tell-tale strip of light might have

shown beneath the door and someone passing by could notice. Even Matthew on his way to the bathroom might have opened it and demanded to know what she was doing, ordering her to hop back into bed or he'd go downstairs and tell Mum. Elder brothers were like that.

From below came the faint noise of the television set and her parents' voices. Praying that the floorboards wouldn't creak and betray her, she tiptoed across to the cupboard and with the aid of a torch located the clothes which she had stacked neatly at the bottom, ready for tonight's expedition.

It was going to be cold out there, she realised, so she pulled on her thickest pullover and two pairs of socks. In the middle of all this, she thought she heard her sister Vicky call out from the room next door and there was a breath-holding few moments while Emma waited to see if either her father or mother would come upstairs. But Vicky didn't call again and all remained quiet. She had contemplated waiting until her parents had gone to bed. But the trouble with that was that they tended to go to bed late and there was a real risk that by the time they came upstairs, she would have fallen asleep and the whole carefully planned mission would be brought to nought at the outset.

The mission was simple. It was to save Maud. No matter what assurances either the vet or Zoë had given her, Emma feared that Maud's days were numbered. The vet had said Maud couldn't see the winter out in present stabling. Zoë had said, more than once, that she couldn't find anywhere else for the animals. *Cogito ergo sum* would have meant nothing to Emma, but her own busy little brain had worked out a similar logical progression. No expensive new stabling: no Maud.

Time too was of the essence. She had to move quickly. If she didn't, she might arrive at the stables any morning now and find the horrid deed done and Maud no more. Nevertheless, she paused to fold her pyjamas and straighten her bed because she didn't wish to be unfair to her mother.

She managed to negotiate the squeaky floorboard outside her brother's room and strained her ears for the sounds of his radio. Sometimes he lay in bed in the dark, listening to the music from his Walkman on the pillow beside him. But tonight all she could distinguish through the door panels was a faint rhythmic tickety-tic, click-click which meant he was listening through his headphones and only the loudest efforts of the rock band concerned penetrated.

Emma crept downstairs. But just as she reached the hall she heard to her dismay her father's voice coming nearer and just had time to dive into the cloaks cupboard to hide among the welter of raincoats and wellington boots, golf clubs and folded pushchair which it housed. Any or all of these things might have fallen causing a clatter which would betray her, but luck was on her side. She heard her father pass the door and then the noise of a kettle whistling in the kitchen and, in due course, her father repassing the door on his way back to the sitting room bearing a tea-tray. There was a sudden gust of sound – the chiming of Big Ben signifying *News at Ten* on the TV. Then it was cut off and all quiet again.

Emma let herself out of the back door and undertook the next part of her plan, the only part about which she had any misgivings. It involved 'borrowing' Matthew's bicycle. It was too far to walk all the way to the Alice Batt Rest Home, especially by night. To take the bus, even if it was running so late which she was not sure it was, might give rise to questions from the driver, seeing her alone at this time of day. The only way to get there was by taking Matthew's bicycle, her own bike having been written off six months ago whilst practising scrambling and not a hope of a new one before Christmas. Matthew cherished his bike. Emma meant to take the greatest care of it and leave it where it could be found.

She fetched it from the shed with many a guilty glance at the curtained windows of the house, pushed it tentatively round to the front, mounted it with some difficulty, it being a boy's bike, and set off, wobbling slightly.

The journey took her longer than she had supposed and was more scary than she had imagined. The country road was lonely but twice cars roared past, picking her up in their glaring headlights and almost forcing her into the ditch. Neither driver stopped, however, and she reached the gates of the stableyard in safety, unchallenged.

Security at the yard was lax. The general state of the animals meant that no one would be likely to steal them. They'd even gone past the horsemeat stage. Zoë lived in the caravan beyond the yard, but she went to bed early as she rose at first light to see to her chores, and the caravan was in darkness.

Emma withdrew the bar-latch on the barn door and dragged it open. The hinges creaked, the noise sounding like a gunshot in the night stillness, and warm air smelling of horses and manure filled her nose. To Schuhmacher it might be a highly objectionable odour, but to Emma it was the most beautiful perfume in the world. She slipped inside and switched on her torch. Straw rustled. Heads turned in the stalls into which the barn was subdivided and surprised eyes gazed at her. One or two animals snickered their welcome.

Emma returned outside to fetch the bicycle, which she wheeled in and propped carefully against the wall. There it would be safe, found first thing and returned to the furious Matthew. She'd make it up to him sometime, buy him a six-pack of Coca-Cola or something equally lavish.

Maud was in the stall at the end, snoozing on three legs and one propped hoof. She lifted her head and stared at Emma in a slightly grumpy fashion, as would any elderly lady rudely awoken in the middle of the night. Emma took the halter from the hook on the wall and slipped it over Maud's head, whispering encouragement and hoping Maud didn't signify her disapproval by uttering one of her ear-splitting brays. Emma tugged at the rope. Maud, resigned to the disruption in her routine, followed her, lurching along in her rheumaticky fashion, probably wondering where they were going but trusting her human friend.

Outside, Emma refastened the barn door and set off with Maud down the lane. At the bottom there was a hiding place in the hedge where she had secreted her purloined store of apples – for Maud – and tins of baked beans – for herself – in an old haversack. It was very heavy, but she managed to hoist it on to Maud's back and balance it there, then they set off again.

The idea was to take to the nearest farmland, make their way across the fields and find refuge in the woods. It should not be difficult to hide Maud there and so far away, even if she did bray, the noise would be faint.

The woods hereabouts covered a considerable area, part native woodland and part Forestry Commission plantation. The former area was a delight to wander in, full of bluebells and primroses in springtime. It was an untidy place where trees jostled for space and curious fungi sprouted. Beyond this wood, a relatively small area, began the regimented close-packed pines, growing dark and tall, blotting out the sky and full of mystery. Here it was exciting to wander too, provided one had a friend to help keep fears away and didn't get lost, which was all too easy. But where it was easy to become lost, it was correspondingly difficult to be found and thus it was to this rustling cathedral of dark pillars that Emma headed.

She'had reconnoitred earlier in the week and discovered a path made by deer. It twisted between the pinetrunks. Following it, Emma had come upon the very place. It was near the stream which ran through the plantation (Maud would need water), and it was a sort of den. Emma supposed it was built by children during the holidays. It was quite roomy, made of interwoven branches dragged in here from the outer ring of wild wood and covered over with an old tarpaulin. She had inspected it carefully and, although a little smelly, it was dry and Maud could just be squeezed inside.

Quite what was going to happen after this, how long they were going to have to remain hidden, Emma wasn't sure. But the plan was working excellently so far and, like Mr Micawber, Emma had every confidence that something would turn up to solve her problems.

The woods lay at the bottom of a steep hillside. Maud found the descent difficult and so, with nothing but the fitful light of the moon and her torch to guide her, did Emma. They stumbled along together, the child gasping and urging the donkey on, Maud uttering occasional disgruntled snorts.

The treeline rose up in front of them, dark, rustling, sinister. Without warning something flew out, straight at them. Emma gave a small shriek and ducked down. Wide wings swept by, almost brushing her cheek and a ghostly form soared up and disappeared.

Only an owl. Emma breathed again. 'Come on!' she encouraged Maud.

But Maud was having second thoughts. She'd gone along with this midnight jape so far but the night was chilly and she missed the warmth of her barn and the companionship of her fellow equines. Besides, she wanted to go to sleep. She stopped.

Emma tugged at the halter. 'Don't give up, Maud! You've got to come on! You don't know what they're going to do to you!'

Maud clearly thought that whatever it was, this was worse. She jerked her head, dragged the rope from Emma's fingers and wheeling round on her sound hind legs, set off determinedly back the way they'd come. Emma plunged after her in the darkness and managed to catch her up. But the haversack of provisions had fallen off the donkey's back in the brief escape and although Emma flashed the torch around, she couldn't see where it lay. It would have to be retrieved by daylight.

A battle of wills ensued. Emma tugged at the headstall. Maud, four hooves planted obstinately, just refused to budge. Even worse, she attempted to give voice to her displeasure but at the first 'hee' Emma grabbed her soft muzzle and the 'haw' turned into a cross groan.

Eventually, after what seemed like ages, Maud gave up the argument and allowed herself to be turned and led back towards the wood. Emma felt relieved but worried. It was all taking so long, she had lost the haversack and was hot and tired. Maud did not like the woods and the whispering voices which came from the treetops in the darkness. Neither did Emma, for that matter. Even the wild wood, which had been rather pretty and exciting to wander in, was now hostile. Things rustled in the undergrowth and fell from the trees. Twigs snapped away between the dark trunks, some of which were stunted and twisted and seemed in the poor light uncannily humanoid. Emma stumbled over the exposed roots and trailing shoots. Eyes watched, the owners unseen but there. Occasionally the torch's gleam caught the luminous reflection of them, a rabbit's or stoat's. Emma didn't these days believe in goblins or fairies. She tried not to believe in ghosts. But the woods raised primaeval fears. Here existed things older than Emma, older than the now standing trees, older than the recorded history of the whole area. Shapeless things, timeless things, forgotten things. They stirred amongst the mossy fallen trunks and peeling bark and rippled the layer of fallen leaves.

And now they had reached the edge of the pine plantation. More by good luck than skill Emma came upon the deer track – she hoped it was the same one and not another. She grasped Maud's headstall more firmly and whispering to the donkey to give herself encouragement, plunged them into the forest of alien woodland.

Sheer blackness enveloped them. The moon could not penetrate the overhead canopy and the torch was inadequate. Emma flashed it ahead of them as they plodded together down the narrow path. Their feet sank in the soft needle-strewn soil and sprang back again, their steps silent, their nostrils filled with the musty odour of decay and the acrid all-pervasive scent of resin. It seemed they would stumble on for ever but, at long last, Emma heard the tinkling of running water and knew they were near the brook. She had marked a turning off here with a pile of stones and pine-cones. With relief and triumph the beam of the flashlight picked up her private cairn. She tugged at the halter and Maud lurched after her into the trees.

There it was, the bothy! Emma approached it with a feeling of rising exultation. They'd made it! After so much time and trouble they were here! It was all worthwhile.

'We're all right now, Maud!' she gasped into one long

drooping ear. Maud stamped her hind hoof, possibly not agreeing.

Emma pulled back the tarpaulin and flashed the light briefly inside. It didn't illuminate the whole interior, just a strip from the doorway but she hoped Maud would realise this was a refuge. She tugged at the halter.

Maud threw up her head and jibbed. Emma struggled to pull her forward. Maud pulled back, snorting. Emma switched off the torch and tucked it into her belt to leave both hands free for the battle. She made a superhuman effort and managed to drag the donkey into the cramped, dark, smelly interior.

The tarpaulin over the door fell down abruptly with a slapping sound, making her jump and cutting off any faint light from outside so that they were in pitch darkness. The stench in here was far worse than Emma had remembered, airless and stale, foul and oppressive at the same time. She began to fear she wouldn't be able to stick it. And then she heard something move in the recess by the entry.

She thought at first it was Maud, stamping a hoof. But pressed against the donkey, she realised that the animal stood stock still. Whatever it was, it moved again. Her heart gave a sickening jolt and her blood seemed to coagulate in her veins. Another animal? Emma ran desperately through a list of comforting possibilities. A badger or fox? Unlikely. They were outside in the undergrowth. A bird which had flown in here and become trapped? Bats? She hated bats. But one thing was sure. She and Maud were not alone in the bothy.

Emma's fingers scrabbled at her waist for her torch and as they did, whatever it was began to move in earnest, moving towards her. She could smell it, fusty and sour, sense its warmth and most terrifying of all, hear its hoarse, laboured breathing. Maud snorted a warning, throwing up her hammer head and taking a step forward as if to place her solid body between Emma and It.

Emma's trembling fingertips touched the metal of the torch. She struggled to drag it from her belt and at the same time find the button to switch it on.

But before she could, a hand came out of the darkness and took hold of her wrist.

left Ellen Bryant out on her own. I wonder if that's significant. Time will tell. Goodnight, off you go.'

Grimsby lived in semi-detached respectability with a row of geraniums in pots on his parlour windowsill, volumes of local history and Dickens in his bookcase, three china geese flying up the wall and a faded carpet patterned with swirls on the floor. The whole room dated from the 1930s. There was even a Marconi wireless set in a polished case, pleated satin sofa cushions and embroidered chairback protectors depicting crinolined ladies in flower gardens.

Markby was offered and accepted an exceedingly small glass of Cyprus sherry and sat uncomfortably trying not to crush the satin cushions or disarrange the flower ladies. It was fairly clear to him that his host lived in the home created by his parents more than fifty years before and had either taken anything from it nor added anything to it except possibly a few of the books.

'I really don't see how I can help you, ah, Chief Inspector,' Grimsby when hospitality had been dispensed. He ed at Markby as if reassuring himself that this really a chief inspector of suitable demeanour and not some stor.

n trying to find out as much as I can about Mrs

nsby looked huffy. 'I'm sure I can't tell you g!'

tell me about the historical society. Who formed llen belong to it for a long time?'

ormed ourselves,' said Grimsby reproachfully. ago. Hope and I were original members together s who for one reason or another fell by the llen joined us about three years ago. I had met

Chapter Ten

Markby had had a tiring day. Whilst Pearce had been interviewing Deirdre, he had obtained a copy of the film shot by the TV company and now he was running it through.

Pearce came back in the middle of it and joined in enthusiastically. As intimated to Deirdre, the sergeant hadn't seen Hope's streak before and regretted missing it. Nevertheless, he was well trained enough to keep most of his attention on the background activity on the film. Well, nearly all of it.

Back and forth they went over the event. Markby rubbed a hand over his eyes and squinted at the screen. He mumbled, 'Go on!'

To an accompanying soft whirring, the film moved onward. Bodies leapt and jostled and one, Hope Mapple in the buff, ran. Spectacular as the sight was, however, she was not the one the two policemen sought on the short length of film obtained from the TV company.

'Go on!' Markby ordered again. 'No, wait! Back, no that's too far – yes, there!'

He leaned forward and peered intently at the screen again. Pearce came forward and pointed at the face in the crowd close behind Hope. 'You're right, sir. There she is, Zoë Foster!'

Markby nodded. 'Okay, you can switch that thing off now. I would say that lets Zoë out. She followed the crowd after Hope, as she told us, and could only have arrived in the cellar after the rest of us. She retreated to the far bay and found the body, just as she said. She didn't have time to kill Ellen.'

'It was a quick kill,' said Pearce doubtfully. 'If Ellen was waiting . . .'

'Zoë wouldn't kill her with all those potential witnesses in the cellar! Ellen was dead when we all raced down there after our streaker and Zoë found her body. However, I have to say I'm rather glad she was caught on the film like that. It gave me a bit of a shock when she started babbling about Ellen's will. I wouldn't have thought her a likely killer, but she does care about those old nags and people have killed for lesser reasons. So a nice filmed alibi is helpful.'

'Gave young Harding a shock too, by all accounts!' said Pearce with a grin.

'Irritating youth! Oh well, time to go home!' Markby hauled himself up with a sigh. 'Or rather, you can go home. I've arranged to go and see Grimsby.' He glanced at his wristwatch. 'I'm to meet him at his house at six-forty-five sharp, he informs me. He's leaving that bookshop of his just after six. That, he also informs me, is solely on my account. Normally he stays there till six-thirty tidying up.'

'Couldn't you have called on him there?' Pearce asked.

'He wasn't keen on that idea. The impression I gained was that he thinks a police inspector coming into his shop might lower the tone of the place. Perhaps he's worried I mightn't wipe my police boots or I'd ask in a loud voice if he stocks porn. He hasn't yet addressed me as "officer", but I suspect that any moment he will.'

'Daft blighter,' said Pearce.

'A member of the public, Pearce, and a pillar of the Chamber of Commerce. Handle with care. I don't mind going to his house. In fact, I'd rather see him on his own ground. You can tell a lot about a person from the content of his bookcase and the pattern of his carpet. However between you and me, I have just about had enough of Society for the Preservation of Historic Bamford for day. When I've seen Grimsby I shall have spoken entire surviving committee within a twelve-hour pe that's enough for anyone!'

Markby heaved an exasperated sigh. 'When I we used to gather round pub pianos and sin version of Longfellow's "Excelsior" with gestures and a few inappropriate ones. It begin "The shades of night were falling fast" and a youth appearing in an alpine village be with a strange device". Well, Hope Map a strange device all right and Eric's gard nearest we've got to an alpine villa everything else is as obscure as the in the poem.'

'What happened to him, the blo

'He got buried in a snowdrift, lucky. I've got to struggle on w historical society. By the way, di bermaid?'

'Deirdre,' said Pearce, rolli Deirdre has to say about Hop He told Markby about the

'Kindest regards, Char 'So within the committe Grimsby and Zoë was a

her before in connection with the Chamber of Commerce but I had no close acquaintance with her. I really must stress that. Robin Harding joined us about a year ago and little Zoë only recently. I have to say I suspect that young lady is less interested in history than in her horses. You know Schuhmacher threatens to evict her and her animals, I suppose? Though not an animal lover myself, I have every sympathy as I feel it's typical of the man's high-handed way. I called on him in London to discuss our objections to his plans. I thought he would at least be civil to a fellow businessman. But he was extremely offensive.'

'Yes, I know – about the horses, that is. But if you and Hope were friends—'

'Colleagues!' corrected Grimsby stiffly.

'But friends too, surely, after six years on the same committee?'

'I admit I did get along well with Hope,' Grimsby conceded grudgingly. His tone sharpened. 'Did until she saw fit to stage that ridiculous demonstration. I have to say my view of Hope changed.'

In more ways than one, Markby found his *alter ego* whispering.

'I cannot afford to be made to look either foolish or disorderly to the Chamber of Commerce! Neither could Mrs Bryant. That, I imagine, was why she left the scene before Hope's exhibition. Why she went down to the cellars I can't even guess.'

'But until that Saturday you and Hope were friendly,' Markby persevered. 'The young people, Robin and Zoë, were drawn together –' Grimsby gave him a slightly furtive look. 'So Ellen had no ally on the committee . . .'

Grimsby had begun to look uncomfortable. 'We were a committee. Committees are supposed to work together. The members do not, Chief Inspector, form alliances!'

'In my experiences of committees, that's very often exactly what happens.'

'I have not your experience of committees, Chief Inspector. May I offer you another sherry?'

This ought to have sounded like an invitation to linger and chat but in fact it sounded quite the reverse. Markby took the hint. He rose to his feet. 'I really am anxious to find out about Ellen's friends and acquaintances, Mr Grimsby. So anything you can remember, just give me a call.'

'I doubt there will be anything!' said Grimsby, opening the door for his visitor. 'Goodnight, Chief Inspector!'

Contrary to his habit, Markby stopped off on his way home for a pint. This murder was beginning increasingly to look like one of those which were resolved at the expense of unpleasantness throughout the local community, as people's private lives were exposed to public scrutiny. Did Grimsby have a secret behind his lace curtains? Did Hope Mapple? Did Eric? Had Hope, more by chance than by any process of deduction, hit the nail on the head when she claimed Ellen had discovered something odd at Springwood Hall?

The mysterious money in the accounts of the craftwork shop begged explanation, but what? Eric was a wealthy man and might have attracted the attentions of a greedy and unscrupulous person in possession of some awkward information. But perhaps the whole idea of blackmail was wrong. Ellen might have been a gambler and won the whole lot on the ponies. She might have been one of those people who saved their junk and took it to car-boot sales; something Markby had been informed was quite profitable. Or she might have sold something more profitable still and in far greater secrecy. An attractive woman, Ellen. Why not a little discreet upmarket whoring? Had Ellen then been the victim of blackmail and not its instigator? Her accounts showed no large sums of money withdrawn. But there were forms of payment other than cash.

'Funny old job you've got!' Robin Harding had said to him, quite rightly. Funny old job, indeed. Suddenly the urge to go to McVeigh and ask to be taken off the case became overwhelming. He no longer wanted to know any more about Ellen, to ask anyone any more questions or deal with people who manifestly didn't want to talk to him and regarded his arrival as an unwarranted intrusion. He wanted to go home.

But home, when he got there, was an empty place. The resounding echo of the front door as it shut behind him, the rustle of uncollected post under his feet, the unwashed breakfast cup and plate still where he'd left them on the draining board in the kitchen, all these things added to his sense of isolation.

He wished very much that Meredith were there. He wondered what she did in London when not at work. He wondered about her friends. He wondered about them quite a lot and especially if there were any particular person. She hadn't said so. He fancied she would tell him if she met anyone else, anyone special. But why should she? She was not accountable to him for what she did nor he to her. But he did wonder, all the same.

Markby cooked up a packet of fish fingers and ate them with bread and butter for his supper. Paul was always telling him how to make quick, nutritional and eye-pleasing meals from fresh ingredients. But Paul liked messing about in the kitchen and Markby didn't. He read the newspaper and then turned on the television for the news, but dozed off before it came on with his feet on the camel saddle footstool he'd gained when he and Rachel had split up. Neither of them had wanted it and Rachel being Rachel, items neither of them wanted ended up forming his share of their divided goods and chattels.

The persistent double buzz of the telephone awoke him. He opened his eyes with a start and looked at his watch. It was a little before midnight. He got up, switched off the television and picked up the receiver. 'Hullo?'

'Thank God, Alan, you're there!' It was Paul, his brother-in-law, clearly agitated.

Markby asked quickly, 'Is something wrong with Laura?'

'No, it's Emma – she's gone! She's not in her room! Laura looked in on the kids on her way to bed as she always does and Emma's gone – just vanished!'

'Hold on!' Markby interrupted firmly. 'I presume she went to bed as usual?'

'Yes, yes! Just as usual! Where on earth—'

'Have you checked the house and garden and are any of her clothes missing?'

'Yes, yes and yes!' Paul shouted down the line. 'She's not in the house and she's wearing her jeans, boots and anorak as far as we can tell. She'd folded up her pyjamas and put them back in her bed—' At this point Paul's voice became unsteady.

Markby said, 'Take it easy, old chap. I'll be right over.'

A missing child. One of the worst experiences to suffer. For him this was a special pain, not only because Emma was his niece and godchild but because she was for him the daughter he'd never had and probably now never would. He was in his forties with a childless marriage and long years of being single behind him and he didn't suppose that now, even if he ever managed to persuade Meredith to marry him, there would ever be fatherhood. Nor that now, at his time of life, could he be sure he would be able to cope with the reality of babies, wet and squawling and being sick on one.

Besides the pain and alarm as he drove, he knew too fast, towards his sister's house, he also felt anger. Anger with himself for all the times he'd kept silent when he'd wanted to say that they encouraged Emma in an independence she was too young to manage, and anger with them, Paul and Laura, because they'd let this happen. And yet he knew he was being cruelly unjust, even as these jumbled thoughts filled his brain. Because Emma had not vanished from that lonely country bus-stop or the lane to the stables, but from her own bed beneath her family roof and there was no rhyme, reason or anything comprehensible in it.

Unless it was a childish prank. He found himself cling-ing to the idea. Yes, a midnight adventure, hiding in the garden, daring herself to be brave . . . She'd come indoors soon, probably by the time he got there she'd be back already. He'd walk in and see her sitting at the kitchen table drinking cocoa and being scolded and kissed alternately by her relieved parents.

And yet some cold frightening little voice inside his head whispered no, that this was a fulfilment of the premo-nition he'd been harbouring three or four days now, an inex-plicable sense of foreboding. He had sensed, known, that some threat hovered over Emma. And he hadn't been able to stop it reaching her.

All the lights in the Danby house were ablaze as he drew up. The front door stood open and he strode in. Laura, pale as death, shot out of the sitting room and hugged him wordlessly. He put his arms round her and said, 'All right, Laurie, don't break down now. It'll be all right.'

What a stupid, feeble encouragement, he thought, but he couldn't manage better.

As his sister broke away and sniffed into a damp handkerchief, he spotted from the corner of his eye his nephew sitting on the top stair in his dressing gown. 'Hullo, Matthew!' he called up. 'You've got no idea where she's gone off to, I suppose? No secret adventure plan? Nothing she swore you to secrecy about? Because it won't be breaking a solemn oath to tell now. Now's the time to speak up.'

'No,' said Matthew. 'I told Dad and Mum she didn't say anything to me.' Passionately he added, 'But she's pinched my bike! Dad checked the shed to see if she was hiding there and it's gone! She's got my bike! I bet she writes it off. She wrote off hers—'

'All right, all right!' Paul had come into the hall. 'You hop off to bed. Go on!'

Matthew got up and trailed morosely along the landing. 'Bet she falls off, bet the chain comes off, bet she scratches the paint—'

His bedroom door closed on this litany.

In the sitting room Markby asked, 'You've checked with immediate neighbours? How about her friends? They might have planned some midnight jape as kids do. You know, a feast in someone's garden shed.' He heard his voice repeat his hoped-for solution and fought to keep the anxiety out, the desperate desire to hear his own fears assuaged.

'Feast!' Paul's face turned pale with consternation. 'Bloody hell! The apples, the baked beans, half a loaf of bread! Stuff's been going missing for a week! She must have been squirrelling it away!'

'We have checked the neighbours and her friends.' Laura spoke, tense but controlled.

'And none of her friends has any idea where she might have gone? You're sure she didn't leave a note?'

'Alan! We've searched everywhere! Of course we're sure! And she's taken Matt's bike, she could be anywhere!'

Markby was only too well aware of that but he said, 'The chances are she's gone to someone she knows and trusts. Was she in trouble at home? Not been behaving herself, been told off? Kids take the hump and go off in high dudgeon but generally come back next day. I've known it happen.'

'Not Emma!' Laura said firmly. 'She wasn't in trouble at home.'

Markby frowned. 'Not at home but elsewhere, perhaps? School is still on holiday. What about the stables?'

The parents exchanged glances. 'She was upset about Schuhmacher giving the stables notice to quit,' Laura said. 'But she wouldn't have gone there at this time of night, surely? The place will be locked up and Zoë gone to bed ... damn it, she's got no phone in that caravan. But Emma wouldn't go there in the middle of the night.'

'Okay,' said Markby, 'I'll phone the station and have them put out a description.' As he lifted the receiver he asked, 'No history of sleepwalking? I know it's a wild guess ...'

'No!' Paul snapped. 'She's on a bike, anyway!'

'Fair enough. This still could be some childish prank, Famous Five stuff.' Markby dialled through and relayed his request. 'Yes, she's eleven years old and riding a bicycle, we think. She has long fair hair and is probably wearing jeans, gumboots and a blue anorak. That's right. Yes, her friends have been checked. No, no, I don't think so . . .' He glanced at Paul. 'Did you try the local hospital?'

'No,' Paul said dully and Laura sat down on the nearest chair and put her head in her hands.

After that it was a long wait through the darkest, chilliest and loneliest stretches of the night, a wait for news which didn't come. At four in the morning, the hour when the human spirit is at its lowest ebb, Markby went to Bamford police station to make sure everything was being done which could be until light. The town was empty and desolate. Everyone was abed even the cats. Empty fish and chip wrappers floated down the gutters and a few aluminium lager cans rolled noisily across the shopping precinct. There was a supermarket trolley wedged among bushes on the roundabout and the window of an electrical goods store was cracked. He supposed the night patrol had already seen and reported that.

At the station they were professional and reassuring. He realised with a mixture of irritation and despair that they saw him at this moment not as one of themselves, much less their chief, but as another worried member of the public.

They offered him tea. They said, 'It's all right, sir! We've had experience of this kind of thing before! Most runaways return home within twenty-four hours. I expect the little girl will be back in the morning. After all, she couldn't have got far, could she?'

He lost his temper at that, crashing his fist on the counter and yelling, 'Don't give me that! She's eleven years old and she doesn't play damfool tricks like this every day of the week! She's got a bike and could have got miles! That's if she hasn't had an accident, been knocked flying by a car which might not even have seen her in the dark! So get moving! This is my niece and I want her found! Got that? Put in a request for that helicopter to be sent up in the morning! Make some use of the taxpayers' money!'

Driving back to Laura's he paused before the dark front of Needles craftshop. Engine idling, he contemplated the windows of Ellen's flat as the steel grey fingers of dawn touched them. Ellen's death was his main case at the moment but now Emma was missing, how to concentrate on it? Impossible.

He sighed and tapped his fingers on the rim of the steering wheel, a wave of discouragement sweeping over him. It had been a salutary experience to be on the wrong side of the counter in his own station. How many worried relatives were plied with tea and platitudes, unable to do as he had done and bawl out the night team? One thing for sure, he thought grimly, from now on, any worried parent coming to Bamford station was going to get maximum practical assistance and pronto! He'd see to that!

He drew away from the silent shopfront and went to reassure his sister, sounding, he knew, much as the night team had sounded when mouthing their reassurances to him, seeing the frustration and anger on his sister's face and knowing how the parents of the missing child felt, unable to do anything more about it.

When it was light he went home, showered and shaved and prepared to go back to work. He was just drinking a quick cup of coffee when his phone rang.

Markby seized it. 'Paul? Has she been found?'

'No, Alan, it's me, Meredith . . .'

Puzzled, he tried to adjust, slurring his words with tiredness and mental confusion. 'I'm sorry, I was expecting . . .

I thought Paul or Laura might . . . why are you ringing?'

'Is something wrong?' Meredith asked. 'I'm sorry to call so early but I'm just off to work . . . Alan?'

He said simply, 'Emma's missing.'

There was a barest pause. Then Meredith said, 'I'll phone in and tell the office I'm taking a few days off. I'll be back in Bamford later on today.'

'Thanks . . . thanks . . .' he mumbled and, putting the phone back on the rest, went into work to organise the hunt.

Chapter Eleven

When Markby walked into the police station, Wpc Jones was on the telephone. He had plenty on his mind without anything new added to it so he walked briskly past her, heading for the stairs. But as he reached the bottom tread, the word 'stable' fell on his ear. Markby wheeled about and strode back, signalling his query to Jones.

She put her hand over the mouthpiece and said, 'It's the young woman who runs the Alice Batt Rest Home. She's calling from a public phone box on the old Bamford road. Someone's stolen an animal, a donkey, and she's in a real old state. She's says the animal's worthless. It hasn't strayed. It was taken from their stableblock last night sometime.'

'Let me have that!' Markby almost snatched the receiver from her. 'Zoë? Chief Inspector Markby here. What's all this about a donkey?'

'I can't understand it,' came Zoë's distraught voice. 'Maud's very old and quite valueless. Who'd want her? She's very bad-tempered too and I can't understand her going quietly with a stranger. And another odd thing. There's a bicycle in the barn. It wasn't there last night. It's a boy's bike, quite a nice one. It looks as if someone rode it here last night, took Maud and left the bike. Is it some horrid practical joke? Because if so, it's not funny. But if it isn't, well, it just doesn't make sense!'

'It does to me!' said Markby grimly. 'I'll be right there, Zoë!'

Zoë was waiting for him at the gate to the yard. She looked more than usually dishevelled and as he drove up began to point wildly at the barn and mime her misfortune. The animals were wandering about the yard in a desultory fashion. Markby got out of his car and she dragged the gate open.

'It's awfully good of you to come so quickly and in person!' she began. 'I thought just a constable—'

'There's something you don't know!' he interrupted. 'Emma's missing.'

'Emma?' Zoë stared at him wildly. 'You don't think – oh no! Finlay Ross!'

'The vet? What's he got to do with this?'

'Emma was here when he called last and examined Maud. I thought she'd gone over to the caravan but she could just have been hiding and listening. Finlay said Maud might have to be put down. Emma's devoted to Maud—'

Markby heaved a sigh and set off towards the barn. 'Where's this bike?'

She showed him. It was Matthew's all right. He recognised the pop group sticker on the saddle bag. Markby swore softly. 'Okay, tell me when you found this. What time do you go to bed? Did you hear anything, any noise during the night?'

She appeared overwhelmed by the questions for a moment. Markby made an effort to calm himself. He must put out of his mind that this search concerned his niece and behave as he would if the search were for any child, be concerned but not incoherent, and above all methodical. 'Just tell me everything.'

'Well, I go to bed early, about nine or nine-fifteen, because I get up very early. Anyway, I haven't got any electricity, only a paraffin lamp.' She looked guiltily at him. 'Actually, Mr Markby, I haven't really got planning permission for a dwelling. I'm sort of squatting in that caravan. But nothing's fixed permanently so the council haven't bothered me yet . . .'

'That's not my department, Zoë. I don't care if you're living in a tent. Did you hear anything during the night?'

'No, not a thing. I sleep like a log. It's so dark and quiet out here and I'm always dog-tired.'

'Speaking of dogs, you don't keep one? It's lonely here. Aren't you frightened at night?'

'No. I used to have a dog but he was very old and he died. I didn't get another because it costs enough to feed me and the horses without a dog. I got up this morning as usual, about six. I had my breakfast and I came out here. I didn't go in the barn straight away because I wanted to fix a hole in the paddock hedge before I turned out any of the animals for the day. It took me about an hour . . .'

She held out her scratched hands as evidence. 'Robin said he'd do it, but I couldn't wait for him to come. Then I went to the barn and found Maud had gone – and the bicycle had appeared. I didn't know what to think. I searched all round just in case the person who took Maud had let her loose. I thought then it must be a practical joker, but I couldn't find her. So I ran up to the road to the call box and phoned Finlay because – I don't know – I thought if anyone had seen an animal wandering they might have called him. Then I phoned the nearest farmer and then I phoned the police . . . I should have phoned the police first, I suppose, but I couldn't

believe it. Maud isn't worth anything and she's got rheumatics.'

'So she couldn't have been taken far?' Markby seized
on this.

'Well, that depends. Although her legs are wonky, she
gets along on them all right. In the course of an hour or two
she could wander a long way even if she was just left
loose.' Zoë bit her lip. 'Do you really think Emma's run
off with her? It would make sense, because if a stranger tried
to take Maud, she'd kick up a devil of a fuss and probably
bite whoever it was. But Emma could do anything with her.'

'It begins to look as if she's taken the donkey. Poor kid.'
One of the Shetland ponies had approached him and was
glaring balefully through a mop of hair over its eyes.
Markby prudently edged away.

'But where could she go? Anyway, what did she think
she could do? She couldn't stay hidden with Maud for ever!'
Zoë wailed.

'She wasn't reasoning like that, Zoë, with a cool brain.
She loves the donkey, she believed it in danger, she rescued
it.' He looked across the fields. 'I'll get the local farmers
to check their outbuildings and put out an appeal for
searchers.' He indicated the Shetland. 'Hadn't you better
put these animals in the paddock or in the barn?'

'Thank you,' said Meredith and tipped the hall porter who
had brought up her modest suitcase.

She looked round the room she had just taken at
Springwood Hall. Staying here would probably make a size-
able dent in her bank balance. Newly and beautifully deco-
rated and furnished, the linen crisp, flowers and fruit on a
table and a range of free toiletries in the bathroom. It would
have been nice to have come here on a happier occasion,

relax, put her feet up. But this was not a holiday break but a grimly serious business. As for the decision to stay at the Hall, some instinct had brought her back here, the memory of that huddled corpse and the white face of young Zoë Foster.

Meredith unlocked her case and took out the binoculars she'd brought along. Going to the nearest window, she pulled back the curtain and surveyed the view. This room was on a corner of the house and there were windows in both exterior walls. From this one in the side of the house she could see green lawns and the swimming pool building. Beyond that were hedges and beyond them pastureland and an enclosure, a sort of yard containing a rickety building.

She put the binoculars to her eyes and twiddled with the focus. The distant building leapt into view. That must be the Horses' Home. A real eyesore, as Eric claimed, unless you were particularly rustic minded. The barn was in a state of near collapse, patched with corrugated sheeting, loose and missing slates on its roof. Just beside it, in the foreground as she looked through the binoculars, was a large steaming midden. A horse trough and old-fashioned pump stood in the middle of the untidy yard and right at the back, half hidden by the barn, was what looked like a rusting caravan propped up on bricks.

In a paddock to the right grazed a motley collection of animals, including a piebald cob, two gloriously scruffy Shetland ponies and what looked like a broken-down racehorse with a faded, sad elegance about its bony frame. The whole place resembled a tinkers' camp. Picturesque and highly individual, maybe, but understandably not the sort of thing Schuhmacher wanted his guests gazing upon.

As she watched a motorcyclist appeared by the gate.

There must be a lane there, disguised from here by an untidy hedge. He got off his machine and opened the gate, lugged the motorbike inside and fastened the gate again. A girl came out of the barn – it looked like Zoë – and the young man took off his crash helmet. The two began to talk together, Zoë gesticulating wildly. The young man put his arm round her shoulders and gave her a comforting hug.

Feeling that further covert observation would be impertinent, Meredith left that window and went to the other, at the back of the house. Beyond the gardens stretched farmland and in the distance a vast expanse of woodland visible as treetops. The ground must fall away over there into a kind of valley. The dark mass suggested conifers and were Forestry Commission planting, no doubt. It would be difficult to search, dark, extensive, and in the way of official plantations, full of identical trees so that to get lost would be easy. But there were some searchers making their way slowly across the farmland in a long strung-out line, like ants. They hadn't reached the woodland yet and long before they did would be out of sight, descending the slope down to the treeline.

A distant buzzing high above struck her ear, growing louder. She peered upward curiously. A helicopter came into view and made its way across the sky like a large bee.

Meredith put the binoculars in their case, changed into jeans, waxed jacket and gumboots and, with the binocular case hung round her neck, set out to join the hunt. She didn't know where Alan was, but ten to one, he was out there somewhere with the search party.

She felt nothing if not out of place clumping along the elegant hotel corridor in her outdoor wear. But there was a surprise in store for her even before she left the hotel.

As she arrived at the far end where the lift was situated

and put out a hand to press the call button she saw by the illuminated arrow that the lift was already on its way up. Seconds later she heard a muffled bump and the doors slid open.

The Fultons stepped out.

They stared at one another in mutual astonishment.

'Meredith?' exclaimed Leah. 'What a lovely surprise. How very nice—'

'To see you again, er, here . . .' Denis, frowning at Meredith in a doubtful way, finished his wife's sentence. He blinked. Perhaps he fancied she was just a hallucination. But there was no reason why he should not be as surprised as Meredith felt.

'Hullo,' she returned inanely and added, 'I've only just arrived. I thought I'd join the hunt. Did you know—'

Leah interrupted. 'About the little girl? Yes, how dreadful. Denis and I just arrived this morning too. Of course we knew nothing about the missing child until we got here. Perhaps we shouldn't have come. But we—' She glanced doubtfully at her husband.

'Things have been a bit fraught between us,' said Denis loudly. He fixed Meredith with a slightly aggressive look. 'I'm sorry about the bit of bother when you came to dinner. I hope you'll come again – I'll behave next time! But Leah and I—'

He fell silent and his wife took up the tale. 'We both needed to get away from London for a while, and we thought about poor Eric who is a friend, after all, and having a dreadful time. So we thought we'd come down and lend him moral support as well as have a break. So here we are. Denis has known Eric for years—'

'And I didn't want him to feel deserted!' confirmed Denis. 'He's sunk everything into this place, you know.'

More than ever, Meredith was reminded of the Tweedledum and Tweedledee aspect of dealing with the Fultons. As they spoke, passing the chain of speech back and forth between them, finishing one another's sentences and anticipating one another's thoughts, she found her head going from side to side like a spectator at a tennis match.

'Do you think we'd be any help with the search, darling?' Leah asked her husband.

'Got no boots,' said Denis.

'Perhaps Eric could find us a couple of pairs . . .'

'I'll see you both later!' Meredith said hastily.

She stepped into the lift and the doors closed on them, each assuring her earnestly and in antiphon that they'd see her in the cocktail lounge before dinner.

Chapter Twelve

It took Meredith a quarter of an hour to walk over the fields to the line of searchers. When she neared she found that a rough track running along a hedgerow was the scene of a command point. Parked neatly were three civilian cars, a mini-bus and two police vans together with a Range Rover. One of the vans was clearly a mobile radio communications centre. A disembodied voice echoed from the barrage of electronic equipment visible through the open back doors.

Alan wasn't to be seen but the Danbys were standing a little way off and Meredith approached them. They both looked dreadful, strained and grey-faced. Worse, as Meredith came within earshot, she realised they were quarrelling.

'You're there at home most of the day!' Laura was saying energetically. 'And Mrs Barnes is there from eight till one. The children love Mrs Barnes!'

'You're talking about them as if they weren't growing up!' Paul snapped. 'Emma's eleven, nearly twelve. She needs her mother!'

'She's got a mother! She's got me! Dammit, I've never neglected the children!'

'You're busy, you're tired! The kid needs someone to

talk to when she gets in from school or back from wherever she's been . . .'

'You're at home!'

'I keep telling you, she needs her mother! She's growing
up! She'll be a teenager soon. I tell you, Laura, when this
is over, there will have to be some changes. You're going
to have to work part-time!'

'I can't believe this! Apart from any other consideration,
we'll all starve to death if I work part-time!'

'I'm aware I'm not a huge earner!' snarled her husband.
'But we'll just have to cut some things out, like – like holidays.'

'We need our holidays! The children like to go away.
Anyhow I can't just walk out on the firm! I'm needed.'

'And you're needed at home! The firm will find someone
else.'

'I don't want them to find someone else!' yelled Laura,
a rush of scarlet suffusing her pallid cheeks.

'That's it, isn't it? The whole point? You love being there,
you love that blasted career of yours and we all play second-
fiddle!'

'Rubbish!'

Meredith cleared her throat and they both whirled round.

'Oh, Meredith!' exclaimed Laura with obvious relief.
'Alan said you'd phoned.'

'Sorry to interrupt,' Meredith apologised. 'No news of
any kind?'

'You're not interrupting,' Paul said tersely. 'We're just
getting at each other because we can't do anything. Emma's
taken off with an aged donkey from the rest home because
she thought it was going to be put down. We're blaming
each other. We knew she was upset about the threat to the
rest home and I knew food was disappearing from the

larder. We just never made the connection.'

'Why should you?' she replied in practical tones. 'Where's Alan?'

'Not here. Wish he was. He's overseeing the search from the station along with all his other cases. He's put a sergeant in practical charge of it all, someone he says is very reliable especially where children are concerned. His name is Harris and he's a middle-aged chap with greying hair. Over there somewhere.' Paul pointed at a group of men conferring in a huddle.

As he spoke there was a distant shout. One man had detached himself from the group and was coming toward them. He was holding a bundle.

'We found this!' he called as he came up. 'Sergeant Harris said to bring it back to the van and ask if you recognise it.' The bundle was an old green haversack.

'Yes!' Paul leapt forward and seized it from him. It fell open and a motley collection of apples, tinned fruit, sliced bread and a packet of porridge oats fell out.

They all stood looking down at these pathetic foodstuffs in silence for a moment.

'Oh, dear God,' Laura whispered. 'Where is she? Paul?'

He turned to her and put his arms round her and she buried her face against his jacket.

Meredith walked quickly towards the knot of men. She wasn't abandoning the Danbys but neither could she comfort them and she was sure their basic relationship was strong enough to weather out this storm. On the other hand, if Emma weren't found safe . . .

Meredith pushed the thought out of her head. The child was out there somewhere. It was a question of finding her.

She had reached the group but the men talking together ignored her. She waited patiently until they seemed to have finished their immediate discussion and then addressed the grey-haired man. 'Sergeant Harris?'

He turned and stared at her distrustfully. 'Reporter?'

'No!' Meredith was taken aback. Briefly she explained who she was. It didn't seem to convince him of her worth.

'Thought you might be a reporter. They'll be here soon enough, sniffing round. Beats me how they get to hear of things so quick! What's brought you out here then?'

'I'd like to help.'

'Oh yes?' He gave her another jaundiced look. 'We got plenty of help, thanks.'

'Look,' Meredith began, annoyance creeping into her tone. 'I don't want to get in the way! I just thought—'

But his attention had been taken and he turned away from her and began to talk briskly to a constable beside him.

It was a situation with which she was not unfamiliar. In his book she was the chief inspector's girlfriend. Wives and girlfriends didn't belong at the scene of operations. They were supposed to be at home, getting ready to fry up the sausages when the menfolk got in at the end of the day's work.

Meredith gave a little hiss and glanced back the way she'd come. From bad to worse. Plodding purposefully towards the group now came two figures she had thought she'd left behind at the hotel.

Denis and Leah had evidently acquired gumboots from Eric. Whether the borrowed boots didn't fit or whether this was just an unaccustomed type of footwear, the Fultons staggered along in them unhappily, clasping one another by the hand for support and mutual encouragement. They looked tiny and frail, even Denis who, although he was inclined to stoutness, was only just of middle height. Two people more out of place in their surroundings would

170

have been hard to imagine. Yet there was something both endearing and admirable in their patent desire to help. Stumbling over the uneven ground, they had British determination stamped all over them. What Sergeant Harris would make of these two new recruits, Meredith did not like to think.

They had spotted her. Denis raised an arm and made the sort of gesture with which Roman emperors once responded to the roar of the crowd in the circus. It wasn't clear whether he was hailing her or asking her to wait for them. Meredith realised with horror that if she once allowed them to join her, she would be stuck with them for the remainder of the day. Her own efforts to help would be dogged by the constant distraction of the Fultons falling into ditches and getting caught up in brambles.

On the other hand, she did not like to run away from them when it was obvious she'd seen them. Fortunately at that moment Denis caught sight of the Danbys and the Fultons turned aside to express their sympathy and encouragement. It was likely they would be talking for some minutes and they could not reasonably be surprised if Meredith set off without them. Meredith turned back and swept the horizon with an impatient glance.

Across the fields and far to the right of the line of searchers, a mass of dark woodland seemed to beckon and she set off towards it. As she did, she heard Sergeant Harris call out 'Oy!' Well, she wasn't going to upset his organised line. She was going well out of the way of it. Assuming that he was busy and if she didn't turn back, he would be content to let her go, Meredith pretended not to have heard and quickened her pace, slipping and sliding down the steep grassy slope, well aware that if Alan knew, he would have condemned this evasion of police instructions in the most forceful terms. But somehow, she felt what she was doing just might be of some use.

'You needn't have struggled with that fence repair!' said Robin resentfully. 'I told you I'd come out today and do it and here I am!'

'Yes, I know. But I wanted to turn the animals out. I am always grateful for what you do.' Zoë pushed her hair out of her eyes. 'Don't start grumbling, Robin. I'm half out of my mind with worry about Emma and Maud.'

'Sorry,' he said contritely. 'Now I'm here, what can I do?'

'You couldn't face mucking out the barn, could you?'

'Sure. Give me a moment to get ready, find me a muck-fork and I'll start.'

He returned a little later in his rolled shirt-sleeves, the fork balanced over his shoulder to find her pushing the bicycle out of the barn into the sunlight. She propped it up and sighed. 'Poor Emma. Just to think of her cycling along that dark road last night. She could have been killed!'

'This is all Schuhmacher's fault!' Robin said with barely controlled anger. He went into the first stall and thrust the fork into the soiled straw as if he had the hotelier pinned helpless beneath the tines.

'It's not his fault Maud's rheumatics have got so bad.'

'I don't care.' Robin paused to look up and wipe sweat from his forehead. His brown eyes glowed. 'Everything was fine around here until Schuhmacher came and bought up Springwood Hall!'

There was a sound of a car engine outside. It fell silent and the gate to the yard squeaked. Zoë and Robin looked at each other.

'It might be Mr Markby,' said Zoë, adding hopefully,

'Oh, Rob! Perhaps they've found Emma and Maud!'

He shouldered his fork again and they went outside. A solid, well-dressed man was picking a cautious path across the muddy yard.

'Would you believe it?' said Robin incredulously, his jaw dropping. 'Of all the nerve!' He pulled himself together and stiffened.

'Good morning,' said Eric Schuhmacher. 'You will be Miss Foster? My name is—'

'We know what your name is!' interrupted Robin furiously.

The Swiss turned his attention from Zoë to Robin. He eyed the young man slowly from top to toe then turned back to Zoë without a word. 'I heard about the child taking the donkey. I see they're still searching so I assume there's no news of the little girl.'

'No.' Zoë cleared her throat and tried to sound businesslike. 'But I'm sure they'll find her soon. It rather depends what time of the night she took Maud. I mean, Maud can travel a fair distance but only slowly because of her rheumatics.'

Eric looked puzzled. 'Who's Maud? Is someone else missing?'

'Maud's the donkey, sorry, assumed you knew. Of course you don't.'

'What do you want, Schuhmacher?' demanded Robin, standing aggressively, feet astride and with the upturned fork resting on the ground. 'Because you're not wanted here! You've caused enough trouble! This is all your fault, you know!'

Eric cast him a look of contempt. 'Surely it's for Miss Foster to say whether or not I may stay? You are what? Her stableman?'

'Oh no!' Zoë said hastily. 'Robin's a friend who kindly helps out.'

'Then he is not the spokesman. As you say, only a friend helping out. Perhaps you should return to your work?'

This last was addressed to Robin. Already angered by the Swiss hotelier's arrival, this high-handed suggestion delivered in the tone of an order, could only fan the flames of Harding's wrath. Over Robin's frank, open features came a startling change. Mouth and jaw hardened. The veins in his neck became pronounced and cord-like. He looked older, decidedly tougher and more dangerous. The look in his brown eyes not only held loathing, it was quite vicious.

'Did you want to speak to me about something in particular, Mr Schuhmacher?' Zoë interpolated, putting a soothing hand on Robin's arm and casting him a worried glance. 'Is it about the lease?'

'No – no, I came only to say I am very sorry about the little girl – and the animal which is lost, of course.'

'Okay, you've said it, now scram!' snarled Harding in a thick, distorted voice. He half lifted the fork.

'You are an ill-mannered young man,' said Eric mildly. 'And also, it seems, slow to understand. I have not come to talk to you.'

'Well, you needn't think I'm going to stand by and let you harass Zoë!' Robin suddenly lunged forward, the fork held bayonet-fashion at the attack. 'Go on, clear off or it'll be the worse for you!' He jabbed the tines of the fork at Schuhmacher's chest.

Zoë let out a cry of alarm, but she needn't have worried. Eric, moving with the speed and dexterity acquired in his ice-hockey days, seized the tines and twisted them expertly. The implement leapt from Robin's grasp. At the same time the Swiss jumped nimbly to one side.

Robin, summarily relieved of his weapon and unable to control his own forward momentum, stumbled and fell flat on his face in the filth of the yard. He scrabbled immediately to his hands and knees. Swearing vociferously he raised his face, eyes blazing furiously in the mask of mud and muck, to the Swiss who stood staring down at him with impassive countenance.

'Young man,' said Eric to him. 'You wish to run before you can walk. Now, Miss Foster, let us go and see these animals over there in that paddock and you can tell me about your charity.' He glanced at Robin and tossed the fork down on the ground beside him. 'You can finish your work!'

The animals grazing in the paddock raised their heads, ears pricked inquiringly, as Zoë approached with the visitor in tow. The piebald whinnied and the two Shetland ponies began to amble in unison towards the fence.

'These two,' explained Zoë, 'are inveterate scroungers. As soon as they see anyone coming, they dash straight over.'

'Indeed?' Schuhmacher said. The Shetlands had reached the fence and pushed their noses over it, snickering impatiently. 'Rather endearing little animals.' He stretched out an unwise hand to pat the nearest neck.

'Don't!' cried Zoë. 'Not if you haven't got—'

She was almost too late. The nearer Shetland had snuffled suspiciously at Eric's fingers and found them empty of any titbit. It flattened back its ears and snapped.

The Swiss snatched his hand back in the nick of time. Surprise showed on his face, followed by bewilderment, then marked displeasure.

'I was about to explain,' said Zoë apologetically. 'They are greedy and if you don't give them anything, they can get a bit aggressive.'

'So I see! I take back the word "endearing". They are obviously treacherous little brutes!' said Schuhmacher with some emotion.

'Not really. They've been teased, you see, in the past. If animals are badly behaved it's generally because humans have treated them badly or carelessly.'

'So where did these two come from?' The explanation did not appear to have mellowed the opinion Schuhmacher had formed of the ponies. He might not know whence they'd come, but he clearly had a place in mind whither they might be sent.

'They were kept in a children's zoo at a pleasure park. The child visitors were fine but the park was on the outskirts of a big city and yobs used to come out and climb the walls out of hours, chase the animals, try and ride the ponies and tease them generally. Both quickly became very snappy which meant they were no longer any use to the zoo. Just imagine what a fuss there would have been if one of them had bitten a child! The people who ran it got in touch with us and asked if we'd take them. They felt they couldn't sell them on because of their uncertain tempers. Slaughter would have been the only alternative.'

'And the others?' Eric pointed at the cob, the thoroughbred and a mealy-nosed Exmoor pony.

'The Exmoor was also saved from slaughter. He had been a child's riding pony but when the child outgrew him, the owners couldn't find a buyer and wanted rid of him. Luckily Miss Batt heard about it and stepped in. Some people are very callous. The piebald on the other hand was the victim of ignorance. People inherited him who knew nothing about horses and thought all you had to do was leave them in a field. It was poor pasture and he got no extra feed and nearly starved. He was in a terrible state when he came.

All his ribs showed and because his hooves hadn't been trimmed they'd grown and grown, so they were like big boots and he could hardly walk.'

Zoë paused absentmindedly to rub the end of her nose, smearing it with mud. 'The chaser broke down and so wasn't any more use. He wasn't going to win any races. Actually he didn't win any before he broke down. He was never any good. But he was a great favourite of Miss Batt's. She used to ride him before her arthritis got bad. He's a sweetie but a bit nervy and can kick. Maud, the missing donkey, was found wandering by the roadside. Someone had just abandoned her and we never found out who. She had awful sores but we managed to clear them up. Now she's got rheumatism. Oh, and look over there, the grey mare under the trees, do you see? She had been kept by an unscrupulous breeder and had foal after foal until she was exhausted. Miss Batt stepped in and rescued her, too.'

Eric grunted. He eyed Zoë thoughtfully and then said, 'You have mud on your face. You do not mind my saying?'

'What? Have I?' Zoë hunted in her pockets. 'I haven't got a hanky.'

'Please.' Schuhmacher offered his own immaculately laundered cambric square.

'Oh, I couldn't use that, it's much too good!' Zoë scrubbed at her face with her sleeve. 'Has it gone?'

'Yes.' Eric returned his spurned handkerchief to his pocket.

Zoë waited but he didn't offer any further observations. She began again tentatively, 'I realise that all the animals are quite valueless in terms of money. They aren't even attractive. Some are ugly. Most bite or kick. Although,' she added hastily, 'they don't bite me because they know me.

And they never behave badly with poor little Emma. I do so hope she's all right!' Zoë's face clouded. 'Where can she be? If only I'd heard her last night. The barn door creaks and she must have made a certain amount of noise. I feel so guilty. Poor little soul, she must have been so worried about Maud.'

Schuhmacher glanced at the rusting trailer in the distance. 'That is your home?' His voice was cold with disapproval.

'Yes. It does look rather old and not very smart.'

'It is old,' said Eric. 'And unsightly. You see, Miss Foster, I don't wish to insult your establishment.' He waved a hand to encompass the entire site. 'But imagine you are a guest in my hotel. You set out for a little stroll. Suddenly, what is this awful smell? What are these flea-bitten animals?'

'They haven't got fleas!' interrupted Zoë indignantly.

He ignored the interruption. 'This ramshackle barn and that wreck of a trailer? This is not the countryside my guests have come to see.'

'It's the real countryside!' Zoë was growing increasingly mutinous before the litany of complaints. 'Or don't they want that? This is what the countryside is like. If people don't like it, they ought to stay in towns.'

He shook his head. 'They don't want reality. They want pleasant relaxation. They pay for it and it is my business to provide them with what they want.'

'But what's to happen to our animals?' Zoë burst out. 'Just because they haven't expensive price tags hung round their necks and aren't beautiful, they don't count, I suppose?'

He met her agitated look with one of stony calm. 'And it is necessary, is it, to prolong their useless lives?'

'They've had rotten lives!' Zoë almost shouted. 'And they deserve to see out their last days in a bit of comfort, or as much as I can give them, with people who care! Your rich people with their picture-book ideas about country life can take their money and go somewhere else!'

'But I wish them to spend their money here,' said Eric with the same irritating calm. 'And they wish to come here. And why shouldn't they? That is their choice. Why should I not provide an idealised country scene? It is what they want.'

'We were here first!'

'But on my land. I own it. It is not yours. Your lease is almost up. So the decision is mine, isn't it? Besides, we are talking of my business, my livelihood and that of all my staff. I have given work to local people. To the chambermaids and garden staff. All these people depend on my hotel and its success. It is not only I.'

Baffled, Zoë glared at him. Then she made an effort to regain some poise and say reasonably, 'But we can't afford to go anywhere else or pay more rent, Mr Schuhmacher.'

'Yes, I understand that, Miss Foster. I am not stupid. But you must also understand that I have invested a great deal of money in Springwood Hall.'

Zoë sighed and thrust her hands in her jacket pockets.

Eric studied her disconsolate figure for a moment. 'Look here, Miss Foster. I have nothing against animals. I admire what you have done here, truly. But it's a business decision, do you see?'

His tone had become unexpectedly gentle. Zoë looked up in surprise and flushed. 'Yes, I see. We just have different goals in life, Mr Schuhmacher. Nothing wrong with either of them separately, but they clash. Incompatible, that's all.'

'Perhaps.' They turned and began to walk back towards the barn. 'You are also a member of the historical society, are you not?' he asked suddenly.

'Yes, I suppose you don't like that either!' Zoë hunched her shoulders. 'To be honest I joined it because I thought there was just a chance they might be able to stop your plans for the Hall.'

'Oh no.' Schuhmacher gave a little chuckle. 'There was never any chance of that!'

Hearing him laugh, Zoë stopped and spun to face him. 'Do you think us comical? I suppose we do seem funny and behind the times and impractical. But this is our world, our home, our corner of the country and we care about it!' Her vehemence became dampened. 'But we should have left you alone. It seems as if all our efforts have brought nothing but trouble. Ellen's dead. Emma's missing and may have had some awful accident. Maud's missing. I'm sorry if I don't join you in your laughter, Mr Schuhmacher, but I don't find anything to laugh at, that's all.'

For the first time in their conversation about the animals Eric looked angry. 'I am not laughing at you!'

There was an interruption. Robin Harding had heard them returning and emerged from the barn. He stood by the door, glowering.

'Your friend is unhappy,' Schuhmacher said stiffly. 'I had better go. Thank you for showing me the animals, Miss Foster!'

He walked quickly away, got into his car and drove off without a backward glance.

'Good riddance!' muttered Robin.

Zoë said nothing.

Chapter Thirteen

Meredith had reached the outer edge of the woodland spied from the distance. She found it ringed with a narrow strip of mixed undergrowth and native woodland represented by weedy saplings. Brambles caught at her clothing, tall nettles leaned out to sting her hands, weirdly shaped fungi broke with a musty odour beneath her feet. There was a dead bird lying on the leafmould beneath a tree, headless. She turned the carcass with her foot and thought it might have been a spotted woodpecker and she wondered what had killed it. It was perhaps a gruesome omen.

However it was unlikely a child and a donkey could be hidden for long in this tangled brush and Emma would have sought safer refuge. If they were anywhere, they were in the pine plantation beyond, now looming ever more sinister.

The tall straight trunks seemed to be formed up like an enemy army to repel any advance on them. Dark and impenetrable, these conifers, aliens in this landscape, had been planted for their commercial value.

Glancing back to ensure she was well clear of the advancing line of searchers and would not be covering the same ground – and also to check that she was not being pursued by the Fultons – she found herself nonetheless comforted by the knowledge that others were not so very far off. She felt as vulnerable as a one-woman scouting party. It might have been better to have pleaded with Sergeant Harris to be allowed to join the organised search. But she had ever been one for striking out on her own. Meredith stepped resolutely forward.

The first lines of conifers were still accessible to daylight and to enter them not so alarming. But very soon Meredith found herself in a different world.

Here the ground underfoot was soft, sprinkled with pine needles and twigs which cracked as she stood on them. Daylight now penetrated with difficulty from above and the air was scented with resin. Nothing grew on the woodland floor. Everything was smothered in fallen pine needles which formed a dry, brown carpet. Meredith advanced slowly through the gloom as if making her way through some nightmare-created castle, full of pillars and corridors running off in all directions. When she glanced back she saw that she could no longer see anything but a receding mass of dark trunks, all the same. She hoped fervently that she wouldn't lose her bearings.

To move a donkey freely among these trees would be difficult and somewhere there must be a path, probably a series of paths. But she could blunder about in here for ever without finding one and Alan wouldn't be pleased if a second search party had to be sent out: she could well imagine Sergeant Harris's reaction. But if she moved forward in a straight line, or as straight as she could make it, she'd eventually come out the other side of the plantation. That made sense even if it wouldn't find Emma.

On the off-chance, Meredith put her hands to her mouth and shouted the child's name. The sound echoed amongst the trees and was swallowed up somewhere in the distant reaches. A bird flapped up from a branch above her head, startling her, but there was no reply.

Meredith went on. After a while the ground grew soggy. Her boots squelched in a dark-brown moisture oozing out of an odoriferous mire. There were hoofprints here but not a donkey's. These were cloven, the marks of deer. They had probably made them on their way to water. Donkeys too need water. Meredith squelched on through the soft ground with the horrid feeling her boots were starting to leak.

At last, however, she was rewarded. She came upon a murky stream, running swiftly in a straight course between the trees. Meredith set out to follow it. At first it was difficult because the poor terrain became even worse and each step took her deep into mud from which she could only extricate herself with a great effort and a hideous sucking noise as her foot came free. Mud was soon plastered up to her knees but eventually the ground began to become firmer.

The stream now ran between banks. It had broadened out and although choked here and there with accumulated debris it was deep enough and the current strong enough to overcome the obstacles. Despite keeping a sharp eye open, Meredith had not so far seen any sign of human presence here before her. There were no dropped sweet papers. No one had brought their domestic rubbish to jettison it here, as often happened in woodland. Its absence added to the sense of unreality.

Visibility was improving. The light was coming from up ahead. Without warning, Meredith emerged into the open air and a grassy drive. This was clearly a firebreak maintained between two blocks of pines. On the far side of it the pine mass began again. But in this open space and beneath the bright sunlight the coarse grass carpeting the ground formed a pleasing contrast to the dark sterile environment of the plantation.

And there, quite alone, right in the middle of the open drive, browsed a donkey.

It was of the large working donkey type Meredith remembered from the Balkans, pale in colour and unlike the small dark grey Neddies of British seaside holiday snaps. It was extremely ugly and obviously very old. It snatched at the coarse grass, tearing it from the roots in a way which suggested it was hungry. If it had been abandoned amongst the inhospitable conifers, it must have had a long search to find this food supply.

'Maud . . .' called Meredith.

The donkey swung up its large ungainly head and pricked long furry ears. Meredith began to walk towards it and the donkey moved awkwardly away from her on deformed front legs. She continued to speak softly and encouragingly and at last managed to reach the animal and pat its neck.

'Where's Emma, Maud? I wish you could speak . . .' Meredith's hand, caressing the donkey, encountered something dry, coagulated. She took away her fingers. A small area of the donkey's hide was matted with something dark. Meredith scraped at it. It seemed to be blood. She parted the sparse hair and searched for a wound but there was none, not even a scratch. Meredith's heart descended to her toes.

She looked up, searching the terrain, and spotted a narrow path running away from the open drive into the pines on the far side. A small neat pile of fresh manure indicated Maud had come that way earlier. Meredith dived into the trees once more, stumbling in her anxiety and shouting, 'Emma! Emma, it's Meredith, your Uncle Alan's friend! Emma, are you there?'

There was no answer from among the dark, inhospitable pines.

Panic now began to take hold of Meredith as she hastened along the deer track. It twisted through the ranks of the pine army, here almost petering out, here clearly marked by the two-pronged indentations.

She became more and more convinced that the path must lead her to Emma. Meredith called the child's name several times but without getting any response, the sound of her own voice disappearing eerily among the dark trunks. Once she heard a distant rustling, perhaps one of the deer trotting away. It was a heart-stopping moment leading her to call out again more urgently, but doomed like her other attempts to disappointment. After she had progressed some way like this, she stopped to take stock.

She could blunder about for ever in here. The uniformity of the trees was disorientating. She could easily have missed some small clue. After several moments spent just standing and straining her ears Meredith, not without hesitation, began to retrace her steps, eyes fixed on the needle-strewn ground.

The way in which it was possible to walk over this dry carpet without leaving a sign of passage was disheartening. But Meredith continued to search the surrounding woodland floor with feverish intent. Somewhere, surely, there must be something which showed the way to the lost child. So absorbed in her task was she that she was aware of nothing else and with a cry of alarm suddenly bumped up against a solid form blocking her path. Hot breath blew gustily into her ear. Meredith looked up and found herself face to face with Maud who fixed her with a reproachful expression in her long-lashed lustrous eyes. She wheezed again.

The donkey must have followed her back into the trees. Meredith patted the mealy muzzle and ran her hand over the coarse uneven mane. 'All right, old girl. Where next? Because blowed if I know. You do, don't you? Can't you take me to Emma?'

Maud groaned, jerked her head free of Meredith's hand and turning, began to plod away with her stiff gait between the trees. She had quit the path and was striking out at right angles to it. After a brief tussle in her own mind as to what was best, Meredith followed.

The bony rump ahead of her moved steadily, unhurriedly on. From time to time Maud's moth-eaten bell-pull of a tail twitched away clouds of midges but the only time the donkey stopped was once when Meredith herself paused, uncertain whether to continue. After all, the animal might simply be looking for something to eat. Maud, however, paused too and looked back, long ears pricked, and rolling her eyes with a distinctly irritated expression. She stamped a hind hoof.

Meredith accepted that she had been told off, donkey-fashion. Donkeys were reputedly highly intelligent and perhaps she ought to trust this one. She called, 'Walk on, Maud!' and they set off again in their curious Indian-file progress.

They were nearing the stream again. Meredith could hear its rippling progress ahead. The ground was becoming softer and the smell of damp rotten wood was in the air. Without any warning, Maud stopped. Meredith saw with some dismay that the donkey stood, head hanging, showing every sign of being about to doze off.

'Oy!' exclaimed Meredith angrily, slapping Maud's threadbare hindquarters. 'Don't pack it in now! Dratted beast, I've followed you this far! Have you been leading me on an utter wild-goose chase?'

Maud's eyelashes drooped and she gave a long-drawn-out hissing noise like an airbed which had sprung a leak. Apart from that she might have been turned to stone, and deaf into the bargain.

Meredith thrust her hands into her pockets and glared at the donkey in exasperation, but at that very moment she heard a faint cry. It came from somewhere quite close at hand.

'Emma!' Meredith shouted, her heart leaping.

The cry was repeated. It came from up ahead. Meredith began to run forward. She stumbled between the trees and suddenly found herself on the banks of the brook. There was a clear area here. To her right was a kind of wigwam made of tarpaulin-covered branches and straight ahead by the edge of the water crouched a small grimy figure in a muddy anorak and gumboots who raised a tear-stained countenance.

'Oh, Emma!' cried Meredith, experiencing the greatest lightening of her heart she could remember in a long time. She flew across the short space between them, fell on her knees and clasped Emma in her arms. 'Oh, thank God! Are you all right?'

The child was shivering, tense as a coiled spring. As she huddled in Meredith's grip her voice could be heard indistinctly, thin and shaky. 'I didn't think anyone would find me!' A sob cut short the words.

'Everyone's searching. I followed Maud. She brought me here.'

At the mention of the donkey, Emma gave a convulsive jerk. She lifted her head and whispered, 'Meredith, something awful's happened! It wasn't my fault.'

Meredith's elation evaporated. She remembered the

congealed blood on the donkey's coat. 'Are you hurt, Emma?' she asked anxiously.

Emma shook her head, her tangled fair hair falling round her white little face. She said nothing but her gaze travelled to the bothy a short distance away.

Meredith released the child, stood up and took a step towards the primitive shelter. Emma caught at the edge of her jacket, holding her back, and cried out, 'No, no, don't look in there!'

Meredith turned back and dropped on to her heels beside the child. 'Why not, Emma? What's in there?'

'He is . . .' Emma whispered.

The wind rustled in the pine trees above. Very faintly, borne on the breeze, the voices of the search party could be heard calling to one another in the distance. They must have reached the edge of the wood.

Meredith said steadily, 'It's all right, Emma. I'm just going to take a look – no! Don't be afraid. It'll be all right.'

She walked slowly towards the bothy, and with considerable trepidation put out her hand to throw back the tarpaulin over the entrance.

A swirl of warm fetid air rushed out and brought instant nausea surging into her throat. She gagged, forced it back and with her hand clamped over nose and mouth, peered inside. It was dark and the air thick with insects. Gradually her eyes became accustomed to the gloom and Meredith saw the huddled form sprawled on the floor. Tentatively she edged closer. A man, clad in dirty clothing, his arms in an old torn anorak with stripes on the sleeves thrown forward as if he'd tried to protect his head, his face—

But there was no face. It had been quite destroyed, battered to a pulped mass in a crushed skull beneath a cloud of hovering midges.

The nausea came back. Meredith gave a choked cry, whirled and stumbled out into the fresh resin-scented air.

For a moment the world turned topsy-turvy. Then the mist and confusion cleared. She saw Emma's white frightened face fixed on hers.

'He's dead, isn't he?' Emma asked in a cold little voice.

Meredith sank, or rather collapsed, on to the pine-needle carpet beside the child and asked as normally as she could, 'Where did he come from?'

'He was in there. I thought – I thought it was empty, a den, you know. I thought it would be all right for Maud. It was dark and I didn't see him until I got inside with her. I think Maud knew he was there because she didn't want to go in.'

Meredith picked her words carefully. 'Did he touch you, Emma?'

'He grabbed my arm. I tried to get away. I fell over and he bent over me and then Maud – Maud did it.'

'Did what, Emma?'

'Kicked him. Maud doesn't like strangers and she was always a bit snappy and difficult but this time she went sort of mad. She kept kicking and stamping and making funny noises in her throat . . . I got up and ran outside.' Emma's eyes filled with tears. 'Maud killed him, Meredith! I didn't think she could ever do a thing like that!'

'She was defending her foal,' Meredith said gently. 'You were her baby, Emma, and he threatened you. What she did was instinct. She knew he meant harm and she saved you. She did it out of a sort of donkey-love.' She took Emma's hand. 'Come on, sweetheart, let's go and find the people looking for you. Your mother and father are waiting and they'll be so relieved to know you're fine.'

Chapter Fourteen

Holding Emma by the hand, Meredith set off back the way she had come. Emma snuffled a little but insisted in a quiet, tight little voice that she was all right, something Meredith doubted. After a few minutes they heard a dull regular thud behind them and knew that Maud plodded along bringing up the rear, probably hoping that after all the excitement they were at long last going home.

As soon as they hove into view, Laura let out an ear-splitting shriek and flew to meet them. Emma let go Meredith's hand and shouted, 'Mummy!', racing across the grass.

On the other hand Sergeant Harris's expression when he saw them would have been hard to depict. Surprise and relief mingled with frustration and outright fury. Meredith was sure she would have been on the receiving end of a number of blunt accusations, but fortunately Markby had arrived at the scene meantime to check progress. She was very glad to see him and his face, when he saw Emma, relegated the sergeant's anger to a triviality.

Emma was borne away home by her overjoyed parents. The search party was stood down. The members of it stood around in groups drinking coffee from polystyrene cups and chatting. Markby left the group by the radio-control van and came to where Meredith sat on the grass resting her arms on her knees. He dropped on his heels in front of her and pulled a wry face.

'Trust you. Why didn't you wait for Harris's instructions?'

'He didn't want me. Thought I'd be in the way. The Fultons came along as well.'

She nodded her head towards Denis and Leah, sitting on the ground and drinking their tea from the polystyrene cups but still managing a dash of elegance, as if they assisted at some upmarket point-to-point or other cross-country horsy event.

'Yes, so I saw when I got here. I don't think poor Harris knew what to make of them, but as it turned out they stayed back here, comforting Laura and Paul. Harris would have found Emma in the course of things, you know, but I can't grumble at you for charging on ahead on your own because it led to her being found the sooner. There's not much I can say, except that another time I hope you'll report your intention to someone before wandering off into the woods. Not that I'm looking to another occasion like this one!'

He hesitated as their eyes met and he went on quickly, 'I am grateful that you came down here so quickly after we spoke on the phone. I was very worried about the kid. I do worry about her sometimes. She's at a vulnerable age, the age when things do happen to little girls. Boys too. Thank you.'

Meredith leaned out sideways to add her empty cup to the pile of such rubbish in a black plastic bag nearby. 'Actually, Alan, there's something else you should know. I told Emma to let me tell you about it and I wanted all the fuss to die down a bit before I did. She's had about as much as she can take. She's a brave child but I think when she gets home she'll break down and have a really good howl.' Meredith swallowed. 'There's a body in those pine woods.'

He stared at her, his coffee cup half-raised and steam from it rising into the air. 'What?'

She explained, watching the gratitude in his eyes fade and his features harden. He rose to his feet without comment, dropped his coffee cup into the bag and walked back to Harris and the uniformed men. She saw him speak a few words and Harris's head jerk round to face her, his eyes bulging.

Markby came back and she got to her feet. 'Lead on, then, MacDuff!' he said. She wished his grim face had matched the casual tone of the invitation.

They set out again, passing Maud who was now grazing peacefully on the outskirts of the group as if nothing had happened.

'Has someone gone to tell the girl at the Horses' Home to come over and fetch that animal?' Markby asked.

'Yes, sir,' Harris answered grimly.

After that no one spoke another word until they reached the spot where she'd found Emma.

The bothy was as she'd left it. Markby and Harris went inside and remained there several minutes which Meredith, recalling the smell and the gruesome sight, thought worthy of some kind of medal. When they came out Markby spoke into a walkie-talkie for several minutes before coming to where she sat on the ground with her back against a tree.

He looked down at her. 'He's certainly a mess. We may be able to put a name to him from the fingerprints if they're on record but certainly no one's going to identify him from his looks! He may be a chap we've been looking out for, in fact. If so, he probably built that shelter after he'd been disturbed in a previous one on farmland. That one was reported to us, but by the time we got a man out to look at it, the bird had flown. Poor kid, a hell of an experience, but it could have been worse.'

Meredith burst out, 'That's the understatement of the decade!'

Looking down at her, Markby said quietly, 'Do you think I don't know that?' She flushed and he went on more briskly, 'I'll have to stay here till the forensic team arrives. Do you mind finding your own way back?'

Meredith got to her feet, dusting herself free of pine needles. She accepted she was no longer needed but felt vaguely resentful at the manner of being dismissed. After all, she had been the one to find Emma. 'I'm staying at Springwood Hall,' she said stiffly. 'I suppose this means another statement. I'm piling them up.' Her voice rang starchily and she realised she must have acquired a matching expression because he said mildly, 'All right, madame consul!'

He was then evidently struck by a suspicion. 'By the way, staying at Springwood Hall won't give you any ideas about investigating Ellen Bryant's death, will it? You know how I feel about amateur detective work! That wouldn't be just barging off to look for Emma on your own. That would be outright interfering in a police matter!'

Meredith glared at him and snapped, 'I've been very helpful to you in the past! And incidentally I'm an ex-consul! I'm just an FO dogsbody in London!'

'I told you I'm grateful you came down to lend moral support and naturally I'm pleased you found Emma!' Then he added impatiently, 'And yes, you've been of help once or twice in the past. But don't push your luck, madame "ex"!'

Markby's attempt to take the edge off his criticism with this faint joke fell flat. Embarrassed by its failure he attempted to explain it as if in some way she hadn't got the point.

'Years ago that term, Madame X, always indicated a lady of vulnerable reputation who appeared in the witness box wearing black with a veiled hat!' He caught the tail end of a chilling glare. 'All right, but you're going to come unstuck eventually. You'll get yourself into a situation you can't handle. Just suppose that chap lying back there with his head kicked in had been alive and holding Emma prisoner? What then, eh?' He saw the mutinous look in her eyes. 'I know you're a very capable lady. But as I've had cause to tell you before, this isn't foreign climes and you don't have consular authority here – as you yourself have just pointed out. Nor do you have diplomatic immunity. Watch it, my girl!'

'I am not your girl!' Meredith snarled and marched off through the pines, head high.

'More's the pity . . .' sighed Markby to himself, watching her go.

Meredith caught up with the Fultons on her way back to the hotel. They must have dallied at the operations point, perhaps just curious at seeing Meredith set off again with the two police officers.

Denis stomped along in the gumboots which could now be seen to be two sizes too big, his hands in his pockets. 'Thank God that's over!' he said.

Leah, walking beside Meredith, murmured, 'Yes, thank God indeed!'

Meredith glanced at her and was struck by the expression on her face. If Emma had been personally known to her, a relation even, Leah's features could not have shown a more heartfelt relief.

As if sensing Meredith's thought, Leah looked up and said, 'She's a lovely little girl, a beautiful child, and nothing so horrid ought ever to have happened to her, to any child. She ran to her mother and father, so pleased to see them. I wonder if Lizzie, my daughter, at that age, even in such circumstances, would have done that. She was always such a contained sort of child, almost unnaturally so. The more I tried to fuss over her, the more she always seemed to push me away.'

Leah had probably just tried too hard, been too possessive, thought Meredith. Leah didn't know, of course, about the body in the woods because Alan had asked her not to tell anyone: the police would release the news themselves at an appropriate moment. Leah must be curious as to what had taken the trio back to the pine plantation, but had nobly refrained from direct questions.

Aloud Meredith only said, 'Emma's had a dreadful fright. I hope she gets over it.'

Schuhmacher was standing in the hotel entrance, awaiting their return. He darted forward eagerly.

'I heard a rumour that they have found the child, is that right?'

'Yes. She's okay.' Meredith eyed him with some curiosity. He also looked agitated and more than normally concerned about the matter.

'That's a good thing, very good!' Eric said. 'I remember such a case years ago in Switzerland. It was the winter there and the snow very deep. Alas, the child was not found in time.'

'I'm getting these boots off!' announced Denis shortly. 'Come on, Leah. I hope the bar's open, Eric!'

When they'd gone, Schuhmacher gave Meredith a sharp look and said, 'You need a drink too.'

'I can't face the bar and to be truthful, don't want to talk to the Fultons any more just at the moment.'

'Then come and have a drink in my office.'

She would have preferred to go straight up to her room and collapse. She was suffering an understandable reaction to the morning's events. A long tiring drive down from London had sapped her energy before starting out and then her emotions had abruptly soared when Emma was found, only to plumb the depths of horror moments later. She wouldn't forget that crushed head. She felt her metaphorical batteries were at an all-time low.

But Eric meant kindly and she wasn't at liberty to explain to him about her finding of another body. And, anyway, he might react very unfavourably if he heard about another body. So she said, 'Thanks!' and allowed him to lead her into an office and seat her in a comfortable chair in one corner of it. In due course an excellent brandy was put in her hand. She wished she was more in the mood to appreciate its quality. As it was, she knocked it back in a disrespectful fashion.

Eric, however, didn't seem to mind. He had taken a nearby chair. 'And the donkey?' he asked unexpectedly. 'The animal is found?'

'Oh, yes – Maud. She's – she's all right.'

'I am very pleased because Miss Foster is naturally worried about the animal.'

This, if anything, was an even more surprising remark than the original question. Meredith's face must have shown her astonishment.

197

'I was earlier at the Horses' Home,' said Schuhmacher in explanation. 'She showed me around it.' He looked thoughtful and slightly regretful. 'It is very untidy.'

'Not very Swiss,' said Meredith, unable to restrain this comment. 'Sorry – rude of me.'

'No, no, quite correct. Not Swiss at all. That barn, so rickety and as for that caravan where she lives . . . I did not see inside it, of course!' Eric fixed Meredith with a minatory look. 'But I could see it is in a bad state. I do not think she has planning permission for that trailer. The whole place has got to go, I'm afraid.'

'Look,' Meredith said. 'I realise it's an eyesore but—'

He held up a large capable hand, stopping her. 'Yes, it is. But I am not unaware of the worthwhile work she does. It is really most commendable. After all, the animals are not beautiful and she depends upon charity. People are more willing to give to attractive animals, abandoned puppies and so on. One of those small ponies which she has there tried to bite me.'

Meredith, for all the nervous exhaustion which was creeping over her, aided by the brandy, had to smile.

'Perhaps it knew who I was!' said Eric with unlooked-for humour. He was turning out to be more surprising by the sentence. 'But she is a remarkable young woman and her work must not be – well, wiped out. To run such a place on so little finance, Miss Foster is also a remarkable businesswoman.' Real respect now echoed in his voice.

'Hullo, hullo, hullo . . .' thought Meredith drowsily.

From somewhere in the distance she heard Eric's voice saying, 'Yes, the Horses' Home really should be saved somehow. The same is not so of the young man, Harding. I have met such a type before. He has to go. He really has to go. I do not trust that young man. I certainly would never give him a job here!'

Eric's words only half registered as Meredith unceremoniously fell asleep in front of him.

Chapter Fifteen

The committee of the Society for the Preservation of Historic Bamford had gathered in its usual meeting place, Hope Mapple's flat. It was its first official meeting since the events at Springwood Hall and the awareness of all that had happened weighed heavily on the air. Earlier that day they had heard the coroner adjourn Ellen's inquest pending police inquiries, leaving it hanging above them like a Sword of Damocles.

The surviving members sat huddled in their seats, not looking at one another and especially not looking at the empty corner chair which was where Ellen Bryant had usually chosen to sit. No one referred to it. The vacant seat was covered in worn, royal-blue Dralon and intended to be Queen Anne period in design. Vaguely throne-like with its wings and cabriole legs, its emptiness seemed to reproach them for some kind of *lèse-majesté*, for daring to assemble in the absence of its former occupant. They were as uneasily aware of it as they had once been of her ironic gaze. From time to time one or other of them would cast it a furtive glance.

Hope, resplendent in a full-length jade green kaftan made of some shiny material embroidered at neck and bosom with sequins, appeared in the doorway. Bearing a tray, she plodded heavy-footed to the coffee table in the middle of the floor, green cloth billowing behind her. They all watched her as she stooped and her strung bead earrings swung like the decorations on the vast Christmas tree she resembled. Each of the observers was plainly hoping that the others wouldn't guess that the image in each and every mind was of Hope sprinting across Schuhmacher's lawn in her birthday suit.

'Tea!' Hope assured them as she proceeded to pour out a beige liquid. 'Help yourselves to biscuits.'

Zoë didn't want a biscuit but took a custard cream, feeling obscurely it would be polite to do so. Robin Harding, aware of pekinese hairs floating on the surface of his tea, grunted, 'No, thanks!' He folded his arms and glowered sulkily at the assembled company. Zoë guessed he was embarrassed and threw him a tentative smile. His expression lightened and he grimaced wrily with a barely perceptible nod towards Hope. Zoë blushed.

Charles Grimsby said loudly, 'I have a motion to put before the committee!'

'You can't, Charles, not yet,' said Hope. 'I haven't declared the meeting open yet. And Zoë has first to read the minutes of the last one and then we discuss matters arising.' She flopped down on a divan among the pekinese and folded her hands in her lap. 'Well now, I suppose we can begin. Secretary, please?'

Zoë opened the cheap exercise book in which she kept the records of their deliberations. 'Present at the last meeting were Hope Mapple, Zoë Foster, Ellen Bryant—' She stopped.

'We know who was here,' said Charles gruffly. 'I think we can cut all that. I want to say something – and it comes under matters arising if you want to be finickety about it!'

'Oh, for goodness' sake, Charles. Go on, then!'

'Right!' He sat up straight and glared at the pekinese opposite him. 'I propose that Hope Mapple be removed from the chair of this committee.'

There was a gasp from Zoë. Robin muttered, 'Shut up, Grimsby, not now!'

Charles went on sternly, 'I consider her behaviour at Springwood Hall brought the name of the committee into disrepute.'

Hope flushed an unattractive puce and tossed back her raven curls. The bead earrings swung so violently they threatened to tie themselves into knots. 'I at least tried to bring our society to the attention of the public!'

'You did that all right!' retorted Grimsby. 'But some of us can do without that kind of publicity! The Chamber of Commerce—'

'Stuff the Chamber of Commerce!' said Hope rudely.

Grimsby's face darkened to a magenta hue which rivalled Hope's. 'It's all very well for you. You're already associated in the public mind around here with the mentally disturbed!'

'And what does that mean?' demanded Hope, adding theatrically, 'Pray?'

'You give art lessons to those poor souls in the psychiatric ward at the hospital, don't you? If you ask me, some of their behaviour is starting to rub off on you, Hope.'

'That,' snarled Hope, 'is actionable!'

'Oh well, if we want to talk lawsuits, I'm not so sure I couldn't claim my business reputation has been damaged because of your antics!'

'Now just a minute,' Robin interrupted. 'You can't complain about anything now, Grimsby. It's too late. You should have said all this at the last meeting. Hope made it

203

quite clear what she proposed to do.'

'I did say it, or something like it. I objected anyway. It's in the minutes. It is in the minutes, isn't it, madam secretary? I particularly asked at the time for my objections to be noted in the minutes!' Grimsby fixed Zoë with a steely eye.

Zoë frantically hunted through her exercise book. 'Yes, yes, here it is. "Mr Grimsby requested his objection to the plan to be noted".'

'There you are, then!' said Grimsby.

'No, we're not!' Robin argued vigorously. 'After you objected, Hope made it clear she was still going to do it. You should have resigned if you felt that strongly about it.'

'It's not a question of *me*, of any of *us*, resigning!' Grimsby yelled. 'It's for Hope to abide by the decision of the committee! And we all said we thought it was a lousy idea, but she went and did it anyway! Hope should resign!'

'Shan't!' declared Ms Mapple in ringing tones. She rose to her feet in a shimmering explosion of jade green and glittering glass beads.

'You haven't got a leg to stand on!' snarled Grimsby.

Zoë, disastrously, giggled.

'Oh, funny, is it?' Charles, stung, turned on her. 'Well, some of us have a regard for decency! We also have a regard for this society, as it was! You have only just joined it, but Hope and I were founder members. Hope sadly seems to have forgotten our original high aims. I have not. You, I suppose, accustomed to the standards of that ramshackle animal sanctuary, cannot be expected to appreciate that.'

'Oy, you leave Zoë out of this!' Robin sprang to Zoë's defence. 'Or you'll have me to answer to. Who worries about a bit of bare flesh these days, anyway?'

Grimsby, at bay, whirled to face him. 'Before you go any further, perhaps you might reflect that if Hope hadn't made a spectacle of herself as she did, Ellen might be alive today and sitting in that chair!' He flung out his hand to point at the Queen Anne armchair now occupied by a slumbering pekinese.

There was a stunned silence and they all looked guiltily at Ellen's former seat. The peke, sensing a challenge, lifted its head and gave a gurgling growl.

Hope, breathing heavily, said, 'That's rubbish!'

'Oh, is it? It's because she didn't want to be present when you made your lewd display that poor Ellen left the main company and went off alone – to her death!'

'You're out of order, Grimsby!' Robin said angrily. 'We don't know why Ellen went down to those cellars.'

'We don't,' Grimsby said nastily. 'But you might!'

This time the silence lasted so long that Zoë felt she would scream if no one spoke and was compelled to break it herself. 'What do you mean, Charles?'

'Ask him!' Grimsby pointed at the pale-faced Robin. 'He was friendly with the deceased lady, very friendly.'

'That's a lie!' Robin said hoarsely. 'Don't listen to him, Zoë!'

'Intimate lunches together. I saw you, more than once!' Grimsby's eyes glittered triumphantly.

'Good grief, I must have lunched with Ellen two or three times at the most!' Robin snapped. 'And they weren't the sort of lunches you're trying to make them out to be. They weren't romantic! If I wanted to lunch romantically with anyone, would I take that person to the sort of quick service cafés you must have seen Ellen and me in?'

'So what were you doing there with her?' Grimsby persisted.

'You're trying to make something out of it, I realise!' Robin thrust his face into that of Grimsby, who recoiled as well he might at the ugly light which had entered the younger man's eyes. 'But it was all completely innocent. More than that, it was trivial! I don't owe you any explanation but I will explain because if I don't, you'll sit there smirking and thinking you've scored some point! Well, you haven't!' He took a deep breath.

'Ellen used to go into town sometimes for her lunch, generally on a Friday after she'd been to the bank. At other times I believe she went upstairs to that flat of hers or so she told me. I don't know it from personal experience!' Robin's glare indicated he wouldn't allow his opponent to make this charge. 'As it happened, I was lunching in town quite a lot at that time. I'd got fed up with sandwiches and an apple in the office. I started nipping out to the nearest cheap café. So that's how I happened to run into Ellen and since we were acquainted and both alone, we sat at the same table. After a while I found it was too expensive to eat out and I went back to sandwiches and a thermos in the office. I don't know what Ellen did. She found eating out tricky because she was a vegetarian. She always had to have the cheese salad or egg on toast. She said to me she could get that for herself at a quarter of the price so I suppose she went back to eating at home, I don't know!' Robin shouted out the last words.

Grimsby gave him an evil grin. 'The two of you looked pretty friendly to me!'

'This,' said Hope majestically, 'has nothing to do with the society. It's personal abuse and now that you've subjected both myself and Robin to some of that, perhaps you'd let the meeting resume? No, I won't resign and as I gather no one is going to second your motion that I be replaced as chair, I take it I'm staying. Agreed?'

There was an awkward silence. Robin and Grimsby had retreated, glowering, to their respective corners. Zoë chewed the end of her pencil in embarrassment.

'Right, let it be noted in the minutes!' Hope commanded. As Zoë began to scribble industriously, she went on, 'Now if we can get back to business . . . Is there anything else we can do about Schuhmacher's use of the Hall? Perhaps, Charles, you could suggest something you'd consider suitable action? Be constructive for once instead of just rubbishing my efforts?'

'No,' said Grimsby curtly. 'We've lost that fight. The odious Schuhmacher has won it.'

'Actually,' said Zoë nervously, 'he's quite a nice man.'

There was stunned reaction and all three stared at her.

She blushed scarlet. 'I don't mean to sound a traitor, but I've met him now, which I hadn't before. I know he's a bit inclined to order people about and he was awfully rude to Robin – but you shouldn't have threatened him with that fork, Rob, I was really scared! And of course he does still want to move the Horses' Home off our present site. But when I showed him round the place the other day he really seemed interested in our work and quite sympathetic.'

'His sympathy,' said Robin, 'won't stop him giving you and the animals the boot! You're too trusting, Zoë. Don't be taken in by him.'

'I'm not suggesting he'll change his mind.' She sighed. 'He explained his point of view to me and I have to say I couldn't disagree. Our buildings *are* an eyesore. I suppose we smell, although I don't notice it. Our animals are very ugly and one tried to bite him. I am aware of all that. If we had the money, I'd do something about it.' She paused. 'As a matter of fact, ever since that national newspaper ran an article on us when Ellen – you know, when that happened – and especially since little Emma got us in the press again by running off with Maud, I've been inundated with cheques from complete strangers all over the country! It's lovely, of course, but it won't last and the money so far has mostly gone on settling outstanding bills for feed and so on. I owed the farrier a huge amount although he'd never asked for it, but I had to pay as soon as I could. I ought to pay Finlay Ross but he absolutely refuses to take a penny. People are very kind.'

'Schuhmacher isn't kind,' said Robin sourly. 'You won't get a penny out of him!'

Zoë reddened. 'I didn't suggest I would!'

'He's buttering you up because he's had a bad press over his persecution of the Horses' Home. Insensitivity towards animals is the one thing the British won't take. Schuhmacher is worried about his image and he wants you to put in a good word for him. And you're doing it, very nicely! You're playing his game, Zoë! Don't!'

'He's not getting kind words from me and I'm not closing our file on Springwood Hall!' said Hope robustly. 'If necessary I shall picket the gates. Like the women did at Greenham Common.'

Grimsby groaned and put his hand to his head.

'Schuhmacher is pally with the local cops,' said Robin. 'He'd only get you moved on.'

'Good! Let 'em try! I shall resist! I shall lie down in the road!'

'If Hope gets herself on the telly again,' said Grimsby hoarsely, 'being carried away to a police van—'

Hope's face had brightened and Robin said quickly, 'Forget it, Hope! Schuhmacher would probably send you out a plate of leftovers with a photographer on hand and get himself good publicity! He's a devious beggar and we know how difficult he is to dislodge. Nevertheless, I'm inclined to agree with Hope. I'm not ready to concede defeat either.'

'You're wasting your time,' said Grimsby.

'He didn't leave you lying in the mud! This is personal!' Robin told him.

Later Harding gave Zoë a lift back to the Alice Batt Rest Home on the pillion of his motorcycle as he usually did. Conversation on a motorbike wasn't possible but when they sat in her trailer drinking Nescafé, they still kept an introspective silence. At last Robin put down his mug.

'It wasn't true, what Grimsby was suggesting about me and Ellen.'

'Doesn't matter . . .' mumbled Zoë.

'Yes, it bloody does!' His tone grew heated. 'I had a couple of humdrum lunches with her during which she lectured me for eating meat and extolled the virtues of a nut diet.'

'It's okay, Robin. It doesn't make any difference to our friendship,' Zoë insisted. 'It's not my business. You can lunch with anyone you like. It's nothing to do with Charles Grimsby either, so just forget about it.'

Robin looked far from satisfied with this answer. After a moment or two he said awkwardly, 'Actually, Zoë, old Grimsby wasn't exactly completely off the mark. I don't mean,' he added hastily, 'that I saw my meetings with Ellen as romantic! But it is just possible that she, well, perhaps she began to get ideas. The last time we ate together she made a couple of come-hitherish remarks. I feel a bit of a fool telling you this and I suppose a gentleman wouldn't, but she's dead, poor cow.'

'That's not very nice!' objected Zoë, startled.

'Well, she was a bit pathetic. Anyhow, it took me aback when she started batting her eyelashes over the brown bread and vegetable lasagne. It's true that I had been finding eating out a bit expensive, but that sort of decided it. I didn't have lunch with her again. I always fancied, whenever we met after that, that she gave me a funny look. It was embarrassing, frankly. But you ought to know.'

'Why?' asked Zoë.

He reddened. 'Why? Because I want you to know the truth and not hide anything from you! Because, oh heck! You must know how I feel about you, Zoë!'

'Me?' She stared at him. 'No, I don't.'

'Oh, for crying out loud, Zoë!' he exclaimed but then fell silent. 'Sorry,' he muttered at last. He got up and picked up his crash helmet. 'I didn't mean to say it, better get going. Good night!'

Zoë listened to the roar of the motorcycle fading into the distance. 'Oh dear,' she said aloud, 'I do hope not!'

Then she sighed and pulled on the ancient Barbour she'd inherited from Miss Batt and went out to check on the animals.

'One draught cider!' said Markby, setting it before Meredith and putting his own pint on the table. 'Budge up!'

She obliged and he squeezed on to the aged oak settle. They had come from a full and dispiriting morning at consecutive inquests held on Ellen and the man in the woods. Ellen's had been adjourned. The other had been declared accidental death. Thankfully the pub was only quarter full and peacefully quiet. Despite it being summer there was a certain coolness in the air today and a small but cheerful fire had been lit in the hearth. The logs spat and crackled and the flames reflected in the polished horse brasses tacked along the blackened oak lintel.

'I like to see it,' the plump woman behind the bar had said when Meredith had remarked on the cheery sight. 'Any old excuse, I light that fire.'

'Thanks,' said Meredith now, sipping her cider. 'Lovely.' She set it down. 'I must say I'm relieved at the result of the inquest on the body in the bothy. I thought they might accuse Emma.'

'Pathologist said she couldn't have struck such heavy blows. His skull was caved in and the shape of the indentations matched donkeys' hooves.'

Meredith shivered. 'Emma seems to be taking it well. A bit pale, but otherwise an altogether different child to the poor scared little scrap I found in the woods.'

'Children are remarkably resilient.' Markby studied the golden brown depths of his glass. 'But I'm not convinced that she's feeling as chipper as she makes out. She doesn't talk about it. That's bad. She ought to get it out of her system, not bottle it up. I suspect she may be brooding over it. I know I oughtn't to criticise Laura and Paul and I don't mean they aren't devoted parents, but they occasionally seem to me to take a superficial view. This will mean a lasting change in their attitude, but paradoxically that's also worrying. I used to think they allowed Emma too much freedom. Now I'm afraid they'll go to the other extreme and be frightened to let her out of their sight.

'It's going to make a big difference to Vicky when she's a little older. She'll never be allowed to roam as Emma was before this happened and whilst there's a plus in that, taken to extremes, there's also a minus. Over-protectiveness is also bad. Both Paul and Laura are having trouble coming to terms with it all. They feel guilty. They say they ought

211

to have known she'd left the house that night; Paul should have inquired more deeply about the missing food from the family larder; they should have realised how upset she was about the donkey.'

'All that's being wise after the event, surely? They couldn't be expected to know she'd try and kidnap the animal.'

'Try telling them that. Outwardly Emma herself seems more worried about Maud's fate than anything else. I was very relieved no recommendation was made for the animal's destruction. It was touch and go but there's a lot of public support for Maud at the moment. She's quite a heroine and you know how the British public is about animals.'

'I would have objected vigorously if it had! Maud led me to Emma! She's not a friendly animal, granted, but she's not vicious. Both Zoë and that nice Scots vet swore to that and normally the public doesn't come in contact with the animal anyway, only Zoë does.'

'More to the point,' Markby observed, stretching out his legs to the crackling logs in the hearth, 'in the confined space of that bothy, with Emma struggling and in almost total darkness, it would seem likely the donkey kicked out and sent him sprawling. The following kicks must have caught the fellow's head.'

'Good luck in my book. I don't feel the slightest bit sorry for him!' said Meredith sturdily.

'Ever done jury service?'

'No.'

'If and when you do, the defence will be worried! The man was sick. He had a long history of mental illness. Blame a society which leaves such people wandering about the countryside. And we can't say for sure he would have harmed her, remember that. That's speaking as a fair-minded man. As Emma's uncle, naturally, I feel the way you do – rather him than Emma.'

'There is one positive result of all this,' said Meredith dreamily. 'It took Eric down to the stables to see Zoë for himself and if you want to know my opinion, I think Eric's developed a *tendresse* in that direction!'

'Surely not?' Markby looked doubtful. 'I can't imagine Eric falling for a girl perfumed by a delicate aura of midden.'

'He has, I tell you! He said she was a remarkable businesswoman.'

'Ah, well, that's hardly romantic . . .'

'It was the way he said it, all glassy-eyed and awestruck.'

'You,' said Markby firmly, 'are exaggerating.'

'Only a bit.'

They fell silent while he turned over this new idea. 'He must be my age,' said Markby at last.

'Hey! Whenever has that had anything to do with it?'

'Nothing,' he apologised. 'And I admit I was secretly cheered the other day when Zoë declared Grimsby not to be "that old" at forty-five! Contrary to young Harding's view! But if you're right about this, it's going to cause a problem, and I don't like the idea. Not that Eric isn't free to dally where he wishes! But I've got enough to worry about already and I rather fancy Harding is carrying the torch for Zoë. He isn't going to take kindly to being cut out. He's known her a lot longer than Eric has and he regularly proves his devotion by shovelling muck at the Horses' Home. He won't readily accept being displaced by someone who is, after all, the sworn enemy both of the Rest Home and of the history society!'

He sipped his beer. 'Of course, the fact that both these

gentlemen fancy the same girl doesn't mean she feels the same way about either of them. I wouldn't have thought myself that she ever thinks about anything except horses and donkeys.'

'Eric,' said Meredith firmly, 'is a very attractive man. He's good-looking, athletic, rich, capable, successful, just a nice touch of a foreign accent and he's used to getting what he wants.'

'You're not falling for him, are you?' Markby asked, alarmed.

'Of course I'm not! But see it from Zoë's point of view. In a straight contest that youth with the motorbike doesn't stand a chance. As for his long service mucking out the stables and old friendship, well, that can go on too long, you know. Probably Zoë no longer thinks of him as anything but a friend.'

'And our friendship, has that gone on too long?' Markby asked evenly.

She flushed. 'That's different.'

'Only I don't fancy playing Harding's role and if at any time an Eric surfaces on your emotional horizon, I'd rather know so I can retire gracefully.'

'You don't have to take it personally!' she said crossly. 'I'm talking about Eric and Zoë and Robin. It's a classic eternal triangle, that's all.' She saw his face and added in mock exasperation, 'I haven't got an Eric hidden somewhere!'

'That's all right, then.' The fire crackled and a few more people came into the pub, their voices loud and jolly. 'I suppose,' Markby said tentatively, 'you wouldn't like to visit the Alice Batt Rest Home and chat up young Zoë? I'm sure she'd like a visitor, especially if you put a fiver in the collecting tin. She might, um, unburden herself, woman to woman.'

'What makes you think women do that?'

'They do,' said Markby grimly. 'They tell each other things while powdering their noses that a man wouldn't dream of telling anyone in the most secure surroundings.'

'That's an old-fashioned and sexist remark and unless you're given to snooping with your ear to the door of the ladies' powder room, which I hope not, you can't possibly know! I would quite like to see the Horses' Home, however. I might go out there. I might just talk to Zoë. I'll see what I can do.' She paused. 'Actually you are right about it being surprising that Eric is smitten. I wouldn't have thought Zoë was Eric's type, either. I'd have thought he'd go for someone more like, well – more like Ellen Bryant, I suppose.'

'It had crossed my mind,' Markby said.

'Alan, when I rang you up the other morning, when Emma was missing—'

'Oh yes!' He set down his glass. 'What were you ringing about so early? I'm sorry, what with Emma and everything else I've not got round to asking you.'

'It was because I was thinking of having a word with you about Denis Fulton. This is a bit embarrassing. I didn't know whether to tell you about it or not and then I thought that if you saw Victor Merle again he might tell you and – I'll begin again!' she said hurriedly, observing the expression on his face. 'I had dinner with the Fultons in London.'

'Very nice. But I already have their statements. Was something said which ought to be added to the file?'

'There was a bit of a scene. Denis accused Victor of seeing his wife. All nonsense, I'm sure. Victor denied it and so did Leah and Denis had obviously got hold of the wrong end of the stick. But it didn't stop him creating havoc. He'd had a few drinks too many, as well.'

'But where's the connection with what's been going on here? I assume there is one or you wouldn't be so keen for me to know this.'

'Denis grabbed a dagger from a wall display and went for Victor. Not very efficiently, I ought to add, but if he'd connected he'd have done Victor serious harm. I grabbed a swagger stick off another display and knocked the knife out of his hand.'

'I see,' Markby said thoughtfully.

'Only Victor made a sort of remark afterwards, outside on the steps. About Denis grabbing a knife under stress and wondering if he'd done it before. I wasn't going to tell you because I think myself Denis was just drunk. But then I thought perhaps you ought to know, seeing how Ellen died. And Victor might see fit to tell you and make it sound worse than it was. I don't care for Victor much. I think he might have a malicious streak and when we parted that night outside the Fultons' house, foolish though it may seem, I found him a little scary. He wore a cloak, if you please, and looked both dramatic and distinctly odd. Theatrical, you'd probably call it and you'd be right. But the whole episode of Denis with the knife was a silly bit of theatricals. I don't suppose Denis could harm a fly intentionally and I'm pretty sure that he's wrong about Merle seeing his wife. But when a person is tiddly and has got a bee in his bonnet that kind of thing can turn nasty. I don't think he'd have done it sober.'

'You're right to tell me about it. I'll bear it in mind – and not make more of it than it is. It was probably a one-off. But knives are knives.'

He didn't seem disposed to discuss this further and

Meredith eventually asked, 'About Zoë. Do you want me to chat up Eric too?'

'No!' Markby said firmly, 'I'll do that!'

Chapter Sixteen

In fact far from visiting Zoë the next day, Meredith, feeling in need of a break, set out for Oxford. She had begun to collect early crime imprints and it seemed a pity, being within reasonable driving distance, not to take the opportunity to look around the city's bookshops. But it seemed that even if she wanted to, she couldn't avoid Zoë Foster. For, wandering by chance into a charity shop, her eye fell at once on Zoë in inevitable jeans, trainers and battered Barbour, riffling despondently through a clothes' rack.

'Hullo,' said Meredith, surprised. 'Do you remember me?'

Zoë started and spun guiltily to face her, putting her back to the clothes as if to dissociate herself from them. Red-faced she mumbled, 'How could I forget—'

'I like these shops,' said Meredith quickly. 'I often come in.'

Zoë looked at her doubtfully. 'Not for clothes?'

'No, mostly for second-hand books.'

The girl appeared to make a decision. 'I – I was looking at these things.' She indicated the rack behind her. 'I haven't got a lot of money for clothes, new clothes. Sometimes on these racks you can find quite good labels and they only cost a pound or two. I don't, um, wear much except jeans and sweaters and if I have to go out somewhere, it's a bit embarrassing because I never have anything.'

'Oh, going somewhere nice?' enquired Meredith.

Zoë turned redder. 'I don't know. I haven't made up my mind.' She fiddled with the racked clothes. 'Can I ask you, do you think you'd know if I turned up wearing something I'd bought here?'

'If I didn't know you'd bought it here and it was a good label and in good nick, why should I?' Meredith returned simply.

Zoë looked relieved. 'Only I was thinking he'd guess and I'd be so embarrassed, I think I'd just sink through the floor.'

'He?' Meredith picked out a tan and white striped two-piece. 'This would suit you.'

'Yes, I've already looked at that.' Zoë fingered the material. 'That is an awfully good label, isn't it? I wonder how it got here?'

'Someone bought it for a special occasion and didn't get the chance to wear it again, or got too fat. Who knows? It wants a decent press but otherwise it's in very good condition. I'd be surprised if it has been worn half a dozen times.'

Zoë held the two-piece up against her and regarded her reflection in the mirror provided. 'Mr Schuhmacher's invited me to lunch at the hotel,' she said bluntly.

'Oh? That will be nice. He's got a marvellous chef.'

'I don't know much about food, that kind of food, and not a thing about wine. I'm really in two minds about accepting. The thing is, he says he might have some ideas about the Rest Home. He wants us to leave our present site, but he's got some idea about what we might do. I feel I ought to go and listen to him. After all, he might have the answer, although if it costs any money it won't be any use to us no matter how good an idea it is.'

Zoë sighed. 'I do feel a bit awkward about going,' she went on, 'because apart from anything else, the historical society wouldn't understand my breaking bread with our enemy.'

'Not their problem, the Horses' Rest Home, is it?' said Meredith firmly. 'I'd go and see Eric, if I were you.'

'But you're not me,' said Zoë dolefully. 'You're very capable and smart and you know how to sit and eat the kind of meal I'll get put in front of me and make intelligent remarks. I only know about animals and if I drink wine I fall asleep.'

'Eric's not an ogre, you know,' said Meredith gently.

'No, he's not, is he? I thought he was until I met him.'

'Then go along to his lunch. Jaw-jaw is better than war-war, as they say.'

'Yes, I will!' Zoë brightened. 'Meredith, would you mind waiting while I try this on and give me your opinion?'

'It looks fine, perfect fit,' said Meredith when Zoë emerged a few minutes later from the cubicle. 'You need some high heels.'

'I've got a black pair, very old but I can polish them up. They are leather – they were quite good ones when new.'

'Get yourself a pair of tights. Turning up with no stockings isn't really a good idea. The suit needs brightening up. Got any jewellery?'

Zoë hadn't, but the shop provided a chunky turquoise necklace for a pound and, a real bonus, a black clutch purse for the same price.

'I know the society isn't going to like this,' said Zoë again when they emerged from the shop. 'It is only a business lunch, after all, but people can be funny. Charles Grimsby made an awful fuss at the last meeting because he'd seen

Robin lunching with Ellen a few times and it was all about nothing. But Robin was very angry.' She paused. 'Robin won't like my lunching with Mr Schuhmacher either. They had a – a disagreement when Schuhmacher came to the Home.'

'So don't tell him.'

'He'll find out,' said Zoë sapiently. 'People always find out the things you don't want them to know, don't they?'

'As far as business is concerned, the murder is proving a nine-day wonder,' said Eric, refilling Markby's glass. 'You said it would be so, and you were right. I was very worried about the effect on trade, as I told you the last time you were here. But I'm glad to say other things have hit the headlines and people forget, as you knew they would.'

'Yes, people forget,' said Markby thoughtfully.

'I am pleased you could come,' Schuhmacher said suddenly, leaning across the table. 'And I'm sorry Miss Mitchell cannot be with us.'

'So is she, but she wanted to go into Oxford to look around the bookshops. She's started collecting early editions of paperback crime novels. You know how it is with collectors!'

They had lunched well and Markby had that sense of well-being and rosy glow that comes from good food, wine, company and pleasant surroundings. 'It was very good of you to invite me.'

'Well, when you rang to see how we were getting on, it seemed only polite to offer you a decent meal, the more so because on the last occasion you didn't, as I recall, get any dinner!

'But enough of that!' Eric dismissed all matters pertaining to the murder. 'My dear friend, I wish to discuss something of a personal nature. I have a great respect for your opinion. I am sure you will tell me the truth. A pity Miss Mitchell is not here to add a woman's viewpoint. However, you are a man who has seen much of human ways so I believe you will not be shocked, at any rate.'

Markby contrived to appear outwardly both bland and encouraging but inwardly he was full of surprise mixed with trepidation. Meredith was right!

'I have now made the acquaintance of Miss Foster who runs the Horses' Home,' Eric was saying. He was displaying unusually fidgety behaviour, realigning all the flowers in the table vase with scant regard to how the finished arrangement looked. 'Previously all our business had been conducted through third parties. When the child – your niece, of course. I am so very glad she was found. The fellow in the woods, the body, he is identified?'

He made this sudden sideways swoop in the direction of the conversation with a kind of intensity which suggested he was grateful for an excuse to abandon his original line of speech.

'Yes – he turned up in the computer with a string of sex convictions.'

'Then he was certainly no loss.' Eric paused to glower at the mangled flowers. 'Sex turns up all the time in life, doesn't it?'

'Er – yes,' Markby agreed cautiously.

Eric gave himself a little shake. 'As I was saying, when the child and donkey disappeared, I called at the sanctuary to express my regret. She showed me round. I never saw such dreadful animals and she's devoted to them! I found her charming, not merely pretty but glowing with enthusiasm! She had mud on the end of her nose,' added Eric regretfully. 'I offered her my handkerchief which she refused and I hadn't the courage to wipe it away myself.'

Markby struggled to suppress his reactions. He wished desperately Meredith were there. Eric, in this men's *tête-à-tête*, showed signs of going completely overboard. Silently he took back everything he'd said to Meredith about women chatting in the powder room! What the dickens was Schuhmacher going to say next?

'She is in fact a remarkable young woman,' Eric declared. 'And really most attractive – or she would be if it were not for the jeans and wellington boots. And the awful haircut. Really, one longs . . .' He fell silent. An absent expression entered his eyes. His fingers toyed with one of the martyred blooms in the vase.

'To do a Pygmalion?' Markby said with a smile.

'Exactly!' Eric came to. 'Take her to a good hairdresser, dress her in some decent clothes – a skirt! I fear this sounds quite disreputable on my part. I sound like some old roué of the Third Empire scouting around the streets of Paris for an innocent girl to establish. I don't mean it so.' He fixed Markby with an earnest gaze. 'I have no dishonourable intentions.'

'Good Lord, Eric, I never thought you did! You like her. That's not a crime.'

'Yes, I – did, do! But she is, I gather, only twenty-four. I am forty-four. It is a big difference in age, do you think?' Schuhmacher looked wistful.

'Nonsense. She is a most mature and capable young woman.' Markby wondered guiltily if he ought to sound encouraging or not.

'Yes, yes!' Eric, somewhat disconcerting his guest, leaned forward and seized his sleeve. 'I have never married, you know. I have always been too busy, always on the move. It is difficult. When I was young I first began in the hotel business because my family was in it. Then I turned out to have some sporting ability so I had a career in sport and then, when that finished, I returned to the hotel business. I have never had time to settle down. Of course in the past there have been occasions when I, you know, especially when I was a sportsman . . . you understand?'

'Yes, yes, quite!' said Markby hurriedly, disengaging himself.

'But never seriously. Now, at forty-four, I do not wish to make myself ridiculous.'

'You won't. Why should you?'

'There is a younger man. Why should she not prefer him?'

'Why not ask her?'

'Hah!' said Eric grimly. He signalled to his head waiter. 'A brandy? I have a special bottle, set aside for me. I bought it at auction some time ago. Very rare. You have been married, I think, Alan?'

'Yes,' said Markby gloomily. He shook himself. 'But don't let me put you off. Every marriage is different. Mine didn't work out, but that doesn't mean a thing.'

'You will marry Miss Mitchell one day?'

'That's undecided. I mean, I'm decided, she isn't.'

'Modern women,' said Eric sadly. 'Perhaps Miss Foster also would not wish to give up her independence.'

Markby, recalling Zoë's rusting trailer, glanced round the sumptuous dining room. One could be tempted to be cynical. But, on the other hand, he was fairly sure this kind of affluence really wouldn't cut much ice with Zoë Foster. She'd see it as money wasted. Money which should be spent on old horses.

'She's rather keen on those old animals, Eric. Whatever she did, she wouldn't abandon them. Any, er, plan would have to take into account her dedication to the Rest Home.'

'One of the small ponies attempted to bite me.'

'They all bite, as far as I can tell. Although my niece tells me it's generally because they've suffered at the hands of men. They don't bite her.'

'Suffered at the hands of men,' Eric repeated. 'And do you think Miss Foster shares this mistrust of men?'

'How,' demanded Markby in some exasperation, 'should I know? If you want to find out, you'll have to – to make your own inquiries!'

'Yes.' Eric sat back as the brandy arrived. 'I have invited her to lunch. She has said she'll come. Perhaps I have made a terrible mistake. She will be insulted.'

Markby, nursing the glass of tawny liquid and letting the aroma fill his nostrils, said slowly, 'Some things aren't found often, Eric. Like this fine old brandy. When you find them it's a mistake to pass them up. At least put in a bid.'

Margery Collins let herself into the shop, closed the door behind her and stood still, letting her gaze wander around the shelves and racks, the bright stacks of wool, the array of tapestry canvases, the little trays full of rainbow-hued cotton reels. It was all hers now. She owned Needles.

She had never owned anything substantial in her life before. She'd been brought up by an aunt. Since the age of eighteen she had lived in a rented room in a large house divided into a warren of lettings. She shared a couple of gas burners on the landing with two other people by way of a kitchen, and the bathroom with the whole house. She'd always hated it there, but now she needn't live there any longer.

Margery raised her eyes to the ceiling. She would live upstairs in Ellen's flat and come down every morning to open up the shop, her shop, just as Ellen had done. That was what Ellen had wanted. Mrs Danby had been right. Ellen had wanted Margery to have Needles, the flat, everything, because Margery would understand and appreciate it, and carry on where Ellen had left off. And the everything included Ellen's secret.

Margery knew now what it was. But she would keep it safe, just as Ellen had known she would. That was why Ellen had entrusted everything to her. Margery would look after it and preserve it as Ellen wanted, running Needles according to Ellen's business ideals, keeping the flat nice – and the secret safe.

At first Margery hadn't liked going upstairs to the flat. It had seemed cold and eerie. Sitting there with Mr Markby going over the books she had felt like the worst kind of intruder.

But no longer. Not since she knew the secret. Now she felt a kind of partnership with Ellen. That was it, a partnership. Ellen had done more than just leave her Needles, she'd made her a partner.

Margery tossed back her hair and set off briskly towards the staircase leading up to the flat above. As she climbed it she was busily making plans. Mrs Danby foresaw no problems with the will and when probate came through, Margery would be free to re-open Needles. She'd have to get herself properly organised first. She had already given notice to the landlord that she would be leaving the miserable cramped room at the end of the month. But there was no reason why she shouldn't leave before. It was only a question of clearing the flat of Ellen's things and moving in her own few possessions.

She would keep Ellen's furniture, china and kitchen utensils. She might even keep one or two of Ellen's suits and dresses, because Ellen had bought some beautiful clothes recently. Not worn them, just bought them and hung them in the wardrobe. She'd shown them to Margery and Margery had understood. It wasn't necessary to wear these beautiful things, just to own them was enough. Just to be able to take them from their hangers and smooth the silky material, holding the garments up against you and parade before the mirror. Of course Margery wasn't Ellen and hadn't Ellen's looks, but in such nice clothes anyone, even Margery, would look better.

All this was probably sinful, thought Margery with a start of guilt. Vanity. But she would wear the dresses, put them to good practical use, and not just keep them to gloat over. And what she didn't keep she'd take along to Oxfam. That couldn't be sinful.

Feeling quite a buzz of anticipation Margery put the key to the door at the head of the stairs. To her surprise, without her turning the key and as soon as she touched the lock, the door swung open.

She hesitated, puzzled and feeling a twinge of alarm. She had locked it behind her the last time, she was sure. Had the police been back?

Margery hurried into the flat and stopped with a gasp of dismay.

Everything lay strewn about in unimaginable confusion. Drawers had been tipped out on the floor and their contents scattered far and wide. The desk had been forced open, the wood around the lock splintered, the pigeonholes gaping empty. Books had been tumbled from their case, the records taken from their sleeves. The chair seats had been wrenched out and the carpet rolled back.

She ran into the bedroom. The same confusion. The mattress taken from the bed and left propped against a wall. All the clothes, both workaday and the beautiful new designer labels, had been pulled from the wardrobe and tossed down like so many worthless rags, defiled. Margery gazed at them in horror, knowing she would never be able to wear them now.

In the kitchen spilled lentils and beans crunched under her feet. A strong aroma of coffee filled the air from the sink, into which had been tipped the contents of a Nescafé jar in a pyramid of brown powder. The empty glass jar rolled away across the floor as her foot struck against it.

Had the police done this awful thing? No.

Margery's hand automatically touched her shoulder bag. He'd done it. He'd been here. He wanted this, Ellen's secret, which lay in Margery's bag, burning a hole in it, shrieking out its presence and the danger having it meant to her. She was in no doubt.

He had searched, in increasing desperation. He had failed to find it and if he thought about it, he would realise where it was, who had it, and where he had to go for it. Even now he could be lurking in a doorway opposite the shop, having waited for her to return. He could be crossing the road, climbing the stair, creeping up behind her, his hands outstretched . . .

She gave a little shriek and ran back to the living room and the telephone. With trembling fingers and her frightened eyes fixed on the door to the flat, she dialled 999. Terror was in her heart and the sure certainty that he would find her.

She stuttered, 'P-police, p-please . . . ! Oh, do come quickly!'

After all, he had already killed Ellen for her secret, hadn't he?

Chapter Seventeen

'Eric's got it bad,' said Markby into the phone. 'You were right.'

'You needn't sound so surprised,' came Meredith's voice tinnily. 'I did warn you.'

'Surprised? I'm shell-shocked. To tell you the truth, it was embarrassing. Oh yes, very funny. You may laugh but you haven't spent the last hour listening to Eric's semi-erotic ramblings. It's in no way a joke! He is very serious about it and he's not a green youngster. He's forty-four. What's he going to do if she turns him down? He'll probably go into terminal decline.'

'Now who's exaggerating? You can't do anything about it, Alan. It's up to Eric to plead his suit.'

'He will. He's invited her to lunch. Lured her in with a ploy about discussing the fate of the old nags' home. If she rejects him, he'll be devastated and if she accepts him, young Harding will have to bite the bullet. Both possibilities make me extremely uneasy.'

'Eric didn't like Robin. A rival, I suppose. I know Zoë's going to lunch with Eric. I met her in town and she told me. Poor kid, she wants to make a good impression and she hasn't a penny to spend on herself. She buys her clothes in charity shops.'

'Don't worry, if she accepts Eric he'll load her down with Paris fashions.'

'She wouldn't want that. That's the trouble, I suppose. I really believe the animals will always mean more to her than any mere human relationship. Clothes are a bit of a nuisance in her view. If you can't muck out horses wearing it, a garment is useless. And you can't really shovel manure wearing Saint-Laurent, can you?'

'She's not a kid exactly, she's twenty-four and self-supporting. Perhaps she just hasn't had the chance to spend money on herself? Given the serious opportunity, she might surprise us all!' returned Markby, sounding hard-bitten and then destroying it by demanding helplessly, 'But what on earth was I supposed to say to Eric?'

He sighed when Meredith failed to respond. 'It was such a change to hear him talking about something other than the hotel business and the damage done to his investment by the murder! He's dismissed all that to second place now. Eric's a person who gives one hundred and ten per cent effort to whatever is claiming his attention. He must have been a terrifying ice-hockey player. Utterly ruthless! Then it was hotels; now it's love. But he still works by the tactics of the ice-rink. He is a tactician, Eric, but a bruiser, too. No wonder I'm worried and not least because I know I encouraged him. You see the one thing Eric doesn't know how to do is how to accept defeat.'

There was still silence from the other end of the telephone line. 'Are you still there?' Markby asked. 'How was Oxford, find any books?'

'None that I could afford and none exactly what I wanted but it was fun looking. Did you see the Fultons while you were lunching with Eric?'

'No, now you mention it. Perhaps they've gone home.'

'I doubt it, not without saying goodbye. Anyway, they're supposed to be staying to support Eric in his hour of need, besides make up their recent rift, I mean the rift between Denis and Leah.'

'From all you've told me, Denis is the last person to offer advice to Eric in his present state. I just hope Eric's got all the knives locked away!'

'Now that really isn't funny!' said Meredith.

Nor was it, Markby agreed silently as he hung up. But it wasn't helpful, nor did he have the time to brood over Eric's problem-strewn lovelife. He dismissed it firmly from his mind. He had problems of his own and the last thing he needed was anything further distracting him from tracking down Ellen's killer. He set out briskly on foot for Bamford police station, mulling over the murder as he went.

The way things stood, almost anyone who was at Springwood Hall on the day of the gala opening could have done it. To drive in a knife is the action of a few seconds. The letter found in Ellen's flat indicated careful pre-planning, a victim lured by pre-arrangement to her death. The murderer knew exactly where to go to find Ellen and at what time of day. Hence the necessary time for the murder was pared down to the smallest possible turn-round. Into the cellars, plunge in the knife, out again. Neat.

In the general milling about both among the uninvited sightseers and the invited guests as they circulated on the lawn, continually changing position and conversation partners, occasionally getting mixed up with the crowd or popping into the house for a variety of reasons, no one could be ruled out. A few minutes' absence wouldn't have been noticed or, if it had, been thought significant.

The only person he could rule out, thought Markby with a wry grin, was Hope Mapple, since she had had nowhere to hide a knife. But that pre-supposed the murderer carried the knife to the rendez-vous in the cellar. Suppose the knife had been abstracted from the busy kitchens earlier and hidden in the cellars? All the invited guests had been on the tour of the hotel which included both kitchens and cellars. The chef, Richter, and kitchen staff had all been in the kitchens and in sight of one another at the time the murder had taken place. Yes, the knife had been taken earlier.

But if this line of reasoning pointed towards one of the celebrities, then the concentration of attention on those same celebrities meant that hardly anyone was taking notice of what any one person in the rest of the crowd was doing. And as soon as Hope started running, of course, all eyes were on her.

'Exactly!' muttered Markby as he pushed open the station doors. 'So did the murderer know that Hope intended to streak, and approximately at what time, and make corresponding arrangements?'

Or, on the other hand, what about the victim, Ellen? She had certainly known of Hope's plan. Had she sent a message to her killer-to-be, indicating the moment when all eyes would be turned to the streaker so that she and her murderer could meet undisturbed?

It was with this uncomfortable mind-picture, of Ellen writing to indicate the cellars as a meeting place and thereby setting her signature to her own death warrant, that he stepped into the reception area.

There was no one at the desk. But voices could be heard from the office area to the rear of it. Above them all came that of Wpc Jones.

'Come on, don't be stingy. We want to get him something decent!'

Markby's heart sank. The murder and Emma's disappearance had combined to thrust from his mind the problem of his impending promotion and the desk-bound glory which awaited him. As he had feared, somehow the word had got out.

A face appeared briefly round a corner and vanished again. A scurry and much whispering. Jones, red-faced, reappeared.

'Good afternoon, sir. We've been trying to contact you.'

'Oh yes?' said Markby sourly.

From somewhere unseen behind Jones came a crash and the sound of coins rolling across the floor. Someone swore. Another person hissed, 'Shut up!' Scrabbling fingers and scraping chairs conjured up a picture of frantic crawling around to retrieve the money.

Wpc Jones looked bland but something in her eye defied him to ask any questions or make any comment on the noises.

'Sergeant Pearce was called out and left a note.' Jones reached out a piece of paper. 'Miss Collins phoned 999 and the sergeant thought he'd better go straight away.'

Markby snatched the note, scanned it briefly, swore and ordered, 'Get me a car and driver! My car's at home, dammit! Go on, snappy!'

'Yes, sir!' said Jones, giving him a look which indicated if he went on like this, his leaving present was likely to be very modest indeed.

Markby ran up the stairs to the flat above the shop two at a time and burst in. As the door flew open, he spied Margery Collins sitting on a chair shakily sipping tea and Pearce, notebook in hand, attempting to take a statement.

At his sudden appearance Margery squeaked shrilly and spilled tea and Pearce spun round. Then he put his notebook away and said with relief, 'There you are, sir! I tried to raise you on your car radio.'

'I was on the phone at home.' Markby's gaze raked the disordered room.

'I tried there afterwards.'

'Then I'd just left – for crying out loud!' Markby threw out a hand to indicate the disarray all around them. 'What the dickens has been going on here?'

'Miss Collins came and found it like this, sir. She's, ah, very upset as you can see.' Pearce rolled his eyes towards Margery.

'I'm scared!' whispered Margery, fixing them both with her saucer-like eyes.

'Yes, yes, very unpleasant but you're all right now!' said Markby rather brusquely.

'He's been everywhere, in the kitchen, in the bedroom – he took out all of Ellen's lovely new clothes and just threw them down on the bed! He's broken the lock of her desk. That's a valuable desk, she told me. It's an antique!'

'Ah yes, well, you might be able to claim on the insurance. Get Mrs Danby on to that. They may or may not pay up now Ellen's dead. Don't see why they shouldn't.' Markby drew Pearce to one side. 'Any idea who? And how did they get in?'

'I can answer the second bit,' said Pearce. 'There's a window forced downstairs at the back. It leads into a storeroom and from there into the back passage leading to the shop.'

'Get it fingerprinted. Any hope of footprints?'

'Yessir, fingerprint chap is on his way. No footprints,

outside area under the window is all concrete.'

'Anyone see suspicious characters hanging about?'

'Haven't had a chance to ask around yet, but sir—'
Pearce glanced meaningly at Margery again. 'Something's
odd. She keeps saying "he" as if she knew who it was and
when I got here she was in a real old state. She'd barricaded
herself in and it was five minutes before she'd open the door
to me! She's terrified, not just scared. I think she does know,
or thinks she knows, who did this. The trouble is, what with
being frightened and shocked and I don't know what else,
she doesn't make a whole lot of sense. I think we'll have
to get a statement later. One minute she's rabbiting about
the clothes from the wardrobe and the next about Ellen trusting her and keeping faith – and then she says she's in
danger.'

Markby stared thoughtfully at Margery who was blowing
her nose.

'Okay, I'll have a word. Chase up the fingerprint chap
and then go and have a word with the shops either side.
Whoever did this might have made quite a bit of noise
moving the furniture and so on.'

He walked over to Margery, pulled out a chair and sat
down. 'Well, now, Miss Collins,' he said cheerily, hoping
she'd relax. 'Feeling a bit better?'

Unfortunately he'd asked the wrong question.

'No!' said Margery fiercely. She set down the cup and
stuffed the bunch of tissues in her fist into her bag. 'It's
awful!'

'It sometimes happens after a serious crime or an adver-
tised death. Some joker reads about it in the local paper
and thinks he'll break in while the place is unoccupied and
see what he can find.'

He was watching her closely as he spoke and saw that,

if anything, her manifest terror had increased. She was slowly shaking her head, contradicting his words. She knows a lot more than she's told us so far! he thought with some satisfaction. Now it'd led to this she didn't know what to do, whether to speak up and ask for their help or run the risk of staying silent.

Encouragingly he asked, 'Have you had a chance to check yet and see if anything is missing?'

She reddened, swallowed and muttered, 'Don't need to.'

'What's that?'

'Don't – don't have to check. I know, I know what he wanted.'

'And who is he, Miss Collins?'

She was scrabbling in her handbag, he supposed for a fresh supply of tissues. Suddenly she stopped and looked up, more mouse-like than ever, her pointed nose trembling. 'It was because Ellen trusted me, Mr Markby!'

'That she left you the business? Yes, I dare say it was.'

'No – yes! Not just the business!' Margery glanced about them in a hunted way. 'I keep feeling as if she were here and could hear us, see us. I know she trusted me. She thought I wouldn't tell.'

'Wouldn't tell what, Margery? Is this something we should have known all along?'

'No, not all along because I didn't know it all along. I only knew it the other day! Look, Mr Markby, when we were looking over the books – I didn't understand it, honestly, not then. Because I didn't know about the other thing then. But since then I've been thinking . . . Ellen was – was doing something she shouldn't, wasn't she?' She fixed him with apprehensive eyes.

'Possibly. We don't know. Someone is currently looking

them over who knows more about that sort of thing than I do. There does appear to be unexplained money paid into the bank through the business. There may be a simple explanation.'

He felt he could almost hear the wheels going round in her head. When she didn't reply he prompted, 'What is it you want to tell me, Margery? You'll feel much better when you have.'

'I suppose so. You see, it's like I said. Ellen trusted me. That's why she left everything, not just Needles, but all her affairs, papers, that sort of thing, to me. She thought I'd be discreet. And so when the bank gave me her safe deposit box and I opened it, I really wouldn't have told anyone what it contained if – if this hadn't happened.' She gestured at the room with her free hand, the other still rummaging in her purse.

'But this means that he knows about it, that I've probably got it because he couldn't find it here.'

'Who is he and what is the thing he wants, Margery?' Markby asked with suppressed impatience.

'You won't be angry? I didn't mean to cause any trouble. I thought it wasn't necessary – that it wouldn't hurt to keep it – to protect Ellen's reputation. It's – I've got it here.'

She withdrew not the expected bunch of tissues, but a stiff folded sheet of paper from her bag and handed it over with a shaking hand.

Markby took it and unfolded it. She watched his face, holding her breath. He refolded the paper and put it in his pocket.

'Okay, Margery, now listen to me. You've done the right thing in handing this to us. You are quite safe and no one is going to hurt you. But you are an important witness so I think perhaps you shouldn't go back to your rented room. Apart from anything else, I think you'll feel more at ease if you stay somewhere else. Have you a friend you could go to for a few days?'

She shook her head and he tried again, 'How about someone from your church?'

'I don't want them to know! I don't want them asking me questions!' She was becoming agitated again.

'All right, all right!' he soothed her. 'Then this is what we'll do. I'll take you to a hotel, we'll try The Crossed Keys. We'll book you a room and you stay put in it. A woman police officer will go to your own place and pack a few things for you, an overnight bag. You can have your meals sent up to your room and we'll keep in touch. You will be quite safe. We'll explain to The Crossed Keys that no one is to be given any information about you or allowed to go up to your room. This is all just a precaution because I don't think he'll harm you. But he is probably frightened himself and he might come and ask you for this—' Markby held up the folded sheet of paper. 'Or he might just try and find out if you do have it.'

'Aren't you going to arrest him?' cried Margery desperately.

'Well, we may. But not just yet. Evidence is a funny old thing, Margery, and unless we find his fingerprints here we can't even prove he was the one who broke in.'

'But that —'

'Now leave it all to us. All right?'

An hour later Margery was safely established in The Crossed Keys and Wpc Jones dispatched to get a coherent statement out of her and to then go to Margery's rented room and pack a bag for her. Markby and Pearce sat in Markby's office. Markby took the sheet of paper Ellen had given him out of his pocket and put it on his desk.

'Give you three guesses, Pearce.'

'Haven't a clue!' said Pearce, painfully and obviously eaten up with a burning desire to know.

'Come on. Official bit of paper. I've had one of these in my time and you haven't yet. You will. Come on, what do most of us do sooner or later? Give you a clue. What are the three occasions which get most of us into church in our lives even if we never ever set foot in there otherwise?'

'Baptised and buried,' said Pearce. He paused. 'Married?'

'Married, Pearce.' Markby held up the paper. 'A marriage certificate, twenty-one years old. An Australian marriage certificate showing the legal conjoining of Ellen Marie Novak and—'

He turned the sheet, holding it open and held up for Pearce to read.

'Cripes,' said Pearce. 'Denis Fulton!'

Chapter Eighteen

There was nothing so blatantly commercial and workaday as a reception counter at Springwood Hall. Instead a tall, slightly horsy female with ash blonde hair expertly cut in a shoulder-length bob, and turned out with understated elegance in Country Casuals, presided over the entrance lobby at a probably genuine antique walnut table. As Markby entered she rose to her feet and glided across the beautiful new carpet towards him with a welcoming smile and sharply assessing gaze.

'I'd like to see Mr Denis Fulton,' said Markby. 'Chief Inspector Markby.'

But she had recognised him now. The sharp look had gone and she had relaxed, her smile less professionally mechanical. She also looked less horsy and really very attractive. Markby realised he was doing his own summing up and mentally ticked himself off. As for policemen of any sort requesting to see a guest, she was well-trained. She didn't bat an eyelid. It might be the most normal thing in the world.

However, just to put the record straight, Markby added with a smile, 'We're acquainted. It's not an official visit.'

'Of course,' she said as if such a vulgar thought had never crossed her mind.

He wondered if she was shrewd enough to realise his disavowal was, in its way, a lie. Not completely so. For the time being he wanted to keep this informal and off the record. Denis was far more likely to cooperate in that way and Denis, after all, as far as anyone knew, hadn't done anything criminal.

Except a trifling matter of bigamy.

Markby thought about Leah Fulton. This was a very tricky situation. 'Is Mrs Fulton in?' he asked casually.

'Mr Fulton went across to the swimming pool, sir, about fifteen minutes ago. I haven't seen Mrs Fulton. Would you like me to ring up?' She stretched out a hand to a phone on the walnut table.

'No, no!' he said hastily. 'It's Mr Fulton I wanted to see.'

'Do you know the way to the swimming pool, sir?' She was all hovering solicitude.

'Yes, yes. I'll find him. Thanks.'

The interior of the building housing the swimming pool suggested a Kew Gardens greenhouse in the middle of which someone had chosen to sink a large rectangular lake. The temperature was tropical. All around the edge of the pool stood tubbed palms and banks of potted flowers lending an exotic jungle touch and spreading heady perfumes which disguised, though not completely, the faint odour of chlorine. Music, faint and pervasive, filtered through some unseen system. It was relaying the Birdcatcher's aria from the first act of *The Magic Flute* and the piece seemed entirely appropriate.

The pool itself was lined with turquoise tiles and clever subsurface lighting was designed to turn the swimmers into golden-limbed naiads disporting themselves in translucent Elysian waters. As it shimmered and rippled, distorting the square lines of the tiles on the bottom, the pool threw strange reflections on to the ceiling. Markby found this ethereal, topsy-turvy world strangely disorientating.

However its only occupant was distinctly unethereal: Denis, swimming slowly and determinedly up and down its length in the way of a man taking exercise because it was good for him and not because he was enjoying it particularly.

'Denis?' called Markby, dropping on to his heels at the top end of the surrounding tile border of the pool. His voice echoed cavernously in the empty chamber.

Denis splashed and briefly disappeared. He popped up again, red-faced and spitting water, and began to trawl back towards Markby. When he reached him he turned on his back and floated, paddling his hands and staring round-eyed up at his visitor in sea-otter fashion.

'Hullo, Alan!' he said unhappily.

'Glad of a word if you've got a moment. Is Leah about?'

'No – no, she's resting. I'll come out. Give me a minute.'

Denis doggy-paddled over to the steps and hauled himself out. He shook his plump body like a spaniel and padded off towards the changing rooms leaving a trail of wet footprints. Gazing after him, Markby judged there was no way Denis would try to make a run for it. He found himself a white-painted wooden recliner comfortably lined with thick turquoise blue cushions and settled down. He wished he had time for a swim.

Denis came back wearing a towelling bathrobe. His hair, ruffled by brisk rubbing, stood up on end. He took the chair next to Markby's and gave him a nervous smile.

'Know what I've come about?' asked Markby gently.

'No!' Denis jerked at the tie-belt of his bathrobe, almost cutting himself in half. 'Well, yes, I suppose I do!'

'You were wasting your time. It wasn't there and as a matter of fact, we have it.'

Denis's face was a picture of misery. He said, 'Will you tell Leah?'

'If she doesn't know, Denis, I think now is the time for you to tell her. I take it there was no divorce?'

Denis shook his head. 'The tabloids will get hold of it. It'll be the end of Leah. The scandal . . . All her friends knowing. I'll have made her look a fool. For God's sake, Alan, does it have to get out?'

'That rather depends on how much it has to do with Ellen's death.'

'Nothing!' Denis shouted and his voice echoed round the pool area like a yodeller's across a mountain pass. 'I didn't kill her, I swear!'

'Well, if it has nothing to do with it, then I'm not bothered but you will have to tell Leah and arrange a quiet remarriage. After all, you are free now. You're a widower.'

Denis's face crumpled. 'What makes you think Leah will agree to a remarriage? She'll leave me. She'll probably sue me. She'll hate my guts for doing this to her. I didn't mean it.'

'Want to tell me about it?'

The sound system was relaying a Lehar waltz, *Gold and Silver*. Denis threw himself back despondently on his recliner and began to speak, staring up at the patterns of light thrown across the ceiling by the softly surging water in the pool.

'It was years ago, more than twenty. I was in Australia researching a book. You see, a lot of people were starting to take holidays over there, visiting relatives and so on, about that time. I persuaded my publisher that a guide to eating out in the major Australian cities and a bit of other general guide-book stuff thrown in would be a good idea. They said go and do it, so I did.

'I wanted to cover the widest possible range of restaurants from the most pretentious to the humblest. I included ethnic restaurants and off-beat ones. I even took in a couple of "barbies". And I included, naturally, a chapter on vegetarian dining out. That's where I met Ellen. In a vegetarian diner.'

Denis sighed. He shifted in his recliner and folded his arms as if he were cold although the temperature in here could well have been turned down a degree or two in Markby's judgement. He took off his own jacket and hung it on the back of his chair while he waited for Denis to go on.

'It was one of those stupid things,' said Denis suddenly. 'She was a good looker, you know. Even later in these last years. But then she was a stunner. She was a dancer of sorts. Well, between you and me, she was a stripper.'

'Was she?' exclaimed Markby.

'Oh yes, but I didn't realise that. She made it sound quite, you know, upmarket, at least *corps de ballet* stuff. I suppose a fellow quicker on the uptake than I was would have sussed out the situation straight away. But I've – I've never been a ladies' man, far from it! I'm not good around women. I say the wrong things or nothing at all. I'm not good-looking. I'm not charming. I'm a bit of a lost cause. But Ellen seemed to like me. It was, as they say, a whirlwind romance. We got married after one week's acquaintance. You can call me an idiot if you like.'

He paused. Markby said in a curiously flat voice, 'No, you weren't the first man to fall head over heels in love at first sight.'

'I don't know if it was love. I was flattered. It was

lonely, eating on my own in all those restaurants, going back to empty hotel rooms to write up my notes. Actually we were both of us mistaken. It was a failure from the word go. Poor Ellen, she thought she was getting a wealthy English author. But although I've earned a fair bit over the years, I admit, I was never able to keep hold of any of it. Add to the absence of money the fact that she actually liked quite a different sort of bloke to me, all muscles and suntan, playing he-man sports. They breed 'em like that out there,' said Denis enviously.

Markby let his gaze roam across the pool and between the palm trees, out through the floor-length windows and across the lawns to Springwood Hall.

'We couldn't even eat out together,' said Denis sadly, 'because she wouldn't eat meat. She found it offensive. For her sake I tried the vegeburgers but they sent me scurrying to the lavatory, something to do with the make-up of my innards, I suppose. It was worse than a mistake, it was a ludicrous farce. We both realised it and we parted company. I came back to England and she, as I believed, stayed in Australia. By the way, I was told they make burgers out of kangaroos but I never had the courage to check that out.'

'Neither of you suggested a divorce to set the record straight?'

'No, well, to tell you the truth, I don't think either of us felt married, if you see what I mean. It lasted a few weeks, that's all. A sort of failed experiment, not a marriage. Anyhow, time went by. I put her out of my mind. It was an embarrassing memory but it was over and done. I met Leah. Again things moved fast and I found we were all set to get married before I'd had a chance to tell her about Ellen. And then I couldn't. I used to wake up at night cold with sweat and shaking at the thought of what I was about to do. Bigamy. I knew I ought to tell her. I ought to get in touch with Ellen and arrange a quick divorce. But there wasn't time. Leah and I were married and I thought, well, who's to know the truth? Ellen has probably forgotten me, probably got an Australian divorce by now and married someone else! She was on the other side of the world. We'd never be in contact again. But I was wrong.'

Denis swung his legs over the side of his recliner and put his head in his hands. 'She was in England. She'd been here several years and never bothered to get in touch with me. Then she saw a photo of Leah and me leaving the register office in one of the society news round-up columns newspapers run. She got in touch then. I never knew anyone could be so spiteful. I mean, why?' Denis turned puzzled eyes up to Markby. 'She was doing all right. She'd got that shop. She had enough money of her own. She didn't want me back. She'd never wanted me. Why put me through hell? Because that's what she did.'

'Blackmail, and you paid up. It's always a mistake,' Markby said.

'What did you expect me to do?' returned Denis fiercely. 'Tell Leah I was a bigamist, that I'd lied to her and tricked her? You know how it is, everyone does. Leah has all the money. A rich woman always has to be on the look-out for con-men and crooks like me.'

'Oh, come on, you're neither! Foolish, possibly. A con-man, no.'

'Try telling Leah that. Try telling her friends. Try telling the press! I'm done for, I tell you, if it gets out! And so is my marriage!' He gave Markby a haunted look. 'I love Leah. I really do. She means everything to me. I'll tell you something. Just now, before you came in, I was swimming up and down that pool all on my own and I thought, how about if I just went under the water and let myself drown? Put an end to it.'

'Don't talk like that. It wouldn't solve anything. There'd be an inquest and I'd have to produce the marriage certificate to show the reason for your state of mind.'

'You see,' said Denis wretchedly. 'No way out. No sodding way out. Not even death. It's not bloody fair.'

'Two questions, Denis.' There was no point in making reassuring statements. Denis was going to have to face Leah and nothing was going to make it easy. There was no point in telling the poor devil lies. 'First, you did break into Ellen's flat. Just confirm it.'

'Yes. I thought she might have it hidden there and as no one had yet moved in or cleared out the furniture, there was a chance. I searched everywhere. I didn't realise what a mess I'd made of the place until I'd done it and then I panicked and bolted. I realised Ellen had probably kept the certificate somewhere else, in a bank or with her solicitor.'

'Second question. Did you write to Ellen and ask her to meet you at Springwood Hall?'

'Meet me? I wanted her a thousand miles away! Of course I didn't ask her to meet me!'

'Mm. Right. Well, I'm going to have to ask you to stay around, Denis. Don't leave the area. All right?'

'All right,' said Denis. He gave Markby a beseeching look. 'Are you going to tell her?'

'Leah? That's your job. Do it straight away. I'll give you twenty-four hours and then I will have to tell her.'

'Not bloody fair . . .' repeated Denis.

Markby left him slumped disconsolately in the recliner.

It all sounded convincing enough, but he had met good liars before. Denis Fulton's story would need careful, meticulous checking.

'So do we believe him?' Pearce asked with brutal frankness when he had heard Markby's account of all this.

'I don't know. It sounded good. I think that's why I'm wary. I dislike things which sound too good, too sensible and reasonable. I find it hard to accept he didn't try to divorce his Australian wife twenty years ago when they broke up. I also find it hard to believe she didn't try to find and divorce him years ago, if only for the sake of any settlement. Is that why she came to England, do you think? With the intention of finding him and divorcing? If so, what changed her mind? He wasn't hard to find. His face appears on the nation's telly screens. His books are in the shops. He tells you in magazine articles how to prepare the dinner party of a lifetime.'

'She found another source of money?' suggested Pearce.

'Someone richer than Denis? Yes, and his name was probably Bryant. We'll never trace him now. She couldn't have married him because legally she was married to Fulton and she was too smart to risk bigamy even if he wasn't!'

'Perhaps she liked having an ace up her sleeve in the shape of her marriage to Fulton?' Pearce suggested, frowning. 'A chance of blackmail one day? She got it, too. She had a longish wait and she must have been a greedy woman. She was making good money out of that shop by that time.'

Markby was shaking his head. 'I don't believe money was her moving force. As I see it, Ellen at the time of her death was a successful but lonely woman. She had been a beauty but was now entering middle age. A brief far-off marriage had failed. If she'd had a liaison with Bryant, that had long gone too. She had no friends as we'd recognise them. Her fellow members of the historical society had formed alliances which didn't include her. Margery Collins was the nearest person to her and she was hardly a confidante! I think Denis has it right when he says Ellen just didn't care about him enough to bother with a divorce. But then, one day, all that changed! Ellen opened her newspaper and there was Denis, middle-aged, portly, balding – and remarried. Remarried to a stunning lady with a vast fortune and an assured social circle. Call it envy, jealousy, spite, what you will. Ellen hated Denis for his good fortune. All her frustrations spilled out and she turned to blackmail to make him pay, not just in money, but in guilt and fear. She made him pay for his happiness and for being able to forget her and behave as though she'd never been in his life. She didn't want him or the money. She wanted revenge.'

'Strong stuff . . .' said Pearce thoughtfully.

'Dynamite. Hell hath no fury like a woman scorned. You might do well to remember that, Pearce, for future reference! Now then, the time has come for us to start calling some of the shots!'

Markby picked up the phone. A few minutes later he said, 'Paul? Yes, Alan . . . No, not to do with Emma. Is she okay? Good. Listen, Paul. Did you once say you had a letter Denis Fulton wrote you a long time ago? That's right. You have? Can you find it and bring it round here? As soon as possible would be appreciated and Paul, not a word to anyone. Thanks.'

He put down the phone. Men may come and men may go – but typewriters went on for ever. Well, several years anyway. Denis had a word processor these days but that was a recent acquisition. The letter he'd written Paul would turn out, with luck, to be typed. As was the letter to Ellen Bryant suggesting a meeting. Individual typewriters could be identified. If Denis's machine had produced that fatal note to Ellen, they'd know soon enough.

Chapter Nineteen

Zoë hesitated in the doorway to the restaurant of Springwood Hall.

The elegant receptionist had deposited her there, making her feel like one of those poor village children of yesteryear, togged up in her shabby best and invited up to the 'big house' for an annual tea-party.

Her heart beat like a drum and she was miserably aware that her nervousness – perhaps blind panic would be a better description – must be obvious to all. Not that at the moment anyone was taking any notice of her. The restaurant was about half full. The patrons seemed absorbed with one another, their food, wine and conversation.

Zoë, on the other hand, could not but be aware of them. They all looked so at ease. How did they do it?

The answer, as she realised almost immediately, was that they were quite unlike herself in every way. They were middle-aged, prosperous and well groomed. Eating in expensive restaurants was for them a common occurrence. None of them had begun the day shovelling manure.

Suddenly she was aware that at least one inhabitant of this alien world had noticed her intrusion: a gentleman of immeasurable presence and dignity who looked at the very least like an Austrian archduke at the turn of the century.

'Miss Foster?' inquired this personage. 'Mr Schuhmacher is awaiting you. Would you care to come this way?'

Zoë opened her mouth but not a sound came out. She followed him obediently across the room, teetering on unaccustomed high heels as she threaded her way between the tables. She was sure now that all eyes had turned to her. Not that she actually had the courage to look into any faces and see their expressions, but she felt certain that was how it must be. In her caravan the charity shop suit had looked positively stylish. Now it seemed drab and its origins as obvious as if she'd left the shop's tatty price tag hanging down her back. She had washed her hair but styling it had never been her strong point and as usual, she had just let it dry as it wanted to. Now she regretted she hadn't broken into the petty cash and treated herself to a visit to the hairdresser. Too late now.

They were approaching a corner of the room where a table was discreetly sheltered from inquisitive gaze by a large potted palm. Schuhmacher's solid form advanced to meet her.

'I am very pleased you could come,' he said, enfolding her damp palm in his capacious fist.

Squeak. Try again. Clear throat. 'Very kind of you to invite me . . .' Now that she had actually managed to say something, she felt better. In fact reaction was setting in and a spirit of rebellion had appeared unexpectedly from some subconscious resource. So what if she was out of place here? He could not have expected otherwise. He'd been to the Horses' Home and seen her in her workaday kit. What use pretending? Suddenly the awful paralysis began to recede. 'I'm dying to hear your suggestion about the home!' she said quite firmly.

'Yes, later. Would you like a drink?'

'No—' she began but stopped. Yes, dammit, she would – a large one. 'Gin and tonic, please!' she said aloud.

'This,' said Schuhmacher when they were settled behind the palm and the gin and tonic had been placed respectfully before her, 'is a compromise between a private dining room and sitting in full view of everyone else. I do not like to be stared at.'

'Neither do I!' Zoë confessed, surprised. She felt herself blush as she remembered the charity shop outfit she wore and wondered if she had drawn unnecessary attention to it.

'You look charming,' said her host. 'Why shouldn't people stare at you? They stare at me because they know that I own the place but run it for their pleasure. They see no reason why they shouldn't walk up to me in the middle of my meal and begin a conversation. That's why I dislike to eat in full view in my own restaurant.' He smiled.

Zoë giggled.

Eric leaned muscular forearms on the table, broad hands folded. The survivor of innumerable past encounters on the ice, of the collisions, roughing, holding and slashings attendant on his chosen sport, now found himself rewarded by an unexpected smile. This was a game in which he felt himself floundering as a novice, none of his former skills any longer the slightest use.

'I am glad you laugh,' he said. 'You see I am not a monster. I should like it if you call me Eric and allow me to call you Zoë. It is a nice name. I mean yours, not mine. Mine is an old-fashioned name now.' He looked faintly melancholy as if this prompted some further reflection he didn't want to put into words.

'Yes, of course,' she said. 'Eric is all right as a name. What's wrong with it?' Without thinking Zoë put up her hand and rubbed at her already tousled mop of fair curls in a habit she had when trying to think of the right phrase to open a tricky explanation. 'Mr Schuh— I mean, Eric, I want you to know I do understand how you feel.'

'You do, Zoë? I wonder.'

'Oh, but yes!' She indicated the room beyond the palm tree. 'All this, it's beautiful and it must have cost so much.'

'It's business!' he interrupted, sounding reproachful.

'Yes, I know. But it means more to you than just a business, doesn't it? I know what the Alice Batt Home means to me.'

'Hm . . . My family has been in the hotel business for three generations. Naturally I'm proud of that tradition. But I am not sentimental about it. Tell me, I am curious, how do you come to be in charge of the horses' rest home?'

'Well,' Zoë reflected briefly. 'It just sort of happened. One thing led to another. I was a pony-mad child, a bit like little Emma Danby, and I used to come and help Miss Batt. She was a wonderful woman!' Zoë's voice gained enthusiasm. 'She founded the home and persuaded the last owner of the Hall here to grant her the original lease at the peppercorn rent we pay. She was very determined, a very strong-minded lady, and she just kept at people until she got her way. I'm not like that, I'm afraid.' Zoë sighed.

Eric made no comment.

'Then, when I left school, Miss Batt took me on full time as stablegirl. It wasn't much money but I loved the job because I'd never wanted to do anything else and I still don't.'

Eric looked gloomier.

'You see, it's all so worthwhile!' She'd forgotten all her shyness now, all her awe of her surroundings. Zoë clenched her fists and beat them on the pristine tablecloth. The gin and tonic rocked in its glass. 'It matters! I'm not sentimental either. I've no time to be. But I do believe it's important to care! Miss Batt was getting on in years by the time I joined her full time and she had awful arthritis, poor dear, and couldn't ride any longer. So she had to give up. She retired to the coast and left the home in my hands. I promised her I'd keep it going. As for the lease, when the Hall was first sold the new owner renewed it on the same terms. After that, although the Hall changed hands many times, everyone seemed content to do the same. We just carried on paying the same paltry rent, not that we could pay any more if it were asked. But that's not the point, is it? You don't want more rent, you want us to go altogether.'

'You know,' Eric said slowly as she ran out of steam at last, 'I too understand. I agree with much of what you say, except in one respect. Do not imagine yourself less formidable or determined than Miss Batt! Your style is different, perhaps, but no less effective! And you are wrong to think I wish to do away with the home altogether. I simply want it somewhere else, out of sight and out of smelling range of my hotel! That is a different situation.'

'But there's nowhere else we can go!' Zoë cried passionately. Her outflung hand knocked the glass and this time the gin and tonic almost spilled. 'We haven't got the money for proper rent somewhere else. I've just told you! Do you know what our feed bills are? And farrier's bills, medicines – although Finlay Ross the vet doesn't charge for his visits. And there's my caravan. If we moved—'

Eric held up one large hand to stem the flow. 'Please, Zoë! Allow me first to explain my idea about the home. When I bought the Hall I also bought the land which went with it. That includes the immediate ground but also a hotchpotch of fields. You see, when the Hall was originally

259

sold, its estate was broken up, farms sold off and various plots of land for development. What was left was what, in effect, no one wanted. It is not all joined together. It is a piece here and another there. One, for example, is the plot on which the Horses' Home is at present.

 –'Now I have been looking at this map . . .' Eric produced a folded sheet from his pocket and opened it out, smoothing it flat on the table. 'Now if you look here—' His stubby finger traced the centre crease of the map and then made a right-angled sweep. 'Here is the river and just here five acres of pasture land owned by me but at present leased to a farmer. That lease is also up and I am informed the farmer is no longer interested to renew it. Something to do with Common Market quotas. He is reducing the size of his dairy herd. I took the liberty, therefore, of instructing my solicitors to make relevant inquiries of the local planning department and I am informed there would be no objection if you wished to move your horses there. You see there is water from the river which runs along one boundary and good access from the road on the other side. Of course, the rent would be the same! I am not interested in making a profit on this and in fact, your cooperation would be worth more than mere money! I wish no more unpleasantness. There has been enough . . .' He sighed.

Zoë was staring at the map, brow furrowed. 'That's Five Acre Bottom. I didn't realise you owned that! It – it's kind, but I'm afraid it won't do.'

'What is the problem?' Eric asked a little sharply, raising his bushy eyebrows.

'There are no barns or outbuildings we could convert easily and cheaply to stabling. You see, we also need proper stables. They'd cost a fortune to build. In normal circumstances horses can live out all the year round, provided they get some extra feed in the lean months and perhaps a waterproof coat thrown over them in bad weather. But ours are not normal animals. They generally reach us in very bad condition, sometimes at death's door. They're weak and often take a long time to recover. Some, like Maud, never get back to full health. Most are old.'

Eric muttered, 'They are not normal, I agree.'

Zoë flushed and went on aggressively, 'Anyway, where would I live? Would the council let me move my caravan there? Actually, I don't think my caravan can be moved! It hasn't got any wheels now, it's just propped up on bricks and if anyone tried to shift it, it would just collapse.'

'You cannot continue to live in that rusting trailer!' said Eric vehemently. 'Nor would it be necessary. There is an old cottage, just here adjacent. It is only two rooms downstairs and another two upstairs and all very dilapidated. But I am prepared to pay for essential repairs, such as a new roof, to make it habitable.' He heaved a sigh. 'But I cannot solve the problem of stabling and you could not move the animals into the cottage with you – although I do believe you would try!' He drummed his fingers on the map. 'You could not launch an appeal?'

'It's not so easy. People are already as generous as you could expect. But we're talking here of several thousand pounds.' Zoë shook her head. 'No. It's a lovely idea and it's kind of you to offer it, the cottage as well. But it's all so much more complicated than it seems, I'm afraid.'

Her companion opened his mouth to reply but before he could speak there was a commotion from the further side of the restaurant. Voices were raised in angry protest. Someone dropped cutlery. Eric frowned. There was clearly a scuffle in progress. Suddenly the palm was violently agitated and a red, furious face appeared amongst its fronds.

'There you are!' the face roared.

'Robin!' Zoë jumped up and now the gin and tonic did tumble over on to its side and spill. 'What are you doing here?'

'As I might ask!' snarled Eric. He reached out into the palm and grabbed young Harding, hauling him into the alcove. 'How dare you burst into my hotel and cause a commotion? Henri!'

The archduke appeared, much flustered, and flanked by a pair of grim-faced waiters. 'Herr Schuhmacher, I am very sorry! He forced his way—'

Eric brushed aside the excuse. 'You will escort this person out!' he ordered curtly.

'They bloody won't, you know!' Robin yelled, diving behind Zoë's chair and putting the table between himself and the advancing staff. 'What on earth do you think you're doing, Zoë? You thought I wouldn't find out, I suppose? Well, I knew you were up to something and I tracked you here! I waited outside for a reasonable time because I thought you might just have come for a business meeting with him – but you didn't come out and now I find you here, hobnobbing *tête-à-tête* in a hidden corner! Are you out of your mind?'

'Hold your tongue, you revolting youth!' growled Eric. To the trio of staff he snapped, 'I shall require explanations later as to how he managed to get in!'

'You're not shutting me up, I'm not afraid of you!' Robin told him, dodging the archduke. 'I know your game! Zoë doesn't because she's so damn simple about this sort of thing! All she thinks about is horses and donkeys! Suave men of the world are right out of her ken! But if you think I'm going to stand by and let you seduce—'

The rest was cut off by a ferocious roar from

Schuhmacher who leapt forward and seized Harding's jacket lapels. He dragged him bodily from behind the table and thrust him into the ungentle embrace of the two waiters.

'Throw him out before I throttle him! And if he tries to get back in, call the police!'

As Harding was hauled away across the restaurant with its mesmerised occupants, he could be heard yelling, 'You haven't heard the last of this! Police? You don't want the police here any more! You've got more than enough to hide! And keep your hands off my girl!'

Silence fell. Eric, ignoring the frozen faces of his customers, put the palm tree straight and sat down. 'I regret!' he said stiffly.

'So do I . . . I mean, I am most awfully sorry.' Zoë picked up her napkin and dabbed ineffectually at the puddle left by the spilled drink. 'Rob is a bit hasty-tempered sometimes. He doesn't mean any harm—'

'On the contrary. He is a bad lot and I am sure he would do any harm he could, provided he thought he wouldn't be caught!' retorted Eric coldly.

'Oh no, you're wrong!' She stared at him, shocked. Then she looked down at the table in some confusion. 'You see, this is quite crazy, but Rob fancies – he thinks he's in love with me. He sort of told me so.'

There was a silence. 'And you? You are in love with him?' Eric asked bluntly.

'No, no, of course I'm not! He's a friend and he's been a good friend. I suppose I – I should have told him not to come to the stables any longer, after he'd said – what he said to me the other evening. But I thought he'd get over it. I am so awfully sorry that he said those dreadful things about – about you and, um, me.'

'Dreadful things?' said Eric, sitting down heavily. 'Well,

perhaps he was not so wrong? No, don't misunderstand, please! This is not the time or the place, but I cannot deny I find you a very attractive young woman. Of course I realise that in the past I have not appeared in a very good light to you. I have tried to repair that. I hoped that we could now be friends. Perhaps even, one day—'

Eric stopped, not because of any sound or movement from his companion but because there had been none. He looked at her and saw that her eyes blazed at him with a fury which far transcended her slight frame. She quivered with rage. Her mop of tousled curls fairly bristled. She resembled a small package of high explosive about to be detonated. 'Mr Schuhmacher,' she said tightly, 'are you saying you offered to relocate the horses' home because in return you were hoping to get me into bed?'

'No!' Eric exclaimed in horror. 'Of course not!' There was an icy silence. 'Well, not as you express it . . .' he went on disastrously.

She did not allow him to finish. She put both hands palm down on the damp tablecloth and leaned pugnaciously towards him. 'I had begun to think you were quite a nice person. I thought perhaps I'd been wrong. Until you came to the home the other day, I expected nothing but opposition from you! I expected underhand tactics, perhaps bullying! I hadn't expected you to make the offer of a new location for the home and I – I was touched for a moment. I thought you were kind! I must be crazy! You weren't making a kind gesture! It was a – a form of sexual harassment! I see Rob was quite right about you! How despicable can anyone get?'

'I am not sexually harassing you!' yelled Eric.

By now the conversation was being conducted at the top of both their voices but neither cared. In the restaurant beyond anyone could have heard a pin drop. No one even pretended to eat or drink and all ears were strained to the enraged voices coming from behind the potted palm.

'Well, I suppose that is a modern term for it!' shouted Zoë, crimson-faced and leaping up and down with anger. 'But here's one your generation might appreciate more! You are nothing but a dirty old man!'

'I am most certainly not!' roared Eric. 'I never heard anything so ridiculous in my life! If I wanted to seduce someone would I try to do it in my own restaurant in front of my staff and guests?'

'How do I know what you'd do? You're capable of anything! I suppose you thought I'd be flattered? Well, I'm not! I haven't got your tacky sense of values! So hear this – you picked the wrong woman! You can try your ploys on someone else, you – you gourmet romeo! Goodbye, Mr Schuhmacher! I'm going to find poor Rob and I hope your thugs haven't hurt him!'

Zoë thrust aside the palm tree and walked head high across the silent room. In the doorway she paused and turned to regard the sea of curious, awe-struck faces turned towards her. In the background, through the green fronds of the palm, she could just distinguish Eric's slumped figure. He appeared to have his head in his hands.

'I am now leaving!' Zoë announced to the assembled spectators. 'But before I go I would like you to know that I bought the clothes I'm wearing and my purse and this neck-lace in a charity shop and the whole lot cost me five pounds! When you've finished stuffing your faces here and are paying the exorbitant bill, perhaps you might remember that other people are struggling on pennies to do good, worth-while work and help those creatures less fortunate than ourselves! Perhaps you might even stick a generous donation in the next collecting tin you see!'

She turned and marched past the once-poised receptionist who now appeared near to hysterics.

Meredith Mitchell, who had been lunching modestly in a far corner, emerged cautiously from behind the menu.

'Oh dear,' she murmured. 'More trouble!'

Chapter Twenty

Eric did not wait for his staff to return. A few moments after Zoë had left the dining room, the fronds of the palm tree quivered and Schuhmacher emerged grim-faced. The diners all immediately averted their eyes and returned to their own conversations and meals. Eric strode across the room ignoring them all until he reached the door, where by some mischance he happened to glimpse Meredith from the corner of his eye. He wheeled round and marched up to her table.

'Miss Mitchell! You have finished your lunch? It was satisfactory?'

'Yes, very, thank you!' Meredith replied promptly.

'May I ask you to join me for coffee in my office?' Eric hesitated and added in less peremptory fashion, 'Please, I would be most grateful.'

It was the last thing she wanted to do, but there was no refusing. Meredith accepted with good grace and allowed Eric to shepherd her from the room, followed by curious stares.

In the entrance lobby, the receptionist had regained some measure of composure and the waiters were returning from having seen Robin Harding off the premises. The head waiter hurried up to Eric and began to apologise again but the hotelier cut him short.

'Later! Bring us coffee to my office!'

When he had settled her in the leather-covered armchair in his office, Eric threw himself into a seat opposite and asked curtly, 'You saw and heard?'

'Yes. I'm sorry.'

'I have made a fool of myself.'

'No!' She leaned forward. 'It happened in the dining room and that was unfortunate. But if the young man hadn't followed Zoë here, it would have turned out differently.'

'We cannot know that, can we?' Eric's glare was both hostile and defensive. 'We often like to think that things would be different only if . . . But she would have rejected me anyway, more than likely.'

Meredith heaved a sigh. 'I don't want to meddle. I feel as if Alan and I have meddled enough already. But you're not going to give up, are you?'

'I was accused of sexual harassment. If I approach her again I shall very likely finish up in court!' Eric fumed silently for a few moments. 'I wanted to help. I had a good plan regarding the animal sanctuary and now that's wrecked as well! I could wring that wretched boy's neck!' Eric's powerful hands closed in realistic mime.

'I suppose he can't be blamed—' Meredith began.

'Don't defend him!' Eric leaned forward, jaw thrust out aggressively. 'Do you know what is the very worst result of all that happened out there?' He flung a hand towards the door and the general direction of the dining room. 'Not that she rejected me, because that is what I had feared anyway. Not that my plan for the animals is ruined, although that's a great pity. No, the worst is, I have driven her into the arms of that young delinquent!'

'You mean Harding?' Meredith eyed Eric thoughtfully

as she mentally reviewed what little she knew about Robin. 'Why do you call him a delinquent? He's never been in trouble with the law, has he?'

'I know the type. Childish, immature, and like a spoiled brat likely to strike out and hurt anyone near him if he's crossed. Worse, there is a kind of intelligence there, but entirely directed towards self! To think that even now she is comforting him!' Eric got up and turned restlessly up and down the little office, pausing only when the coffee arrived.

When they were alone again, he asked urgently, 'Will you go and talk to her?'

'Oh no!' said Meredith promptly, putting down the cup she had just raised to her lips. 'Not me. I don't want to get involved in this any further!'

'She'll listen to you. You are a woman of the world. I mean that as a compliment.'

'Even if she does trust me, that's not a reason for me to go and talk to her, it's a reason for me to stay away! Eric, let her simmer down and then you go and see her. Give her time.'

'No, there isn't time!' He stood over her, large and pugnacious. 'The boy Harding can be the only one to profit by delay. He will have time to fill her head with vile suggestions about me. He is a member of that historical society, too. The whole lot of them have formed a united and vicious conspiracy against me!'

'Zoë's a member,' Meredith pointed out.

He dismissed this crossly. 'Only because of the animals. I don't include her. There was no need for her to join with them! If she had come to me herself at the beginning . . .'

'Or if you had gone to see her at the beginning instead

of just sending lawyer's letters threatening the home!' Meredith interrupted.

'Very well, I was at fault!' Eric slapped his massive palms irritably against the arms of his chair. 'But now I am trying to put matters right! Do you want to see her hurt? Do you want to see the animals carted off to be destroyed because she won't move them to the new site?'

'No, of course not, and stop trying to twist my arm!' Meredith retaliated. 'You could just leave her there, you know, with the animals on the existing site.'

'Rubbish. It isn't suitable. Even the veterinary surgeon has told her so. I checked with him, too. And that rusty old trailer? You want her to continue living in that? She will end up with arthritis at thirty! She will finish like the woman who founded the home, Miss Batt! Unable to run it at all because of her health!' He jabbed a forefinger at her to mark his argument and glowered.

There was a long silence. 'If I go,' said Meredith firmly, 'it's on the understanding that this is a one-off visit. I'm not going to be your permanent courier!'

'Of course!' said Eric impatiently.

As Eric and Meredith talked, Zoë was running down the drive of Springwood Hall as fast as she could in the stupid high heels. But tight skirt and heels between them defeated her and cursing both, she slowed to a walk. At the gates she saw that the gardener had been posted already to raise the alarm should Robin try and get back in. She stalked past him, head held high.

With less assurance she began the trek back along the roadside towards the Alice Batt Rest Home. The breeze brought a whiff of its familiar odour and led her heart to rise briefly. When she got back, everything would be all right again. She would be herself once more. No more silly pretence. She'd be back with the animals, in her creaky trailer by the ramshackle barn, out of these clothes and into familiar, comfortable ones. Best of all, out of these ridiculous crippling shoes.

'Out of them now, dammit!' she said aloud. She stopped and took them off and holding them in her hand, resumed her way along the grass verge in stockinged feet. The return of freedom was not enough however to buoy up her brief feeling of release. Deep depression overcame her. What an awful mess.

There was a rustle in the hawthorn hedge. Zoë gave a cry of surprise which became an exclamation of relief as Robin emerged from a gap accommodating a five-barred gate. He was red-faced and tousled, his expression grim. His motorcycle was propped up behind him.

'Oh Rob!' said Zoë. 'Are you all right? They didn't hurt you?'

He ignored her query after his well-being. 'So you've come to your senses?' he demanded truculently.

She flushed. 'Meaning just what?'

'Pretty obvious, I should have thought!' He thrust out his jaw. 'What the hell did you think you were going to gain by hobnobbing with that bully?'

'You've got a damn cheek!' The force with which this burst from his slightly built companion caused even Harding to recoil. 'Who do you think you are? What gives you the right to tell me what I may do or where I can go or whom I may meet? What business is it of yours?'

He rallied. 'I happen to think it's my business because of the way I feel about you!'

'Keep your feelings to your damn self! It isn't your business. The animals are my concern! If I need to talk their welfare over with Eric, I will!'

'Eric? Eric!' roared Robin. 'So it's first names now! You silly little bitch, are you so thick you can't see—'

There was a resounding crack as Zoë's palm met his cheek.

Silence followed. Then Harding dragged his motorcycle to the road and flung himself on to the saddle. 'Right!' he said hoarsely. 'So that's the way of it! Well, nobody makes a fool of me! Not him, not you, not – anyone! You remember that!'

He pulled on his helmet, kicked the powerful machine into life and roared off down the road.

The yard of the Alice Batt Rest Home was deserted when Meredith reached it a little later. The animals grazed in the paddock and raised their heads curiously as she closed the squeaky gate. The two Shetlands moved together to form a mini-phalanx against the intruder and the piebald pony rolled a white eye. No, they were not attractive good causes, more's the pity!

Meredith peered into the gloomy barn but it was empty. The trailer door, however, was ajar, swinging in the breeze and she approached it. 'Hullo! Anyone home?'

Zoë appeared in the doorway. It struck Meredith that she looked briefly apprehensive before she exclaimed, 'Oh, it's you. Come in.'

'Sorry to intrude. Is – is anyone with you?'

'No. Rob's stormed off in a bad temper. I suppose I can't blame him. We had a dreadful row. Rob is normally the most easy-going person, but when he does lose his temper, it's really quite frightening. Anyway, he was very rude to me and I wasn't going to stand for that!' She shrugged, dismissing the subject. 'I was just going to make coffee, only instant. Would you like some?'

The interior of the trailer was by no means as bad as the exterior suggested. Zoë had done a good deal to make it comfortable. All the same it was a poor place and Eric would never be persuaded this was a suitable place for Zoë to live. Nor, thought Meredith, was it. Eric was right. His trouble was that he was generally right but had problems persuading people of it.

Zoë sat with her feet up on a long seat which probably doubled as her bed, with her back against the wall of a cupboard, nursing the mug of coffee. 'I went to that lunch with Schuhmacher. It was a disaster.'

'I know,' Meredith confessed. 'I was in the dining room and heard.'

'Then I don't have to explain. Rob was right about Schuhmacher! Do you know what bugs me most? That I'd actually begun to think better of that man and he turned out to be a creep after all!'

'I think you're being unfair, you know. Robin turning up like that threw Eric a bit and you can't be surprised. Eric said things he ought to have saved up to say another time. I'm quite sure he didn't mean to make his offer of a new site for the home depend on a return in personal services! That wasn't his meaning at all!'

'Wasn't it?' Zoë glared at her over her coffee mug. She looked like one of the pugnacious Shetlands in the paddock glaring through its tangled forelock. 'Well, it doesn't make any difference now, does it?' Her aggression faded and dejection entered her face, voice and whole manner. 'I can't accept his offer of the new site, not after all that, even if we could have raised the money for stabling somehow. Which is unlikely. I'm having to face it, Meredith. The home is finished. When the lease is up, the animals will all be put down and I – I don't know what I'll do . . .'

'It would be stupid if that happened only because of pride!' countered Meredith vigorously. 'Just because you wouldn't go back and say, yes, I'd like to move to the new site.'

'I told you, it isn't just because of that. It's because even if we moved, we haven't money for new stables. I've been thinking about Ellen. I suppose I was wrong to expect she might have left us something. But I do think she ought to have done! She knew how badly off we were and she could still have left the bulk of it all to Margie Collins! I mean, it isn't as if Margery will spend the money! It will sit in the bank! I know Margery!' Zoë stared into space. 'Life's bloody unfair.'

There was no answer to that.

Markby stood in the street as Meredith had done and looked up at the elegant, well-maintained façade of the Fultons' Chelsea house. But now it was early afternoon and, unlike Meredith, he was not alone. For company he had a metropolitan colleague by the name of Chirk.

DI Chirk had just reached forty but looked a few years older. Whereas Eric Schuhmacher represented the type of former athlete who had kept his physique, Chirk represented the other extreme, the man who had largely given up strenuous sports and had gone to seed. He was overweight with heavy shoulders, a bull neck and jowls. His face was red and his hair receding. He had an ill-trimmed moustache. About him hung an air of general disillusion and mistrust towards human kind. If he resembled anyone, he resembled a particular type of nightclub bouncer. And he gave the distinct impression that it would be unwise to argue with him, a suggestion given further credence by a long, black leather jacket of Eastern European type belted round his ample midriff.

Markby was, however, grateful for Chirk's awesome appearance. He suspected that despite the warrant in Chirk's pocket, entry to the house wasn't going to prove easy and as for removing items . . .

'Nice place,' observed Chirk with a touch of resentment. He rubbed a sausage-like finger over his walrus whiskers and peered over the railings into the basement. 'Looks like a separate flat down there.'

'Staff probably,' said Markby. 'I understand there is a Filipino couple in residence.'

'Speak English, will they?' asked Chirk as if the greatest number of obstacles was being placed in his path by malign Fate.

'Oh, I should think so. This house, incidentally, belongs to Mrs Fulton. She already owned it when they married.'

'Wish my old lady had owned something, anything!' said Chirk, further incensed by the unjustness of life. 'Mind you, we did get her dad's allotment eventually.'

'Gardener, are you?' said Markby, brightening, and pleasurably surprised to find he had something in common with his lugubrious companion.

'Gets me out of the house!' said Chirk meaningfully. 'I keep us going with veg from the allotment. Of course that's not my real interest. Dahlias are that. I belong to the Dahlia Club. That's all I grow in our house garden.'

'Get much trouble with earwigs?'

'You can't help it. The missus doesn't like cutting the blooms and bringing 'em indoors for fear of earwigs dropping out and running over the table. She's dead scared of creepie-crawlies, is Eileen. Screams blue murder at the sight of a spider. But her uncle, he kept snakes in glass tanks. Had 'em all over the house, even in the bedroom. So she doesn't mind snakes. But insects, any sort, she goes barmy.'

'I'd like to see the dahlias,' said Markby.

Chirk cheered up for a couple of seconds but then relapsed into his habitual gloom. 'Yes, I'd take you if you had time today. If you come again, we'll make time. Pity.'

'Yes, it is. Oh well, let's see how we get on here.' Markby walked briskly up the steps and beat a loud rat-tat on the door.

Silence followed. Chirk, still leaning over the railing and peering down at the basement, said, 'Someone's just taken a gander up at us from down there.'

'When the houseowners are away I expect the staff get nervous. Do you think we look like coppers?' They exchanged furtive glances. 'Can't be helped!' said Markby with a sigh.

There was a scrabbling at the front door which opened two inches on a chain to reveal a strip of features, mostly nose and mouth.

'Good afternoon!' said Chirk loudly, stepping forward and, with a professional sleight of hand, producing the warrant and his identity card from his black jacket. 'Police. Detective Inspector Chirk. Take a look at the card. Okay? I have a warrant here. We'd like to come in.'

'I ask my husband!' said the voice. 'You give me paper.'

'You – bring – husband – to – door!' returned Chirk, speaking even more loudly and slowly than the British normally do when faced with foreigners. He thrust his battered face towards the crack. 'I show paper to your husband, savvy?'

The door was slammed shut, just missing his nose.

'Silly bitch!' growled Chirk, starting back.

'Scared,' said Markby with some sympathy.

Voices could now be heard on the other side of the door. The chain chinked and the door opened wide. The maid had been joined by her husband. They stood side by side blocking the entry and gazing apprehensively at Chirk and Markby.

Chirk displayed his card and warrant again and explained in pidgin English just what it represented. When he'd finished Markby felt that, if he hadn't known already, even he would have been at a loss to know what it was.

'Mr and Mrs Fulton not at home!' said the husband.

'You will be Raul?' asked Markby cheerfully, anticipating Chirk. He owed this nugget of information to Meredith. 'The cook, right?'

The man looked slightly more at ease. 'Yes, I am Raul. I am cook. Mr and Mrs Fulton are not at home.'

'We know. But we come in.' The pattern of speech was catching. Markby mentally checked himself. 'We have a warrant, permission, to come in. Do you understand?'

There was a flurry of conversation between the two servants in a tongue quite strange to Markby and which he supposed might be Tagalog. Then they moved reluctantly aside and allowed the two police officers to enter.

'Study,' said Markby. 'Where is Mr Fulton's study? The room where Mr Fulton works.' He mimed typing.

More Tagalog. 'Come, please!' said the maid, moving off down the hall.

From the corner of his eye, Markby saw Raul edging towards the telephone. 'No!' he said firmly. 'No telephoning. We all go to Mr Fulton's study.'

The four of them progressed down the hall. At the far end Dolores tapped at a door. Markby and Chirk exchanged startled glances.

The woman opened the door and the sound of slow, inexpert typing could be heard from within. Dolores leaned through the crack. 'Gentlemen come from police, señor. They got paper.'

The typing stopped abruptly and a voice uttered a soft exclamation of surprise. The newcomers were equally surprised.

'Thought they weren't at home?' muttered Chirk hoarsely.

'Watch those two!' retorted Markby. He slipped past Dolores and Raul, threw open the study door wide and strode in, Chirk at his heels.

Victor Merle had risen from the table at which he had obviously been working at an old Remington.

'Good grief, Chief Inspector!' he exclaimed. 'What are you doing here?'

'We might ask you the same, Dr Merle!' Markby replied sharply.

Merle flushed but did not lose dignity. He carefully disengaged the sheet of paper from the platen of the Remington. 'Just writing a note for Denis. I hadn't realised they were out of town. The staff know me well so I asked if I could just pop along here and write a letter. I don't think there's anything wrong in that, Chief Inspector!'

Markby silently held out his hand. Merle's flushed cheeks deepened in colour. He looked as if he was about to make some sharply worded refusal but then thought better of it. He handed over the half-typed letter and retreated to stand before the marble fireplace, his hands clasped behind his back, his head tilted attentively as if Markby were a student about to read out a piece of written work for comment and correction.

Markby scanned the sheet.

'My dear Fulton,' it read. 'I am sorry to miss you. I do not want us to continue on bad terms, especially as it was all a misunderstanding. If I have offended you, I regret it deeply. But I must insist that on all occasions when I have met with Mrs Fulton none has been in any way in the nature of a *tête-à-tête*. As she will in no doubt confirm, she and I have never lunched out together (one cannot count a cup of coffee during a chance encounter at Burlington House), and I am at a loss to comment on the occasions to which you refer. Reference to my diary shows that on two of them I was not even in London and on one I was in America—'

At this point the letter writer had been interrupted by Chirk and Markby. Markby handed the letter to his colleague and glanced round the room. The word processor, bane of Denis's life, was set up in the corner, a battery of screens and leads suggesting the Starship Enterprise. All of Markby's Luddite instincts led him to a momentary sympathy with Denis.

'I'm sorry, Dr Merle,' he said politely. 'I wonder if you would mind writing out your note by hand?'

Merle had been watching him closely as he read. His expression was no longer offended but wary. Clearly he was working out how to deal with a man who now knew that Merle was seeking to extricate himself from threatened scandal. 'Why is that, Chief Inspector?'

'I'm afraid we need to remove the typewriter for a couple of days.'

Chirk walked across to the table and picked up the bulky machine. Either Markby's calm air of authority or the ease with which Chirk manhandled the weighty Remington impressed Merle. It also gave him food for thought.

'Quite so . . .'

'And we'd be obliged if you didn't mention this to anyone.'

'Yes, of course.'

'Just one little thing,' Markby raised his hand holding Merle's original typed letter. 'You don't mind if I borrow this?'

Merle was regaining poise and his normal colour. He adjusted his cuffs, the light shining on the gold links. 'I have every objection. It has nothing to do with any of your inquiries. It's a private matter and concerns only Fulton, his wife and myself.'

'I understand, but possibly you may be wrong. We are interested to know about Mr Fulton's recent behaviour.'

'Then I shall consult a solicitor.'

'Why should you do that?'

'Why,' asked Merle, smiling thinly, 'should you want Fulton's typewriter?'

'Do you think,' Markby asked him directly, 'that Denis Fulton has been altogether himself lately?'

'Ah . . .' Merle looked thoughtful. 'Now that's another matter. I think perhaps Miss Mitchell has already told you what happened here at a recent dinner party?'

'Yes, she did. Fulton attacked you.' Markby eyed Merle curiously. Something had entered his expression, a hint of malicious glee which called to mind Meredith's misgivings about the man. 'Perhaps you could show us where the incident took place?'

'Certainly.' Merle led them from the study, followed by Markby, Chirk bearing the Remington in his arms like a baby and with the two Filipinos sullenly bringing up the rear.

In the dining room Merle indicated the ceremonial daggers on the wall. 'He threatened me with that one with the filigree handle.'

Markby moved towards the display and lifted his hand. But before he could touch it, the maid spoke unexpectedly.

'You not touch. Mrs Fulton not let anyone touch. Knife very sharp. I only dust with little brush.'

Markby turned to her. 'How long have you worked here?'

'Five years.' It was the husband, Raul, who spoke now. 'We have work permit, all in order.'

'Yes, I'm not worried about that. But you were here during Mrs Fulton's previous marriage? When she was Mrs Keller?'

They were nodding in unison. 'Mr Keller very nice gentleman.'

'And these knives? Do they belong to Mr Fulton, Mrs Fulton or were they Mr Keller's?'

'Mr Keller, he collect all things military. Mrs Fulton, she not like them. She say, nowhere in house, only in here. She say, knives unlucky.' Raul pointed at Chirk. 'You take away typewriter?'

'Yes, that's right. I'll give you a receipt.'

'I can telephone Mrs Fulton now?'

'When we've left. But I shall be seeing Mr Fulton.'

'You tell him it not our fault you come in house and take typewriter?'

'Yes, I'll tell him. And you tell him,' Markby smiled genially at Merle, 'you tell Mr Fulton that Dr Merle was in the house at the time and can verify everything.'

Merle gave him a very dirty look. Markby ignored it and moved over to the window, beckoning to the two Filipinos to follow him. There, out of Merle's line of sight, he took a magazine clipping from his pocket.

'Just answer "yes" or "no", understand?' They nodded. 'Good. Has this person ever visited this house?'

They stared nervously at the picture in the clipping but both answered quickly, 'Yes!' Dolores adding, 'Many time.'

'Thank you,' said Markby, slipping the picture of Eric Schuhmacher he had cut from Springwood Hall's brochure back in his pocket. 'We'll be leaving now.'

As he walked towards the door, Merle started after him. 'Just a moment, Chief Inspector! That letter of mine . . . obviously its contents might be misconstrued if any unauthorised person read it! You will be discreet?'

'Rest assured, Dr Merle.'

Merle looked neither assured nor likely to get much rest.

'Yes, I see . . .' said Superintendent McVeigh. He spread out on his desk the three sheets of paper, the letter received by Ellen Bryant, the letter sent by Denis Fulton to Paul Danby and the unfinished letter by Merle. 'Even to my untutored eye, these all seem to have been typed on the same machine.'

'They were, and so was this one.' Markby produced another. 'It's by me. I tried out the machine when we got it back to the office. And I've had an expert look it over. He says all the letters were typed on it. It's a very old machine and several letters are distinctively worn. If you look, you'll notice the s, t, n, e and r. And alignment is out. The full stop drops below the line and the 4 and dollar sign are slightly above it. Denis doesn't like his new word processor. His wife told Miss Mitchell so and he tells anyone who cares to listen. For short letters he obviously still turns to his trusty old Remington.'

'And you believe he wrote this to lure Ellen Bryant to a meeting in the cellars where he killed her with a knife filched earlier from the hotel kitchens, taking only a matter of minutes to commit the crime?'

'He could have done it. He was absent from the drinks party on the lawn for a few minutes at least once. Miss Mitchell noticed. And in the general crowd and confusion, he had ample opportunity to slip away more than once. It was a quick kill. He could have been lurking in the recess by the wine racks waiting for Ellen. She walked in and before she had time to realise it, he jumped out and—' Markby made a graphic gesture.

'Hm. So what do you want to do?'

'I want to bring him in and hold him for twenty-four hours. I'm sure he can tell us more. I believe he'll crack. He's edgy. Scared.'

'You're more likely to find his solicitor there within the hour, protesting his client's right to silence!' growled McVeigh. 'And he is a well-known personality. The press will get hold of it.'

Markby leaned forward. 'He had motive. Ellen Bryant could have exposed him as a bigamist. She was blackmailing him. He admits it. We have their marriage certificate. We have the letter written on his typewriter. He's a panicky chap, given to sudden outbursts. He attacked Dr Merle with a knife because he thought Merle was having an affair with Leah Fulton. Denis is passionately in love with Leah. But he's got a chip on his shoulder the size of a pit-prop. There is nothing he wouldn't do to save his marriage – his second marriage, I mean, calling it that for the want of anything else even though it was – is – bigamous. I mean, he's a widower now. But the marriage to Leah is invalid. Also his public reputation would be shot to pieces if it were known he was a bigamist. No more TV shows. No more invitations to speak to women's groups about food and wine. He had everything to lose and the story he told me leaks like an old lilo.'

'This chap, Merle, he doesn't want to press charges against Fulton for assault?'

'No, he assures me it was all a misunderstanding. You know the sort of thing. He doesn't want that kind of publicity.'

'Pity. It would give us an extra reason for taking Fulton in. Think Merle really was having an affair with Mrs F.?'

Markby hunched his shoulders. 'Leah Fulton is very attractive and wealthy. She married Denis very quickly after her second husband died. Perhaps too quickly. She may have decided she made a mistake and have found someone else.

'Merle is anxious to deny he's the man and give himself alibis for the clandestine trysts with Mrs F. Denis accused him of having. If Merle's telling the truth and he wasn't meeting with Mrs F. on the dates in question, where was she and with whom? She must have been with someone and she doesn't want to say who because she's been lying to Denis about that, claiming to be with her daughter when she wasn't. I owe all this information to Miss Mitchell. It was Denis finding out from the daughter that Leah's story was false which precipitated the attack on Merle. This brings us to Schuhmacher, another frequent caller at the house. Eric's recently fallen for a girl in gumboots but he could have been having an affair with Leah before that.

'Suppose Denis originally thought the lover was

Schuhmacher? What a chance to kill two birds with one stone! Get rid of Ellen and do it at Springwood Hall, ruining Eric's opening gala and leaving him with an embarrassing corpse on the premises? Denis's been under near intolerable pressure. It would be little wonder if he was driven to the extreme action in an attempt to extricate himself. All the more so if he knew there were other men, or at least one other man, in Leah's life and that if she'd found out about the bigamy, she didn't lack consoling arms to run to.'

McVeigh sighed. 'That Remington is covered in fingerprints, I suppose?'

'Every print in the household except the cat's. Plus Merle's, plus mine and Chirk's. Plus the maid dusted it once a week and wiped off a dozen others.'

'Okay, pull him in. But don't come to me to authorise an extension after that because I won't. I don't even like this. I am overseeing this investigation and it's I who'll take the flak if nothing comes out of it.'

'I wouldn't suggest it, if I didn't think it was necessary,' Markby said quietly.

McVeigh muttered, 'Just bear in mind that if you can't make anything stick at the end of it, the civil liberties lot, Fulton's lawyers and the press will all have a field day.'

'Don't they always?' returned Markby.

McVeigh sighed again. Then he sat back and placed his hands on his desk. 'Let's turn to another matter.'

'I can guess!' Markby said sharply. 'I don't want to leave Bamford. I'm not bothered about promotion. But I do want to know who leaked the possibility! They're passing the hat round already for my goodbye present! They think I don't know.'

'Alan, we need good senior men taking overall control.

I don't need to tell you that morale is pretty low in some quarters of the force. Too many scandals recently. It makes my blood boil. Don't these idiots realise the harm their stupidity does the image of the police?'

'I feel as strongly as you do. But the crime rate in and around Bamford is rising. Town's expanded in the last few years. Villages are losing their old social cohesion. We're understrength. This isn't the moment for me to walk out on it all!' said Markby stubbornly.

McVeigh glared. 'There'll never be a good moment! Like it or not, decision time comes and we can't duck and dive for ever, hoping to avoid it! I retire in three years' time. Approaching retirement has the effect that Dr Johnson said the knowledge of being about to be hanged did: it concentrates the mind wonderfully! I'd like to think that you'll be sitting at this desk one day. If you take a transfer now it could set you up for just that. I've worked hard during my time here. I want to hand it all on to a safe pair of hands. Think it over from that point of view. It could be that you're being selfish as well as short-sighted!'

There was a silence. Markby said, 'I appreciate what you've said. It's not a question of dodging the issue. I'm just not ready for that particular change in my life yet. I don't like sitting at desks. I do more than enough of that already. The higher you go the fewer the opportunities for getting away from paperwork and chairs. That's life. In a couple of years' time, maybe, I'll feel differently.'

'You're getting older too, Alan,' McVeigh said brutally, 'whether you like it or not! You may still be mentally alert but you must be physically slower and less tolerant of irregular hours. Not to mention lack of sleep and missed meals! Take the step now!'

'That's probably what the hangman said to Dr Johnson's man on the gallows!' Markby retorted. 'But I'm like the condemned man. I'll only go when I'm pushed!'

Chapter Twenty-One

When Markby returned to Springwood Hall to inquire again after Denis Fulton, he received the same answer: that Mr Fulton was at the swimming pool. But this time the information was accompanied by a beaming smile from the elegant receptionist which, in view of his mission, troubled his conscience.

In another respect, his luck was out. Denis was not alone at the pool. Both Leah and Meredith were with him and Markby cursed silently. All three of them lounged in the poolside recliners chatting. They looked quite relaxed and happy which surprised him a little. Surely news of his visit to the Fultons' town house and the removal of the typewriter had reached them? And if Denis had confessed his bigamy, Leah was taking it remarkably well. Markby's heart sank. Somebody, somewhere, was playing games. He glowered at Denis's round, pink, shiny face, as innocent as a plaster cherub's.

Apart from that, the smell of chlorine was stronger today. The water must have been treated that morning. It reminded him of the formaldehyde smell of forensic laboratories. The music tape had been switched off. Sub-surface light still rippled through the pool's turquoise depths and led to the distracting *trompe l'oeil* effects he had noticed on his previous visit. There was altogether a baroque feel to this place, as if one ought to be able to raise one's eyes to the ceiling and behold a painted heaven of cloud-borne saints. He found himself looking up and was oddly disconcerted only to see plain white paint across which grotesque shapes gyrated, caused by the undulating water below.

He looked down and saw Meredith, her short brown hair wet and clinging to her scalp like a glossy cap. 'Hullo,' he said, his guilt returning.

They all chorused delighted greetings, rendering him in his own eyes a complete Judas. But he saw that a slightly wary look had entered Denis's expression.

'Coming in for a swim?' Leah invited.

'Sorry, not today. Business call. I'd rather like a word with you, Denis.'

'Then Meredith and I will take the plunge,' said Leah amiably. 'And leave you to it!' She twisted her long hair into a rope and, coiling it on top of her head, stuck in a couple of pins to secure it. 'Come on, Meredith.'

The two men watched the women descend into the pool and swim slowly away towards the far end. Meredith looked as though she might be a strong swimmer and Markby wished he had the time to sit and watch her. Leah had a leisurely, elegant stroke which conserved energy and suggested she found the exercise basically boring.

He asked bluntly, 'Have you told her yet?'

Denis looked sullen, his lower lip jutting petulantly. 'No! And I've been thinking it over. Why should I? Ellen's dead! Whether or not I married Leah bigamously doesn't matter tuppence now. It's no one's business, not even yours!'

'You're deluding yourself!' Markby told him unkindly.

Denis scowled. 'If I'm deceiving anyone, it's Leah.

Surely that's a matter between her and me? I think I'm doing right. Sometimes deception is kinder than truth.'

'I'm only interested in truth!' Markby said. 'That's the way police investigations operate, for better or worse! And this is, I ought to remind you, still a murder investigation.'

'And searching for truth leads you to invade our London home and make off with my typewriter, does it?' Denis demanded nastily.

'I realised you'd have heard about that. Your wife seems pretty calm despite it.'

'That's because she doesn't know.'

'I thought either Merle or the cook, Raul, would have telephoned the news through to you?'

'Both did, as it happens. By pure chance I took the call from Raul and Victor phoned me personally, so Leah is still in blissful ignorance of your uncouth behaviour! Pinching my typewriter and who knows what else! Frightening Raul and Dolores into fits, also, I might add. Merle said you were damn high-handed and had brought along a heavy from the Met, presumably to kick in my front door if need be.'

Markby felt his annoyance growing and his feeling of being a snake in the grass distinctly lessening. 'For crying out loud, how many more secrets are you going to try and keep from your wife indefinitely? It can't be done, man! The whole bally edifice is about to come crashing down and the more your wife has to discover when the collapse comes, the tougher it will be on her! You should have told her about Ellen by now. I gave you fair warning and plenty of time! As for our visit to your London address, she'll find that out as soon as she gets back.'

Across Denis's face had come the obstinate expression of a wilful child, refusing to admit that to adult eyes his infant behaviour is unacceptable. 'Well, it can wait then, can't it? What did you want the wretched typewriter for, anyway?'

'That, Denis, is among several things I'd like to discuss at the station. I've come here to ask if you'd accompany me there. I believe you can help us with our inquiries and I don't believe you've been entirely frank with me up till now.'

Denis's face was a picture. Shock, anger and wounded vanity all appeared on it in quick succession. 'You've got a nerve! Suppose I refuse? I've told you everything I know. Told you freely!'

'Come off it!' Markby returned brutally. 'You've been anything but forthcoming. The only things you've admitted are things I'd already found out and you couldn't deny. Your marriage to Ellen. The blackmail. The break-in and damage at Ellen's flat. I could charge you with that if I wanted to hold you officially, remember! You may have been reasonably successful deceiving Leah to date, but you're not going to be anything like as successful if you try and hoodwink the police! The game's up, Denis!'

The reflection from the disturbed water of the pool caused a weird effect of light and shade to play across Denis's face. But behind this, he had changed colour. The angry turkey-cock red had drained away to a sickly pallor.

'Are you, then, charging me?'

'No. I'm asking you to come in with me. I'm trying to make it easy, or as easy on you as I can. I could have sent a police car and a couple of uniformed men.'

'And you will, I suppose, if I refuse to accompany you now?' Denis said spitefully.

'Spot on, I will.'

'Am I allowed to express my personal opinion of your behaviour or would that go on the charge sheet with everything else?' Fulton snarled.

'What everything else?' Markby countered coolly.

There was silence, broken by a splash from the two swimmers at the far end of the pool. Their voices echoed around the walls.

'What do I tell Leah?' Denis asked, suddenly deflated.

'Sooner or later you'll have to tell her everything. For the time being, I suggest you simply say you're leaving with me.'

'She won't leave it at that! She's not stupid! She'll ask—'

'And if you'd told her the truth before, she'd be better prepared now!' Markby snapped. 'It's your ruddy problem, not mine! Go and put some clothes on.'

Leah and Meredith were holding on to the bar running around the edge of the pool and treading water.

'I'm not the sporty type,' Leah was saying. 'I take a dip occasionally like this, indoors. I never swim in the sea. When Marcus was alive we went to the Côte d'Azur every year. He loved the place. But lying around on the beach or pool-side has always bored me stiff, all those bronzed bodies cooking in suntan oil like rows of sardines. I'm a city girl. I like to shop or go to restaurants, theatres, exhibitions. Marcus had a yacht for a while and I'd make him go down the coast to Monaco so I could visit the casino. I am, I admit, a bit of a gambler so I enjoyed that.'

'I like the south of France,' Meredith said. 'But I'd rather go inland than stay along the coast, although I do like to swim.'

Leah turned her back to the edge of the pool and rested her outstretched arms along the rail. She allowed her feet to float out straight ahead of her. From the new position she was looking directly down the pool towards the two men.

'What are they talking about?' Her voice was suddenly sharp.

Meredith took a look in the same direction. Markby and Fulton certainly seemed to be arguing. A twinge of unpleasant apprehension seized her. 'I don't know.'

'Well, I'm going to find out!' Leah pushed herself away from the rail and began to swim back to the further end with far greater determination than she had shown on her leisurely breast-stroke progress down. Meredith followed her.

As they climbed, dripping wet, out on to the tiled surround, Markby and Fulton got to their feet.

'What's going on?' Leah asked in a clipped voice. She took the pins from the coil of hair and shook it loose about her face.

'It's okay,' Denis said quickly. 'I'm just going to change and then I'm going with the chief inspector here.'

'Going where?' Leah glared suspiciously at Markby. 'Why do you need my husband?'

'Don't be alarmed,' Markby said soothingly. 'Your husband has agreed to come down to the station so that we can discuss certain matters in more suitable surroundings than here.'

'What matters?' She stepped forward aggressively. 'Denis, what on earth is going on? Why can't you talk here? Why must you go to a police station of all places?' She switched her head to Meredith, hair flying. 'Did you know about this?'

'No, nothing.' Silently Meredith cursed Alan. She didn't know what was going on and she didn't like being landed in the middle of whatever it was without the slightest hint to guide her. She treated Markby to a furious glare of her own.

'You're not going anywhere, Denis!' said Leah furiously. She snatched up a towel. 'I'm going to get changed and we're all going up to the Hall where we'll telephone our solicitor and take advice on this! He can't make you go with him, can he? I mean, you're not arrested, for pity's sake, are you?'

'No,' said Markby. 'But I think it would be better if your husband were to be positive about this.'

'Positive!' Leah shouted. 'I'm being positive! Positive he's not going! What do you want him for?'

Denis spoke, his voice loud and echoing above the gentle splish-splash of the water. 'It's about Ellen, Leah, the murdered woman, Ellen Bryant. I didn't tell you this before, and I'm sorry, but she and I – we knew each other, long ago.' He glanced at Markby. 'It's complicated. I'd rather tell you later, in private.'

Leah was obviously dismayed but was adept at thinking on her feet. 'But if it was so long ago, why does it matter? So you knew her? I have a nodding acquaintance with hundreds of people. If anything happened to any one of them, would the police haul me off just because of that?'

'I'd been in touch with her recently!' Denis's voice became pleading. 'Please, Leah. I'll explain it all later. I'm just going with Markby now. Meredith, take care of my wife, won't you?'

The two men turned and walked away. With exquisite bad timing the canned music suddenly burst into life amongst the potted palms. Soupily the crooning voice informed them all that once, the singer had had a secret love . . .

Zoë straightened up with a sigh as she eased the crick in her neck. She put down her pen. Trying to balance the books of the Alice Batt Rest Home was difficult at the best of times. 'A challenge' was how some might charitably have described the task. 'Hopeless' others might have said. Zoë's emotions generally veered between the two views. Usually she sat down filled with determination to make the Home come out on the credit side and by the end of half an hour's grim calculations, ended up with a substantial sum firmly in the debit column. However she juggled the figures, their outgoings always exceeded their income.

To make things worse, she was so tired. The truth was that she missed Robin's practical help about the place. Not that he had come regularly or for long hours, but he had turned up whenever he could and always pitched in willingly no matter how disagreeable the task. Thus in the past it had always been possible to leave a heavy or awkward job 'till Robin came'. But since their quarrel it seemed fairly certain Rob would appear no more. At least, not in friendship.

'Drat!' said Zoë miserably, erasing a set of pencilled numbers and beginning to add up her columns of figures again.

It was getting dark in the caravan and she could hardly see what she did. She got up and lit the oil lamp which provided her lighting. The Home was nearing the end of its existence. She had to admit it. They could no longer afford to take in any more animals and yet, if another sad case appeared on their threshold, there would be no way she could refuse. But how to pay for it all? Costs couldn't be pared down any further and her own lifestyle could not be simpler. She was sorry, on reflection, that she had marched out of the luncheon with Schuhmacher before they'd eaten. She could have done with the free meal. Now thoughts of the hotelier added to her gloom and filled her with mixed emotions of anger, frustration and regret.

Outside in the gathering gloom an engine coughed and died. Zoë froze, listening. Rob's motorcycle? She glanced apprehensively around her. She wasn't exactly afraid of Robin but, recalling his expression after she had struck him and also on the occasion he had attacked Schuhmacher with the fork, her confidence in being able to deal with Harding was severely shaken.

She had been feeling nervous lately. In the daytime things were all right but when night fell, it was different. This sense of being less secure probably dated from Ellen's death. It had increased since Emma and Maud's adventure in the pine plantation. Moreover, something Chief Inspector Markby had said had also made things worse. Poor man, he hadn't meant to alarm her. But when he'd asked if she were ever afraid out here and did she keep a dog, it had set her thinking about her situation in a way she hadn't done before. The animals had always filled her thoughts, and their welfare. She had never had the time to worry about herself. But now Schuhmacher's offer of a new site with cottage appeared more and more desirable and more and more an unrealisable dream.

But she had definitely heard an engine quite near at hand. Not Rob's bike, though, different-sounding. Zoë hesitated and then went to the door and opened it. She peered out into the twilight. It was a little misty. Swirls of fog curled across the ground and a gauzy haze hung over the treetops. Was she imagining it or did a figure move by the corner of the barn?

Suddenly Zoë realised that with the dull glow of the oil lamp behind her she was silhouetted in the doorway making a perfect target. She gave a gasp and pulled the door shut.

It was stupid but her hand was shaking. She sat down

and tried to pull herself together.

Crack!

Zoë's head jerked round. That was no sound to be explained by a falling twig or some loose object bowled along the ground by the wind.

Tap – tap – tap.

The blood in her veins curdled. Footsteps – and coming nearer. Hesitant steps which stopped and then began again.

A dislodged stone rattled away just outside the door. There was a scraping and scuffling at the fabric of the trailer and then a knock so loud that she almost jumped out of her skin. It was repeated more urgently. A female voice called, 'Miss Foster? Are you in there?'

She had no idea who it was but it was neither Rob nor Schuhmacher nor some ill-intentioned vagrant such as Emma had disturbed in the pinewoods. It was company and as such, it was welcome. Zoë grabbed the oil lamp and holding it high, jerked open the door.

Margery Collins' white face and pointed features leapt into the flickering circle of light, eerily illuminated. She was still wearing black or another dark colour and in the gloom and swirling mist only her face and hands could be distinguished. They were fish-belly ivory and appeared to hover detached from her body so that she resembled some macabre disjointed marionette. Zoë stared at her with instinctive revulsion.

'Miss Foster?' Margery repeated. 'Can I come in?'

'What? Oh yes, of course.' Zoë ushered her in and offered her a seat. 'I'm so sorry. I wasn't expecting a visitor.'

Not quite true. She'd half been expecting an unwelcome one. She asked. 'How did you come?'

'In my little car, my runabout. Well, it was Ellen's, you

remember it. But now it's mine. I parked in the lane. It was quite difficult to find my way across your yard. The fog is closing in and obscuring the moon and, stupidly, I didn't bring a torch.'

'You didn't—' Zoë felt foolish asking it but had to check. 'You didn't see a motorcycle on your way here?'

'I don't think so.' Margery sounded puzzled.

'That's all right, then. Would you like some coffee? I'll just light my little calor gas-stove. It will give out a bit of heat, too.'

'I'm disturbing you,' Margery apologised. 'I would have rung but you haven't a phone. It's just that I've made up my mind about something and I wanted to tell you straight away.' She fell silent, offering no explanation of this mysterious statement.

Zoë, nonplussed but prepared to let Margery get to the point of her visit in her own way, fetched mugs and put the little tin kettle on the gas bottle's ring. 'You didn't disturb me. I was just doing the books.'

'Oh, the books . . .' Margery glanced at the papers scattered across the bunk seat. A shadow crossed her face. Then she blinked as if she'd just woken up. 'No, please don't put coffee in that mug for me. I don't drink it. If you've got any fruit squash I'll have that, with hot water if you like. I quite like it that way and I don't drink stimulants.'

Zoë fetched a bottle of orange squash and obliged.

Margery asked her, 'Where do you get fresh water?'

'From the standpipe out in the yard. It fills the horsetrough and I draw off my water. I suppose it's not really meant to be used for humans but I always boil it and I've never been sick. Do you still want this drink?'

'Oh yes, I don't mind. I'm sure it will be all right.' Margery twisted her thin hands and fell silent again.

Zoë's patience at last gave way to lively curiosity. She ventured a blunt, 'What can I do for you, Margery?'

'It's about Ellen's money.'

Zoë, mug half-raised to her lips, stared. 'I'm sorry?'

'Ellen's money. You've heard, I expect, that Ellen left everything to me. The shop, her car, her clothes, her furniture and her money. She was quite well off.'

'Yes, I did hear.' Zoë hoped she didn't sound envious.

'It was a great shock. I mean, Ellen's death itself was a shock but then when Mrs Danby told me I was her heiress, it was worse. I felt so guilty.'

'Why?' asked Zoë, surprised.

'Because I didn't deserve it. I wasn't a relative. I wasn't really a friend. I just worked at Needles. I've hardly slept since I knew about it.' Apparently at a complete tangent she added, 'I'm staying at The Crossed Keys. It was Chief Inspector Markby's idea.'

Zoë began to wonder whether a combination of shocks had slightly unhinged Margery and if she really was quite right in the head.

'Is it true, do you know, that they've arrested someone at the hotel?' Margery's next question seemed to confirm Zoë's suspicions.

'I don't know, I haven't heard. But then I wouldn't, out here. At the hotel? Are you sure? Who told you?'

'Someone came into the shop and said so. Perhaps it's just a rumour. But I hope they have arrested him. I've been so scared he'd come after me.'

'Why on earth should anyone bother you?' The words burst from Zoë's lips in complete incredulity before she realised how rude they must sound.

'Yes, me. I can't tell you why, but ever since I inherited all of Ellen's belongings it seems nothing has gone right.

Although I want to keep the shop going. But in every other way it's been a miserable time.' Margery's voice grew louder and more vehement. Her pale face flushed. 'Even the shop, for that to be mine poor Ellen had to die first and so horribly! And I've become deceitful, keeping things from Mr Markby, and vain, dreaming of wearing Ellen's clothes as if I'd look anything but ridiculous in her things! It's all wrong and I want to put it right. I'll keep the shop because I know how Ellen would have wanted it run. But not the money. I can't keep the money.'

She straightened her back and pushed her dark hair from her eyes. 'I've wondered and wondered what to do. Then I heard about the little girl taking the donkey and her dreadful ordeal in the woods. It seemed somehow to be giving me the answer, as if it had happened just for that reason, to show me what to do.' Margery leaned forward earnestly. 'I want you, I want the horses, to have the money.'

'Oh no . . .' Zoë whispered. She shook her head. 'It's kind, Margery, and of course we're always broke. But I couldn't. Ellen wanted you to have it.'

'I don't believe,' Margery said firmly, 'that Ellen had really thought about it at all. How could she? She wouldn't have left it all to me if she had. What should I do with so much money? No, it's right that the Home should have it. You do need it, don't you?' Margery indicated the poverty-stricken surroundings with an innocent cruelty.

'Yes,' said Zoë.

'Then I'll tell Mrs Danby in the morning. She can do all the necessary legal business. Of course, I'll keep back a certain amount to cover buying new stock and so on for the shop. But Mrs Danby can help us sort that out.'

Zoë nodded. With an effort she managed to say, 'I can't

think how to thank you, Margery. It – it seems unreal. Too good to be true.'

'You don't have to thank me. I want to do what's right and this is right.' Margery got up. 'I'd better be going before the fog gets any thicker.'

'I'll walk with you to your car and bring my torch!' Zoë offered.

The mist outside had thickened, swirling about them and reaching out to touch their faces with clammy fingers.

'Take care!' advised Zoë anxiously as Margery prepared to drive away.

But as she walked back to her trailer she suddenly felt so elated that she hardly noticed the fog or the dark or remembered her earlier fears at all. From nowhere, literally out of the dark and mist, had come salvation. She felt as if she floated across the ground, borne up by her happiness. In the caravan again, she picked up the papers on which she had so painfully calculated their debts and threw them up into the air. She wanted to celebrate but had no way of doing so other than to sit and joyfully imagine all the things they could do now with the money.

She was so elated that she quite failed to hear, shortly after Margery's departure and muffled by the fog, the stuttering roar of a motorcycle engine start up in the lane.

Chapter Twenty-Two

Meredith had also witnessed the thickening mist slowly descend over the landscape from early evening onward. Now, at a little after ten p.m., she stood at a window in the lounge of Springwood Hall and peered out between the heavy drapes.

She was alone in the long narrow room with its high ceiling and dusky nooks. The main lights had been switched off and only two table lamps and the glow from the embers in the hearth bathed the room in a subdued rosy haze. Two couples of fellow guests who had shared the lounge earlier had long bid her goodnight and retired. One elderly man had remarked that he was glad he hadn't to be out and about on the roads that night.

There was a rustle from the grate as the skeletal remains of the logs which earlier had crackled so hospitably now fell in upon one another with tiny showers of golden sparks. The air was warm and heavy. A clock ticked softly. It was as if time stood still at the Hall. It might have been 1890 or 1909 or 1990, it made no difference. Perhaps she wasn't alone, but watched from the shadows by the ghosts of former occupants, curious but not unfriendly.

Outside, in startling and sinister contrast to the comfort within, everything was blanketed in a wet, grey-white chill mass. The fog besieged the house, swirling malevolently at the windowpanes as it sought some chink through which it might seep. The row of Victorian-style lamps which illuminated the main drive and should have been visible from here could only be located by fuzzy yellowish smudges in the murk. Trees and shrubs were invisible. Meredith shivered and turned away, letting the velvet curtain fall back into place.

Although she was tired she was unwilling to go up to bed. She returned to her seat by the fire, picked up a copy of a countryside magazine and sat with it unopened in her lap, staring down at the flickering remains of the fire. A sudden spurt of flame sprang up and almost immediately died.

If the household spirits did still hover over the place, she thought drowsily, they had plenty of scandal to amuse them! It had been as exhausting a day as any since murder had first come among them. After Denis and Alan Markby had left, Leah had descended on a telephone and spent the whole afternoon furiously contacting influential personages of all descriptions. She had joined Meredith at dinner, but only to fulminate, over congealing food, against the British police, the system of justice and Chief Inspector Markby in particular, promising retribution once her solicitor got on to it.

Trying not to tuck into her own meal too obviously and thus appear unsympathetic, Meredith had listened patiently. She had defended Markby as best she could whenever she was able to get a word in edgeways. But she could not feel she had defended him well. How could she, when she didn't know what he was up to? she thought now a little crossly.

Thinking it over in the quiet warm gloom, it seemed

incredible that Denis Fulton, of all men, should have been
requested to 'help the police with their inquiries'. Denis,
for pity's sake? But still waters run deep and Denis, it now
seemed, had a colourful past.

Where, wondered Meredith idly, had he known the late
Mrs Bryant and in what circumstances? And what had
been the nature of his recent communication with her? No
use asking Alan who certainly knew but wouldn't tell.
Leah, too, was presumably in ignorance since Denis had
been hauled away making vague promises of future explanations. No wonder Leah was upset. Not knowing the full
truth and being left to speculate wildly was far harder to
bear than any complete knowledge, however shocking.

As if by thinking about Leah Meredith had somehow
established a telepathic contact with her, there was a click
from the door which opened to admit the lady herself.

'Hullo!' said Meredith, surprised. 'I thought you'd gone
to bed. Everyone else has.'

Leah smiled mirthlessly. 'Perhaps they can look forward
to pleasant dreams! Mind if I join you?' She took the seat
opposite Meredith and gazed down at the crumbling ashes
with some dissatisfaction.

'Hang on!' said Meredith. She got up and fetched one
of the smaller pieces of wood from a basket by the hearth
and pushed it into the flames. After a moment it caught,
crackling and sending up a little Mount Etna of sparks.
Meredith prudently pulled the mesh fireguard across.
'There, that's better. I'm sure they won't mind us burning
another log and it's quite safe.'

'You see, you're practical,' said Leah moodily. 'You're
a useful person. I mean that as a compliment.'

'Thanks, but it does make me sound a bit of a workhorse.'

'Don't scorn it. It's better than being a useless ornament

like me!' The speaker's voice was unexpectedly bitter.

'Come on,' said Meredith gently. 'You're just feeling down in the dumps because you're worried about Denis. You must be tired. You ought to go to bed, really. Take an aspirin. I've got some if you haven't. Sleep and stop thinking.'

'I've got pills, thanks. But I don't want to stop thinking. I want to work it all out and get it straight in my mind!' Leah sighed. 'I don't know why Denis didn't confide in me that he had troubles. I really don't understand it. Why did he feel he couldn't tell me? Am I an ogre?' She raised dark-ringed eyes in her pale beautiful face, fixing Meredith with a questioning and embarrassingly direct gaze.

'No. I don't know what's wrong but I am sure he loves you. I expect he wanted to protect you.'

Leah's clenched fists beat on the arms of her chair. 'I don't want protecting! I'm not a bit of Dresden china! I'm not stupid, incapable of understanding! But that's what people think when they see me, isn't it? Just another rich bitch, thick as two planks. A clothes-horse, drenched in French perfume, tricked out with expensive gems, incapable of earning a living or standing on her own two feet. Always kept by a rich man. Someone whose status is midway between a decorative statuette and a pet pug!'

Meredith couldn't help laughing. 'That's rubbish!' At the same time she couldn't help recognising the element of truth in what Leah said. Of course no one expected anything of her. And, yes, one did notice the clothes, the jewellery, the perfume. Meredith could smell it now. It was a shame: Leah was an intelligent woman. She'd never really given herself a chance.

'It isn't rubbish, it's true!' said Leah calmly. 'You know it is. I can see it in your face. No, don't argue. I don't mind.

I've never made the slightest effort to achieve anything in my own right. I was Bernie's wife, Marcus's wife, now Denis's. That's it. Someone's wife.'

'I'm not laughing at you, only at the words you used.' Meredith hesitated. 'Being a successful wife is an achievement too. I don't know I could fulfil that role.'

'You haven't tried. Marry your policeman and then you'll find out, not before. As for me, I'm not a successful wife to Denis or he wouldn't have felt he needed to keep secrets. He was afraid to tell me, that's it. I'm not proud of myself.'

'Look,' Meredith began. 'We don't yet know why Alan wants to talk to Denis at the station. It may all be cleared up by tomorrow morning.'

'Cleared up or not,' said Leah with sudden vigour, 'Denis will be out of police clutches! Our solicitor is coming down first thing in the morning. He wasn't free to come this afternoon, he had to be in court, and with fog and poor driving conditions forecast for tonight, he thought it best to leave it till tomorrow. But he'll be here and get Denis released well before the time when, as I understand it, they'll have to let him go anyway if they can't show good reason for holding him! The solicitor is quite sure there will be no problem and he's a good man, a friend of Marcus's. He won't let us down.'

Marcus. Dead but not forgotten. Poor old Denis, married to Marcus's wife, spending Marcus's money and living in Marcus's house, now to be sprung by Marcus's lawyer. Meredith commiserated with Fulton even though she did find him a rather irritating man.

'Leah,' she asked, feeling a little ashamed of herself. 'What was Marcus Keller like?'

'Marcus? A good man, very successful, and tough in

business but honest. Devoted husband. Generous to a fault, spoiled me. Never wanted me to be anything but a doll. Perhaps if we'd had children . . . but we didn't. My daughter, Lizzie, is Bernie's child. Bernie was my first husband and is still around, remarried with more children from his present union. All I've got is Denis. I don't want to lose him.'

'You've got your daughter,' Meredith pointed out.

Leah shrugged eloquently. 'She doesn't need me. In more ways than one she's Bernie's daughter! Bernie was always utterly self-sufficient. If he could have managed to have babies by himself he'd never have bothered to marry me! He wanted a son, of course, and I couldn't give him that. We parted amicably enough. I left him free to try again for a son with someone else. He was correspondingly generous in our divorce settlement.'

They sat in silence for a while, watching the log Meredith had put on the fire as it was slowly consumed by the flames.

'I wish . . .' said Leah quietly.

'Wish what?'

'Just that. I wish. Are you one of those people, Meredith, who believes in reincarnation?'

'That we've all been here before?'

'Rather that we'll all be here again, get another chance.'

'Not really,' confessed Meredith. 'Anyone who ever admitted those sort of views to me seemed to believe they were Cleopatra or Julius Caesar. None of them believed they were previously a complete nonentity. It's comforting, I suppose, to think we'll get another crack at life. Most of us think we've messed up this time round.'

'Yes. That's why I hope it's true, the reincarnation theory,' said Leah. 'Then perhaps I'll do better next time.

I hope I do.' She smiled suddenly, her wide beautiful smile which Meredith recalled had been so striking when she had first met Leah. 'It's late. I think I will go to bed, go to sleep and stop thinking. Yes, you're right. Goodbye, Meredith.'

'Goodnight,' said Meredith. 'Sleep tight.'

'Oh yes, I'll do that.' Leah got up and walked across the lounge. At the door she hesitated but then, without looking back, turned the handle and walked out. A faint aura of perfume lingered in the air, a testament to her presence. Meredith frowned.

Markby tapped on his niece's door and put his head round. 'Your mum sent me up to say it's time to stop reading and settle down.'

Emma was sitting up in bed, pink as a freshly boiled shrimp from her bath, frowning over a venerable tome with yellowed pages.

Markby came in and sat down on the rather uncomfortable beanbag on the floor. 'What's the book?'

She held it up silently.

'Oh, *Black Beauty*, about a horse. I should have guessed! That looks like a pretty old copy.'

'It was Mummy's when she was a little girl.'

'Oh, yes, I seem to remember it. It made her cry.'

'That's because it's sad.' Animation entered Emma's tense little face. 'They were horrible and cruel to cab and carriage horses in the Victorian days!'

Markby laced fingers and said gently, 'Being horrible and cruel is sadly part of human nature sometimes. But only a part. Humans also do lots of fine and good and beautiful things.'

'Zoë does lots of good at the Rest Home.'

'Yes, she does. But you know how some of the animals

there have been damaged by bad handling in the past? That can happen to humans, too. If so, it's much better if it's dealt with straight away and put right.'

She looked away, back at her book, but she wasn't reading. Her mouth quivered.

'It's better to talk about it than think about it all alone, Emma.'

'I don't want to.'

There was a silence and then he said, 'I think your mum coloured in the frontispiece of that book.'

Emma turned back to the picture facing the title page, luridly crayonned purple and green by a childish hand. 'Vicky does that to my books. She does it to Matthew's as well. She mucks things up.'

Markby, well aware of his younger niece's predisposition to wreck everything, sighed. 'I know. She'll grow out of it.'

'He was sort of ill, wasn't he? The man in the woods.'

'Yes. Ill. An unhappy person. Do you dream about it?'

'Only once, the first night after I got back home.'

'We all have bad memories of one kind or another, Emma. The thing to do is to let them go. It's not easy. But it can be done. Just think of them being like boats. You untie them and let them float away out of sight.'

'It's already a funny fuzzy sort of memory. I never saw his face. But I don't like the dark much. I imagine shapes in it. Will you light that little lamp for me? I leave it on all night.'

'Sure.' He got up and switched on the little lamp with its lower-wattage bulb. Then he turned out the main light. 'Good night, sweetheart. Sleep tight. Even in *Black Beauty*, things all turned out all right in the end.'

'Yes, I know. Good night, Uncle Alan.'

* * *

Laura waited at the foot of the stairs. 'Did you switch the lamp on?'

'Yes, yes. Don't fret. She's a sensible kid. It will take a little while but she'll get it out of her system eventually. It's a pity she's reading such a lachrymose book – *Black Beauty*!'

'She only reads about horses.' Laura rubbed her forearms.

'You too,' her brother said. 'You'll get over it.'

'No, never!' Laura said fiercely and tossed back her long fair hair. She looked for a moment very like her own little daughter. 'Alan, did I hear right that you've hauled in Denis Fulton?'

'You legal eagles have wonderful ears. But he isn't asking for legal aid. He's got his own solicitor coming down from London tomorrow.'

'You take care!' she warned. 'You can't mess around. You have to follow all the rules, Alan!'

'Dear little sister, I'm well acquainted with the Police and Criminal Evidence guidelines! I can hold him for twenty-four hours. I am obliged to fetch his solicitor once he requests him and I may not ask him any questions till that solicitor arrives. If I want to hold him longer, I have to get authority from above and if I want a yet further extension I have to get it from a magistrate. But it won't come to that. Twenty-four hours will do it.'

'It won't come to that because Fulton's legal adviser won't let it!' Laura opened the front door and a swirl of fog drifted into the hall. 'Ugh! Thickening fast. Drive carefully and mind how you go!'

Springwood Hall and its gardens slept in a silent cocoon.

Down at the Alice Batt Rest Home the animals hardly stirred. The distant pine plantation was wrapped in eerie gloom. The whole countryside was held motionless as if suspended in time.

Only one creature was wakeful. He kept a lonely vigil, yet comfortable enough because he'd broken into the building housing the swimming pool. Inside, warm and safe from the unhealthy mist, he relaxed on one of the poolside recliners with his hands behind his head. Occasionally there came a gurgle from the pool's pipe system. Odd creaks and rustles sounded among the potted palms and the cooling central heating system. A tap dripped in the shower by the changing rooms.

He waited patiently. He even dozed off for an hour but awoke at an inner reveillé call set into motion by his own pent-up excitement. He consulted the illuminated dial of his wristwatch. Twenty to three in the morning. An excellent time to make his move. He got up, stooped to retrieve the plastic bag which stood by his chair and set off with it for the hotel.

As he quit the pool building the cold dank night air struck his face and the intrusive fog filled his nostrils. But he didn't mind. The murk could only help him. Marooned out here in clammy cottonwool amidst invisible fields, the Hall was at his mercy and any help summoned from Bamford would be hampered by the poor visibility and slow in arriving. He counted on that.

The ground plan of the whole place, Hall and gardens, was imprinted on his memory, the result of endless visits here during the period of the Hall's conversion to hotel. He turned his steps confidently towards the Hall and when he reached the spot he judged to be the corner of the building, he stopped and stretched out his hand. His fingers made contact with rough masonry. No more than he had expected but all the same, he smiled to himself in the darkness, a smug, self-congratulatory smirk of satisfaction because everything was going according to his plan.

Now it was easy. He had only to follow the wall of the house along to the next corner, turn right, along past the kitchens, turn right again – and now he was on the further side of the house alongside the dining-room windows.

A desire to keep the character of the old house had led to retaining the original frames and windows. Modern ones might have given him more trouble. Historical accuracy and old world charm have their price. Reflecting censoriously on this, he set down his bag and felt inside it, withdrawing a glass cutter and a roll of heavy duty sticky tape. He used the glass cutter to incise a neat circle in a pane by a window latch. Careful, now. Cautiously he picked up the sticky tape and affixed it to the pane covering the scored circle. A single sharp tap in the centre and the glass circle came away but, held in place by the sticky tape, did not fall. With infinite care he peeled away the overlapping ends of the tape and it lifted out the glass circle intact. He laid it on the grass, reached through the hole in the pane and released the catch.

Noiselessly and painlessly, he had obtained entry to the house, and taking a large bottle from his bag and holding it clasped to his chest, he climbed in.

He was in the dining room. This he knew but he took a flashlight from his pocket and splayed the beam around. There were two sets of doors. One led into the kitchen for staff use; the other, admitting the diners, into the corridor which ran to the front entrance hall and main staircase. The tables were ready, set with crisply ironed damask cloths and napkins. He unscrewed the top of the bottle and splashed the paraffin it contained freely across a line of table linen to the doors into the corridor. These doors he then propped open using a dining-room chair.

Stepping through them into the corridor, he was confronted by a small staircase, the former servants' back stairs. He ignored it and set off down the ground-floor corridor, splashing paraffin as he went. Half way down was a fire door insulating the back half of the house from the front. This too he wedged open, using a handy fire extinguisher.

A few more steps and he emerged into the main reception hall at the foot of the wide main staircase, an impressive sweeping construction intended to accommodate crinolines. Here he splashed the rest of his paraffin across the carpet, across the walnut antique table at which the snooty receptionist presided by day, across the lower treads of the staircase and up the carved oak banister.

The paraffin container was empty. Now speed was of the essence. He darted away, running back the way he'd come, down the corridor, through the opened fire doors, through open dining-room doors into the dining room. There he tossed aside the empty bottle. He fumbled, a flame flickered in his hand as he stooped. There was a sudden whoosh, a rush of heat and a sheet of blue and yellow flame which leapt into the air, its violence causing him to spring back at first in alarm and then with exultation.

He wished he could have stayed here to watch it, but its heat already scorched his face. He ran across the dining room and scrambled panting from the forced window out into the open air. Even as he did the alarm bells, activated by smoke and heat detectors in the dining room ceiling, began to ring shrilly.

But they could not quench the progress of the fire he had

left behind him as it retraced its creator's steps. It danced from table to table fuelled by the paraffin-soaked linen and out of the dining room doors. Drawn faster by the draught of air rushing from front to back of the house through the opened doorways and broken window, it hopped nimbly down the corridor along the trail of paraffin, ran across the carpet and licked up the banister of the staircase. Well away now, it seized on the walnut table making the polished veneer crack and split as the flames chuckled throatily and the smoke billowed about their skirts and rose to blacken the ornamental plaster of the ceilings.

In the garden and safe from its hungry progress, the man who had set it and run from it could no more have left it to its devices than he could have flown. It was his creation and he would stay to watch it grow and do its work. Perversely the fog had started to lift and the house appeared as a dark block against the lightening skies. But it was still cold and damp, eating through his heavy leather jacket and into his bones. He was oblivious of it as, at a prudent distance, he stopped, drawing deep, ragged breaths, and crouched down among the bushes to watch Springwood Hall burn.

Chapter Twenty-Three

Meredith was dreaming she was back in her early years at boarding school. She was in the dormitory asleep in one of its neat little white-enamelled iron bedsteads and someone had decided to hold the once-a-term fire drill. The alarm bell had been set ringing, awakening her from slumber and ordering her out of the snug spot under the bedclothes to face the rigours of the chill corridors and eventual night air in the school's quadrangle.

She woke up and for a split second believed it was all true, she was back at school and the fire-drill bell was ringing. But for some extraordinary reason she was alone. Everyone else had already quit the dormitory and left her there to sleep on.

Then reality struck and she sat up with a gasp. It was a fire alarm all right. But it rang in Springwood Hall hotel. Meredith threw back the bedclothes and jumped out, her toes feeling for her slippers. It took a further second to switch on the bedside lamp and grab her wristwatch. It was nearly half past three in the morning.

The bell still rang insistently. It could be a malfunction but if so, surely someone would have shut it off by now? She pulled on her dressing-gown and set off towards the door, tying her belt as she went and muttering at the inconvenience.

The corridor was empty but from below came the sound of a shout and doors slamming. A twinge of alarm dismissed her first thought, that the bell had been set off by some electrical quirk. It seemed there was some minor emergency or other. Memory of a previous injunction against using lifts in the case of fire led Meredith to run to the top of the main staircase. There was a curious odour in the air and a sinister crackling from below. She began to descend to see what was wrong and suddenly found herself met by a wall of smoke which sent her coughing back up to the top.

Now there was no doubt. Springwood Hall was on fire. But that was not a reason to panic yet. There was another staircase, the small back stairs at the other end of the corridor which ran down the side of the house and a fire exit indicated by arrows at the other lateral end of the building. But first she had to find Leah.

Leah was, she knew, the only other person sleeping on this floor at the moment and her bedroom door was shut fast. Meredith ran to it and beat on it with her clenched fist.

'Leah! Leah, wake up!'

There was no response from within. The smell of smoke grew more intense. As yet it was all coming up from below and on this floor there was no fire. But there was no way of telling the extent to which the ground-floor conflagration had taken hold. Meredith hammered on Leah's door again to no avail. She seized the handle and tried to turn it but the door was locked.

'Damn!' she said forcefully. She remembered now with sinking heart that she had advised Leah to take an aspirin and that Leah herself had spoken of having pills. Presumably she had taken Meredith's advice and a couple of pills and was sleeping like a baby.

If so, she could well be suffocated by smoke as she slept. Already it was creeping up the main stair as Meredith, casting a wild glance in that direction, saw. Curling grey wisps floated out on to the upper landing.

This was no time to respect the fabric of the hotel or Eric's property. Luckily the doors of the bedrooms were of traditional type with panels. Meredith seized a particularly hideous ormulu clock, probably part of the Hall's original furnishings, from a table in the corridor and, holding it by the chaste Diana the Huntress who perched atop it, swung it as hard as she could at the door panel by the lock.

Two more blows and considerable damage to Diana's hounds and the clock's innards, and the wood splintered. Meredith thrust her hand through the gap, oblivious of scratches and splinters, and felt for the lock, praying Leah had left the key in the door.

Thank goodness, she had. Meredith turned it and burst into the room, her fingers fumbling for the light switch. 'Leah, wake up!'

The electrics on this circuit were still unaffected and the room was bathed in light. Leah sprawled sound asleep on one of the twin beds. Denis's untenanted pyjamas were set out neatly and pathetically on the other. How on earth could Leah still sleep on?

Meredith ran to the bed and shook the sleeper's shoulder. 'For God's sake, Leah—'

And then she saw the empty pill bottle on the bedside table and the envelope propped against the lamp and addressed in a large, free hand to 'Chief Inspector Markby, Bamford CID'.

There was no time to panic. Meredith snatched up bottle and envelope and thrust them into her dressing-gown pocket. She hauled Leah upright and, supporting her with one hand, ruthlessly slapped her face with the other.

'Come on, dammit, you've got to wake up!'

Leah moaned and turned her head which then flopped forward on to her chest.

'No, no! You can't sleep! It's not allowed, do you hear? On your feet!'

She dragged Leah bodily out of the bed, coughing as a wisp of smoke snaked its way into her lungs. Somehow she hauled Leah to the bathroom, feet trailing across the carpet, turned on the shower tap and shoved Leah's head under it.

Leah jerked, shuddered and made a faint, incoherent protest.

'Good enough!' said Meredith grimly. 'Now then, you can walk – come on! It's me, Meredith, and you're going to do exactly as I say!'

'Sleep . . .' muttered Leah, sagging.

'Oh, no, you don't!' Meredith manhandled her charge back to her feet and propped her against the wall while she took brief stock of the options open to her.

The main staircase was blocked. That left the narrow back staircase and the fire escape, a metal rung ladder. She might just, with God's grace, get Leah down the small back stairs. She'd never get Leah down the fire escape. The back stairs it was.

She propelled Leah across the bedroom and out into the corridor. Leah alternately sagged forward and lurched back. Meredith's arms ached and she would have been surprised at her own language had she had time to consider it. Luckily the back stairs were not far away but if getting Leah there was awkward, getting Leah down them promised to be a nightmare.

Meredith draped one of Leah's arms round her neck and encircled Leah's waist with one of her own arms. Gripping the banister rail with her free hand they began the hair-raising descent.

They didn't get far. Leah lurched down a couple of steps, twisted out of Meredith's grip and sagged in a dead weight to the ground, propped against the banister. Desperately Meredith hauled her up and they tried again. This time Leah toppled forward and there was nothing Meredith could do but let her go or she would have lost her own footing and been carried down with Leah head-long.

Leah rolled and bumped to the foot of the stair and lay there inert amid a cloud of swirling smoke. Meredith, her heart in her mouth, hastened down and was met by a blast of heat. Spluttering and wincing, she bent over the fallen figure. Leah opened her eyes and moaned before cough-ing and then closing her eyes again, her head lolling.

However, as far as Meredith could tell, it seemed that completely relaxed like a drunk, Leah had managed to take a potentially dangerous fall without seriously injur-ing herself. But the new danger in which they found them-selves made short shrift of any relief Meredith might have felt. The bottom of the staircase debouched into a corridor and a little way down it was the guests' entrance to the dining room. Not that Meredith could see it because they had reached the scene of the fire.

The heat was intense and the smoke swirled ever thicker. She could hear the flames crackling in the dining room and see flickering long tongues of sinuous flame darting in and out of the smoke haze. The corridor leading past the dining room to the front entrance hall of the house was similarly blocked by smoke and flames. But off to the left ran the corridor leading to the kitchens. This, Meredith saw when she staggered to the corner and peered round it, was still free of flames and less smoke-filled.

Somehow she managed to get Leah to her feet by dint of the kind of superhuman effort only dire emergency calls forth. She began to haul her along, away from the roaring inferno behind the dining-room doors. Sweat ran down Meredith's body. Her eyes wept copious blinding tears from the effect of the smoke and she could hardly draw breath. Her sense of direction was letting her down and for the first time she really began to believe they were not going to make it. She yelled hoarsely, 'Leah – come on! You must try and walk!' But Leah slumped down again and this time did not move or make a sound and Meredith's muscles no longer had the strength to wrestle with her.

Then a voice answered, not Leah's but a man's and it came from the kitchen corridor. 'Miss Mitchell!' it roared.

'Over here!' cried Meredith painfully, her throat feeling as if it were stripped raw.

A dark shape loomed up and a body crashed into her, knocking her sprawling. Arms seized her and dragged her upright. 'This way!' ordered Eric hoarsely. He gripped her forearm and urged her forward.

'I've got Leah Fulton with me, she's unconscious—' Meredith gasped.

Eric pushed past her. 'I've got her . . . Hold my sleeve – come on!'

She stumbled blindly after him, the blood pounding against her temples. As far as she could tell he had slung Leah over his shoulder like a sack of potatoes. As they blundered along Meredith could hear the fire gaining strength behind them. This whole wing of the hotel was burning, well alight, she thought. The horror of it seized her and she almost fell.

'Nearly there!' gasped Eric. 'Keep going!'

A sudden blissfully welcome blast of fresh air hit Meredith's face, its icy cold touch like a slap. She staggered towards its origin and suddenly they were out of the building through the rear entrance.

Other hands seized her and guided her forward but the tears streaming from her stinging eyes prevented her seeing the faces. Then she found she was sitting on the damp lawn and Leah was stretched on the grass beside her with Eric kneeling over her. Behind them the horrid crackle of the flames and the dull roaring of the fire sounded like a whole pack of wild beasts clawing at their cage for release.

Eric raised Leah's head and gasped, 'She's inhaled the smoke!'

'No!' Meredith fumbled in her pocket. 'She took pills – these! Overdosed, do you understand? We must get her to hospital!'

Ulli Richter the chef was a poor sleeper. He lay awake that night in his tiny flat at the top of the building and thought about his kitchens and the next day's menu. He was a man whose entire life revolved around his profession. When Ulli thought about anything, he thought about food, its preparation and presentation, the efficiency of the kitchens, the manifold shortcomings of his underlings.

He also thought now, as he had done many times, about the murder. A murder committed with one of his knives! His knife! A cherished implement of his trade and now sullied by being used to butcher a stupid woman! He, Richter, the master chef, associated with a sordid crime! At the thought of the insult, he sat up in bed and swore aloud in his native Schywzer-deutsch.

Whenever he couldn't sleep, Ulli got up and made

himself a tisane in the tiny kitchenette of the flat. But often he took his herbal infusion downstairs and sat in the hotel kitchens to drink it, calmed by the familiar surroundings. Away from his kitchens, Ulli always fretted. They were his refuge, his place of safety and he crept into them as a hermit crab into a convenient shell and was happy.

Richter switched on the light, wrapped himself in a voluminous towelling robe and set off downstairs to his beloved domain. He would make a tisane down there. Potter about amongst the shining surfaces of stainless steel, of mottled marble and brightly polished tiles. He would realign all the pots on their shelves, check the store cupboard. He would find peace.

It was not to be. He was nearly there before he realised something was wrong. A faint odour wafting up the stairs. Smoke? Was it possible? And then the fire alarm bells began to shrill their warning.

Ulli broke into a clumsy run. Other people might be concerned with the rest of the hotel but he cared only for his kitchens. He descended the stairs at breakneck speed and found himself, as Meredith had done, faced by the smoke and flames from the dining room. What fool had left the doors open?

Ulli wheeled and darted down the corridor to the left leading to his kitchens, fearing that the fire had taken hold there. Surely it could not have done? Had some idiot left heat under a pan of fat or some such elementary error? No, impossible! He, Richter, always made the final safety check of the day before closing up his kitchens for the night. Not a speck of grease or puddle of water, not an unwiped surface or dripping tap escaped his eagle eye.

But the fire had not begun in nor yet reached his kingdom. Now that he saw the kitchens were blameless and not as yet afire, Richter was at last moved to think of others. With the idea that he might have to smash his way through some barrier to effect a rescue, he took a large, metal-headed meat hammer from a hook and grasping it at the ready, turned back into the corridor and collided with his employer.

'Out, Ulli!' shouted Eric peremptorily. 'Out, dammit! Get out of the building and see how many of the staff you can account for!'

Richter, still clasping the meat hammer, stumbled towards the back exit and out into the gardens. From this vantage point he was now able to see that only the east wing was ablaze. Nearby clustered the guests who had been sleeping in the west wing and who, together with the staff also lodged there, had made a safe escape through the emergency exit on that side of the house. Missing were the two ladies from the first floor east, the one whose husband had left with the policeman and the other, the policeman's girlfriend. Ulli feared that Schuhmacher had returned to the burning east wing to look for them. Mindful of his orders, however, he made a rapid head count of the staff and was satisfied no one was missing.

Uneasily he returned his gaze to the flames licking at the east wing's windows and horror at the appalling deed filled his soul. He did not doubt for one moment that some criminal hand had done this. Filled with incoherent rage and lit by the rose glow of the flames, he stood on the lawn, a short, broad, muscular figure in a dishevelled robe, and brandished his meat hammer in the air like a wrathful Thor as he called down imprecations on the rogues and villains responsible.

'Bloody history people! Bloody Fat-Woman Mapple! All bloody, bloody people! Devils, yes, devils, all of them! I find you, who did this thing, I find you and I kill you, yes, I kill!'

At this point his eye caught a movement in nearby bushes. He peered into the red-lit murk and growled suspiciously, 'Who is there?'

The dark shape which, like him, had been watching the fire, did not reply but turned and ran, crashing a way through the shrubbery.

Ulli didn't hesitate. He plunged after the fleeing figure, shaking the meat hammer threateningly and roaring, 'You stop! You come back here!'

Not surprisingly, the fugitive ahead of him did not obey. He careered on wildly, intent only on escape until his foot caught a trailing root. He stumbled and fell on to his hands and knees. Ulli gave a shriek of triumph and leapt towards the crumpled form. He grabbed a handful of hair and wrenched round the head and the crimson glow was enough to allow him to identify a face he was sure he recognised.

'Ah! So it is you! You are with that damned history society, I remember!' he yelled. 'You try to burn hotel! You try to burn my kitchens! I fix you! You can join that other one, that woman in our cellars!'

He raised the meat hammer on high and the prostrate and helpless Robin Harding on the ground let out a high-pitched scream of pure terror.

It was swallowed up by the sound of the fire engines arriving from Bamford.

Chapter Twenty-Four

Meredith stood looking up at the geometric white shapes of the hospital complex with some apprehension. The breeze ruffled her hair and an empty, crushed cigarette packet bowled a short distance across the surface of the carpark. It was a cool, overcast day. From time to time during the morning the sun had made an effort to squeeze its way between the cloud cover but had now given up and was sulking behind an impenetrable veil. The rows of windows in the architectural blocks gleamed dully and there was an abandoned look to the landscaped lawns despite the numerous cars parked around hers. Signposts pointed the way to various units, indicating Maternity, Radiology, Casualty and a host of others, but if all these departments were bustling with business it, like the sun, was all well out of sight.

She wasn't looking forward to making this visit but it had to be done. Get it over with, that was the thing. Meredith set off determinedly towards the nearest plate-glass door.

'She's feeling a little bit iffy,' said the young nurse. 'Not surprising. It's nasty, being pumped out and, of course, she's been given the standard antidote. You sound a bit hoarse, have you got a cold?' She looked at Meredith dubiously.

'No, I inhaled a lot of smoke and it's left my throat sore and affected my voice.'

'Oh, I see – like Mrs Fulton. She's croaking, too. Were you caught in the same fire?'

'Yes. She is all right, though, Mrs Fulton?'

'Oh, yes, dear! She didn't take enough to really kill herself! They seldom do, you know.'

'Oh,' said Meredith. 'I see.'

'So she's just a bit groggy!' The nurse smiled brightly. 'And just a teeny bit down in the dumps. She'll be pleased to have a cheerful visitor. You won't tire her, will you?'

Alerted by the nurse's emphasis on 'cheerful', Meredith asked, 'Has her husband been to see her?'

'Oh, yes, he's been! But between you and me, he wasn't exactly good for her, if you know what I mean. He was in such a state himself. They're like that sometimes.'

On this cryptic note the nurse ushered Meredith into a small private room. Leah lay propped on pillows wearing a pink bedjacket, its lively hue contrasting grotesquely with the greyness of her complexion.

'Hullo, there,' said Meredith. 'How's it going?'

'All right. I feel lousy. So I should, I suppose.'

'I brought a couple of magazines and some barley sugars. Good for the throat. How is yours? Mine's sore.' Meredith set her offerings on the bedside locker and took a seat.

'It's not too bad. I have to thank you, don't I, for saving my life?' Leah sounded more resentful than grateful.

'Not if you'd rather not,' Meredith told her.

Leah threw out her hands and exclaimed abjectly. 'I'm so sorry! I didn't mean to be churlish. You were so brave and resolute, hauling me downstairs like that! And so unselfish! You might have been trapped yourself.'

'Eric carried you outside. Without his help neither of us might have made it!'

Leah burrowed back into her pillows and sighed. 'Poor Eric. All his work literally up in smoke!'

'In fact only the east wing and kitchens were put out of action. But he's got plans for fixing it all up again. Eric's a determined sort.'

'Yes.'

An awkward silence fell. Meredith asked with some hesitation, 'Has Alan been to see you?'

'Not yet. He sent along a nice young policewoman and she said he sent his compliments – very formal, your police chum! – and he'd call on me later when I felt better.' Anxiety entered Leah's dark eyes. 'Meredith, when you dragged me out of bed, I know you retrieved the pill bottle because the doctor here said so. He said it was very helpful knowing exactly what I'd taken and you were to be congratulated on your presence of mind. But I don't know whether you noticed a – a –' Her voice trailed off and she fixed Meredith with a questioning look.

'A letter? Yes, I picked that up too. I've still got it. It's here, in my bag.'

'You didn't give it to your boyfriend, then? It's addressed to him.'

'No.' Meredith shook her head. 'I was going to ask you if you wanted it back. After all, you weren't exactly *compos mentis* when you wrote it, were you? It was just before you swallowed the pills.' She opened her shoulder bag and took out the envelope retrieved from Leah's bedside table at the hotel. 'It's got a bit grubby, sorry about that.' She held it out.

Leah stretched out a hand which appeared incredibly frail, blue veins showing through alabaster skin. She touched the edge of the envelope. 'You didn't read it?'

'Of course not!' said Meredith indignantly. After a moment she added, 'I didn't need to.'

Leah raised her eyebrows. 'You sound very sure. Do you really know what I wrote?'

'I think so.' Meredith folded her hands in her lap. 'Why are we humans so loath to trust our sense of smell? Animals trust theirs. We only use ours when we have to and we only feel it's telling us right if it's really obvious, quite over-powering. The message does register subconsciously, but we ignore it. I mean, if one human tells another he smells, that's an insult. But of course we all smell different. Dogs can tell us apart by our smell, track us cross-country by it, pick one object out of a pile by it.' Leah, she noticed, had begun to look wary.

'You know what I'm getting at, don't you?' Meredith said. 'When I came on Ellen's body in the cellar, I dare say shock affected me. I disliked those cellars anyway, I found them claustrophobic and there was a musty smell of old stone and new whitewash. That was strong enough for me to recognise it straight off. But there was another smell too, sweetish and not unpleasant, a bit flowery. I registered that subconsciously but I didn't take proper notice of it. I should have done because it was telling me something very important.'

Leah's gaze was cold. 'Yes?'

'It was telling me a name, giving me an identity. It was your perfume, Leah. Your smell, if you don't mind me putting it like that. It was telling me you had been stand-ing where I was, only a little time before me.'

The woman in the bed said nothing.

'I should have twigged earlier because only a very little later I smelled it again. I went along to your room to fetch your wrap as Denis asked me. It was while we were all waiting downstairs in the dining room, remember? The same perfume filled your room, very strong. And again in your house when I came to dinner. And in the lounge of Springwood Hall as we sat talking. You even made a reference to it yourself. "Drenched in French perfume", you said. I laughed because it sounded so funny. But it jolted my memory. Why did you kill Ellen?'

'She was Denis's wife.'

Leah spoke the words so calmly that Meredith could only stare open-mouthed until she realised she was gaping and closed it.

'Yes, really. Your copper boyfriend knows. He's been telling Denis to own up and tell me but of course, poor Denis just hadn't the guts. Nor would he have had the guts to kill her. Oh yes, our marriage was bigamous and now the cat's out of the bag, he admits it.'

'Did you, did you know all along?' Meredith whispered.

'Of course not. Denis said he'd never been married and why shouldn't I believe him? He didn't act like a man who was used to having a woman around. I thought he was a typical middle-aged bachelor until he met me, and at first I put down all his anxiety to that. But I soon realised there was something specific worrying him, something outside our home, and he wasn't going to tell me what it was. I kept giving him the opportunity, creating neat little openings in the conversation, but he utterly refused to take them up. Like all the men in my life, I suppose he wanted to keep unpleasantness from me because he thought I wouldn't cope! It really makes me want to spit!'

Leah scowled. 'So I had to hire a private detective, a very good man whom Marcus used from time to time, and he found out for me.'

Marcus again. Denis was truly doomed to be haunted by the man, even his follies exposed by Marcus's detective. Marcus, guarding his wife from the grave.

'Those absences I couldn't account for, when I lied and said I was with Lizzie and Denis thought I was with Victor, I was conferring with the inquiry agent. It took him a while but once he got on to Ellen he used his contacts in Australia to trace her background there.'

'And you decided to kill her?' Meredith asked incredulously.

'Not straight away, of course not. I negotiated with her via the inquiry agent. But clearly it wasn't going to get us anywhere. I would have paid her off handsomely. I made that quite clear to her. But she didn't want the money. What she wanted was to make Denis jump when she pulled the string. She seemed to think Denis had ditched her and she was out to get him. I realised she wouldn't let go. But I wasn't going to let go either! She should have realised that.'

Leah frowned and reached up both hands to push back her tangled hair. 'I don't know quite when I realised I would have to kill her. Coming down to the opening of Eric's hotel just brought things to a head. I made an arrangement to meet Ellen face to face. I told myself I would make a last appeal but I knew it would be a waste of time. She wasn't going to change her tune.

'We were given the grand tour of the hotel. Do you remember how we traipsed through the kitchens and got in the way of the cooks? The chef was showing off his *batterie de cuisine*, and I saw the knife just lying there unattended. I had some idea of frightening Ellen. I picked it up and put it in my purse. But once I'd done that, I knew I'd have to use it. It was too late to go back.'

Leah met Meredith's horrified gaze and her expression became mulish. 'Ellen left me no choice. It was her own fault. She should have taken the money I offered, it was much more than the pathetic pay-outs Denis had been making her. She should have let Denis alone. I did it for him.' She saw something in Meredith's face and burst out, 'All right, I did it for me! Denis is all I've got! I haven't got anyone else to love! Do you know what it's like, having so much love bottled up inside you and no one to lavish it on? No one to cherish? No one who needs you?'

These last words came out in a vehement croak as Leah's throat succumbed like Meredith's to the after-effects of smoke.

Meredith said lamely, 'Have a barley-sugar. They help.'

'Thanks. Have one yourself.'

There was another silence broken by the rustle of sweet-papers.

'But Denis himself nearly got arrested for her murder!' Meredith accused suddenly.

'Well, I didn't know your boyfriend was going to be so officious and stupid, did I?' Leah rolled her sweet-wrapper into a tiny ball and hurled it at a distant wastepaper basket. It missed and bounced across the polished floor. 'No, he's not stupid, your Chief Inspector Markby. He's too damn bright. I hadn't counted on his finding out who Ellen really was. Denis says the police got hold of his and Ellen's wedding certificate. He said he ransacked her flat trying to find it but all the time that kid she had made her heiress had it. So, anyhow, now I'll have to come clean and own up to the dirty deed. Blasted nuisance.' Leah's voice sounded resentful but resigned.

'What about the letter?' Meredith indicated it lying on the bedspread.

'My confession? Histrionics. Telling all and then swallowing pills like that. I always was a bit of a show-off. It comes of my mother having told me that whatever I did, I should do it with style. Pity my style is so corny.'

'You're a gambler, too. You told me that. You liked Marcus to take you to Monte Carlo. That's why you thought you stood a fair chance of getting away with it. Only a gambler would have had the nerve to kill Ellen like that, under our noses.'

'Exactly. That should have told the police that Denis didn't do it! If he'd even tried he'd only have ended up cutting himself as he did at my dinner party or making a fool of himself as when he threatened Victor. Oh here, take the wretched letter back and deliver it to Markby! I'll tell him all about it when he comes but he might as well have the letter since you rescued it so daringly from the flames!'

'And Denis?' Meredith asked quietly. 'Does he realise you killed her?'

Leah's tired smile was a mockery of its usual brilliance. 'Oh, yes. I think Denis suspected quite early on. But he couldn't bring himself to face up to it. That's Denis's problem, you know, facing up to unpleasant facts.' She turned her face towards the window and the dull vista outside. 'All such a pity, really.'

'The pity,' Meredith heard herself say, 'is that Marcus is dead but won't lie down.'

'That's Marcus for you.' And for a moment, a glimmer of amusement lightened Leah's doleful countenance.

Outside in the corridor again, Meredith tried to marshal her thoughts. What she had heard was what she'd come to hear but it had still been a shock, listening to the actual words on Leah's lips.

Her attention was attracted by squeaky footsteps and, looking up, she saw to her great surprise Hope Mapple plodding down the corridor towards her.

Hope was wearing a flowing dark blue garment and carrying a large shopping bag bulging with rolls of coloured paper and balls of string. She wore plimsoles and their rubber soles adhered to the wax polished floor in a series of protesting squeals.

'Hullo!' she boomed cheerily. 'Visiting the sick?'

'Yes. What are you doing here?'

'It's one of my therapy days. Arts and crafts, you know, help post-operative blues no end. I see Mrs Fulton is in here today. Do you think she'd be interested to learn macramé? There's something very satisfying and therapeutic in all those knots.'

'I really don't think,' said Meredith firmly, 'that she's up to macramé today. Better leave it for a while.'

'Right-o.' Ms Mapple paused and the blue tent quivered. 'Pity about the damage to the Hall. Pity about young Robin, too. He always seemed such an excessively normal sort of boy, bit intense perhaps. It might have been a mental breakdown. Wonder if they'll put him in the psychiatric ward here? I do a lot of arts and crafts with the confused.'

'I don't know about that. I think he probably knew what he was doing. It was a wicked act and a mercy no one died.'

'It's the end of the historical society, anyway,' said Hope. 'Charles and I held a winding-up meeting. But we've heard of a plan to clear the last big area of native woodland round here and plant another of those ghastly commercial conifer plantations in its place. There's talk of forming a protest committee and mounting a really cracking campaign. Charles and I feel that with our experience we ought to offer ourselves.'

Clearly an offer the woodland committee could not refuse. 'I hope you have better luck this time.'

'Oh, I think we'll stir things up a bit. I must be on my way. Collage day in the children's ward.'

Meredith waited as Hope squeaked her way out of sight and then set off on her own errand, to deliver Leah's letter to Alan Markby.

Chapter Twenty-Five

They consigned Ellen Bryant to ashes in the presence of few mourners.

Chief Inspector Markby and Sergeant Pearce attended as the investigating officers into her death. The Chamber of Commerce sent a deputation as a tribute to a late colleague. Fidgeting in their black ties they were obviously ill at ease and anxious to be out of the plain little crematorium chapel. Hope Mapple in purple and Zoë Foster were there as Ellen's fellow history buffs. Charles Grimsby came and stood together with his business friends, well away from both women, obviously signifying to anyone who was interested that he was there as a member of the business community and certainly not as one of the now defunct historical society. Of them all most grief was shown by Margery Collins who snuffled loudly throughout the brief address into a damp handkerchief.

Denis Fulton didn't put in an appearance which did not surprise Markby. But he was slightly shocked that Denis had not even sent a wreath to his former wife's obsequies. Perhaps Denis was simply too embarrassed in the circumstances. Embarrassment, thought Markby wrily, was an emotion not to be underestimated. It influenced people's actions powerfully.

* * *

Later in the day, he and Meredith Mitchell sat side by side on a fallen mossy tree trunk, on the edge of the wild wood which bordered the pine plantation. Before them the land dropped away in a steep grassy slope. Springwood Hall, its east wing heavily scaffolded, lay ahead and below. A short distance from the hotel the sun shone on the unsightly buildings of the Alice Batt Rest Home. The animals grazing in the paddock looked from this point like the wooden beasts inhabiting a toy farm. Only Maud was identifiable, even at such a distance, by the distinctive lurch of her progress towards a patch of fresh grass. It was even clear enough today to make out, on the horizon, a tiny exclamation mark which was the spire of Bamford church.

Meredith picked at a loose piece of bark on the tree trunk. It came away and a beetle ran out, fell off and disappeared among the dry leaves at her feet.

'You've heard about the Save our Bamford Woods committee?'

'Haven't I just . . .' said Markby gloomily. 'My sympathies are with their aims. It's the presence of Hope Mapple in their ranks which worries me! I understand Hope proposes to chain herself to a tree if there's any attempt to fell it.'

'I rather like Hope. I think she's all that's endearingly eccentric about the British and she's very kind. She spends hours working with the disadvantaged. I'm more worried what will happen to Leah.'

'Save your sympathy. Leah Fulton has the best legal representatives and eminent medical men galore to testify to her having been under intolerable strain. And whatever she may have said to you, she's now claiming she took the knife for self-defence because she was afraid Ellen might attack her. Leah is a shrewd and resourceful woman.'

'You know, she'd be so pleased to hear herself described like that. She hates being thought a butterfly. Will they get her off?'

'I trust not entirely. But I suspect they'll minimise the repercussions. That's only my opinion.'

'And did you really think at one time that Denis had killed Ellen?'

He pursed his lips. 'Put it this way. I was sure one of the Fultons had. Taking Denis in shook the truth out of the woodwork.'

'You took a heck of a risk!' said Meredith accusingly. 'Leah might have died! It was only the fire which made me break into her room and find her. You played ducks and drakes with her emotional state. She was devastated when you marched Denis away!'

'I didn't think she'd swallow pills!' he defended himself. 'But I had to break up the double act. They were too good at it.'

Meredith picked out another piece of loose bark. 'Why were you so sure the killer had to be either Denis or Leah?'

'They had motive,' said Markby simply. 'People don't usually murder for no reason.'

'I still think you took an unwarranted risk. You walked awfully near the edge, Alan. Suppose Robin Harding hadn't been eaten up with jealousy and set fire to the hotel?'

'I know,' said Markby abruptly.

They sat in silence for a while. 'Poor Eric, all that work to be done all over again,' said Meredith, gazing down at the damaged hotel.

'Eric assures me that Ulli Richter is the mildest man alive outside of his kitchen, but he managed to give young Harding a terrific fright!' returned Markby with every sign of satisfaction. 'When Eric came on them, Robin was fairly gibbering, sure Richter meant to bash his skull in. Arson endangering life is a serious crime and Harding will have plenty of time to reflect on the error of his ways when he gets sent down.'

'Hope thinks he blew a mental fuse. I suppose he was driven by jealousy. But this has all been about jealousy, hasn't it? Robin jealous of Eric. Denis jealous of Victor Merle. Even poor Ellen jealous because Denis was happily married and had forgotten her. Then Ellen's jealousy collided with the sort of frustrated mother love Leah has for Denis. How frightening that kind of obsessive love can be. Leah was prepared to kill for him almost instinctively, just as Maud killed to protect Emma.'

'Oy!' interrupted Markby firmly. 'Leah took the knife and hid it in her purse knowing she'd arranged a secret meeting with Ellen later. Premeditation – good and proper! However, as I've already indicated, it's not for you and me to argue that one out. Lawyers and doctors will.'

'Alan . . .' Meredith said slowly after a while. 'I don't want to sound conceited but you're never, well, jealous, are you? Of me?'

'Of you? Of course not!' said Markby robustly.

'Oh.' Well, that's plain enough! thought Meredith. Made a fool of yourself, Mitchell! Why should he care what you do?

Suddenly Markby beside her blurted, 'Yes, of course I am! Not exactly green-eyed with it. I recognise you're a free agent. I don't have any rights. But I do sometimes wonder if you've got anyone in London.'

'No, I'm not seeing anyone else. Are you?'

'What? Lord, no.'

'That's all right, then. Alan, have you heard any more about promotion or leaving Bamford? You've been very quiet about it.'

'I'm not going. I've told 'em so. It's all on ice for the time being. Jones will have to give everyone their money back.'

'I wondered because I've been thinking of taking a little holiday. Just a week, perhaps, not going far. Just somewhere quiet.'

'Somewhere quiet, eh?' said Markby. 'Sounds pretty good to me.'

Zoë straightened up with a muffled groan and rested on her muck-fork, one hand clasped to the small of her back. A mountain of soiled straw surrounded her and did not seem to have got any smaller for all that she'd been toiling for ages. She'd have to get Finlay over again about the piebald cob's digestive problem. She hoped it wasn't due to grass. Mostly the horses got upset if they didn't get grass; but the cob had always been an oddity. All around the evidence of his oddness was clearly visible, to say nothing of the smell. Average mucking out was bad enough. They didn't need complications.

It would be nice to have help. But Emma had gone back to school and no one else had volunteered. But anyway, perhaps it wasn't for much longer. The six months was nearly up. They'd get their marching orders any day now.

From outside came the distinctive screech of the yard gate. When she had a moment, she really ought to get round to oiling it. Zoë went to the barn door and peered out to see who the visitor might be. To her surprise and dismay she saw Eric Schuhmacher striding purposefully across the yard towards her. He was wearing old cord trousers and yes, wellington boots. And he didn't look like a man who'd come to waste words.

So sentence of execution was about to be delivered. She hadn't seen Schuhmacher since storming out of his dining room. She'd thought about going over to see him and apologising for Rob's actions. Not that it was her fault Rob had set fire to the hotel, but she was in a moral sort of way responsible.

She'd even got as far as the hotel drive and then the sight of the burned out east wing and the men clearing out the charred furniture from the dining room had filled her with such horror and guilt that she had simply turned and run. Facing him had just been impossible.

But she had to face him now. He'd reached the barn door. 'Miss Foster?'

'Good morning, Mr Schuhmacher.'

'We could perhaps have a word?' Eric paused and sniffed the air. 'Outside in the yard would be preferable.'

Zoë trailed out, still holding the fork. 'I realise why you've come, Mr Schuhmacher. I haven't been able to make alternative arrangements for the animals.'

But she had the money now, thanks to Margery. That was the awful part. She had the money for new stable buildings but not the nerve to ask Schuhmacher if he was still willing to let her lease the new site and the cottage. He'd refuse. Of course he would. Especially since Rob had burned down half Springwood Hall! And the awful embarrassing scene she'd made in front of his guests. How could he forgive her that? How furious with them all Schuhmacher must be.

He said rather testily now, 'Alternative arrangements are available as I made clear to you some time ago!'

Zoë's heart rose and then plummeted. 'You – you'd still consider leasing us the new site?' No, of course he didn't mean that. He couldn't, surely?

'Of course, why not?'

'I thought you'd be too angry.' She gazed at him, bewildered.

He scowled at her in a most ferocious and alarming

manner. 'And why, Miss Foster, should I be so angry as to go back on my offer? It is not my habit to do such a thing. I am a man of my word!'

'No, I wasn't suggesting you – I mean, I made a scene at the hotel and Robin tried to burn it down. I am so very sorry about all of it. If you're still willing to let me lease the new site, it's incredibly generous of you. I'm so grateful. Will you rebuild the hotel?'

'Yes. I've already engaged a builder. It is a set-back but it is not your fault. I shall begin again.'

'That's very courageous of you,' said Zoë simply.

Eric stared at her. Then he said very quietly, 'I am not the only courageous one. You too have a great deal of courage.

'Zoë, when I was a young man, your age –' He paused and shrugged resignedly. 'I dedicated my life to a sport and spent all my time perfecting my skills at it. I didn't worry myself what I was going to do twenty years later when the sporting life was well over and I'd be in situations calling for quite different skills which I hadn't had time to learn. To learn them now in middle age is difficult. On the ice I was quick and clever, with you I'm clumsy and stupid. Old dogs don't learn new tricks and I doubt I'll ever learn these now! But you have time for so many other cranky old beasts, so perhaps you can find it in your heart to be kind to this one? The hotel is not the only thing in which I should like to begin again – if it's possible.'

Zoë shifted her feet and drew a line in the dust with the upturned handle of the fork. 'Um, yes. So – so would I.'

'In fact, to show I am quite willing to adjust my ideas completely, I have come here today to work.'

'What?' She gaped at him.

Eric removed the fork from her grasp. 'I shall finish this task. Only show me where I am to begin.'

Zoë warned, 'It's a bit smelly. One of them's got an upset tum.'

Grim resolution crossed Eric's face. 'Nevertheless, I shall do it.'

He did blench slightly when she took him into the barn but drove in the fork and began shovelling straw with a will.

Eric worked all morning. He cleaned out the barn. He not only oiled the hinges on the paddock gate but took the whole structure off and rehung it, pointing out that it always would squeal like that if it were left sagging. He also mended the handle of the pump and tidied up the yard. The yard, thought Zoë, had never been so tidy. It had acquired, even in its ramshackle state, a faint air of a model Swiss farm, all the buckets in a row. Even the animals seemed to sense a new hand on the tiller. When Eric strode towards the paddock, they all came to the fence and lined up, waiting quietly with ears pricked. Except for Maud, of course, who turned her back on him.

'I should at least offer you some lunch,' she said tentatively when he finally stopped work and came and stood before her. 'I can cut some sandwiches.'

'No, no. I cannot eat sandwiches. They lie too heavy on the stomach. No, it would please me very much if you would let me take you to lunch somewhere.'

'I'm all scruffy.'

'Yes. But you can clean up a little, can't you? I cannot, of course, invite you to my restaurant because Harding set it afire. But there is a little pub in the next village which, I am told, serves quite adequate light lunches. And they will not require smart clothes, only clean ones. It is a very quiet place.'

'I should like that!' Zoë said and smiled. 'Somewhere quiet would be just fine.'

Now you can buy any of these other bestselling books by **Ann Granger** from your bookshop or *direct from her publisher*.

FREE P&P AND UK DELIVERY
(Overseas and Ireland £3.50 per book)

Shades of Murder	£5.99
Beneath these Stones	£6.99
Call the Dead Again	£6.99
Keeping Bad Company	£6.99
Asking for Trouble	£5.99
A Word After Dying	£6.99
A Touch of Mortality	£6.99
Candle for a Corpse	£6.99
Flowers for his Funeral	£6.99
A Fine Place for Death	£6.99
Where Old Bones Lie	£5.99
Murder Among Us	£6.99
Cold in the Earth	£6.99
A Season for Murder	£6.99
Say it With Poison	£6.99

TO ORDER SIMPLY CALL THIS NUMBER

01235 400 414

or e-mail <u>orders@bookpoint.co.uk</u>

Prices and availability subject to change without notice.